She'd been shot twice in one day.

This time, she heard the pop of gunfire right before the window shattered. She fell to the floor.

"Adriana!" Levi called out, and she felt his weight pressing on her, sheltering her.

More bullets flew. She didn't know how many. The shots were loud, echoing. She huddled closer to the couch, desperate for some kind of cover.

"We've got to crawl to the other room." Levi's voice was breathless. "Ready? Go." He lifted himself up and they crawled together. Even as they stopped in the kitchen, she felt as if her heart was running away from her chest at a dead sprint toward somewhere far from bullets and bodies in lakes.

"Who is doing this?" she cried.

"The serial killer. Or someone doing his dirty work."

Whoever was after Levi was monstrous, Adriana realized. Completely monstrous.

And by offering to help track down the killer, she'd put herself right in his path.

Sarah Varland
and
Sharee Stover

Tracking the Truth

2 Thrilling Stories

Alaskan Showdown and *Cold Case Trail*

LOVE INSPIRED
INSPIRATIONAL ROMANCE

LOVE INSPIRED®

INSPIRATIONAL ROMANCE

Recycling programs
for this product may
not exist in your area.

ISBN-13: 978-1-335-42733-5

Tracking the Truth

Copyright © 2022 by Harlequin Enterprises ULC

Alaskan Showdown
First published in 2020. This edition published in 2022.
Copyright © 2020 by Sarah Varland

Cold Case Trail
First published in 2021. This edition published in 2022.
Copyright © 2021 by Sharee Stover

For questions and comments about the quality of this book, please contact us at CustomerService@Harlequin.com.

Love Inspired
22 Adelaide St. West, 41st Floor
Toronto, Ontario M5H 4E3, Canada
www.LoveInspired.com

Printed in U.S.A.

CONTENTS

Sarah Varland lives in Alaska with her husband, John, their two boys and their dogs. Her passion for books comes from her mom; her love for suspense comes from her dad, who has spent a career in law enforcement. When she's not writing, she's often found dog mushing, hiking, reading, kayaking, drinking coffee or enjoying other Alaskan adventures with her family.

Books by Sarah Varland

Love Inspired Suspense

Visit the Author Profile page
at LoveInspired.com for more titles.

ALASKAN SHOWDOWN

Sarah Varland

Trust in the Lord with all thine heart; and lean not unto thine own understanding. In all thy ways acknowledge him, and he shall direct thy paths.

—*Proverbs* 3:5–6

To wilderness search-and-rescue workers,
unsung backcountry heroes.
Thank you for all you do.

ONE

They'd been searching for the missing twenty-something hiker for days and Adriana Steele had thought this time all was going to turn out well, that maybe they'd have that happy ending that search-and-rescue teams dreamed of.

Then she had climbed into the boat with her dog, Blue, and Blue had come to alert in the middle of Haven Lake.

Not the alert she used for people who were still alive. Blue did search and rescue—that was why she'd brought her along—but she was also the best cadaver dog she'd had the privilege of working with. One of the only ones she knew of who was able to sniff out the decay of a body, even when it was underwater. She'd done it before.

And that was her signal. Someone was dead.

Adriana had radioed the discovery in to the dive team, who had been waiting, and navigated her search boat back to the lakeshore.

She had done her best to push past the clench of pain in her chest. She knew what the family was going to go through now from personal experience. Saving people made facing her own personal demons worth it, but she paid a heavy price every time there was someone she couldn't rescue.

Blue whined. Adriana reached down and petted her behind the ears. Finding people took a toll on the dog, too.

She waited with her at their truck, sat right there on the tailgate and watched the activity. The team had recovered the body from the lake, and law enforcement was over there with the search-and-rescue team members who had stayed in the immediate vicinity. The last thing Adriana had heard before she walked away, far enough away to give her some emotional distance, was that the body matched the description of Lara Jones, a hiker who had disappeared from nearby earlier in the week. A roommate had reported her missing, no foul play had been suspected before now and her car was parked at a trailhead not far from the lake.

It was tragic, but familiar. These cases happened too often, where hikers went missing and ended up dead, from some accident or another, enough times that Adriana knew how this worked. Someone was going to have to give a statement and since Adriana had found the body—well, her dog had—they'd want to talk to her specifically.

As long as it was a reasonable individual, she'd be fine. As long as it wasn't... No, she pushed aside the thought.

It's just there was one officer she'd rather not work with.

At this point, though, she'd talk to anyone if she could just get out of here. She could only hold it together for so many more minutes. She and Blue both needed to decompress. Maybe go for a run.

Adriana looked toward the group that had gathered around the body covered with a sheet.

She swallowed hard.

The landscape morphed. She no longer saw the fall leaves, changing on the trees from dull green to browns, golds and reds. Instead she saw winter in her mind. A lake like this, but frozen over. A recovered snow machine.

We're sorry, but he went through the ice and didn't make it...

Adriana stood so fast her head spun, dizziness making her weak.

She sat back down, reaching her hand out to steady herself.

"Whoa, are you okay?"

Levi Wicks grabbed her arm. He was the last person she wanted to see here. Well, maybe second to last. At least Levi gave some kind of credence to the idea of using dogs in search-and-rescue teams, even to assist law enforcement, whereas his brother thought they did no good at all. No, it wasn't that part of Levi that bothered her. He was a laid-back "good old boy," as they'd have called him where she was from, easygoing and unconcerned. Nothing flustered him. Nothing made him upset.

Adriana didn't understand him. Being easily invested emotionally—wasn't that part of what made her such a good search-and-rescue team member?

At the moment, though, he was all that was between her and passing out, maybe hitting her head on a rock on her way to the ground, so she should probably be a little more forgiving of his personality flaws.

"Adriana? Can you hear me?"

Yes, she could hear him. She was having a panic attack; she wasn't deaf. But when she opened her mouth to answer, nothing came out. Anxiety choked her, cut off her airway, and she started to see spots again.

Not now.

But panic and the past never listened to her, never stayed where they belonged stuffed deep down inside, behind all the other thoughts and feelings she had. No, they had to intrude, unannounced and very much uninvited on days like today.

We can recover his body, but he's gone, Adriana.

Her first love. Only love. Taken by a lake like this.

Adriana felt her eyes fill and for a horrible minute thought she might cry in front of this man. He was certainly the *last* person she'd want to cry in front of, not even second to last. How could someone like him possibly understand her feelings?

Besides, she'd never cried about Robert's death. Not in the entire five years since it had happened.

She certainly wasn't going to start now.

"Adriana." She felt his weight settle beside her on the tailgate and blinked several times to clear her vision, to banish memories of the past and remind herself that she wasn't back there, that today wasn't *that* day. She needed to remind herself *these* feelings needed to stay buried at the bottom of her heart, where they belonged.

Her head spun and she squeezed her eyes shut, feeling herself start to give up on talking herself down from this attack. Maybe it was better to just let the emotions come, awful as it would be. She couldn't fix it, couldn't change the past.

She felt Levi's arm brush against her back, then her shoulder, and come to rest on her upper arm.

"Hey." He pulled her close to him. "You did your best. It's an awful way to die and I'm sorry you had to see it."

He was talking about today, and the body. Adriana knew that. But he didn't know about Robert. Couldn't know...

"It's not that." She heard her voice, watery though it was.

"Other...?" He trailed off. "Bad memories?"

Was that his voice breaking? Almost like he was fighting emotions of his own? Adriana took a breath, steadied somehow by his unsteadiness.

"My fiancé drowned. Five years ago."

No. No. No. She heard her voice. Yes, that was *her* that had said that. She'd carried the secret with her from Wasilla, where she'd lived before "the accident," as all their friends called it in hushed tones. Then she'd moved to Anchorage, taken some search-and-rescue classes, given up her work as a dog trainer and moved to Raven Pass to work with the team.

And she'd not told a soul why until now.

"You are the strongest woman I know." His voice was still rough around the edges, heavy with something that made Adriana realize she wasn't the only one with old hurts.

He might have only just found out. They might not be close at all.

But he understood. And somehow, right now, it felt like enough.

For the first time in five years, Adriana started to sob.

"I couldn't save him."

He pulled her closer.

"You can't save them all."

* * *

Officer Levi Wicks hated failure with every fiber of his being. Especially when he wasn't ready to quit on something and giving up was forced on him, the decision taken out of his hands.

Sorry, Officer Wicks. There's just not enough to keep the case open.

His chief's words from the night before played again in his mind as he held Adriana while she cried. He'd finished his shift and kept his mind on patrol—the people of Raven Pass didn't deserve a distracted law enforcement officer—but once his shift had ended he hadn't been able to stop thinking about the serial-killer case that had occupied all his spare moments for the last few years.

Probably it would have helped if he'd left the police department and gone home, but to do that would be to admit that the last few years of work were really over and had come to nothing.

Levi hadn't worked exclusively on a single case for the last several years. It was a small department, so there was a lot of multitasking, but when he could he'd been looking into the most recent string of unexplained murders in the area. Two deaths had taken place in Raven Pass, with a third in nearby Girdwood. There'd been a fourth farther down on the Kenai Peninsula in the town of Hope, ironically enough.

This case hadn't been his only. But it had occupied enough space in his mind over the last few years that it felt fully like *his* case.

Levi had been on this assignment since his second year in the department. He'd worked it with his partner, Jim Johnson, straight through until Jim's retirement last spring.

He was letting Jim down. Letting the victims' families down. They deserved closure.

The night before, he'd been heading for his truck, ready to head home, but turned around and walked instead to the cold-case room.

The door was cold and the handle opened easily after Levi had unlocked it. He'd signed in on the clipboard that hung by the door and stepped into the room, which felt cooler than the hallway had been. That made sense. The evidence related to these cases was stored here to avoid decomposition.

Pieces of peoples' lives, those odd discordant details that reminded him that nothing about his job was natural. Levi and his brother Judah had both become police officers to deal with the darkness in the world. Their eldest brother, Ryan, had become a pastor.

He supposed everyone had their ways of coping with the broken world they lived in.

Every box in the room represented a cop who hadn't been able to do his job, who'd walked away feeling like Levi was.

He hadn't known why he was there exactly, but still he'd walked around the room, removing a box here and there, looking through the case files, setting them back down.

It was all he'd been able to think to do at the time.

The next box had been a missing-persons case. It had gone cold in 1977, not long after the Raven Pass PD had been established. A man, midthirties at the time, had gone hiking and never been seen again.

Heaviness had settled on him again, so he'd set the lid on top of that box and slid it back onto the shelf.

He'd needed to leave and do something to get his

mind off his work. It wasn't like him to wallow in a sense of melancholy.

As he had walked toward the door, Levi took one last look behind him, imagining his case on these shelves.

Then one more box had caught his eye. The label was faded, the edges peeling slightly.

Women in Their Twenties. Twenty Years Ago.
Serial Killer.

He'd slid the box off the shelf.

It stung, how many criminals were never found and brought to justice.

Levi had settled the box on the table. Opened it.

The first folder was about a girl named Jessica. Average height, he had noted, taking in the features on the photograph of her like this case wasn't colder than ice itself. Blond hair, past her shoulders. She looked friendly. Pretty.

She'd been killed at twenty-two and found on a popular hiking trail near Anchorage. Investigation had revealed that she'd been killed near Raven Pass.

The folder had slid back into the box easily and Levi had grabbed the next one. Its details were similar to the first, except this one specifically mentioned that the victim had been abducted from a coffee shop. Just like the victims in his case over the past three years. All women in their twenties. Usually early twenties. Bodies found buried.

He'd swallowed hard. There were a lot of coffee shops in Alaska. Had anyone at the department worked there for more than two decades? Levi hadn't thought so.

Still, he wouldn't know if there was significance to what he'd found until he looked at the next folder.

Another woman. Annie. Disappeared from a coffee shop. Presumed dead.

Chills had run down his arms, down his spine.

And last night's realizations hit him all over again.

The women in the case he'd been working had all disappeared from coffee shops…

Either someone knew of this case and was copycatting…

Or the killer had stopped for more than a decade and then started again.

And Levi thought this body might be another one of his victims.

Levi shook himself from his memories to the crying woman he still held in his arms. He was in way deeper here than he'd meant to be. He'd only meant to check in at the scene that had been causing chatter on the police scanners to go crazy. When a body was discovered, it wasn't something that required multiple police officers. Levi could have let someone else handle it, but something had told him to go down there.

But when he'd gotten there and seen the state of the body, he'd known.

It was another death related to the serial killer.

The zip ties around the hands were the same. Levi was willing to bet the victim hadn't died from drowning at all, but rather had been suffocated somewhere else, like the others, and then moved.

But if she'd been a missing hiker, then she didn't fit the profile of his victims, since she hadn't been taken from a coffee shop. Her age was right. Her general build was right—most of the women killed had been medium height and weight. Could a serial killer deviate that much from his preferred MO?

And if so, why?

More than anyone else on the team, aside from his buddy Jake—who was out of town on his honeymoon—Levi trusted Adriana Steele to shoot straight with him. The woman didn't know what it was to step lightly around a subject. When you went to her, you got the truth. So he'd left the busy scene at the water's edge, where other law enforcement agents had gathered, and trekked around the lake a bit to where he saw Adriana sitting by her truck with her dog.

Alone. With a look on her face that almost made her seem...

Human. Breakable.

Even so, he hadn't expected to find her on the edge of falling apart, so needing her information for his case had taken a back seat.

Levi had never seen her like this and if someone had asked him if he could picture her anything other than in control and too bossy for her own good, he'd have said no.

But here they were.

Adriana let out one more shuddering cry and then took a deep breath.

"I didn't want to save them all, I only want to be able to go back and save him."

Her voice came out in sobs, but Levi knew better than to believe the words. She was more like him than he'd realized. It hurt—every person he couldn't find justice for, every person he couldn't save by preventing their death. Sometimes he wondered why he'd chosen this job, what made him face that kind of defeat over and over.

He didn't always have answers for himself.

"You can't." Levi didn't try to soften the words—she wasn't the type who would appreciate that. Instead he held her higher, close enough that he could smell the berry-scented shampoo she used. Close enough to almost be able to feel her heart beating against his chest.

Levi swallowed hard. He hadn't held anyone like this in years. Hadn't wanted to.

Now…

He wished Adriana wasn't upset and would give anything to fix her pain, but the idea of her in his arms… He didn't hate it.

He should hate it. They were nothing alike.

Everything had been normal and now something in his mind, his heart, had shifted.

Please don't let me mess up everything between us for work's sake, God. Levi breathed out the prayer and inhaled again, begging for strength he wasn't sure he had to act completely normal. The words felt funny, like rusted metal trying to work again. His relationship with God was…

Well, he had one. Some days that was all he could say about it.

Long minutes passed. She kept crying. And then she finally stopped and looked up at him with her brown eyes wide.

"I'm sorry. I've never… I don't usually…" She cleared her throat, brushed at her tears, looked away. "I'm sorry."

"You don't have to apologize. Tears aren't a crime, Adriana."

She looked up at him and there he was, staring into

those eyes again, uncomfortable awareness coursing through him.

Movement to the left caught his attention. He broke eye contact and looked that way.

Just as a bullet whizzed into the ground, a foot or two from their feet. Closer to Levi's.

"Behind the truck!" he yelled at her, pulling her with him as he ran for cover. She pushed away.

"Blue!" she shouted. The dog followed and she sped up again, her speed matching Levi's. They dove behind the truck and Levi pulled her and the dog close.

"You okay, buddy? It's okay. Such a rough day, sweet-heart."

Her voice was thick and sweet, like fresh honey. Of course, she would talk to her dog that way, even after someone had shot at them.

Though he'd never heard her talk to people without a little more spice in her tone.

Another shot. Across the lake, he could see the incident team taking cover also, even though the shots weren't near them. Good. They were following protocol.

Though if Levi had to guess based on the proximity to his shoes…

They were aimed at him.

"Why is someone shooting at you?"

Apparently it hadn't escaped Adriana's notice, either.

"I don't know."

But didn't he?

Had the killer been watching the site where he'd dropped his latest victim? Or had Levi been followed from the police department?

Neither option was good.

Another shot. This one hit the ground, too, kicking up rocks and dust.

Levi's radio crackled. "Unit thirty-four. I've found where the shooter is and I'm approaching."

Unit thirty-four was his brother.

He pulled the radio from his waist. "Unit thirty-four, this is unit thirty-seven. Approach with caution. The suspect may be our serial killer."

Radio silence for a solid ten seconds. Then a crackle. "Ten-four."

The shots stopped. Coincidence? Or was the killer on their radio frequency?

Levi slowed his breathing, started taking deeper breaths in and out and waited.

"Is it safe to move?" Adriana's voice was breathless, too.

"I wouldn't yet."

"I couldn't if I wanted to, anyway," she pointed out, some of the sassiness that had been missing earlier returning to her voice. "I can't move with your arms around me, holding me like this."

She had a point. He suddenly let her go like he'd been burned, and maybe he had been. Or could feel that he was about to be. Surely she hadn't thought his proximity was about anything more than keeping her safe. It hadn't been. He was just bothered by the fact that he felt more aware of her, was conscious of her presence, that she was an attractive, intriguing woman close to his age.

He watched her as he waited to be convinced everything was all right. She was collected now, the only traces of her earlier episode being some shadows of eye makeup around her eyes. It was faint, not too obvious, but it gave her a worn appearance.

How had she managed to be part of that recovery when she had something in her past similar enough that the memories gave her a panic attack? He hadn't been exaggerating when he'd told her she was the strongest woman he knew. He'd meant all of it.

Sometime he was going to tell her again, when he was sure she would believe him. Because it was true.

"So what now?" she asked after a minute.

"Well—" Levi began. Just then, the all clear came over the radio. "It's probably safe to leave our cover. You don't need to give any kind of statement about the shooting. I was here." He smiled wryly. "I do need a statement from you about…today."

"I'm assuming you don't mean my hysterical crying."

"The part right before that, I believe."

Adriana nodded. "Okay. That's fine. But actually I meant 'what now,' like what are you going to do about this? Someone is trying to kill you? Surely you're not going to just ignore that."

Well, when she put it that way.

"No. I'm not going to ignore it."

"So who is it?"

"I don't know."

She stared at him.

He stared back. Then looked away. Sighed.

"It's a case I'm on." That was all he could say. While he still needed to talk to the chief, a new discovery of a body connected to that case surely warranted keeping it open.

Adriana nodded. "The serial-killer case."

She shouldn't know about that. He hadn't been publicly mentioned in connection with the case in over a year, since the chief had fired the department's press secretary for giving out his and Jim's names. They'd done a good job since then in keeping coverage of the investigation from any of the press.

"I remember the article." She shrugged. "I rarely forget anything. It's a blessing." She looked away. "Sometimes."

"Yes, it's that case." Levi trusted her. Telling her wasn't against any kind of department policy—it was just smart to be wise with who knew the information. His safety depended on it.

Although apparently it was a little late for that.

She nodded. "I thought so. If I remember, not all the bodies have been recovered, isn't that correct? Like, weren't there some women who were assumed to be victims but their bodies were never recovered?" Her mind was spinning. This might be a way to help Levi out, regain some of her dignity, help families get closure in another way.

"Also correct, yes." Levi stood. "Okay, so I'll get back in touch with you about a statement for today, but I think for now—"

"I want to help you." Adriana blurted the words as they both stood, facing him straight on. "I want to help you find the bodies of those missing women in case it helps you solve the case."

Levi blinked. "I can't... The department isn't doing well financially and I can't afford to hire a consultant. I appreciate the thought, but—"

"I don't need to be paid. I'll work around my search-and-rescue schedule. I want to do this, Officer Wicks."

Come to think of it, she'd never called him Levi. He thought of her by her first name because everyone called her that, but she called him by a title. It was a good reminder that any relationship they had was strictly professional, and any further thoughts of her berry-scented hair, shiny in the sunshine, were fully and completely inappropriate.

"It's Levi," he said, which made no sense when he considered all the thoughts he'd just had about keeping professional boundaries.

But she nodded, still looking up at him. How could someone have such big innocent eyes and be knowledgeable about the ways the world could break a heart all at once? Looking at her eyes was like looking at her heart. Levi didn't want to look away. Didn't know if he should keep looking.

He felt like he knew her better from five minutes of face-to-face conversation than he'd known Melissa in all the months they'd been married.

So strange.

But with Melissa, what went wrong there had been his fault. He needed to remember that and not rush into a similar situation.

"Okay," Adriana said. "Levi. Please, let me help you."

He considered her again, thought about his brother out there in the woods risking his life. Looked down at the dog that he knew would do anything to keep Adriana safe.

Then he nodded his head down, just slightly. "Okay, I'll promise to think about it."

Her eyes narrowed like she was ready for a fight.

He tried not to smile. "Thinking about it is the best I can do."

That seemed to be enough. She nodded once. "Okay."

Then she walked to the front of the truck, opened the door for her dog and climbed in. "I'll be at my house when you're ready to talk. It doesn't matter how late—come by, okay?"

Levi nodded and then watched her drive away. When she was safely out of sight, he walked toward the other officers.

Could he do it, let her help him?

If he did, then he might be risking her safety, too.

But if he didn't he was risking the lives of countless other people who might be the serial killer's next targets.

Some days the weight of the job felt too heavy to carry. So for now, as he walked he worked on passing some of the weight back to Jesus, who'd promised to carry his burdens, and did his best to put Adriana Steele out of his mind.

Even while he wondered whether she'd somehow snuck past just his mind straight to his heart.

And whether or not she'd put herself in danger by doing so.

TWO

Even though she was fairly certain the shots had been directed at Levi, Adriana checked her rearview mirror almost as much as she paid attention to the road in front of her all the way home.

When she finally got to her little town house, she pulled her truck into the garage, then she and Blue walked into the house.

Babe, her other dog, met them at the door.

"Baby, did you have a good day?" She bent down to ruffle the animal's ears. She'd used Babe as her main dog even into this summer, when she and the Raven Pass search-and-rescue team were searching for Cassie Hawkins's missing aunt, but it had become apparent over the last couple of weeks that it was time to let Blue do more of the work and let Babe rest.

Blue and Babe sniffed at each other, what Adriana always pictured as one dog asking the other about his day. Some people would probably say she spent too much time with animals, but could she help it that animals made more sense than people?

Leaving the dogs to their greetings, she walked to the kitchen. Her stomach had started growling halfway home and she'd realized then that in the midst of the search she hadn't had much to eat today. All she could remember having was a granola bar for breakfast and a can of LaCroix sparkling water around midmorning.

Probably not enough food to actually count as sustenance.

As she reached for the fridge handle, though, she caught a glimpse of her hand. Her skin was filthy— whether from the search itself or from being pushed to the ground by Levi, she wasn't sure, but it didn't matter.

Shower first, then food. And maybe the shower would help erase some of the embarrassment that flooded her again when she thought about Levi.

Adriana hurried up the stairs, feeling her cheeks heat up. Had she really broken down in front of him so completely? She wanted it not to be true, but it was, so she had to find a way to move on. Whatever else could be said about her, Adriana tried not to be the kind of girl who got bogged down in the past.

She frowned as she turned on the shower. Was she? She didn't think of herself that way, but was she wrong? She'd just spent the last hour or so trapped in the past in a way that she hadn't been able to overcome. Shame burned her cheeks again and she climbed into the hot shower, letting the water wash over her. She'd had panic attacks before, it wasn't like she hadn't known the whole…situation had a hold on her.

But it was controlled, right?

Suddenly Adriana wasn't sure.

She finished her shower, though she didn't know how she managed to focus when her mind kept going back to the comfort it had been to have someone to listen to her tears.

It was strange that it had been Levi. Of all the people it could have been, he was the one around whom she'd have chosen not to show any weakness.

Maybe that was why she'd been so insistent on helping him with the case he was working on. She had the skills and, as far as she was concerned, she owed him. Helping him find some of the victims he hadn't been able to include in his investigation, those women who were missing and fit the profile of the victims but whose bodies hadn't been found, would get him closer to identifying the suspect in the serial-killer case, and then maybe Adriana would feel like the field was level again.

She toweled off and got dressed, this time in yoga pants and a fleece pullover. She didn't have any intention of leaving the house again today, and if she changed her mind she was going to pull on some tennis shoes and let people assume she'd been exercising. Or doing more SAR training. The Raven Pass Search and Rescue team had a core of full-time members, including her, but they spent part of their working hours training volunteers to make sure there were always enough people in a crisis.

Her cell phone rang just as she'd finished dressing.

Not a number she knew.

"Hello?" She felt her shoulders tense. It wasn't every day someone shot at her, or more accurately, at someone next to her. Maybe that was what was getting to her now, but seeing an unknown number made her uncomfortable.

"Adriana, it's Levi."

Oh. That would explain why she didn't have the number in her phone. She made a mental note to save it after the call. "Levi." It was the second time she'd called him by his first name. It was hard to be too formal with him after what had happened today.

"Are you doing okay?" she asked and then almost smacked herself in the face. He'd been shot at. How good a day could he really be having? Her question had been unnecessary.

"All things considered." His voice was even, no hint of mocking her somewhat ridiculous question. She felt her shoulders relax. How did he do this? She'd never had someone in her life who could talk her down from her ledges of drama...

Well, she had. And then he'd died.

She swallowed hard, tried to ignore the tightening in her throat.

"Did you need something?" she asked, trying to make sure her voice sounded casual.

"I still need to talk to you about the search today and its result." Levi almost sounded apologetic. The last thing Adriana wanted to do was make him feel bad. She sat up straighter, took a deep breath.

"I can talk whenever." She only hoped that was true, and that she could do it without falling apart.

"Great." He paused, but something gave her the sense he wasn't quite finished. "Can I swing by your place now? I'd like to talk to you about it as soon as possible."

"There was something wrong, wasn't there?"

"I'll be at your home in ten minutes, if that works for you."

She nodded, though he couldn't see her. "Okay, ten minutes."

She ended the call after giving him her address, the churning in her stomach telling her that in ten minutes, whatever he was going to say could turn her life upside down. Maybe even more than her earlier offer to help him with his serial-killer case.

Because if he was this interested, the case of the missing—now deceased—hiker, Lara Jones, might be connected...

And if it was, she was already involved without her permission. And, somehow, for Adriana, that was harder to wrestle with. Having her life be in danger because she'd offered to help was one thing.

Knowing she might truly have been watched yesterday because she'd walked unaware into a case connected to a serial killer?

She shivered. That was terrifying.

THREE

As Levi drove down Adriana's street, he tried to figure out how to frame his questions. He'd talked to several other searchers after she'd left the scene earlier, but since she'd been the one to find the body—well, her dog had, since she'd probably correct him if he tried to give her the credit—he really wanted her perspective on Lara's death.

And there was more than that, if he was honest, he admitted as he pulled into her driveway. He was scared for her personally. Everyone involved in the search for the killer was in more danger than they'd been when they woke up this morning. With every detail he gathered, the more certain Levi was that the hiker was the latest victim of the serial killer he'd been tracking.

Even his boss had agreed. He'd called the chief after arriving at the scene, and seeing the body and the zip ties, the chief had agreed that he could have more time for this case.

But not a lot. He'd been clear that this was the last try. Levi had to make the most of it.

All of that was making him consider Adriana's offer. Another reason he'd wanted to talk to her in person. He couldn't gauge her facial expressions over the phone, or read her body language.

He suspected several other undiscovered bodies were still out there, and Adriana could help him find them. Not everyone missing had a point last seen in their case file, so there might be more women who could have gone missing from coffee shops but not been added to his list to investigate. Even though Lara hadn't disappeared from a coffee shop, Levi didn't think one deviation was enough to say that the killer had deviated from his or her MO. Rather, it suggested that killing Lara Jones might not have been preplanned. He wouldn't know till he investigated more. There were still a lot of variables. But if accepting Adriana's offer of help meant he found more of the bodies he suspected were out there, then he'd have several potential chances to catch the killer in a mistake, forensically speaking, or in relation to DNA. One mistake. That was all it would take to find the kind of evidence that could be invaluable.

Levi couldn't give up. Not yet.

He parked his squad car, climbed out and locked the doors, then walked toward Adriana's front door.

She opened it before he could knock. "Come in."

Her hair was wet—she must have showered right when she got home and he couldn't blame her for it. When he had days like this a shower was the second thing he did, the first being a really long run while he prayed and asked God why He let bad things happen to good people.

"Thanks." He stepped in and reached down to take his shoes off.

"I'm not from here. It makes sense to me in the winter when our boots are covered in snow, or mud, but during the rest of the year I figure that's what the vacuum is for." She gestured to a nice model vacuum that sat behind the front door.

Levi had grown up in Anchorage, so he understood Alaskan culture well and the way it dictated taking off shoes when entering a house.

"Thanks for letting me come over," he said, not sure how to fill the awkward silence. His mind was tangled already because she was even prettier than she'd been earlier and he'd never noticed before, and he didn't understand why he was noticing now.

"So she wasn't just a missing hiker, was she?" Adriana asked as she walked out of the room. Levi followed her. She was heading for the kitchen and he could hear a coffee maker percolating.

If he drank another cup of coffee he'd probably start to see noises, after all the caffeine he'd had that day already. But if she was making it he wasn't going to turn it down. The machine made noises in the background as the coffee continued brewing.

"I don't think Lara Jones was just a missing hiker." He answered as honestly as he could.

Adriana nodded, then turned away from him. He wished he could see her face to read her facial expressions. He stepped toward her and reached out a hand, though he didn't know why.

She stepped away and opened up a cabinet that was crammed full with coffee mugs stuffed beside each other, on top of each other, as full as it could possibly be without them all falling. "Are you going to tell me more, or did you have questions? I'm not quite sure how this works."

She tossed a glance back at him and Levi just stood there, met her eyes.

Adriana stopped moving. Her eyes widened as their gazes connected and held there, the pull between them almost palpable, at least to Levi.

He swallowed hard.

He didn't even know how to explain what he could feel passing between them. Levi felt more *seen* than he had ever before. It was an awkward, exhilarating closeness they shouldn't have felt because they barely knew each other. But they'd shared so much earlier when she was having her panic attack, and then they'd been shot at...

"Is she why you were shot at?"

Her question confirmed that letting her help him was a good choice. Adriana was smart, observant to the point that he almost wished she'd been a little less good at putting pieces together.

"I believe so." He nodded, still feeling the power of her gaze on his. "Yes."

"You need to let me help you, then." She said it quietly, then turned away, breaking whatever strange moment had happened between them, when they'd been fully facing each other. She reached for the full coffee carafe, grabbed a mug out of the cabinet and handed it to him. "Coffee?" she asked as she filled two cups.

"Thanks." He accepted the mug the offered and took a sip. Much stronger than he usually made, but this wasn't a woman who did anything halfway or average. Definitely not someone who tended toward "weak" as a word that described either her or her coffee, apparently.

He opened his mouth to continue their conversation and she abruptly moved toward the living room.

"Let's sit."

"Okay." He followed her into the other room, then waited while she sat down. He stayed quiet until she finally looked up at him.

"How are you doing?" He kept his voice calm as he sat. "How are you *really* doing?"

This time, rather than look away, she met his gaze head-on. "I've been better. This afternoon wasn't like me, I hope you know that. I don't usually..." She trailed off.

"I know." And he did. Especially after his relationship with Melissa had fallen apart, Levi knew what it was like to put on an "I'm okay" face for the world. Someone could only keep that up for so long before it cracked.

Especially someone who saw people at their worst like he so often did; she must in her job, also. It was emotionally exhausting, making having a relationship even harder than it was for most people.

He watched Adriana's expression.

She seemed to appreciate his understanding, but something still seemed to be on her mind, so he waited.

"I don't know what else to say," she finally confessed with a shrug that she probably didn't realize was as cute as it was. "I'm embarrassed. But if we are going to be working together, I want to clear the air."

"Are we going to be working together?"

"I would like to."

He still needed to know. So he asked. "But why?"

"Because..." She took a long sip of coffee and turned her head to look out the window. Her gaze was pensive, and then her eyes narrowed. Became more focused.

"What?" He leaned forward, turned to look at whatever she saw.

"Nothing. I…I'm stressed from today is all, I think."

Levi sat back, exhaled. If that was true, he had no business dragging her into this investigation. Today, he feared, was only a glimpse of what the next few weeks or months could hold. If every discovery hit Adriana as hard emotionally as today had, he didn't think he could do that to her. Or her dog, for that matter.

Or himself. Seeing her hurt… It shouldn't affect him so much. They were casual friends at best.

But something about today had made it feel like more than that. Not romantically, though he was undoubtedly attracted to her. But on a deeper level than just friends. Like they knew each other somehow, in a way that mattered.

It would be better for both of them if he'd just ask his questions about the body she'd found and leave. They wouldn't get any closer, there would be no awkwardly charged moments like whatever had happened in the kitchen.

"Adriana…"

Glass from a window shattered on the living-room floor just as he heard the pop of gunfire.

And Adriana fell to the floor.

Two times in one day. She'd been shot at twice in one day.

Adriana was pretty sure she could count this one as being "at" her because it was *her* couch that was likely going to have a hole in it. Or her wall or floor or something. She hadn't seen where the first bullet hit; she'd just fallen to the ground as soon as she heard the glass breaking. Levi had cried out like she'd been shot and she'd been too frozen to reassure him or say anything until she felt his weight pressing on her, sheltering her, and then she managed to say "I'm okay," though it did nothing to make him move.

She'd shut her dogs in her bedroom before, when she'd heard Levi pull up; that was the one positive aspect of this situation. They were safe.

Herself? She couldn't say the same for sure. More bullets flew, she didn't know how many. The shots were loud, echoing. A rifle, she thought. She'd been around enough of them in her life, when her parents were in the military.

She huddled closer to the couch, desperate for some kind of cover and not sure where to go to find it.

"Can you crawl to the other room if I move?" Levi's voice was breathless. Adriana nodded, then realized he might not be looking at her. He was probably looking out the window. The one she'd said just minutes before didn't have anything interesting out of it. She'd blamed her imagination rather than her senses and it had nearly cost them both their lives.

"Yes," she said, swallowing hard.

"Ready? Go." He lifted himself up and they crawled together for the door to the kitchen. One more shot was fired and Levi heard a lamp fall off the table beside Adriana's couch. He made a note to have the crime-scene team check that spot for bullet casings.

The gunshots stopped. There evidently were no more easily available targets.

Levi was already pulling his phone out of his pocket. She listened as he reported the incident to the police department, his voice out of breath like he'd been running, but not betraying a hint of emotion or terror.

He must feel nothing like she felt. Her heart was fleeing her chest, headed in a dead sprint toward somewhere very far from here and bodies in lakes and bullets and men who were confusing and comforting all at the same time.

Or… She studied him closer. Could it be that having a happy-go-lucky personality was how he dealt with being in situations like this?

She might have misjudged him.

"They'll be here as soon as they can be." He looked to her as soon as he ended the call. "You okay? I'm going to stay in here with you until my team gets here. Tempting as it is to go straight outside and try to see if the shooter is still there, it would be foolish and it would leave you alone. I'm not going to do that."

That he'd ask her that question meant a lot. And further shattered her Levi-doesn't-care-about-anything thoughts. Yes, she'd certainly misjudged him.

Was she okay? That had been his question.

Would she ever be again?

How much could one person take?

She started to cry. *Again.*

"Hey, it's okay."

She braced herself for him to wipe her tears, to tell her to stop. Robert always had done that, and she'd loved him for not wanting her to hurt. It had been sweet.

"Go ahead and cry. It's been an awful day."

Again, this man was not what she expected or understood. He wanted her to cry? She didn't understand, but cry she did, over everything she could think of and none of it all at the same time. She was shaking, her body drained of energy from the shock. Her living room had become a crime scene.

Whoever had been after Levi was after her now, too.

"At this point, I'm…already…involved." She choked the words out between sobs.

"I know." He reached his arms out for her and she didn't protest, but scooted closer on the floor and leaned toward him. He wrapped her upper body in his arms— arms that clearly spent time at the gym or rock climbing, she wasn't sure which—and she felt herself finally relax.

"Thank you," she said to him.

"We really should stop meeting like this, though," he joked. There was the Levi that drove her crazy when they searched together on occasion. The unflappable guy whose never-takes-things-seriously attitude usually infuriated her.

She knew now, though, that it wasn't that he didn't feel things as deeply or take things as seriously.

It was just that he held things in and dealt with them differently.

Interesting. She wasn't sure how to feel about that.

"What happens now?"

"The department will send guys here to process the scene, check if the shooter's still out there and see if we can gather any evidence or ballistics. They should be able to find the bullets in the living room."

"But it's…" She couldn't make herself say the rest.

"The serial killer. I think so. Or someone he's sent to do his dirty work. It's hard to say." Levi shrugged like he didn't have the weight of the world on his shoulders.

"So if I'm working with you, tell me what I need to know. About this guy, I mean. What are we dealing with?"

Levi took a deep breath. "Three years ago…well, let me explain. We thought the case started three years ago. I was looking through some cold cases recently and think it may have started before that... But I'll tell you about the recent ones first. Three years ago, a woman disappeared from a coffee shop here in Raven Pass."

"Disappeared? You don't disappear from a restaurant, Levi. Maybe from the woods, or from somewhere isolated, but you don't leave a coffee shop without leaving witnesses to your disappearance."

He shook his head. "I don't know how. I just know it's true. No one in the shop remembers noticing anything out of the ordinary. People saw the victim there, but didn't notice anything else."

She frowned. "Okay, go on."

"She disappeared from a coffee shop. Later she was found dead. A few months later, the same thing—another woman, same coffee shop. Then a similar disappearance from a little coffee place in Girdwood. Then one at a diner in Hope that served coffee and was the closest thing the town had to a coffee shop."

Adriana was already frowning. "So someone...kills women that were last seen at coffee shops?" She shook her head. Why?

"Serial killers are tricky," he began. "They're not killing in fits of passion or rage, like so many murderers. They're more purposeful and calculated than that. Some of them are trying to right what they believe to be societal wrongs. Some of them are transferring feelings of rage toward someone to other people who look like them. Some of them killed once, maybe even by accident, and now feel compelled to repeat it."

"But Lara Jones wasn't last seen at a coffee shop." Adriana commented.

"No."

"So the killer is changing his MO, or...?"

Levi shook his head. "I'm not jumping to conclusions yet. It's possible that they're shifting a pattern, but this could also just be an outlier. There are other reasons that could explain why the killer deviated from the pattern. They're difficult to figure out or box in."

He shrugged again, but Adriana shuddered.

Whoever was after Levi was a madman, Adriana realized before Levi was even though explaining. The killer's possible motives were nothing short of insanity. Did she want to get involved in such a miry mess?

At the same time, could she do otherwise?

Still, the magnitude of the danger was growing clearer the longer Levi talked. This person had killed multiple times not because he—or she—was angry, but because he believed somehow he was in the right. He'd even tried to kill her and Levi.

Heinous madness.

And Adriana was offering to try to track him down by uncovering his past sins right in front of his eyes, unburying corpses he'd thought were dealt with.

God help me, she prayed, and meant it. Because she felt like she was staring death in the face. And to live, she was going to need help from beyond herself.

FOUR

It didn't take long for Judah to show up. For all their budget woes, Raven Pass PD had excellent response times. Although the fact that it was Judah's younger brother who'd been shot at—twice now today—might account for the speedy arrival. All Levi knew was that within five minutes of calling the station, Judah was banging on Adriana's front door.

"What happened? And what are you mixed up in?"

There was that big-brother tone. Levi shrugged it off with a grin, or at least tried. The truth was it got tiring, having his sibling looking over his shoulder all the time, treating him like, well, a kid.

Maybe it was why he worked so hard, why he'd felt his whole life like he had something to prove.

"My serial-killer case just heated up," Levi said.

"That's an understatement." Adriana stepped up beside him. "I'm glad the case won't go cold, though. How awful for families, not to have that closure."

It felt nice to have her stand next to him while he talked to his brother.

As much as he wanted this case solved and could see huge value in her helping him find bodies, he didn't want her in danger. If he could go back, not talk to her today at all and keep her safe instead, he would in a heartbeat. No case was worth her safety.

As soon as the thought materialized, it hit him like a punch to the gut, but he shook it away. Of course he wouldn't want her hurt. He would feel that way about any civilian getting involved in a case, right?

Wrong. But he could try to deny that Adriana meant a lot to him for a little longer. Maybe.

But the decision about her being involved or not had been taken out of his hands.

Now what did he do?

"The shots came from where?" Judah looked around for evidence of the attack.

"We were back there in the living room, but they came through the window. So I'd say the backyard," Levi answered. Adriana started that way and Judah followed. Levi brought up the rear, trying to work out the best way out of this situation he'd unwittingly placed Adriana in.

"We were sitting here." She was already giving him a walk-through, back in that room, and still she seemed unshakable. How was she the same woman who'd broken down today over a body? Levi wasn't minimizing the value of life, but he did wonder how she could be so strong most of the time and then just…break like she had today.

And she hadn't seemed surprised at her outburst, really, just embarrassed that he had been there to see it.

"…then the shots." Adriana finished what she'd been saying and Levi focused back in, realizing he'd missed part of that conversation.

"Did you tell Judah you thought you saw something out the window before the shooting began?" he asked.

She raised an eyebrow. "Of course. Not paying attention?"

Okay, yeah, she didn't appreciate that. He got it.

"She did," Judah answered, "and she also mentioned something about helping you on your case?"

His brother's tone left no question about what he thought about that idea.

"I told you, I offered. Insisted, actually."

"That may be a plan you want to rethink." Judah started out looking at Adriana, but it was Levi's gaze he held as he finished his statement. More like a command.

"It's not like I'm safe if I'm not involved, am I, Officer Wicks?" Adriana asked Judah. She'd folded her arms over her chest, almost like she didn't appreciate Judah blaming Levi for both shootings.

But she met his gaze and again, he felt like she understood his complicated relationship with his brother.

Levi looked away. It was starting to be disconcerting to be read so well. And how did she do that, anyway? A woman who spent more time with her dogs on her days off than other people, if rumors could be trusted.

"I can see your point," Judah finally conceded, his voice rough. "Levi, is this something you've run past the chief?"

A question he would have preferred to discuss *not* in front of Adriana, but sure, why wouldn't they talk about that now, too.

"I need to run it past him."

He braced for Adriana's judgmental look, but nothing. Just a small nod.

"Do that." Judah's gaze swung between the two of them. "I'm not sure I think it's a good idea, but…" Levi opened his mouth. Judah held out a hand. "It's not my choice, Levi. I get it." Another look at Adriana. "But if I were you I'd think extremely hard before I started literally digging up the past. It might help with this case, but is it going to hurt you?"

"That's not the question here." Adriana's tone was still pleasant enough, but her shoulders were tense. "And someone's already tried to hurt me."

Judah nodded. "All right, I'll process the scene and ballistics here, see if I can get any clearer of a picture of where the shooter might have been. There are a couple of officers outside." He motioned out the window. "And we'll try to pinpoint where he or she was in case we can get any forensic evidence from whatever was essentially a sniper's perch."

"I'll come with you." Levi was ready to keep working on this. "If you're okay here?"

Adriana nodded. He should have known she would be. Part of him wanted to stay and talk to her more, but frankly, at the moment he was too off balance. He needed space and not to feel helpless. This was the closest he'd ever been to being the victim of any kind of crime and it had happened twice in one day. It was unacceptable and working was the only way he knew to deal with it.

He followed Judah back down the hall toward Adriana's front door, promising himself he'd check in with Adriana later, as well as make sure someone sat in her driveway in a patrol car that night. He'd do it himself, but that would probably just attract more trouble since he was the main target.

"You're sure about this?" Judah asked when they were outside.

"Helping with the case?" Levi shrugged. "I don't

think it's a conflict of interest. If we left a case every time someone tried to intimidate us, we wouldn't get a lot done, would we?"

"You know that's not what I mean." Judah was walking toward the woods behind Adriana's house. It was mostly spruce trees, with some hardwoods, too. Full, leafed out from summer, but the leaves were changing now in the middle of September, starting to fall down.

"Adriana is an adult, Judah. And she's the best cadaver-dog handler in the area, maybe the state. I've talked to people, asked for recommendations in case I ever had the money to hire someone to help on a contract basis, and it's her name that comes up, even as far away as Anchorage."

"She looks at you like it's morning and you're a hot cup of coffee."

"That is the strangest thing I've ever heard you say." Levi shook his head, feeling a rush of heat come to his cheeks. Why would how she looked at him affect him at all? She was helping him with a case. That was all. If she was prettier than any of the partners he usually had, smarter, more intriguing, none of that mattered, right? "Not only does she look at me completely normally, but that's just a weird expression."

"Think what you want. She doesn't look at you the same way she looks at me."

Snarky comments hovered on the tip of his tongue. Saying them would be admitting that Judah was right, and while Levi didn't know how Adriana looked at him, he didn't think it was like his brother said.

Actually, he desperately hoped it wasn't. Because as much as he'd felt *something* between them today—the flickers of something, anyway—Levi wasn't the kind of guy who was going to settle down. No, he had tried that once and it had gone wrong. All wrong and it had been all his fault.

At least Judah hadn't brought that up. His brother must have understood that some wounds went too deep to be thrown into someone's face so casually.

Together they walked into the woods and the general area from where the shots had come as they searched for evidence. Levi glanced back at Adriana's town house. The angle was wrong from here, but the distance might not be.

"How did the shots have any chance of hitting us, fired from an upward angle like this?" Levi asked his brother.

"You don't think someone was set up in a tree?" The tall spruce trees were high enough to be a possibility, but they were thin trunked and not something a person could put a deer stand in.

"Here," Judah called a minute later. The grass underneath one spruce tree had been tamped down, like someone had been lying on it.

Levi frowned. Not what he'd been expecting at all. He turned around.

The view into the room from there was good enough. Adriana's oversized windows that went almost to the floor had provided the shooter with enough of a vantage point to be able to tell when they were there and when they'd crawled to another room.

But the angle of the shots would have made it difficult for the shooter to hit them. It wasn't an impossible trajectory, and they'd still been in real danger, but it was strange. Had whoever fired the shots been unable to set up in a more viable sniper's perch? Or had the shots only been intended to scare them?

Did that change how they investigated?

"Someone was rushed," Judah said when he walked over.

Levi nodded his agreement. For all the tension be-tween them, Levi knew his brother was a smart guy, a good cop. It was why Levi had followed him here to Raven Pass after his life in Anchorage had blown up in his face.

Literally.

"So whoever is after me isn't a professional killer or a hit man..." Levi said slowly.

Judah's expression said that he agreed. "No..."

Levi suggested, "It's the serial killer himself."

The officers working to process the scene had told Adriana that her leaving the house wasn't necessary, but asked that she stay out of the living room while they processed. So she went to the kitchen and started cooking dinner.

She had friends who would argue that if ever there was a night for takeout, the day you'd been shot at more than once was it. But cooking had always helped Adri-ana calm down, even from the time she was a little girl. There was something about having her hands busy, about seeing all the ingredients come together to make a meal, feeding not just herself but other people. All of it gave her life and helped her cope when...

Well, everything had fallen apart. Again.

Adriana reached into the fridge, grabbed an onion and set it down on the cutting board she'd already placed on the counter. She took a knife from the knife block and started the reassuringly monotonous chopping process as her mind ran through the day.

Their missing hiker was dead. She assumed the cops always got called when bodies were unearthed, but she also assumed there was evidence that the death had not been accidental.

Chop, chop, chop.

She'd been shot at in her house. Her living-room window was in shards on her nice floor.

Chop, chop.

Most unbelievably, she'd broken down in front of Levi. Cried. Had a full-blown panic attack.

Chop, chop, chop, chop, chop.

Adriana blinked moisture out of the corners of her eyes and blamed it on the onion. Never mind that it was a Vidalia sweet onion.

Having finished chopping, she continued pulling ingredients from the fridge. Spinach. Ricotta cheese. Pasta shells from the pantry.

A day like today called for carbs and cheese. Adriana had never been one of those women whose goal was to be thin. She just wanted to be fit enough to do her job well and enjoy Alaska.

She put the pasta on to boil and wondered for half a crazy second if Levi would stay for dinner if she asked. It wasn't that...

Well, she knew better than to let herself feel...

She didn't like him like that!

Adriana dumped the spinach in a bowl and slammed the cabinet shut behind her.

He'd been patient and understanding today; that was why her mind was all weird and confused. He'd been a decent human and he hadn't made fun of her little break-down. She'd been feeling the same about…

Well, no, she couldn't imagine having this kind of… pull toward Judah even if he'd been in the same situation.

She couldn't have a crush on Levi. Could it even be called a crush when both people were adults and should be above such things as "listen to your heart" or "follow your feelings"?

Or when falling in love wasn't an option for her?

Adriana had let it happen once, and her heart had been crushed so badly it had only just started to heal. Or at least she'd assumed that it had until today, when she'd been crouched on the cold dirt next to a man she only knew in a professional capacity, trying to remind herself how to breathe.

She couldn't afford to let that happen to her again. She'd seen what love could do to people when she was growing up. She didn't want to be that way. She had goals, dreams.

A solid determination to be better than previous generations of her family.

She wouldn't invite him for dinner, wouldn't let him get any closer to her.

Would. Not. Be. Like. Her. Mother.

Levi walked in. "Wow, something smells good."

She had just put the now-stuffed shells into the oven. "It's dinner…" She turned and her eyes caught his.

"Want to stay and eat with me? I made too much for one, anyway." Was that really her voice, her traitorous voice?

He didn't answer right away. She felt every kind of stupid. Her cheeks heated and she looked away from him.

"I'd love to stay."

Oh.

Well.

"All right." She nodded, pulled two plates from the cabinet and busied herself setting the table in her adjoining dining nook.

"Do you want to know? What we found out in the woods, I mean?"

If she ignored him, would he go away? Or at least not follow her to the table but give her a minute to collect her thoughts? She was used to being competent, maybe even a bit intimidating to people.

She still was, according to her search-and-rescue team. Apparently it was just this…weirdness of today that was turning her this way.

Some help here would be great, God. Praying hadn't occurred to her earlier, which she felt bad about. There had been a time in her life when it was the first thing she did in any situation that made her uncomfortable, but Robert's death had changed that. She and God… well, it wasn't that they had a bad relationship, but Adriana just didn't quite trust Him like she had before. He'd let her down, hadn't He? Not come through when she'd needed Him to.

"You can tell me if you are allowed," Adriana finally answered, glancing over at him. His expression looked relieved. That was one thing she appreciated about Levi—at least he wasn't difficult to read.

"We found the place where he had been sitting. Not sure what significance it has yet, and we didn't find any solid forensic evidence so far. But there are still officers out looking it over. If there is something to be found, they will find it."

Adriana nodded. "Good."

Levi grabbed the silverware she'd set on the table and while she was setting out napkins, he started to put it down.

"The woman you found in the lake today?" he said as he did the chore, not looking at her. Something in his voice warned her that they were still talking about the case.

"Yes?" She did her best to brace herself even though she felt her chest tighten, her breathing become more shallow, as she imagined the scene.

"I believe she's tied to my case because her hands were zip-tied, Adriana. She didn't drown, not on accident the way…" He trailed off but she knew what he meant and heard every single word that he was merciful enough not to say.

Did that make her feel better? She didn't know. A life had still been lost, wasted. And zip-tied…

A life had been stolen, as she'd suspected and he'd hinted at earlier, the way he'd implied that the serial killer had something to do with her missing—now murdered, it turned out—hiker case.

"So this is for sure tied to your case," she clarified.

"I'm almost certain."

"How do you want to start the search?" she asked him, finally daring to meet his gaze. He shook his head, regret lining his features.

"Let's talk after dinner. We both need a break."

He'd been the one to start the discussion, did he realize that? Adriana wanted to point that out to him, but it didn't seem polite. Instead she just nodded and brought dinner to the table.

They sat to eat and as Levi prayed over their food, Adriana felt herself wondering what the next few days—

make that even just the next few hours—were going to hold.

The gunshots confirmed they were making progress on the case. If they weren't, then whoever was behind all this wouldn't take the risk to attack them, possibly being caught in the process. It spoke of a criminal who was desperate.

But desperate criminals were often the most dangerous. And Adriana knew she and Levi were the ones in the crosshairs.

FIVE

Levi had barely been able to focus during dinner.

He had so much he wanted to talk about, details of the case he'd gotten permission to share.

But she'd been starting to look pale when she was setting the table and he'd been concerned they were going to have a repeat of this morning.

So he'd told her they'd talk about it after dinner. And he'd spent the entirety of the meal making plans, thinking of areas they should search, information he should give her.

He tried to keep up a polite conversation with her, said goodbye to the officers who were processing the living room once they'd finished, and headed out. But as he did all that, he was debating what he was about to do—and asking himself how much he should tell Adriana. How much she needed to know.

She'd seemed relatively unaware of his internal struggle. Her color had turned back to normal and he was feeling fairly confident now that she wasn't going to...

What, fall apart again? Levi was sure Adriana wouldn't appreciate even being thought of in the terms he'd been pondering.

"So what were you thinking? " she asked him once she returned from clearing their plates and going to let her dogs out. She'd kept them locked up while the officers were processing the scene. He'd started to stand up to help with the dishes but she had waved him off.

"Thinking about what?" he asked as she sat back down.

"The..." She took a breath. "The murders. The investigation. Where do we start?"

"You really don't have to do this." The words came out before he could take them back, charging ahead without his permission. He couldn't afford not to have her help, so he wished he could yank back the offer, hold her to her promise.

But when he looked at her, her eyes were shooting sparks and it appeared he didn't need to backpedal. She was going to help, anyway. Regardless of how much it cost her emotionally.

"You aren't seriously trying to get rid of me already, are you?" She met his gaze head-on, immovable in front of him.

"I can't..." He trailed off and then decided honesty was always the best policy, but especially with Adriana. "Listen, are you sure about this?"

"How many times do we need to have this conversation?"

"I know, but—"

"Earlier. You doubt that I can handle it because of earlier, right? Is that how it's going to be, Levi? One mistake, one time that I accidentally break down..."

She stood up and walked to the coffee maker.

"Adriana..." He started to talk but she pressed the coffee grinder.

Kind of hard to talk over that.

He waited.

She turned to him when it was done. "Listen, the way I see it we have two choices. One, I can help you, and you can treat me like a functioning adult who is doing you a favor and is capable and strong. That panic attack was an *exception*." She emphasized the word, but her facial expression wavered. Was she doubting herself? Was that why she was coming down so hard on him? "Or," she continued, "we can forget it. I'll try to stay safe, you can try to solve the case without critical evidence. But I will not tolerate being treated like a child in any way."

He was pretty sure that she'd have walked out by now if it wasn't her town house.

Levi nodded. "I'm sorry. I didn't mean to make you feel that way."

She eyed him, finished making the coffee without a word and then set the two mugs down on the table.

"So…coffee?"

He nodded.

She got the carafe, poured out the coffee, then sat. "What's the plan?"

"I don't think we should try to do much tonight." This wasn't his usual way of doing things—telling people to take some time, to rest. When he was on a case, he was driven. Focused. Determined. And that had helped him in the past. Professionally, anyway.

Personally…

It had been what his ex-wife had blamed all their struggles on.

He couldn't be trying to correct for that now, right? What did it matter if Adriana thought he was hyperfocused? He wasn't trying to start any kind of relationship with her. And besides, she'd made it clear more than once that she didn't have regard for his focus at all. Actually, she'd looked at him judgmentally before when he'd tried to affect a laid-back attitude.

She let cases affect her personally. That much was obvious after today. He couldn't do that, not the way she did, and expect to keep doing this job. He needed to have some emotional distance.

"Okay." She just nodded, not seeming to mind either way.

Levi didn't comment. No need to stir anything up if they were both happy.

"So I should probably let you get home, then, huh?" Adriana took a sip of her coffee and then stood, moving back toward her coffee area. "I've got a to-go cup here somewhere."

Levi stayed quiet again. That hadn't been what he was going for, but if she didn't want him here…

He stood up. "I'll head home. You're okay here on your own?"

She nodded.

Should he tell her that he'd already talked to Judah, who had promised he'd stay in the driveway in a patrol car that night? It would be foolish for Levi to sit on her house when he had a target on his back.

But there wasn't any chance he was leaving her unprotected.

Finally, honesty won out. Adriana wouldn't appreciate things being kept from her. And on a practical level, she was likely to notice a car in her driveway. Might as well explain now.

"An officer will be in your driveway all night, keeping an eye on things. You should be safe."

It was that *should be* that was going to make it hard for him to sleep. If he knew her better, he might ask to crash on her couch downstairs, just to reassure himself. At the moment, though, it made more sense to let his brother handle it. He'd have to just trust someone else to keep an eye on her.

She met his gaze then, but rather than argue, she just nodded. Her expression softened, ever so slightly, and he wondered if she was regretting essentially kicking him out.

"So we're good?" she asked as she handed him the coffee.

It was probably as close to an apology for the brush-off that he was going to get. And that was fine. He didn't deserve one, really. He just couldn't help that the way she'd clammed up on him and asked him to leave had hurt his feelings some.

He nodded. "We're good."

He took the coffee from her and headed to his car, waving to Judah as he climbed into his cruiser.

Tomorrow they'd compile a list of women who'd gone missing between the first wave of serial-killer cases and the second. There had been some talk at the time of whether or not those disappearances could have been linked to the serial killer, but nothing conclusively linked them. In Alaska, people went missing often, sometimes from trips into the wilderness gone wrong, with no foul play.

With the help of Adriana and her dog, they might be able to find a lead there.

The possibilities were bright enough that he almost didn't want to go to sleep. But if he didn't, he wouldn't be able to give his best to this case.

And he needed to give it his best or Adriana would be in danger.

And that was unacceptable.

Darkness hadn't fully come until Levi left, well after dinner. Adriana always appreciated that even though darkness had finally come to Alaska at night after several months of mostly daylight, they still had more daylight than many other parts of the country in mid-September.

Now, though, it was after ten and she was trying to go to sleep. The darkness outside was heavy. Inky-black and suffocating.

But not suffocating the fear that had come when night had fallen.

Adriana always slept with her blinds open and had crawled in bed with them that way tonight. Now, having tried to sleep for a long half hour, she stood up, walked to the window and pulled them down.

Having an officer in her driveway reassured her somewhat.

But…what if the shooter was still out there?

Murder was difficult enough to imagine. But the concept of a serial killer, someone who committed a crime over and over…

She shuddered and returned to bed. Tried to pull the covers up higher, but Blue and Babe were lying on them. She patted the spot next to her and the dogs moved closer, giving her a chance to yank at the covers.

She relaxed a little, her pets having moved closer. But her eyes kept drifting to the window. How could someone commit crimes like this? And how could she have gotten involved?

It was one thing to try to get some kind of closure to families. Another to help bring a serial killer to justice.

She wasn't ready for this.

Or was she?

Of course, she thought as she rolled over, giving up would prove that Levi had been right to doubt her. It would be succumbing to fear.

And Adriana didn't do that.

Ever.

She sighed. Turned over again. And prayed morning would come quickly, and with it, some kind of resolution that would make this case easy to solve.

She wanted to be free from this fear. And the only way to do that was to figure out who was behind these murders and put them in prison.

By the time morning finally came, Adriana had managed to sleep some. She hesitantly walked down the stairs, let her dogs into the backyard to do their morning business and then went back inside to make coffee.

Her unease from the night before had been partially chased away by the light, but only partially. They'd been shot at it in broad daylight twice yesterday.

Her cell phone beeped a text-message alert as she sipped her coffee.

In your driveway now. Let me know when you're awake and ready—Levi

She glanced down at her sweatpants and sweatshirt.

No point in pretending she was the kind of girl who woke up looking like she'd stepped out of some kind of fashion magazine.

I've got coffee on if you want it, she texted back and waited. Five minutes later he was knocking on the door.

"Ready for today?"

"As I can be." She hoped her smile made up for the uncertainty of her words. "What's the plan?"

"How about we talk about it while we drink that coffee you mentioned? I ran out of the house this morning so I'd appreciate it."

"Sure." Was it her imagination or was her heart beating a little faster than it should have been?

She walked to the coffee maker and poured him a cup, her mind racing as she tried to imagine what today was going to look like. She'd already talked to Blue about the day; while some people would probably think it was strange to talk to a dog, Blue was her partner. Besides, she had read some study saying dogs knew thousands of words.

"I thought we'd start off by going to some of the burial sites to see if there's further evidence buried there that we missed and see if we can find anything else…with your dog." He added the last part like it was necessary. Adriana knew her K9 was the valuable one here and it made her laugh. Levi's face turned red. A man who blushed. Interesting. She didn't mind that at all.

Clearly he felt things much more deeply than she'd ever thought he did.

"I didn't mean you aren't a necessary part of the search…"

As well trained as Blue was, she worked with Adriana, who, as her handler, was the one with the skills to assess her cues and make human judgment calls on what they might mean. It was part of why she'd been drawn to dog handling when she'd decided to get involved in

SAR work after Robert's death. She figured that being able to help people—and to do that with animals she loved—would bring her closure. Adriana might not be as cute as her dog, but she was essential to the team. She knew it well enough not to need the reassurance, though the way he was stumbling over himself was sort of cute.

"Relax, Levi. You're fine." She sat back down and took a sip of her coffee. "Do you have any more plans for finding them? Like, any kind of system for how to canvass those areas?"

He shook his head and had the good grace to look a little embarrassed. She appreciated that. He wasn't running the search the way she would and it was nice that he knew that.

"So rather than do that..." She wasn't sure how he'd react to her idea, but she'd thought about it last night and the idea wouldn't go away, so it might be one that was worth considering. "What if we plotted out where you've found all the bodies so far? See what I mean? Like a map that shows the killer's preferred burial locations—they were all buried, right?" She realized she wasn't sure.

He nodded, confirming her assumption. Other than the one they'd found yesterday in the lake. She wondered what it could mean, that the killer had started deviating from his pattern of burying his victims, or that something had been different about this murder.

"So if they're all buried, besides that one, and you said not to draw conclusions from one outlier," she continued, doing her best not to let her mind settle on the memories of the empty expanse of lake and a water logged body, "then I think it would be useful to see them on a map. The killer must have had some kind o pattern, right?"

Levi seemed to consider it for a minute. "I can see what you're saying. It's different from our usual approach." He was frowning now, his eyebrows pulled together, maybe in concentration, maybe in frustration. Adriana didn't know him well enough to be able to tell.

"Is it worth it, though?" she asked it in a soft voice as she took another sip of coffee, and he nodded almost immediately.

"Yes." Levi kept nodding. "Yes, I think it is." He set down his coffee mug. "Okay, do you have a piece of paper? I like to visualize things."

Adriana reached for her iPad, which was sitting on the counter, and handed it to him. It was open to one of her favorite drawing-and-plotting apps.

He raised his eyebrows. "Do you have any of the old-fashioned kind of paper that comes with a pencil?"

She smirked. Handed him the white Apple Pencil.

He shook his head. "Okay…" His fingers looked adorably clumsy—she noticed without wanting to. The adorable part, anyway. Finally, she laughed, stood, walked to one of her kitchen drawers and pulled out a yellow legal pad and an actual pencil.

"Thanks." He laughed. "We aren't exactly that tech friendly at Raven Pass PD, so my tech skills are behind."

"We use it when it's useful." Adriana shrugged. "Sometimes it's not and the old-fashioned way is better, but I do like having it."

"I'll take a legal pad any day."

"There's probably an app for that." She laughed.

Levi started sketching out a rough map: just the main road into Raven Pass, some general areas, like parks, shops, trailheads and hiking trails. "It's not superdetailed," he explained, "but I think it'll give us a start, anyway, to see if there are any obvious clusters, features, things like that."

"Features?" She knew the word, clearly, but wasn't sure what he meant in that context.

"Like sometimes killers will bury bodies next to water, or by a certain kind of tree—things like that can be part of a signature or MO."

Adriana nodded. She hadn't known that. "Makes sense. So where were the bodies?"

"Here…" He marked one *X*. Then another. "Here… Here."

"Okay, and the women who disappeared and whose bodies were not found? The ones you suspect could be tied to the case but aren't sure about? Those women went missing in between the first killing spree and this most recent one, right?"

Levi nodded. "I have those details back at the police department." He glanced down at her sweatpants. Adriana looked at him, a smile tugging at the corners of her face as she waited for his comment.

"Are you, uh, ready to go?"

Bless his heart. He was trying so hard not to ask the obvious question, which was "Are you wearing that?" Half of her wondered if he'd grown up with sisters to know that such a question wasn't a good idea, or if he was just an extraordinarily smart man.

"I do have to go change first," she told him, letting a small smile creep up.

He laughed. Not a small laugh, but a full-out loud one, like he was zero percent ashamed of his humor.

"Sorry," he said again, but unlike earlier, he didn't seem sorry. Actually, since she'd suggested different search techniques, the mood between them had shifted.

Like he was finally comfortable working with her, like they might be part of a team.

Huh.

She was already part of the search-and-rescue team, but it was different than this, the respect she saw in his eyes now.

Why did Levi's opinion matter so much?

"I'll be back in a minute." She took a long, last sip of coffee and hurried up the stairs, without waiting to hear what else Levi had to say.

Suddenly the idea of spending all day today with him, not to mention the many more days it would take for them to solve this case, seemed overwhelming. How was she supposed to keep a grip on these feelings, whatever they were, when they were in such close proximity so often?

She wasn't sorry she'd volunteered, though. Adriana needed to remember that, and no matter how distracting Levi was, she needed to keep her eyes focused on what they were doing.

Stopping the killer before anyone else became the next victim. Getting a criminal behind bars.

Making their world safe again.

Yes, that should be enough to keep her focused. Even with a distractingly handsome officer on the case with her.

SIX

Sitting in Adriana's kitchen drinking coffee she'd made was a little surreal, since up until yesterday they'd had very few conversations with each other. It had always seemed like she'd avoided talking to him.

All he knew was that he liked how things were now and he had no desire to go back to the strained relationship they'd had before.

Interesting.

He took another sip of coffee. His phone beeped and he pulled it out to check it.

Jim, his old partner.

Heard you had some excitement yesterday. Everything all right?

What did he want to say to him? Levi respected the years the man had put into the case, but Jim wasn't an officer anymore and it wasn't appropriate to discuss it the same way he would have in the past.

Maybe that was the wrong way to think of it. Levi was still stinging from yesterday's close call, and the fewer people who knew about the situation, the better.

It was strange, counting his old partner as one of the people he couldn't talk to, though.

And probably an overreaction. But, Levi justified, part of why Jim had retired had been to spend more time with family. He knew from the man's vague comments that he and his wife of something like forty years had been through some rough patches. Likely due to the stress that police officers' jobs put on their marriages.

Everything's okay. Gotta have excitement now and then to have a job and some of us can't afford to retire yet.

Levi sent the message and smiled to himself. Jim's dry sense of humor had rubbed off, which was just fine with him. It was standard police-officer humor.

His brother's face then came to mind. Half the time he wasn't sure Judah *had* a sense of humor.

Or it might just be that Judah was still hurting from the rough time he'd gone through years ago, when his fiancée had died. Part of him thought he should ask about that, but lately he didn't feel like he knew his brother well enough to know what would help him or how he'd respond to things.

No, better to let it go. Continue with this weirdly cordial relationship they'd had since Levi moved up here. Levi sure didn't want Judah prying into his past relationship with his ex-wife, so maybe Levi owed it to him to let him grieve in peace, if that was what had caused his moodiness lately.

"I'm ready." Adriana took the last few steps quickly and then skidded a little in her socked feet on the hard floor.

Her dark hair swung as she skidded and her arms

flailed out to catch herself, and then she turned to him with a grin.

He had to muffle another smile. He did that a lot with her, he was noticing. Funny, for someone who'd accused him of being too lighthearted about his work, she was pretty funny and easygoing herself.

He took that thought back just over an hour later. They'd loaded into his car—him, Adriana and her dog Blue—and started for his office. There they'd picked up his files and case notes, and then they'd headed to the location where the first body of the most recent string of murders had been found. If Levi was correct, that would make it the fourth body out of eight. Three from the first string of killings, four from the more recent and now Lara Jones. Not to mention the gap in time where Levi was still wondering if more women could have been killed whose bodies just hadn't been discovered. He had told Adriana not to jump to conclusions about the burial location changing with Lara Jones. But if they found another body that hadn't been buried, that would change.

On the other hand, if all the other bodies they found had been buried, then they'd know this hiker's burial had been an exception for some reason. Something nagged Levi's brain about that, told him that this exception could tell him something about the case, but he didn't know what yet. They were nearing the parking lot for a trailhead when Adriana, who'd been quiet since they left the police department, spoke.

"So this was the first murder?" Adriana frowned, like she was trying to put it all together.

"I worked on a set of serial-killer cases that started with this one. Of those, yes, it's the first. But two days ago, in the cold-case room, I found several old cases, from more than two decades back, that look extremely similar to the cases I've been working. There were three of those. If this one is related, it would be the fourth chronologically. That we know of."

"So you think the same killer was killing years before you were on the case or started working here?"

Levi nodded. "Yes, but somehow they hadn't been connected before."

Her frown deepened and this time it was less concentration and more judgment. "How did someone not notice that?"

He shrugged. "You have to understand, cases have many pieces, important details, so it's easy to overlook connections if you don't have a reason to suspect any. In this instance, no one who was at the department back then is still at the department. So no one made the connection and the boxes sat in the cold-case room."

"Until you did."

He nodded.

"Then you found them and then got shot at." She frowned. "And then…"

He could see the wheels in her head turning. Yes, then she'd discovered the missing hiker at the bottom of a lake, and the woman's hands had been tied in a way reminiscent of his serial-killer case.

"My missing hiker."

He didn't like the way she used personal pronouns and took ownership of her search. No wonder she carried the toll so heavily if she took every single loss personally, like she was losing someone she cared about again. He understood it might be some kind of PTSD related to her loss of Robert, but he still wondered if it was the healthiest way to deal with it. He'd found in his line of work that you had to be able to step back emotionally to survive. It didn't mean you cared about people less. It just meant that you knew that separating yourself was sometimes necessary in order to help others.

"You mentioned her hands were zip-tied," Adriana said with too much calm in her voice. Levi felt his shoulders tense as he watched her grip on the handle on the side of his car tighten. He'd agonized over how much information to give her, but she had insisted she could handle it and she was an adult.

"Yes."

Her eyebrows pulled together. "Definitely not typical. So your thought is…" She waited for him to explain.

Levi opened his mouth to explain that it was too soon to draw conclusions when his mind finally landed on the implication that had been nagging at him.

He'd been right to tell her that the killer's MO hadn't necessarily changed. When multiple bodies had been discovered buried and only one in a lake, it didn't make sense to assume everything about the pattern had changed.

Which should make him ask the question—why had this hiker been found in a lake? Why hadn't she been last seen at a coffee shop?

The answer hit him with the force of a slap.

Because Lara Jones hadn't been one of the killer's intended victims.

"I think," he continued as his mind kept working out its conclusions, "that while Lara Jones was hiking she found something she shouldn't have, like another body or the burial of one. Either would fit. And to keep her quiet, after zip-tying her to stop her from leaving, the serial killer murdered her also. But disposed of her in a lake because it was convenient and she wasn't one of his or her typical victims, so the MO mattered less."

He waited for her to comment, but she said nothing. He pulled the car into the trailhead parking lot and drove into a spot, noting that the lot was fairly empty, which made sense for a weekday. Searching here made less sense to him now that he'd had his realization about Lara Jones, but he needed more information from Adriana first before he figured out their next move.

"Where was her car found?" he asked.

"The Evergreen Point trails. Near the lake."

Close enough that there were trails where someone could dump a body into the lake without ever being seen.

There. That was where they needed to start. He was sure of it.

"Do you mind if we come back to this search?" Levi asked her, not waiting for an answer before he put the car back in Drive.

"You don't want to search around here first and see if the killer hid more bodies near the first you found?"

There she was, frowning again. She did that a lot when she was thinking, he'd noticed, which explained why he'd assumed their personalities were completely different. It turned out that was her thinking face.

Seemed like maybe she wasn't the only one who had made incorrect assumptions about someone. He was guilty of that, too.

"Oh…" Her voice trailed off and she looked up at him. "You think there is a new body, a new death in this latest round of serial-killer cases. And that Lara Jones discovered the body."

Her voice was grave, her face utterly expressionless in a way Levi would have thought wasn't possible.

"And then was killed because of it. Making her not an intended victim that would fit the killer's MO, but just someone who was in the wrong place at the wrong time and needed to be silenced." He nodded as he spoke.

Adriana's eyes were wide. "Go. We need to find out."

She felt it, too—the need to give people closure, to stay on top of things.

And talking things out with her had helped clarify the case in his mind, helped him piece things together. If they were going to work together, he needed to keep reminding himself that she was in this just as much as he was. *Trust her. Work with her like a real partner.*

But he would also try to remind himself that this was only for one case; that soon enough he'd be on his own again and she'd be back to rescuing the living.

Everything made sense, now that Adriana had all the pieces.

Levi had a case involving a serial killer. He discovered similarities to a cold case. He hurried to the lake when the strangeness of the missing hiker being zip-tied had been discovered, or in any case he'd discovered that soon after he got there.

The killer, then, must have been watching. Even before he—or she—had shot at them, Adriana realized with a force that made it hard to swallow. How close had they been?

Since the shots had missed, it couldn't have been too close.

Could it have been?

Unless the shots were meant to warn.

For a minute, Adriana wanted to call this all off. She stared out the window, wondered what her team was doing today and if they needed her. Levi had texted last night and told her that he'd talked to her team leader, Jake Stone, about her taking a break from her search-and-rescue duties to work as a contractor for the police department. She had some vacation time saved up so she'd be able to take it for a couple of weeks, and if she needed to work after that ran out, her savings account was healthy enough that she could take a small hit financially.

She felt like she was doing the right thing. But this was hard, looking for bodies someone had left on purpose. Before now, she would have said she'd seen the heaviest things life had to offer, what with all the searches she'd done that hadn't ended well. Alaska was a harsh place, where the line between adventure and irresponsible risk was as thin as a razor's edge.

But the people she and her team had found dead in Alaska hadn't been killed maliciously. Their lives had been seemingly stolen, but not literally. They had just… died. Risked too much, gone too far.

These people she was looking for now had been murdered, in cold blood.

The difference was huge.

She scratched Blue behind her soft white ears. The dog looked into her eyes and Adriana would have sworn Blue could read her thoughts.

How would this different kind of search affect her K9 partner? Would it be too much for the sensitive Alaskan husky she'd come to love so much?

Adriana hoped not.

She exhaled deeply.

She couldn't quit, though. Not knowing that her work could help end this sooner and save someone's life before it was threatened.

She'd gotten into search-and-rescue work in the first place to save people like Robert—people who had accidents in the backcountry and needed to be rescued. Even though working with Levi wasn't quite the same, it fulfilled the same kind of catharsis she was looking for.

She hadn't been able to save the man she loved. But there were people she could save.

Starting now. Lives might depend on her involvement.

Because the killer would keep killing. There was no doubt about that, after what Levi had told her this morning.

"Adriana."

She looked up, realized the landscape outside the car window was no longer moving, but was still. They were here.

"Sorry. I was…" What could she say? Distracted? Preoccupied?

Terrified about what she'd gotten herself into, yet somehow eager to get started so it would all be over?

"I was thinking," she said as she swallowed hard. This was enough, this living with her emotions so very close to the surface. There was a job to do, and it was time to go into work mode and focus in.

Lives were at stake.

She sat up a little straighter, then petted Blue behind her ears, something that had always seemed to calm both of them down.

"The Forest Lake system has more than twenty miles of trails," he told her. Adriana had already known that— she'd searched this area a few years back after a little kid had gotten separated from his mom while hiking. The child had been found within an hour or so of the SAR team being called, thanks to her dog catching the scent.

The feeling of satisfaction and victory from that would help her now; at least she hoped so.

"So do you want to start here at the entrance?"

"Let's get into the woods a bit, where the scent would be more preserved," she suggested.

She walked into the woods, and when she was sure no one else was around, she let Blue off her leash. The dog trotted ahead of her, her body language relaxed, her eyes focused. She was keeping alert, Adriana could tell.

"Can you talk while she works, or is that against some kind of code?" Levi asked from where he hiked beside her, matching her pace close to perfectly.

"I can talk." Adriana glanced at him, seeing that he was smiling slightly. She turned her eyes back to Blue. "I just have to watch her in case she alerts."

"How does she do that?"

His voice sounded genuinely curious, with none of the skepticism she'd heard in the tones of some people.

"Technically she's trained for a bark alert, since she's an air-scent dog and works off-leash," Adriana explained, glancing at Levi now and then to make sure he was really interested. He still seemed like it. "But sometimes I notice her body language before she actually barks."

"She stays pretty close to you, then?"

"Blue does. That's not necessarily typical of air-scent dogs. Some of them will run a good bit away, then alert, and the handler has to chase them down." She laughed. "Blue likes to keep me where she can see me."

"Even when she finds a scent?"

Adriana nodded. "She'll typically stay within sight

of me no matter what. I guess she figures the scent will still be there, even if she waits for me."

He nodded and they kept walking. Adriana figured he must be tired of making conversation when he was working, which she understood. She hoped he didn't feel like he had to talk to her. Sometimes walking through the woods with someone else with no conversation was actually welcome.

"What made you decide to become an SAR handler?" Levi asked.

The man was more of an extroverted conversationalist than she was. It was kind of nice, though. With so many people she knew, she was the one who kept the conversation going. She felt the opposite with Levi, and it was a welcome change.

"I didn't even know it was a job until I was halfway through college."

Had she meant to admit that? She hadn't really stopped to think before she spoke, a fault of hers for most of her life.

Even her search-and-rescue team didn't know this part of her story. They just knew that she came highly recommended from the SAR training team in Anchorage, where she'd learned her trade after Robert's accident.

They didn't know about the accident, either. And Levi did.

He might as well know everything.

"I went to college in Oklahoma, where I'm from. When I lived there I met this guy who was from Alaska. We fell in love, got engaged, and when he wanted to go back to Alaska, I went with him. I'd have followed him anywhere."

She stopped talking.

"Adriana, if you don't want to…" He trailed off.

He'd asked a simple question. One that should have been safe for small talk, Adriana knew.

But there was no way she could explain how she'd ended up with the job without going this far back.

She shrugged like it didn't matter. Like she didn't hesitate to open up like this.

"Really," Levi said again, his voice firm.

Maybe he didn't want to know. Or didn't want to know her?

"Anyway, I heard about the concept of using dogs for searches when a student disappeared from our campus and then was found because of a dog. That stuck with me and later on, after Robert died, I decided that was what I wanted to do with my life." She kept her voice light and gave him the CliffsNotes version.

Then why did she feel a sting, like she'd come close to having someone to trust with her whole story?

She looked ahead, watched Blue's shoulders tense. *Come on, girl. Find it. Do you have the scent?*

Still, the dog didn't alert. But she did pick up her pace. Adriana picked hers up to match, careful not to look at the man beside her who was, and would always be, strictly a coworker.

Because right now, her tense relationship with him, her feelings about the past, her desire to have someone want to know her: none of that mattered. Somewhere in these dark spruce woods, Levi believed there was a new body. That would not only provide another starting point for his investigation, it would also bring with it the heartache of knowing someone else had lost a family member.

The least she could do was bring closure.

Adriana watched the dog closely and kept walking.

SEVEN

Levi had done something wrong or said something wrong, that much he'd figured out. But what, he wasn't sure. For now, it was all he could do to keep up with Adriana and her dog. They were walking through an area where the trail had narrowed. He could still walk beside Adriana, but only barely. He was fascinated by her use of the dog and wanted to see how the whole thing worked.

So far all he'd seen was a dog on a hike through the woods, off-leash. Blue had sped up a little, but did that mean anything? Levi wasn't sure. He wasn't sure about any of this, really. Not that he was a critic. He believed she could help, didn't he? He was counting on her.

But it was still a bit hard to imagine, that a dog could...

The dog barked.

"Is that the alert?" He turned to Adriana. Her eyes were straight ahead, on the dog. She was focused and alert, with no hint of a smile. The opposite of relaxed.

"We'll talk later, okay? Or not, Levi. Whichever you prefer, but right now I am working."

Ouch. Yeah, he had definitely said something wrong. And later he'd figure out what, but right now her dog had taken off and she was running, too. Levi ran after them, hand on the sidearm he wore on his hip. He was pressing it against himself to keep it from bouncing around.

The dog took a bend in the trail to the left and Adriana and Levi were close behind. Then Blue took off into the woods. Adriana was pushing past branches and Levi kept his hands out to deflect them, since she was in such a hurry she wasn't slowing them down as she pushed through.

And he didn't blame her. Since the dog usually kept her in sight, this was extremely odd behavior.

They all kept running. For two more minutes? Five? Levi didn't know, only knew that he was glad he made outdoor recreation and being in shape such a high priority because their pace was intense.

The dog skidded to a stop, then started pacing. Whining.

Adriana bent down next to the husky, to catch her breath, it looked like.

Levi stayed back and waited, looking around to make sure they were alone. Though the woods were thick with trees and he didn't see anyone else around them, he didn't feel protected. He felt exposed.

Worse, he was worried Adriana could be in danger.

The further into the woods they hiked, the more their options for escape were limited. Alaska's woods weren't as thick with brush as some he'd hiked in during his time in the Lower 48, but they still had their fair share of weeds and brush. Here, tall devil's club and cow parsnip still bloomed, their branches reaching almost as tall as he was. In an emergency, they would block many of the other possible trails.

Levi glanced at Adriana. If it came down to it, she'd

have the presence of mind to run. But that didn't matter if they got so deep into the woods that there was nowhere to run.

He looked around. Again, nothing out of the ordinary.

Still, a sense of foreboding pressed on his chest. The darker the woods got, the worse the feeling grew.

"What did she find?"

The dog whined again, then lay down.

Adriana looked at her, then back up at him. "She found exactly what we came to look for."

Levi raised his eyebrows. An hour of hiking and they'd found the body the killer must have been burying when the hiker stumbled across them? It seemed too good to be true. His eyes narrowed.

"Unless…"

Surely there was no way to confuse a search dog, right?

Also, shouldn't the ground be messed up? Obviously dug up and then recovered? If the hiker who had disappeared had walked up on a body being buried, it should be freshly buried enough that the ground wouldn't have settled.

If this was a body, it had been here much longer than a week.

Was there more than one body in these woods?

What had he walked Adriana into?

"Get down," he ordered her, not stopping to think about anything aside from what was happening right now and the uncomfortable feeling he had that something was wrong.

Adriana frowned and kept standing. "Levi…"

"Down," he said again, this time more firmly, just

short of raising his voice, but in a way that was clear he meant what he said.

She called Blue to her, rubbed her ears and crouched beside her. Levi moved toward them, ready to shield her with his body if necessary, but...

Nothing happened.

No gunshots. No crashes through the trees.

Nothing.

"What's wrong?" Her voice didn't waver, so she must have trusted him; that much was clear in the steady tone of her voice.

And Levi didn't know how to answer her.

Was it just him? He'd never reacted like this before.

"I..." Nope, he still had no good explanation.

"Am I okay to stand back up? Because kneeling beside a buried body really makes me uncomfortable."

"Yes, sorry, go ahead."

"What's wrong, Levi?" Adriana stood back up carefully, looking around like she was keeping her eyes open for anything strange.

He had overreacted.

Yesterday's conversation with Judah was haunting him now. His brother had told him he had no business letting a civilian help him. Maybe it wasn't just because Judah was concerned that doing so would be dangerous for Adriana. Maybe he'd also been able to tell that Levi wouldn't be able to avoid making this personal.

He'd just started to get to know her yesterday and today. At the very least, as a friend, a coworker, she intrigued him. And also kept him on his toes. He didn't have anyone to do that for him very often.

It made sense he'd been extra jumpy.

"Levi?"

"Sorry." He shook his head. "I thought I saw something, but I didn't."

She studied him for a moment. For signs that he was falling apart? After a short time, she nodded, then continued. "So," she began, "what now?"

"This is supposed to be a body? Buried right here?"

Adriana nodded.

"But it's not fresh."

"Right. So you have two choices." She was keeping her voice quiet, but it still echoed in the chilly autumn woods, without summer's full leaves on all the trees to insulate their words. The echo gave him chills and made him wish he could whisk her away somewhere safer.

He wasn't sure what she meant. "Okay…"

"Either our guess was wrong, and the killer didn't get caught burying a body and then murder the hiker, or he or she did get caught, but not burying this body. Or—I guess this is three choices—the hiker got too close to this spot and it made the killer nervous, though why he would be here essentially guarding a burial site I don't know. So that option is my least favorite."

She had a head for this, he realized. How much of that was because there were commonalities between working a search-and-rescue mission and solving a crime? Levi wasn't sure, but she impressed him.

He nodded, testing out the theories for size in his mind. "All right, I can see those, though I agree you're right—the last is the least likely."

"For now, though." Now it was her turn to seem uncomfortable. She looked around nervously. "Could we handle this and get back somewhere inside and well lit? This whole place is frankly kind of creepy, knowing what we are standing on or near."

Levi raised his eyebrows. *Huh*... He wouldn't have thought she would be bothered.

She shrugged. "I can help Blue find them, but I don't really love the whole thought of what we are doing if I think too hard about it."

"That's fair." Levi pulled his phone from his pocket. "Let me call this in and get a team out here to excavate the body."

"Should we mark it or something?" Adriana asked. He was already pulling out his GPS device, which he'd used many times in the backcountry just exploring, but it would also come in handy now.

"I'll mark the coordinates. A team will come out as soon as they can. I'm messaging them and the police department now."

"What kind of team?" she asked.

He did his best to answer while getting the coordinates marked. "It's really just someone I know..." He trailed off and finished what he was doing, then looked back up at her. "In Anchorage. She's a forensic pathologist and she's qualified for this kind of work."

"Makes sense."

Levi put the device back in his pocket. "Ready?"

"Ready for what?"

"In case our suspicion earlier was correct, that the hiker was killed because she stumbled on a recent burial, we should keep searching. We should hike around some more. If there is a body here—"

"What do you mean, if?" She sounded annoyed, he noted. "If Blue alerts, there is a body."

"I just don't want to jump to conclusions."

"She's a cadaver dog, Levi. She knows what she found. Give her the benefit of the doubt here."

Levi considered it for a minute and then nodded. "Okay, even though there's a body here, it's not the one we are looking for. If the hiker was killed because of a recent murder or burial, the ground would be more disturbed. The scene would be fresh."

Adriana nodded.

"Is there a way to, like, clear the dog?" Levi asked, looking down at the husky, who had set down her head on her paws, brown eyes looking mournful.

Did the dogs know what they found? He found himself wondering. That would be tough on them, he imagined.

"Clear the dog?" Adriana's eyebrows were raised and if he wasn't mistaken, she was trying to suppress a smile.

And failing. Quite spectacularly.

Levi shrugged. "Reset her? I don't know, tell her to try again? Is there a way to say 'Yes, good dog, that was a body, can you find another?' Or is it like a once-per-day kind of thing?"

He had expected her to look at him while he talked, but she was gazing at the dog and he found he didn't mind. Actually it fascinated him, her partnership with the dog and the way she had a working dog whose needs she was so in tune with.

"I think another today would be fine. We can't do too many at once because it can depress them, but she could probably look for one more and see what we turn up. Hopefully that will be enough for today."

She looked so hopeful that Levi didn't want to point out all the things that could go wrong. Like, for example, this body might not belong to a serial killer's victim at all. It could be much older. He knew from the Google search he'd done on search-and-rescue dogs last night that they could recover even much older remains. This may not be one of the sites they were looking for at all.

But it might be. And he hoped it was. Especially because Adriana looked like she needed a win.

So did her dog.

"Come on, Blue," she said gently, moving the K9 away from her place on the ground. Once she was twenty feet away or so, back on the trail—Levi had followed her—she stopped and petted the dog, then reached into her pocket and showed Blue a toy.

Blue wagged her tail and her eyes looked slightly less sad.

"Yeah, you get a new toy, don't you, good girl? You did such a good job today."

"Does the baby voice help?" He did nothing to keep the amusement from his voice.

Adriana wrapped her arms around the huge white animal. "Listen, if it makes my baby happy and my baby keeps doing this job for you, I don't think you should mind."

She had a point. But it was still cute. Levi laughed.

"All right, ready?" she asked the dog, then bent down toward it. Had she said something? Given some kind of command?

Levi wasn't sure, but the dog moved down the trail farther, ignoring the site they had left behind.

"Can we walk toward the lake on purpose? Will that throw off her search?" He was keeping in mind the fact that he really didn't know what kinds of remains were in these woods to discover. If the serial killer had dumped the hiker in the lake rather than bury her, it would make sense for the lake to have been extraordinarily convenient.

"If that's the area where we want her to search that's fine. We can move that way."

Adriana moved to her dog and called her that direction, then headed toward the lake, on the right-hand side of the woods.

The dog's pace picked up slightly, but not enough that Levi was sure if she'd smelled something.

Of all the things he'd seen during the years he'd been doing police work, this was unquestionably one of the most interesting. While he had worked on cases with the SAR team before, and even seen Adriana and her dogs at work, he'd never paid *this* much attention. It was almost unbelievable, except he was seeing it, and did believe it.

He followed behind silently and they hiked for about another ten minutes. The dog's pace seemed to vary. She would slow, then speed up.

Finally her speed increased dramatically, just like the last time, and she let out a bark as she hurried for some unseen spot ahead. She turned back around, ran to Adriana, then ran back up ahead.

"Legit, that's just like Lassie," he said, remembering old reruns he'd watched as a kid at his grandma's house.

"Good girl, Blue." Adriana ignored Levi for now and followed her dog.

Levi followed both of them.

Please, let this be near the lake. Really, really near, Levi prayed.

They twisted through trees, fallen leaves crunching underneath their feet, toward what he had to hope was a body because they needed to solve this case and it would be another lead. According to what Adriana said earlier, it had to be. She believed if her dog alerted, it was surely a body.

Still, he hated to know it was another body because even as he thought it, his chest stabbed with hurt for some family out there that was already missing a relative. And whose hopes for a living person were about to be crushed.

Adriana couldn't possibly be more proud of her dog.

As a general rule, Blue didn't find more than one body a day. There just wasn't a need for it as they were usually searching for one missing person, and so she just didn't have the opportunity. She'd heard about the working dogs of 9/11 and the way some of them burned out and were depressed after the carnage they saw; she'd always been thankful she didn't have to worry about that with hers.

But two in one day seemed like it would be okay and so she'd taken a calculated risk in letting the dog continue on.

Blue dropped to her stomach and whined at the ground—it was a patch of earth that sat on a slight rise, overlooking the lake.

It was a spot that would be perfect for someone to bury one body, then dump another into the lake if discovered.

She was so, so proud.

"Good girl, Blue." She kneeled next to her K9, rubbed her ears. And looked back at Levi.

He looked as happy as she felt. Their theory had just gotten more plausible.

"Is it fresh, though?" Adriana looked at it.

Levi walked over, gently nudged some of the leaves with his foot.

The spot did seem to have more leaves over it than

the rest of the area. In fact, some of the trees had less foliage underneath them than she would have expected.

He scraped the leaves away from the spot next to Blue.

The ground underneath was freshly patted down. Like someone had dug it up with a shovel and then smoothed it back out.

Then covered it with leaves.

The wind whistled through the trees, rustling a few fallen leaves up from the ground, and Adriana shivered.

"Good girl," she told the dog again.

It was easier in some ways for animals to find a missing person. When a person was rescued by a search dog they tended to be thankful, excited, and that passed onto the dog. When a cadaver was found, the energy was completely different. And the dogs noticed.

Levi was marking the coordinates on his GPS tracker again.

"When is your friend coming? Did you say where she's from?" Adriana couldn't remember.

"Anchorage. But she headed down earlier today when I told her I thought we might find something. So she's staying in Raven Pass and should be here soon."

Like talking about it had made it happen faster, Levi's phone rang then. He gave someone directions to where they were, then hung up.

"That was her?"

"Yes."

Adriana nodded. Should it bother her that him having a female friend he talked about made her feel almost…? Not, like, jealous, but…

"So tell me about your friend," she finally said, hoping her voice stayed normal.

"Wren is actually my cousin," he said as he lowered himself down to sit against the base of a tree.

Oh. Cousin.

There was no reason for Adriana to feel relieved, but...

Okay, sure, yes. She felt relieved.

He was a handsome, outdoorsy man who had a desire to bring justice to the world. And she wasn't completely immune to that. Especially now that she had spent enough time with him to realize that some of her assumptions about him had been off.

Levi was on the phone now with the police department, judging by his end of the conversation that she was overhearing. When he hung up, he turned back to her.

"She always wanted to be a forensic anthropologist, and when she got her degree, she found a job up here." He shrugged.

"Are you from Alaska? I can't remember," she admitted.

Levi nodded. "From Anchorage, originally. Judah moved here first, then me."

"It didn't bother you to follow your brother?"

He raised his eyebrows and she wished for a minute she hadn't asked. "Sorry—"

"No, it's okay." He looked away from her, then back again. "I know what you're asking. And in some ways, yes. But it's also worth it to be around family. However much of a hard time they can give me."

Not something she understood at all, but she didn't know him nearly well enough to open up that can of worms. Talking about her loss of Robert was one thing. Her family was definitely like a twentieth-date kind of topic.

Or twentieth year of marriage. She would be okay just not talking about them for that long.

Sudden noises in the forest drew both of their attention. A crackling branch? A rustling leaf? The noises were just small enough Adriana couldn't identify what they were, and they might not be out of place, but in a situation like this it was still enough to make her jumpy. Adriana looked up, back toward the direction from where they'd come.

Levi had stood up, had his hand on his side. Over a weapon? She couldn't see but guessed so. Even though it was likely it was Wren, she appreciated that he was being careful and not taking any chances.

Even if it did lead to some odd situations, like earlier when he'd told her to get down and nothing had happened.

A small woman with blond hair tangled around her shoulders looked up and smiled. "You must be Adriana. Levi, good to see you."

"Thanks for coming." He walked over in her direction.

"Is this the scene?" She gestured in front of them to the forest floor.

Levi answered. "Yes. Adriana's dog found it."

"How does that work?" Wren seemed genuinely curious.

"She alerts to the spot by barking and lying down." Adriana motioned to Blue, who was still lying down. "Come here, girl," Adriana called her to her and Blue looked back at the spot but then ran to her.

Carefully, Wren started to work. She cleared the area first, after suggesting that Levi check it for evidence that might have been left, which he already had. As she meticulously removed the leaves and then started to measure the approximate area, Adriana watched her. Seeing her work was fascinating, but Blue looked like she needed a break. Her ears drooped a little more than usual and her eyes looked sad.

"I need to take Blue somewhere else." They didn't usually stick around for this long and she wasn't comfortable with the dog's mood. If they stayed too long, she could get depressed.

"I can come with you in a few minutes. I'm still waiting for another officer." He glanced at Wren. "I don't want either of you alone right now."

Which made sense to Adriana. While neither of them was at a coffee shop, they did fit the profile of the victims. It would be wise to be extra careful, rather than getting into trouble.

But her dog couldn't wait much longer.

Thankfully, another officer walked up after only a few minutes.

"This is Officer Quinn Koser."

"Nice to meet you," Adriana and Wren said at the same time.

"I've really got to go." Adriana glanced at Levi. "Sorry."

She put a leash on Blue and headed into the thick woods, back onto the trail. She could hear Levi behind her, could feel him watching her, but never glanced back.

"You okay?" he finally asked.

Was she? Blue's mood seemed to have affected her. Or maybe it was the other way around. All she knew was that this wasn't the type of work she wanted to do all the time.

"I don't know," she finally answered honestly, then

shrugged as she inhaled a deep breath. The air was crisp and cool.

"You did good today." He said it and then walked along quietly, maybe sensing she needed the space.

No matter how many deep breaths she took, though, her head didn't clear. It felt fuzzy. Like there was too much pressure in it.

She kept walking. Kept breathing. She felt him behind her.

One thing Adriana appreciated was the fact that he seemed to understand that she couldn't put her feelings into words if she tried. She liked that he didn't try to keep talking until it made sense, or until she could say what was wrong.

Maybe that was the reason she liked hanging out with her dogs so much. Most people pressed for answers. Levi didn't seem to be like that.

Interesting.

She kept walking in silence until the clearing at the end of the trail, where the parking lot was, came in sight. Then, finally, she exhaled, feeling her spirit lighten as the sunshine found its way through the trees more.

"I think it's just that... I don't know. It affected me more than I thought."

"Finding murder victims?"

When he did talk, he didn't mince words. He got right to the point, to the center of the issue at hand.

And yet she somehow didn't wish that she was alone with her dogs. It was right that he was here.

"Yes." She nodded. "Someone did this."

"Someone did."

And as she inhaled, she felt herself become even more determined to solve it.

She looked up at Levi, admiration building in her. She'd thought he was laid-back, didn't take things seriously enough.

How much of that was self-protection? Was he just trying to keep his work from weighing him down?

After spending today doing this work with him, it seemed like that.

It was possible, very possible, that she'd misjudged him.

And that thought was dangerous to her in an entirely different way than a killer who might be after them both.

EIGHT

Levi had wanted, with almost everything in him, to stay at the crime scene. This was his case, and he was finally getting somewhere. He felt like they were closer now than they'd ever been to ending this.

The idea that the killer had been targeting victims years before, when Levi himself was still a kid, was still mind-blowing, even though the idea'd had a couple of days to sink in. The initial cases he'd found in the cold case file had been women whose bodies had been found, whom investigators had linked to a common serial killer. And now there seemed to be a link to the four bodies he'd been investigating for the last few years. Were there more buried somewhere? Had the killer committed any other murders in all those intermittent years? Or had there truly been a pause?

And if the latter was true, then why?

Much as he'd wanted to stay, he knew he could count on Officer Koser to handle it and he needed to get Adriana home. She wasn't a responsibility he could delegate, not with the possible threat against her. He was still fairly certain the attacks had been against him, but she was working with him now. He couldn't afford to take chances, not where her safety was concerned.

"Thanks for driving me home." She'd finally spoken as he pulled into her driveway.

Levi nodded, half of his mind in the present, half back there in the woods wondering what Wren was finding right now and how it would change how they worked this case.

If they got a break now, it wasn't because he'd earned it, but he'd take it anyway. He'd thought that morning that he would come up with a solid plan for how to approach this, but Adriana had offered different ideas—good ones—and then he'd had some of his own realizations, and at the end of the day, nothing had gone as he could have predicted.

Was that good or bad?

That was something he'd have to think about more. Right now, his mind couldn't handle a single other thought than all the ones he'd stuffed into it throughout the day.

"Thanks for all your help today," he finally said.

"Do you want to come in? I could make coffee," she offered.

It was the first solid olive branch she'd proffered since he'd done or said something to offend her in the woods hours earlier, before Blue had alerted to the first body. What had they been talking about? He'd asked how she'd chosen her career and become a search-and-rescue dog handler.

Nope, he still couldn't figure out what he'd said wrong there. Unless it had something to do with the loss of her fiancé? But it had seemed like more than that. Either way she'd pulled back, for sure. Now she was asking him to come inside for coffee.

Did he say yes?

He glanced in her direction, trying to figure out if this was an obligatory kind of invite, or if maybe she was scared to be alone. But, no, he saw no fear in her dark brown eyes, just a tiny spark of friendship, or what could be friendship if he didn't mess it up.

"I can't stay long, but I'd love to for a little while if that's okay." The words were out of his mouth before he'd finished deciding that's what he was going to do.

Adriana nodded. "Okay."

She led the way to the front door and let them both in with a key. "So coffee?" she offered.

This time, he shook his head. "No, but water would be great. You don't have to get it, I saw where the cups were last night."

She looked like she wanted to argue for half a second, and that's when he remembered she'd said she was from down south somewhere. Maybe down there people served guests, but up here in Alaska, at least among Levi and his friends, it was a sign of real friendship to know where things were and serve yourself.

He watched her let Blue off her leash. The dog happily bounded into the house and was quickly joined by Adriana's other dog. Adriana pulled another toy out of her vest pocket, one he hadn't seen earlier.

"You're such a good girl. The best girl." She handed the dog the toy and Blue ran off with it, looking half the age she had earlier.

"And you're the best boy," Adriana told the second dog—Babe, he thought his name was—and that one ran off also.

"Blue seemed different earlier," he commented aloud.

"Bodies depress her."

And her owner, too, unless he'd missed his guess about Adriana's reaction earlier. She'd seemed shaken, especially after the discovery of the second body.

"Is she still okay to search tomorrow or does she need a day off?"

She looked at him with surprise. He tried to read what was behind her eyes, but couldn't.

"I don't want to make this take any longer than it has to."

Levi opened his mouth to reply, but his phone rang before he could. He made an apologetic face. "I'm sorry, just one second, okay?" He didn't like to answer calls when he was in midconversation, but they were in the middle of a case. It was necessary.

"Wicks, it's Koser."

"Thanks for calling, what did you find?"

"It was a woman. Midtwenties, probably. Blond hair. Her prints are in the system—Raina Marston."

If he was mentioning hair, it must not have been an old body. The chances had just gone up that this had been the site and victim they assumed might be there— the one that presumably Lara Jones had stumbled on, maybe even seen the killer burying, that had led to the hiker's death.

"Why do we have her prints, do we know?"

"Looks like she was printed for a substitute job with a school district."

"Okay." Levi took a deep breath. "What else?" He waited, wondering what else they had learned.

"Zip tie around her hands. Orange. Same brand as the others."

Levi knew most of the officers at Raven Pass PD were familiar with the case, even though he'd been the one primarily working on it. Quinn knew the orange zip ties were part of their serial killer's MO.

"Can we establish any kind of time of death yet?" Levi asked, thinking that the ME probably hadn't gotten there yet. Only the medical examiner could establish an approximation with any kind of certainty. That was one of their specialties.

"The ME just got here. He won't say for sure yet, but these aren't old bones, Wicks."

So very, very likely their theory about the hiker interrupting a burial was correct.

Which would mean adding a fifth body to the serial killer's recent tally.

And there was still the body that Bluc had found first today to consider. Was it coincidence the two were buried in the woods? Or had the killer buried them together in the same general location?

And if he had…

Were there more? Were all the burial sites by twos and they only had half the victims accounted for? Even though Raina's body and the other hadn't been in close proximity, they'd been located within half a mile of each other.

It was a terrifying thought.

Levi felt Adriana watching him and wondered how many of his thoughts she could read on his face. He held up one finger in a one-sec kind of sign and walked toward her front door, back into the entryway, where he'd have a little privacy.

"Has anyone been able to work on the scene we found first?" He'd called that in, too, along with the coordinates he'd marked, but it had been necessary to start with the most recent burial. Vital evidence was more likely to be found in the most recently killed body.

"Not yet, but I'll keep you posted. I just wanted you to know this part. The ME is taking her to Anchorage."

"Thanks, man, I appreciate it."

"All right. Bye."

Levi hung up the phone and stood for a minute, thinking.

The serial killer had killed again. A blonde woman, midtwenties. They'd know more soon, hopefully.

But the thought of the killer burying bodies in twos still lingered. Was there a possibility that more bodies were buried in twos? Maybe one older corpse and one more recent? That was just a guess as he didn't know anything about one of the two they'd found that day, but it was possible. Worth investigating further.

Tomorrow, they'd give the dog a break and spend the day finding out all they could about Raina Marston. But the next day, they'd go check the four sites where he'd found bodies before, and see if they'd been the only ones buried there.

Adriana had been running through the day in her mind, over and over, while she drank her coffee, but she still couldn't truly make sense of it or reconcile her mind to it.

She hated the fact that people killed other people. Yet she knew it was true. She'd seen enough violence during her time in Oklahoma to know that and had lost one of her favorite cousins to senseless violence.

That was when she decided she'd follow Robert to Alaska and never look back. She'd needed to distance herself from everything back home and Alaska had seemed like a pretty good place to do it.

Then, when she'd lost Robert, becoming a search-dog handler and reinventing herself had seemed like a good idea, too.

This—helping out Levi—was a little too close to reminding her of everything she'd tried to escape.

Pasts, she knew better than most in her line of work, did not stay buried well.

"Sorry about that," Levi said when he walked back in. "That was Officer Koser, the guy we left there."

"What did he say?" Because news, she could handle more of. Anything that told her this would be over soon.

"We know the woman's identity, and if it is okay with you I think we should spend tomorrow talking to her family and trying to establish what we know about her."

"Is that a step backward in the case, though?"

"No, I don't think so."

"Okay, if you're sure." Adriana couldn't deny that a day with less adventure sounded good to her. It would still be emotionally exhausting, she knew from experience with the SAR team, to talk to the bereaved family. But it was still easier than going out and looking for more bodies.

She could use something a little easier after today.

From her place in the passenger seat of Levi's car the next morning, Adriana's eyes widened and she gripped her coffee tighter. The earth on the other side of Levi's car dropped off into a ravine, the road itself literally crumbling at the edges into...

Well, air.

No guardrails. That would provide an illusion of some

kind of safety. Adriana swallowed hard and tried to ignore the pressure in her chest. She was not having a panic attack today, definitely not in front of Levi, where he sat at the wheel calmly driving the road to Raina Marston's parents' house like it was a normal subdivision road.

She guessed the sign at the entrance that said Wilderness Heights should have been her first clue. It was definitely wilderness. And they were very, very high up.

This was not what she'd been expecting.

Adriana set down her coffee in a cup holder, not taking her eyes from the road. Now she gripped the top of her to-go coffee cup with her left hand and the handhold grip of the car door with the other.

"It's really fine." Levi glanced in her direction.

"Do not look at me, look at the road!"

So, yes, she was scared of heights. She may have left that tidbit out of her about-me section because really, who hired a search-and-rescue team member who was scared of heights? It didn't affect how good a job she did as she was always able to push through the fear when a search required it, but she still hated it, like her own personal thorn in her flesh.

"Hey." His voice was quieter now. She felt his hand settle on top of hers. Warm. Strong. "It is going to be okay."

Simple words like that shouldn't have the power to release the tension from her shoulders, to ease the grip she had on the handhold. No, instead she should be embarrassed that much as she may have tried to keep her acrophobia a secret, Levi had just uncovered it.

But she wasn't. She felt...similar to yesterday. Known.

Adriana swallowed hard as something awfully similar to butterflies danced in her stomach and not from the height. It had been so many years since she'd felt more than a passing bond with someone. This felt…like more than passing.

The second she'd decided she liked his hand there, that maybe she was ready to take the risk to open her heart just a tiny bit, he yanked it away. Like somehow he hadn't been conscious of what he had done until that very second and now he was, and regretted it.

"I'm sorry." He shook his head. "I shouldn't… Yeah." He cleared his throat. "This is their house, on the right."

Better than on the left. Because even though it meant they had a steep driveway to drive up, they weren't driving essentially off a cliff, so she was thankful for that.

"So what's the plan when we go in there?" Mainly she asked to try to keep her mind focused on what they were doing, instead of imagining the possibility of something developing with Levi.

She still wasn't sure why she'd come today. She appreciated his understanding about Blue needing a day off. They'd pick up looking for burial grounds tomorrow. But why did she need to be here? She wasn't a regular partner, not in any sense of the word.

Unless it informed the search somehow? Adriana guessed she could see how that would be a possibility. And it was always better to have a second set of ears hearing people talk, in case someone missed something.

"I just want to talk to them and see what insights they can offer. Sometimes the tiniest details end up being useful to a case. Besides, don't you think they deserve to know that someone is looking for their daughter's killer?"

Yes, of course she thought so. She wanted them to have closure.

Did that mean she was ready to go look people facing loss in the eyes?

No, not at all.

Yet he was reaching for the door handle, clearly expecting her to follow. "Ready?"

No. Yes? She would try to be. Rather than say any of it, Adriana nodded. She was as ready as she was going to be.

Levi opened his door and stepped out and Adriana did the same. The air was a little warmer today, almost like a Lower-48 fall day, and the sun was shining, clear and bright in a vibrant blue sky.

She loved Alaska. Had since the first day she'd stepped out of the Ted Stevens Anchorage International Airport. She might be from Oklahoma, but she was pretty sure somehow that she was Alaskan at heart.

They walked to the front door, rang the bell.

A woman, probably in her midsixties, answered. She looked like someone who had been crying, but who had tried to pull herself together. Adriana knew Levi had called yesterday to set up this appointment, so at least they weren't showing up unannounced, but she still felt uncomfortable stepping into someone else's grief when she always wanted to be left alone with hers.

"Mrs. Marston?" Levi held out a hand, and Adriana noticed not for the first time how much of an impression he made in his tan Raven Pass Police Department uniform. She'd seen him in it before, obviously. But he didn't wear it every time he worked. She guessed an occasion like this called for it, to lend some legitimacy to their coming by, and maybe to reassure people, too. That the police were working on things. That their daughter's killer wasn't going to be left to roam free.

Mrs. Marston's face relaxed into something resembling trust as she took in Levi's appearance and nodded her head. Her shoulders relaxed, like his being here was a reassurance in and of itself.

"You must be Officer Wicks. Thank you for coming by. We are glad to get to talk to you. My husband is upstairs and should be down in a few minutes."

The words, about being glad they could talk to him, struck Adriana as odd. They wanted to talk about things? Maybe some people did better when they talked about what was hurting them.

"This is Adriana Steele. She's part of the Raven Pass SAR team—search and rescue—and her dog was responsible for finding your daughter's body."

She felt herself bristle, though she held out her hand and attempted a smile. Surely learning that Blue had discovered the body wouldn't bring the woman joy the way search dogs did when they found people who were alive and had just been waiting for rescue. Maybe it was silly to feel so overprotective of her dogs, but she didn't want anyone thinking badly of them.

"We are so thankful for you, dear. And your dog. To have had no closure…" She stopped talking, then took a shuddery breath and sniffed. "We are glad you do what you do. What a difficult job."

The woman's words sounded genuine, despite the fact that they were foreign to Adriana.

"Thank you."

It was all she could say, the only words she could force from her lips. She tried another small smile and prayed that Levi would take the lead with the conversation here because being in a room this heavy, with grief that didn't feel suffocating or dark, was confusing her.

"Sorry about that. I'm Dave Marston." A man about the same age and height as his wife came down the stairs and walked toward them, holding out his hand for both of them to shake.

"Thanks for meeting with us," Levi said.

The man's face was a little harder to read, but he nodded. "Thank you for coming by."

Strange, how everyone handled grief in different ways.

"Please, come in and sit. Would anyone like coffee?"

Adriana couldn't drink anything. Not right now, when she could barely even focus on taking breaths, in and out.

"I'm okay, thank you," she said, wondering if that counted as a lie.

Levi glanced at her, a strange sideways glance.

"I would love a cup," he answered, still looking as relaxed as if they were…well, anywhere but here.

Mrs. Marston poured it for him and then they sat in the living room. Adriana sat down first, at one end of a couch, and Levi sat beside her. Not on the other end, as she would have expected, but right beside her. Close enough to reach out to for support, except she wouldn't do that, and shouldn't even think that way.

She wasn't the only one who had a past, that much was clear to her. Something had happened to Levi to make him hesitant to trust.

And despite the fact that it wasn't her business, not as someone who only occasionally saw him in a work capacity, Adriana wanted to know.

She felt awareness of him spread through the blush on her cheeks, and she swallowed hard.

Levi cleared his throat and began. "Mr. and Mrs. Marston, I wanted to say first that we are sorry for your loss."

They both nodded. "Thank you."

Levi took another sip of coffee. "Your daughter seems like she was a wonderful person. I looked at her social-media profiles a bit last night. You were really blessed with her, I think."

What on earth? Did he think this was a good tactic, reminding them of all they had lost? Adriana felt herself pull away again. Only internally. Externally they were still sitting almost close enough to touch.

But how could he talk about Raina like this, like she was still there, sitting in the living room with them, instead of in a morgue somewhere, probably midautopsy? Gone forever.

Adriana was not surprised at all to watch Mrs. Marston's eyes pool with unshed tears. But she was surprised at what she said. "Thank you. Thank you for seeing her as more than a victim, and for your words. So many people…" The tears fell now. "So many people haven't said anything."

"They don't know what to say," Mr. Marston said to his wife, in a tone that made it sound like this was something he'd said before.

"I know, but…" She sniffed again. "Thank you."

Levi nodded. His face remained unreadable, but Adriana wondered how he did this. And then found herself wondering how *often* he did this. She'd never once considered the feelings of the law-enforcement officers who had to deliver bad news over and over, who saw people on their worst days.

But they had to be made of something special, or gifted

by God in some way. She usually slipped away before other people got involved, in the guise of Blue needing a break.

Truly, it was Adriana who wouldn't stand that close to death for too long without feeling it threaten to overtake her hope.

Her dog held it together better than she did.

She didn't hear most of what was said for the next ten minutes. She tried—she really did. But she was overwhelmed. Why had this all started to affect her so much? For years, she'd been fine.

She wanted to pull out her phone and text someone. Ellie, maybe. While Adriana had held herself at arm's length from the other members of her SAR team, she and Ellie had connected a bit more. Maybe because Adriana was under the impression that Ellie was hiding things from her past also. Not bad things, but personal ones.

Shadows. Darkness.

Oh, how familiar Adriana was with those.

Okay, no, she hadn't "dealt" with her feelings like some friends had suggested. She hadn't talked to a counselor, or anyone who didn't have four legs and a tail. She was pretty sure the late-night conversations she had with her dogs weren't what her friends had in mind.

"Can you tell me more about your daughter? Any friends she had that might help us track down her killer, places she hung out?" Adriana heard Levi ask the questions as she tried to focus back in.

Something flickered on the face of both Marstons.

Something, some internal nudge, told her that these people held the answers she was looking for. They were facing death without flinching, facing loss and still looking ahead to their future.

As she held her breath and waited for their answer, she wondered for the first time if one day she could get there, too. To a point where she could only look forward and not be constantly pulled back to her past.

To be here, to be listening to them, was like being emotionally unprotected. Vulnerable.

And sitting next to Levi made that feel even truer. The man had seen her at her worst more than anyone else had.

But nevertheless, Adriana was ready. She leaned forward to listen.

Ready, maybe for the first time, to find out how to move forward with her own life—and the case itself.

NINE

"We've told the police everything already, when Officer Koser and Officer Smith came by right after they positively identified her body," Mr. Marston began, after clearing his throat, "but something about the way you asked reminded me they mostly asked about where she was the day she disappeared."

Levi had read the reports already. Raina had been at work, at a nearby elementary school, the day she disappeared. People had seen her until just after four, when she'd left. She hadn't shown up to a Pilates class at seven. There were hardly any traffic cameras in the area, since Raven Pass had one stoplight and even it was fairly unnecessary, so looking at that hadn't yielded results. They'd asked on social media, had run the search from every angle they could think of.

But the three-hour window remained.

"She was at school, right?" he asked to prompt Raina's father, though he started to question his coming here. These people were grieving.

His time might be better spent elsewhere. Even while he waited for the man to speak, he began to plan his exit strategy.

"But it's where she didn't go that is interesting to me."

Levi looked up. Waited.

"We talked to her that morning, just a few texts. She was talking about how riled up her students were, and that she hadn't had coffee. She'd been running late. Now, she may have had it at school—teacher's lounges have coffee makers, you know, but…" He glanced at his wife. "Maybe she stopped at her favorite coffee shop after school."

"Which was?"

"Raven's Rest. The one on Second Street, near the woods." He shook his head. "It seems like an awfully easy place to go missing."

Levi perked up at that comment. He had said nothing about the pattern of women to disappear from coffee shops in this area.

So there was no reason for the Marstons to link the coffee shop for that reason. But the fact that Raina's dad had remembered she'd not had coffee that day was important.

"I do appreciate knowing that." He kept his voice even so he wouldn't give them false hope if this lead didn't go anywhere.

But they had just given him something to work with.

They talked for a little longer. Levi did his best to update them on the progress of the case and to listen. Adriana joined in very little and unless he missed his guess, he thought she might be a little pale.

She'd lost her fiancé. She'd told him that the other day, but her anxiety was bigger than even her panic attacks, wasn't it? It had been years ago, surely…

No, there was no time limit on things like that. He knew that better than most. He might never be like a guy who hadn't gone through what he'd gone through, no matter how many years passed between his wife's infidelity, and then desertion, and now.

No, what people went through changed them. Forever.

"Thank you again for your time." He told the Marstons when they'd wrapped up their conversation and been through the careful dance of "thanks for coming," "thanks for having us," and all that society had declared had to happen before a conversation could end. They'd all moved to the entryway and then back to the front deck.

"Thank you. We really liked talking about her." Mrs. Marston's smile was genuine, even with the tearstains on her cheeks. "I appreciate what you are doing to find whoever...did this." She glanced over at Adriana, then looked straight at Levi. "Be careful. And make sure that she is careful." The older woman nodded, like she'd given him some kind of official order.

"Whoever did this is still out there. I can't see them appreciating being caught."

"Adriana, could I talk to you alone, just for a minute?" Mrs. Marston asked as they crossed the deck.

Levi's eyebrows rose and Mrs. Marston shook her head. "Just here, on the deck. I know you probably don't want to let her out of your sight at all. I know my daughter isn't the first young woman to disappear here in the last decade."

Adriana nodded, so Levi nodded, too. Adriana did fit the profile, though in her late twenties she was slightly older than many of them. Mostly he didn't want her out of his sight because of the direct threats against both of them.

"I'll go start the car," he said, watching out of the corner of his eye as he walked away.

What would it be like, he wondered, to have been involved with a woman who would still grieve years after he died?

Not that he would ever want to cause someone that much grief. But still, Levi couldn't imagine being loved that way, knew too well that he hadn't been in his past relationship.

But Adriana had a huge capacity for love. That was something else he'd learned over the last few days.

And Levi, despite his hesitations, all the reasons he knew it was a bad idea, still wondered what it would be like to be loved that much.

He sat in the driver's seat while Adriana and Mrs. Marston talked, then watched as the couple waved and Adriana walked to the car. She climbed in. He tried to keep his tone light as he navigated down the hill. "You up for a trip to the Raven's Rest coffee shop? I can drop you at your house if you need me to, and get someone there to watch you."

She looked near her breaking point and Levi didn't want to be responsible for her breaking.

"I'm not fragile, Levi. I can handle working this with you, okay? Let's go to the shop. But let's go home and get Blue."

He raised his eyebrows. "We're not looking for…"

"She's also a regular search dog. And the fact that we aren't looking for bodies today will make it so she doesn't need a break. Searching for the scent of someone who was living doesn't put as much strain on them." Adriana held up a pair of worn socks. "These were their daughter's. She wanted to give them to me, just in case

I could figure more out from using them with Blue. Where Raina was taken from, why, anything like that. It's not too late to search for evidence of where she might have been."

Levi nodded.

"That makes sense. Okay, home to get your dog?" he asked.

Adriana nodded. "And then to the coffee shop."

Something in her voice was determined. Dark.

And he wondered, was she doing this only to get closure for the families affected by the serial killer and to ensure no one else died? Or was she somehow trying to get closure for herself as well?

Making cases personal was never a good way to handle things. He'd seen officers break down mentally because they took on the emotions of victims' families and got too close to situations. Compassion was important, but so was some distance.

He only hoped he could help Adriana avoid those mistakes.

"I'll be right back out," Adriana promised, leaving Levi alone in the car once they returned to her house. Her heart was pounding in her chest, much too rapidly to be normal, and she felt her hands beginning to sweat.

She'd had one panic attack in front of Levi already. She certainly wasn't planning to have another.

Good thing she legitimately needed to get her dog for this next job.

The house was empty, except for Babe and Blue, who both met her at the door. Adriana had felt some hesitation about coming inside alone, but even though Levi had offered to clear it for her and walk from room to room and confirm that the house was empty, she'd turned him down. If he came inside to check the house, he'd want to wait for her to gather what she needed and get ready, and she needed to be alone. To think.

She went through the motions of getting Blue ready. Grabbed a snack and a treat for later. Picked up the bag that held her SAR-K9 vest to put on her later as identification. Gave her some water in case she wanted one more drink before they left, though she had a portable bowl as well. Really, it was a stalling tactic to give herself a little more space from Levi and his gaze that seemed to see through to her soul. She need a little more time to try to breathe and calm herself down.

But it was like someone was gripping her chest with a vise and no matter how much she struggled, Adriana couldn't quite breathe.

She couldn't get over the attitude of the Marstons. Why hadn't they hated her and Levi for not being able to give them answers? While they shouldn't hate them, she knew all too well that grief turned sadness into anger in strange ways.

Hadn't she spent days, weeks after Robert's death blaming the rescue workers? Wondering whether, if they'd gotten there earlier, they could have helped?

Hating how calm they had seemed when her whole world had fallen apart? Maybe that was why she got so invested—too invested, according to Levi.

But they hadn't seemed affected by any of those negative emotions toward her or Levi. They'd been kind. Concerned about her safety.

Your daughter is dead. She'd kept thinking in her mind. *Your daughter is dead and you're worried about me?*

How did they move on? How did they keep caring

about other people after what must be one of the worst losses, the most devastating?

No matter how hard she tried to swallow normally, slow down her heart rate, she couldn't. Finally, Adriana sank to the ground on the floor of her kitchen and leaned her head back against the pantry door.

In her pocket, her phone started buzzing. Adriana took another breath, then another, and finally decided to check it.

It was her SAR colleague Ellie.

Adriana considered, and then answered. "Hello?"

"Hey. Are you doing okay?"

How could she ask that question? Had Levi called her?

"Did Levi ask you to check on me?" she asked.

"No, but I was curious about that, too. I heard you're working with him right now. How's that going? We miss you here."

Ellie's voice was normal, completely free of pity, and if Adriana didn't know better...well, it really did look like no one had told her to call.

Adriana glanced up at the ceiling, seeing in her mind's eye the heavens. Did God prompt people to make phone calls? Ellie was one of the people she could trust. And here her friend was, offering to talk to her.

She was past pride at this point, as nausea had crept in to join a variety of symptoms. "I'm not great," she admitted, her voice wavering.

"Is it Levi? I know he's always driven you crazy."

He had, hadn't he? But, no, working with Levi had been fine. It was her. Only her.

"I can't... I don't..." She struggled for breath. "All those people, Ellie. All those people I've been thinking about, that I'm supposed to be helping him find, they were murdered. And it's different than SAR work."

Her friend was quiet for a minute and Adriana worried she'd crossed some invisible line.

"That would be different. Do you want to talk more about it?" Ellie's voice was soft. Not demanding. Even though they were in different places, Adriana felt like Ellie was sitting next to her.

In that moment, Adriana felt like she wasn't alone. Her next breath came easier and she felt some of the pressure on her chest ease.

"I just don't know what to do. I don't know how to handle this."

"Have you told Levi? I'm sure he won't hold you to helping."

He wouldn't, she knew. He'd let her walk away right now. But Adriana didn't want that. She wasn't a quitter.

Yes, she'd walked away from her entire life near Anchorage years ago and started over here in Raven Pass, but that hadn't been about running away.

Or had it?

"I don't want to do that," she admitted. "I want him to see me as strong."

Ellie was quiet. Adriana heard her own words, felt a question rising in her own mind.

Then Ellie asked it aloud. "Are you…? Do you have feelings for him? You don't sound like this is just an obligation to a sometime coworker."

She didn't. Even to herself. Adriana couldn't argue. She thought about watching Levi work a case, about the way his green eyes weren't always playful as she'd once thought. He lightened up life, that was true, but when he was focused, he gave all his attention to his job. He was actually one of the most driven people she'd ever met and she'd never realized it before.

A tear fell down her face as she felt her shoulders relaxing.

Yes, she had feelings for him.

"You don't have to answer," Ellie said. "But if you did…"

Adriana waited.

"It would be okay. And you wouldn't have to hide those from him. And Adriana?"

Still, she didn't say anything back. Ellie didn't seem deterred. "I will talk to you whenever. I know we haven't always been super close, but you've always been one of the people here that I trust and I hope you feel the same."

"I do," she assured her friend.

"But," Ellie continued, "I think you can trust Levi with your anxiety, too. He won't see you as weak. If anything, he'll see how strong you are for not quitting."

It was something to consider.

The idea of relaxing, of telling him how she really felt about this case, instead of trying to wear a face of unbreakable confidence, reassured her.

Adriana blew out a breath, wiped one more tear. And felt her heartbeat return to normal as the tension in her shoulders dissipated.

"I'll try," she promised her friend.

"Good. You can trust him. He's a good man."

He was, Adriana knew, as she said goodbye and hung up. But the problem wasn't Levi. It was the idea that if she grew closer to him, then she'd be opening herself up to getting hurt again.

Losing someone she loved had almost destroyed her the last time. She couldn't do it again.

Still conflicted, she petted Blue one more time, then stood up and walked back outside, all evidence of what had just happened hopefully missing from her face.

"Everything okay?" Levi asked when Adriana opened the car door and climbed back inside.

She nodded. "Yes. It is now."

He looked at her. She waited for him to put the key in the ignition and head to the coffee shop where Raina had likely gone the afternoon of her death, but he didn't. Instead he just watched her.

Yes, she had to admit to herself as his green eyes searched hers. She felt something for him. More than friendship.

She offered a small smile, tried to find a scrap of bravery. "This is hard," she admitted. "It's hard to see how lives have been destroyed. It's hard knowing that no matter how hard Blue and I work, we aren't going to be able to give any of these people back to those who loved them. They are all gone. And they were all murdered."

Instead of being concerned, or making a big deal out of the fact that she was half admitting to having a meltdown, he just nodded. With that came a sense of connection. To Levi. Because he responded the way she hadn't even realized she wanted him to—just acknowledgement.

"It is hard," he said. And then he put the car in Reverse and backed out of her driveway. Then drove toward the coffee shop.

Raven's Rest was typical of an Alaskan mountaintown coffee shop. Woodsy, with lots of log and wood architectural details, but with quirky local artwork.

That aesthetic usually made Adriana smile, but today she was having to wrestle with the idea that cheery places like this could have been related to something so depressing.

Life was like that. Good and bad, high and low, all mixed together. Alaska itself often reminded her of those kinds of contradictions of life. Beautiful and dangerous at the same time. God was the same even when either extreme was happening in life. That was something else she was learning, slowly.

She and Blue were standing outside the shop now, Levi with them. She'd told him he should just go in by himself to ask for information, while she let Blue smell around outside. Sometimes people watching her work made her nervous, and since her realization earlier today of the slight…attraction she had toward him, Levi watching her wouldn't help.

"I'm not leaving you out here alone. At the last place we think a murder victim was seen? Yeah, no."

Why abduct women from coffee shops? Did the killer hang out at these places often and were they just where he saw potential victims?

Or was it more than that?

She'd stayed up researching last night, serial killers in particular, and had learned more than she'd ever wanted to about them. Their habits still didn't make sense to her—which was good since by definition they were not normal, clear-thinking people—but they generally followed a pattern. Their killings weren't completely random, not in their twisted minds.

The coffee-shop element had to factor in somehow.

"Different coffee shops, right?" She turned to Levi.

"What?" He looked at her. He'd been studying the shop, like the storefront held the answers he needed.

"They haven't all been this one." She didn't think so. Surely he'd have mentioned that.

He shook his head. "None have been here. Two were in the same coffee shop, but it doesn't appear there's any pattern with which shop or how often. Just that it's a coffee shop."

So not a location issue.

It still didn't make sense to her.

"We can both go in. This is Raven Pass. No one is going to bat an eye at a dog in a shop."

Maybe he was right. Alaska was extremely canine friendly, especially in quirky mountain towns of just a couple thousand people, like Raven Pass and neighboring Girdwood. But there was a difference between a standard-size dog and her sixty-pound Alaskan husky, which many people told her looked like a wolf.

Tall and rangy, with pointed ears and varying shades of creamy white and gray...

Yeah, she could see their point.

"You think no one is going to bat an eye at *her*?" Adriana raised her eyebrows and glanced down at her dog, who sat obediently at the end of her leash, looking for all the world like a sweetheart and not like an animal who'd just that morning stolen an entire cucumber off the kitchen counter and eaten it.

"If they do, we'll leave. Come on." Levi reached for the heavy wooden door, with its carved wooden handle, and held it open for her. Reluctantly, she walked inside, pausing for him to follow her once she'd stepped in.

The room was large, with high ceilings that sloped up toward the apex of the roof. At one end, a fire roared in a hearth beneath a mantel that spoke of warmth and made her want to cuddle up in one of the chairs near it, maybe with a blanket.

In front of the entrance was the bar area, with a pastry display case.

Oh, those looked really good.

Maybe this shop would help her get her appetite back. It had been somewhat absent since the awkward conversations with the Marstons and her growing…awareness of Levi.

If anything could, it was the blueberry crumble in the pastry case right there. Or the chocolate-chip banana buckwheat muffin.

"Hi, can I help you?" The woman at the counter had long dark hair and looked to be in her midtwenties. She was gorgeous, Adriana noted and looked over at Levi without meaning to.

Though why, she didn't know. Even if she was developing a slight…crush or something on him, it was still silly. She had no claim on him. None whatsoever. They were *barely* more than coworkers, probably not even that. She needed to remember the way he'd pulled his hand away from her, and the way he'd backed off after realizing a question he'd asked had been personal the other day—

Everything about their interactions made it clear he wasn't looking to get to know her. Her own feelings were something she could deal with. And she could trust him enough to share her anxiety struggles—she thought Ellie was right about that.

But that was different than making him aware of her feelings about him.

She needed to try to ignore how she felt about him.

However that was. She didn't want to think too hard about it.

Levi smiled at the woman at the counter, but with his regular, normal amount of warmth. "Hi."

The woman looked disappointed. At least it wasn't just Adriana who couldn't catch his attention.

"We have a couple of questions about a woman who was here earlier this week," he said.

The barista's eyebrows raised. "We get a lot of people in here."

"This was a woman, blonde. Raina Marston." Levi held up his phone, which had a picture of her on the screen. It was a picture from social media, Adriana could see. He must have saved it when he'd been looking at her profiles earlier.

"She's come in before. I don't know when, though." The woman shrugged, looking at least a little apologetic. "Like I said, we're busy."

"Can you try to remember the last time she came in?" Levi asked it in a much nicer voice than Adriana would have. It was taking all the self-control she possessed to stay quiet when this employee clearly didn't feel compelled to help them.

"I think it was Tuesday. I remember seeing her in here talking to a man." She frowned. Then opened a drawer and shuffled through a binder.

"Nathan Hall." She pointed at a receipt. "I remembered because he was really cute and I was thinking if she didn't go out with him again I sure would." She shrugged.

So Raina had met a man here, someone she might have been dating.

And then Raina had never been seen by anyone again.

But that accounted for at least part of the missing hours they had.

And there was a man involved. Interesting.

"Thanks so much for your time." Levi smiled again. "Could we get a couple of lattes to go also?"

They stood in silence while the woman made them and then handed one to each of them. Levi paid.

"Thanks," Adriana said. The two of them walked back out of the shop.

"Well?" Levi turned to Adriana as soon as they were outside.

"'Well' what?" she asked and then took a sip of her latte. She was usually a caramel macchiato sort of girl, but this was nice. Sweeter than she thought, with just espresso and milk.

She glanced at Levi. *Huh.*

"What did you think?"

Levi had made it pretty clear he was going to treat her like an actual partner. She may as well just take a deep breath and do her best to swim. She'd been tossed in the deep end of this investigation, so it was that or sink.

Adriana was tired, so very tired, of letting herself sink.

"I think it's strange she met a man here and no one knew. No best friend noticed? She hadn't mentioned him?"

"Online dating, maybe?"

Adriana shrugged. "Possibly."

"Let's go find Nathan Hall," Levi said, heading for the car.

"Wait." Adriana found the nerve to interrupt, since they'd brought Blue all the way out here and the dog hadn't even gotten a cup of whipped cream for her trou-

bles. That was probably okay, since too much dairy wasn't
good for dogs, but Adriana didn't want the trip out to
be for nothing. Blue was wearing her vest, so she knew
she was working, or would be soon. "I still need to look
around. As long as we're here, let me give Blue the scent
and see if she picks anything up on the trails right here."
Adriana nodded to the woods next to the coffee shop,
which had trails running through them. "That way we
would at least know if whoever took her did so by car or
walked her into the woods."

It made sense to go ahead and check, Levi thought.

"You're right." Levi stopped. Nodded. "Okay, let's do
that, then."

Adriana petted Blue for a minute, then reached down
with the socks.

"Ready, girl?"

TEN

Once again, to Levi it looked almost like magic, how the dog and her owner worked together. Or maybe his thoughts were just clouded by the fact that Adriana herself looked like magic. Her eyes were sparkling, and he could tell she loved this part of her job—the search, her dog as a partner—and her hair was in loose curls around her shoulders, dark and shining in the sunshine.

He was supposed to be getting her help with this investigation, not noticing her hair, her curls, or the way she looked at life. But he kept finding himself distracted.

Not enough that he felt it interfered with his investigation. But he did need her. He just had to let her help and somehow keep his emotions in check, hold her at arm's length, and that was getting harder to do.

He'd actually grabbed her hand that morning. He remembered how it felt under his. Warm. Soft. And then he remembered the exact moment he'd realized what he was doing, that he couldn't do that, and had yanked it away.

She'd looked almost hurt, just before her face had become unreadable, but surely...

So maybe she was attracted to him, too. In that case, it was just a mutual case of "what a bad idea." A cop and an SAR worker? Not exactly a perfect match. Twice the stress, twice the danger, twice the heaviness. Levi needed to find a sweet…preschool teacher or something. Someone who didn't snark at him, who didn't make him feel so…

Alive. Because when someone made you feel alive like that, and then they left?

Yeah, he knew what that was like. Although had Melissa ever made him feel quite like Adriana did? He honestly wasn't sure.

Either way, the way he was drawn to her wasn't something he should act on, he knew that. He wasn't ready to try again with love. Not yet. Maybe he never would be.

Because even though he knew he hadn't been to blame for all that had gone wrong in their relationship, part of him still wondered… What if it was him? What if he wasn't a good enough husband?

What if he tried again, fell in love with Adriana and then wasn't enough for her?

No. He definitely wasn't ready.

He followed her into the woods after she'd given Blue the scent from the article of clothing the Marstons had given her.

"The idea is that she'll get the scent and I'll be able to tell from her behavior if Raina was here, and if she was taken deeper into the woods or not," Adriana explained.

Levi just nodded and tried to keep up as Blue walked on one of the established trails. Raven Pass was crisscrossed with them. Many of them became ski trails in the winter and he thought this might be one of them with how wide it was. There was plenty of room to walk beside Adriana, so he did.

He sensibly resisted the urge to grab her hand.

Besides, she was working right now. She wouldn't want that.

Then again, he didn't know *what* she wanted. He'd studiously avoided any kind of conversation that could get too serious or make them feel too close to each other.

Because the fact was he just couldn't take getting hurt again. And Adriana was so *much*. In a good way. So much sunshine. So much fire. Spark. So much potential to break his heart and he just couldn't do that again. Not right now.

"She was here." Adriana said it quietly. "Somewhere near here."

"You can tell that?"

She shrugged. "Technically, not for sure. Blue hasn't alerted. There's nothing objective to say that I'm right. But from knowing my dog, I would say yes."

Levi nodded. "Anything more solid than that? Should we keep looking?"

Adriana shrugged. "Give me a bit longer, but I'm thinking no." She turned around, made her way back toward the parking lot, watching the dog's behavior carefully.

"I think she gets the scent almost just as strongly out there. Now you'll understand this is my interpretation, but I think probably it's just that the scent got trapped in the trees. I don't think she was ever in the woods. I think she was probably only here in the parking lot."

Levi stepped a few steps away and looked around. It was easy to imagine the day much like this one. Some cars in the parking lot.

"If she didn't leave the parking lot on her own, then our best course of action is to find the guy she was with."

"Did she mention him to friends? On social media?" Adriana asked.

"Friends have been interviewed and didn't mention anything. Officer Koser conducted those earlier today and texted me to say that nothing new turned up. Social media didn't have anything definitive either."

"Wouldn't she have mentioned him to her parents? If she'd been meeting him?" Levi raised his eyebrows. "So you think she met him and he took her?"

Levi shook his head. "No."

"No?" She waited.

"Did you hear what the barista *didn't* say?" Levi asked as he opened the car door.

She opened hers while she thought and let Blue climb in first.

Adriana had just started to shake her head when he continued.

"The barista didn't mention their meeting being strange. If this is the same killer who began committing crimes more than twenty years ago, he couldn't meet with a woman that young without sticking out. See what I mean? The killer has to be years older. The cashier at the coffee shop would have been more specific, about her meeting an older man. And unless it was Harrison Ford's doppelgänger, she wouldn't have made the comment about him being handsome."

All of which made sense. SAR puzzles just made so much more sense to her than the law-enforcement kind. Not for the first time, she couldn't help but think how eager she was for this case to be over, to get back to her normal job.

Although she wouldn't see Levi as often. Although

their paths crossed on occasion, it would be a rare occurrence. Not every day.

She would miss him, she realized. Which made her aware of another truth. Even if they were only friends, it would still hurt her if he disappeared from her life.

Was there no way to protect herself from all possible pain?

Please don't let me get hurt, she prayed, while trying to focus on the task at hand.

"So who is the guy?" she asked.

"No idea," Levi admitted as he put the car in Reverse. "But hopefully that's what we're going to find out. Let's go to the police department, get his address and then go talk to him."

At Adriana's request, they dropped off Blue at her place on their way to the police department. While they were there, Adriana offered to fix some lunch for them. Her stomach had started growling earlier and she was sure he must be hungry, too.

"No, it's fine. You don't need to do that."

"I'm happy to." She was already halfway through the assembly of two roast-beef sandwiches. Each of her dogs had also had a tiny piece of roast beef, even though they couldn't have much since the sodium wasn't good for them. A little for a treat was okay, though.

"I just feel bad. It's not your job to feed me."

And yet, packing two lunches felt so good to her. It was nice to consider someone besides herself and to feel like she was helping to take care of him.

Had he had a previous girlfriend make him feel bad for requesting that she make him food? Or something similar? Even as she thought it, Adriana was surprised at how much she disliked the concept of him ever having had a significant other. Of course, he would have, though. Men as handsome as Levi didn't stay single their entire lives.

"Why are you being so weird about this?" She finally couldn't hold back the words, even knowing it wasn't really her business.

He seemed comfortable around her. Comfortable in her house, sitting at her table with coffee. He was personable, at least on a professional level.

But there was some kind of line he'd drawn in invisible sand that he wouldn't let himself cross.

Of all things, *that* should make her back off. Leave him alone.

But some flash of insecurity in his kind, light eyes had her feeling like whatever the line was about, it wasn't what he really wanted.

He was looking at her now, hesitation in his gaze.

She stepped closer. Handed him the bag with his lunch in it. "Here."

He nodded and took it from her. "Thank you."

She made herself step back. The last thing she wanted to do was jeopardize their working relationship.

"Ready?" he asked. She nodded and followed him outside onto her front deck.

Maybe she'd been right. Maybe making lunch was too personal a thing.

She turned to lock her door, then opened her mouth to apologize as Levi, who was standing beside her, held his remote up to unlock his patrol car.

The car exploded in a concussive blast, the fireball sending out a wall of force that punched and pushed them backward.

Adriana stumbled back, or flew, she couldn't tell. Or

had Levi shoved her? They landed hard on the wooden deck, and Adriana could feel a bruise forming on her hip where she'd taken most of the impact. Her ears were still ringing from the blast and a thrumming headache had started pounding.

For a second she was lying there, her mind trying to grapple with what had happened and make it make sense. But there wasn't much chance of that. Nothing about this made sense.

"Book inside, now. The house." Levi's breathless voice beside her left no room to argue.

She scrambled behind her for the doorknob, scooting back toward the house for safety.

Her keys. Where were her keys?

The car in the driveway was still burning, a creaking, crackling heap of useless metal.

She had been in that vehicle half an hour ago. So had her dog.

Keys. She had to focus on getting inside. She blinked away a fresh wave of dizziness and fumbled across the front deck on her hands and knees.

There they were.

She reached for them and unlocked the door. "Come with me," she said to Levi and surprisingly, he didn't argue.

They both stepped into the house. Both dogs were barking, dancing in a frenzy of excitement. Adriana almost couldn't breathe. They'd almost been killed.

Incinerated.

No.

"What happened?" she finally asked, her heartbeat still in a tangle in her chest.

His face didn't reassure her. For once, his expression

said nothing about having this under control, and only hinted at confusion.

Even fear...

"Someone is taking this awfully far." At least that's what she thought he mumbled. It was hard to hear, from the way he clenched his teeth.

"Should I call 911?" The words felt silly. A cop was standing here with her and he hadn't been able to stop the attack.

"Yes," he said, again surprising her. He held up his phone, which was vibrating. "I'm sorry, I have to take this."

If he could ignore the look on Adriana's face and just do his job, Levi knew he'd have a much better chance at solving this case.

"Hello?" he said into the phone as he walked away from her, despite the look of sheer, unmasked fear in her wide eyes.

There was no answering voice at the other end. But the "unknown number" on his caller ID had made him ready for anything. Expecting anything.

"Officer Wicks."

Prepared or not, it was still spine-chilling to hear his name uttered by a genderless, heavily computerized voice.

"This isn't your fight. You don't have all the information. It is necessary to do this. Stop getting in the way. Next time, the bomb goes off with you in the car."

He fumbled in his pocket for a piece of paper, to write down the caller's words. But, of course, he had none when he needed it.

The phone clicked. No more voice. No more words.

"I called it in." Adriana walked toward him, her voice shaking. "Who was that?"

"I need paper." He ignored her question for now, trying to focus on what had been said to him. "Do you have some?"

Her eyes widened even more at his short tone. He would apologize later, but not right now. Right now he needed to write down the message as best he could remember it.

"What on earth?" Adriana muttered under her breath as she handed him the paper. Levi scrawled down the message, knowing he was forgetting some of the word choices and hoping he was close enough.

The part that had stuck with him most was the fact that the caller—theoretically, the serial killer he was after—felt justified in his or her actions. Not that it surprised him. Serial killers often felt they were righting some kind of perceived wrong, or helping the world in some way, according to their warped perspectives. But this person's words hadn't sounded crazy, which was perhaps the creepiest thing about the call.

He'd been on the phone with a person who had killed over five people. That person was now after *him*.

It was more than he wanted to grapple with right now. Especially with his shell of a patrol car burning in the driveway.

"The caller said next time I'd be inside," he mumbled. That implied that his unlocking the door hadn't set off the mechanism of the bomb, as he'd assumed. Instead, someone had chosen when to remotely trigger it.

The killer apparently had triggered it right when they were close enough to be in real danger, to have *almost* died.

"Why does this person appear to keep halfheartedly attempting to kill me?"

"Because they don't have the same kind of compulsion to kill you as they do the other victims." He heard Judah's voice as his brother stepped inside the front door, which Adriana had apparently left open. "You really should shut that. The fire department is outside putting the fire out, but that doesn't mean leaving the door unlocked is a good plan with a serial killer."

Levi hadn't meant to ask the question aloud, but nodded at his brother anyway. "Thanks for letting me know. Didn't mean to leave it unlocked. So tell me what you think of this—the killer keeps doing things that might kill me, but doesn't try too hard because he'd rather I just back off?"

Judah nodded. "Exactly. You are in the way of whatever his plan is. But you aren't one of the ones who is 'supposed' to die, according to him."

It was a sick train of thought to consider. But it made sense.

The problem for him was that he wasn't going to quit. Which meant he would stay in the way and still be in danger.

And the more Adriana pitched in on the case, the more she would be in danger, too. Because the killer didn't have anything against him personally. He was just a liability. And she was, too, now that she was helping. Serial killers, while they murdered people who fit their profile, also were known to kill people who didn't fit the profile but who got in their way. Like law enforcement.

And, he feared in this case, like search-and-rescue workers who had volunteered to help with the case and had the skills to blow it wide open.

"I came as soon as we got the call." Judah was speaking to him again. Then he turned to Adriana. "Thanks for calling it in. You did a good job giving details and staying calm. The dispatch worker was impressed with that."

Adriana offered a small smile and Levi felt proud of her. That was weird, wasn't it, like they were something more than friends?

"Thanks. I didn't feel that calm, but I've learned in SAR work that panic doesn't get you anywhere," Adriana said from where she stood petting her dogs. Blue had barked when they'd come inside, but almost seemed to sense that Adriana needed her to be calm now. Both Blue and Babe stood by her like sentries, letting her pet them.

"The killer called me," Levi said, wondering if he should have waited until Adriana had left the room to tell his brother.

"And said?" Judah asked.

Adriana asked nothing. She just stared, eyes wide.

"Essentially warned me that next time I'd be in the car." Levi showed Judah and Adriana the words he'd jotted down.

"Give me the phone number it came from?"

"Blocked." Levi shook his head.

"Not that hard to do these days," Judah said.

"So he's trying to give you a chance to live by stopping the investigation," Adriana chimed in. "And you can't take it because it would mean other people dying."

Well, when she put it that way, he sounded like some kind of hero, and if he was honest with himself, he saw a spark of something in her eye that seemed to imply she almost thought of him that way, too.

But she couldn't, surely. She must see the way that he worked too much, like his wife had said. And the way he tended to be a bit of a lone wolf. He'd worked well with Jim in the past, but he got tired of waiting for other people sometimes and preferred to just charge ahead alone when he had an idea. All of those things made him imperfect and she was *still* looking at him that way.

He didn't deserve it. And somehow never wanted it to stop.

When this case was solved, what was he going to do? Adriana would still be a coworker, so not anyone he could afford to casually date, lest they break each other's heart and make their jobs awkward.

But he'd gotten so used to having her at his side during the course of these last few days that he would miss her.

Maybe more than as just a listening ear. If he let himself, he could admit that he enjoyed spending time with her just as a person, as a woman, which was something he hadn't let himself feel in years.

"You must be getting uncomfortably close," Judah offered, "for the killer to be willing to escalate things this way."

"Or they are just getting unhinged." Adriana didn't look pleased with that idea.

Levi couldn't say he was, either. And Judah's tightened jaw spoke for itself.

"I've got guys outside ready to look at the car when it's cool enough," Judah said finally. "To see what type of bomb it was and if there is any kind of forensic evidence that could help us out."

"Are you expecting to find any?" Adriana asked.

"Not really," Judah admitted. "Not easily, anyway.

Whoever this is has been killing for years. They could get sloppy. But only if they're desperate."

"I like the idea of someone getting desperate enough to leave evidence, but not enough to actually want them after me like that," Levi said, attempting a joke.

His brother, as he should have known would be the case, was not amused.

"Is this some kind of joke to you?" Judah's voice lowered and his tone darkened. "That your car got blown up, the first Raven Pass cruiser ever to be destroyed—by the way, I heard that tidbit from Officer Clark on the way here—and that someone is after you? That's just funny?"

"I'm going to go make sure Blue got enough food earlier." Adriana cleared her throat.

Great. They'd made her feel awkward in her own house. That was another level of being a bad guest. Bad enough that she'd made him lunch today, like it was her job to take care of him.

No one had taken care of him since the day he'd moved out of his house after high-school graduation. No one. Not like that.

It still stung that the marriage he'd thought might have that kind of love hadn't. No, instead it had only left him with betrayal from the discovery of her unfaithfulness and a deep sense of cynicism that he couldn't shake no matter how lighthearted he tried to be about life.

And rather than thank Adriana for the sandwich, for thinking of him, and actually find the guts to tell her why he'd acted so weird, he'd gotten his car blown up in her driveway and interrupted her safe world with this entire case.

Yeah, he might miss her when this was all over, but she would undoubtedly be glad to be rid of him.

"Of course I don't think it's funny," he said now to his brother, doing the best he could to keep some of the pure anger from his tone. Judah was still his brother, no matter what kind of stupid things he might say sometimes. "I think it's awful and I want it to end—that's why I'm barely sleeping and I'm working this case every single second I'm awake."

"So don't make jokes."

"It's what I do, okay? Some people drink too much, some people find a hobby, some people make jokes to handle it. Let me do things my way."

Judah stared at him in that way only older brothers could, and then Levi really heard himself.

"Yeah, okay, I could make jokes and also handle it better, too. Pray about it? Is that what you're thinking?"

Sometimes Judah was a lot like their eldest brother, Ryan, that way. Levi followed Jesus, too—at least he sure tried his best—but it had never been quite the same for him as it was for his two older brothers. For all his gruff attitude, Judah loved Jesus in a big way, the same with Ryan.

Levi…followed Him. Knew a lot about Him. And had trusted Him to save him.

He loved Him. Sure. Just not, you know, in a squishy, overly emotional kind of way.

Something that was hardly Judah's business. He didn't care what his brother thought, or that he might disagree.

"Let me handle my life, Judah," he said, and pain flashed in Judah's eyes.

"Fine," his brother said and walked away.

ELEVEN

She wasn't trying to eavesdrop, truly she wasn't, but Adriana could hear every word from the kitchen. Neither of the brothers were trying particularly hard to be quiet.

It made her uncomfortable beyond belief that the killer had probably called Levi. It was even worse knowing that the person had insinuated that the bomb had been triggered remotely, which meant someone had to have been watching them.

She looked around the house, where she'd always felt so comfortable, and ran her eyes over the ceilings, down the walls. Looked at the room full of furniture.

Were they listening, too? Surely her house hadn't been compromised. No one could have gotten inside without the dogs alerting her to it.

Right?

"Sorry you had to hear that," Levi said as he walked into the kitchen and sighed. The sound came from deep within, less frustration and more heaviness. "I assume you did, based on the fact that you're just standing here, looking alarmed."

She was literally caught in the act. Adriana felt her face color, but she shrugged, refusing to feel bad for overhearing a conversation that had taken place in her own house.

"You guys will work it out. Families do that." TV made it seem like that, anyway. Her family fought and threatened and stormed out. Her parents had divorced when she was two. Her siblings had more drama in their lives than a daytime TV show. So she didn't know from experience. But deep down, Judah and Levi both seemed to care too much about each other not to want to patch up their differences. She suspected faith made an impact on that. She was the only Christian in her own family, and while it certainly didn't make her perfect, it did make her want to live her life a certain way, to be at peace with other people.

"We'll see. He's gone outside to keep an eye on the scene until more officers get here. Right now I'm more worried about who blew up my car."

His voice was more gruff than usual, a low, gravelly growl. He was taking this personally and she understood and didn't blame him.

Someone had crossed a line today. Several lines.

"What now?" she asked him, watching his expression as he thought about her question.

His facial muscles relaxed, and Adriana felt relieved that she'd said the right thing.

"When they finish looking at my car, we're going to look at the list of known victims in this case and try to figure out why the killer feels like he or she is justified."

Not what she'd expected. "What?"

"Whoever is after me seems to think he is doing some kind of service. It's a mission to rid the world of people doing something wrong."

"That sweet woman you looked up on social media,

that we heard her parents talk about for hours?" Adriana shook her head.

Levi shrugged. "Listen, I'm not judging any of the victims. Obviously, no one actually deserved to die and our killer is absolutely crazy. But people aren't what they seem. You get used to that, especially working in the job that I do."

Maybe that explained his cynicism. Still, Adriana felt like it must have more to do with a past relationship than just cases Levi had worked. He held on to his hesitation to trust too tightly for it to be just work related.

At least she thought so. Would she ever have the chance to ask him about it?

The memory of his hand on her flitted across her brain, entirely inappropriate to the situation, and she swatted it away.

"Are we going to talk to Nathan Hall, the man who was having coffee with Raina?" Adriana asked because she felt like they were jumping around. In SAR work, she didn't just leave the search grid and run off to someone else's unless she had an exceptionally concrete reason to do so.

Nothing the caller had said to Levi sounded like that kind of reason to her. No, it felt like they should stay focused on what they had been doing before.

He stared at her for a minute, and the hard planes of his jaw showed no hint of softening into a smile. For a second, she wished she hadn't offered her thoughts at all. After all, as she kept reminding herself, she wasn't an equal partner in this. She was a K9 handler, a small aspect of the case, and for Levi to involve her in any more than that was giving her a glimpse into a world and a case where she didn't fully belong. He was the one who had the training and knew what he was doing. She needed to trust him to do it.

"You're right." He nodded once. "Let's eat some food and go talk to that guy. You're right, that's where we should have started."

Their sandwiches were still in the bags on the front deck, but going outside to retrieve them would have done nothing for Adriana's appetite, so she remade them, offering Levi one and biting into the other.

"I'll let you buy me ice cream for dessert after we talk to him," she said around bites, still uneasy with how serious Levi was being. She had truly misjudged him. If anything, he was *too* focused when working a case. He didn't take anything lightly at all.

Why did she insist on assuming things about people she didn't know? It was a bad habit she needed to break.

"That sounds like a good plan."

There, she'd almost gotten a smile from him. It was enough for now. She finished her sandwich. Levi had finished before her and was already getting ready to leave.

"Would you mind if we took your car?" he asked her.

Adriana smiled. "I had assumed."

"Someone is dropping off another patrol car for me later. But they're not here yet, clearly. Before we go anywhere—" his voice had no hint of humor and neither did his face "—I want the crime scene team to check your car for us and make sure there's nothing...wrong."

Interesting, roundabout way to say that he wanted them to make sure there wasn't a bomb inside it anywhere, but in some ways she could appreciate him not wanting to say that out loud.

She didn't particularly want to articulate those thoughts, either.

More officers arrived soon, including the crime-scene team Levi had mentioned. Their check of her car revealed that it was fine. Adriana hesitated before they left, trying to decide whether it was safer for the dogs to stay or come with them, but in the end she decided that law enforcement would probably have a presence outside her house for most of the time they were gone.

"Smart choice," Levi told her when they were finally driving away. The shell of his car still sat in the driveway. "They'll be safe there."

Adriana hoped so. While it was no secret to anyone who knew her how much she loved her dogs, she doubted her friends fully realized that the animals were all she had left.

Yes, technically her mother was still alive. But her being in prison didn't exactly lend itself to a close relationship. Adriana thought she might have a sister in there, too, at this point.

If anyone understood her family situation, they'd know multiple things about her. First, why she'd so willingly followed Robert up to Alaska. Second, why her dogs meant the world to her.

That was what happened when the people you should have been able to count on in life couldn't be counted on for anything.

"So did you get Nathan Hall's address?"

Levi had left her alone before they'd left her house and had gone outside to talk to his fellow officers.

"Yes, we were able to call the station and they looked it up for me."

"Was he in your system?"

"He had a parking ticket a couple of years ago. But mostly they know how to research online." He smiled at her, the first real smile she'd seen of his in what felt like hours.

How long had it been since they'd been at the coffee shop? This day would not end.

"What did they find out?"

"He's twenty-nine, works on the north slope with an oil company two weeks on, two weeks off. Has a dating profile on at least one website," Levi said.

"Does he know we are coming?" She wasn't sure how cops did it in real life. Did they show up unannounced, hoping to surprise people?

"He knows someone wants to talk to him, but not that we are coming now."

She nodded, trying to take it in. She hadn't had nearly enough time to think before they were pulling into a driveway of a nice house on Blueberry Street, one of the residential areas of Raven Pass, with twisty, narrow neighborhood roads and a lot of houses close together.

It wasn't the kind of place she pictured a serial killer living. But that didn't make Nathan Hall innocent.

"I should have brought Blue to sniff out the area, to see if Raina was ever here," she said, mostly thinking out loud. She climbed out of the car once Levi had parked and followed him to the front door.

"She wasn't here. Really. I think you're going to agree with me that he's not part of the equation at all when we are talking about the disappearance."

"So why are we talking to him?"

"He was likely the last person besides the killer to see her alive. That counts for something. And a guy she was meeting for coffee—whether they met online like we wonder, or in some other way—might have some different kinds of insights than her parents had. I still want to figure out what the killer was saying on the phone when he said they 'deserved it,' or however he phrased it."

The words still gave Adriana chills, as did the fact that Levi had really talked to him in person at all.

"Okay, makes sense." She stood beside him at the door, waiting for him to ring the bell.

She wondered if the next half hour or so was going to give them another lead. And how close they'd be to a killer before this was all over.

Levi had beaten himself up all the way to Nathan Hall's house, even as he'd talked to Adriana and tried to seem relatively calm. He'd lost it, back there at the house. Something about seeing his car incinerated in Adriana's driveway and getting a threatening call inside her house...both had messed up his head.

Of course he needed to talk to Hall. This whole case had him so messed up, so out of order, that more than once he'd broken procedure and rather than go in a logical order, bounced around.

His panicked investigation wasn't going to help anyone. It could hurt. He needed to make this less personal, and fast.

Adriana was...

They were...

Yes, he wanted her to be safe. But he had to get her out of his head, had to get rid of this sense of urgency.

Deep breaths, solve the case. One logical step at a time. Like his brother would.

"Can I help you?"

The man who answered the door was a few inches taller than Levi. Average build, nice enough looking, he would guess, though he didn't really know what women considered attractive these days. In any case, there was nothing glaringly wrong with him that disproved their working theory about Raina having met him on an on-line-dating website.

"Officer Wicks, Raven Pass Police Department." Levi flashed his badge. "We have some questions for you about Raina Marston."

The man's face went pale.

"She never texted me back. Is she…okay?"

If he was acting, he deserved an award because Levi was familiar with the genuine signs of shock and he could see them all on this guy's features.

"Can I ask how you met her?" Levi ignored the question.

He named a popular online-dating site, not the one Levi's coworkers had found his profile on. Apparently he was a member of more than one.

Levi nodded, made a note to call the police department and have someone confirm his story later, that Raina had an account on that site.

"Is she okay?" Hall asked again.

This time Levi didn't ignore him. "I'm sorry, no. She was murdered and we need to ask you some questions. You may have been one of the last to see her alive."

His eyes widened and he nodded, stepping out of the doorway and back into the house just enough to motion them in. "Come inside, I'm happy to talk to you."

They stepped in.

"Have a seat." Nathan Hall motioned to the dining room table. They followed him and sat.

The first thing Levi noticed was the mess every-where. Not a serious mess, like he'd seen in some child-abuse or drug cases he'd worked, but clutter. The house itself was nicely decorated.

Levi waited. "Is anyone else here we should talk to?"

"No, not right now… She's not… I don't…" Nathan Hall pulled at the collar of his shirt.

And bingo. He'd found what the man was hiding.

Adriana was looking around also, but the slight frown on her face said she wasn't quite where he was yet in his thinking.

"So, to clarify, you have a…girlfriend who lives here also?"

Hall shook his head. "She doesn't… No one else lives here."

"No girlfriend?"

Maybe he'd pushed it one question too far, but the embarrassed man finally squared his shoulders and glared back at Levi.

"The decor is my wife's, okay? She isn't here because she left me. She isn't coming back."

And yet, the place mats on the table said the breakup must have been recent enough that the man probably shouldn't have been on an online dating site.

"You were just on a casual kind of date with Raina, right?" Adriana asked in a calm voice.

Levi almost cut her off. First of all, they didn't need to lead him to any kind of answer. Second, he couldn't believe the way she was talking to the guy. Like he was worth any kind of compassion. The guy had cheated on his wife. Levi had no sympathy for anyone who would do that.

No, it wasn't that. Everyone needed compassion. Years in law enforcement had convinced Levi of that and he was used to showing it to people who didn't seem to deserve it.

It was the fact that she seemed to have some sympathy toward him. Like she understood?

The only reason Levi was able to keep his own voice calm was that he knew that would put the suspect at ease, make him more likely to give them more information. It was basic police knowledge. Surely Adriana's casual lack of reaction was the same thing. She couldn't really understand that kind of thing. At least he hoped not. Sure, it was his business as a friend to hope she had better moral standards—at least that's what he told himself.

"Yes. Casual." Nathan's shoulders fell. "I didn't mean for her to get hurt."

His wife, or Raina?

Levi didn't say anything but Nathan met his eyes. "Either of them," he said and answered the question like it had been asked aloud.

"So did one of them find out about the other?" Again, Adriana's voice was soft. But now that Levi had calmed down he could hear the probing quality in it. She was trying to get information. The least he could do was be quiet and thank her later for doing his job for him.

Nathan shook his head. "Not as far as I know." He blew out a breath. "Yeah, well, maybe. I mean, my wife suspects—that's why she left—but…" He caught himself quickly. "She wouldn't. You don't think…?"

That his wife had tried to punish his sorry self by killing the woman he admitted to having one date in a coffee shop with? No. Besides, they were chasing a serial killer.

Adriana looked to Levi. He shook his head.

"Listen, ask me whatever you need to, okay? But I want to get that part of my life over with and keep trying to work things out with my wife."

Considering it had been less than a week since Raina's

disappearance, it seemed an awfully quick about-face of that lifestyle, but Levi reminded himself that deciding that really wasn't his problem.

"Did you know her before you saw one another at the coffee shop?"

Nathan shook his head. Then paused. "Well, sort of, yes. We met online. We had been text messaging back and forth for about a week. She'd asked if we could meet, but I was still deciding. The day we met for coffee, I had decided last-minute that I did want to meet. I sent her a text and she agreed to meet and suggested Raven's Rest."

It seemed consistent with her parents' story. If she'd been planning to get coffee that afternoon, anyway, then using that as a meeting place made sense also. Still. "Can we see the messages?"

The man reached in his pocket for his phone, punched the screen a few times and handed it to Levi.

He read through them. Fairly standard. They felt closer than they were because they were talking online, they'd decided to finally meet...

Reading the messages sent chills up his spine. Not because there was anything strange about the messages, although it still bothered him to know that Nathan had sent them when he'd been married. It wasn't that he felt like he was perfect and got to sit on a throne and judge other people. But trust and faithfulness mattered to Levi. It hurt to know not everyone felt that way.

"Thanks." He handed the phone back to Nathan. It supported the story as he had told it.

The man wasn't full of integrity. But Levi doubted he was a killer. They'd keep him on a person-of-interest list out of an abundance of caution, warn him they might need to talk to him again, but he hadn't been an adult long enough to have been the one who'd committed the crimes decades ago.

It might not be someone from Raven Pass at all.

It might be time to pull in some guys from other agencies, maybe talk to the FBI in Anchorage about the situation. The last thing Levi wanted was to turn the case over to anyone else, but he also didn't want his pride and determination to get in the way of it being solved.

"Thanks for your time," he said as he stood. Adriana looked surprised but she stood as well. "We'll be back in touch. Don't leave the state without talking to someone."

His eyes widened. "I'm not like a suspect, right?"

"You're still part of the investigation."

Nathan's face fell but he nodded. "Okay, I hope you find out what happened. She seemed really sweet."

He'd been planning to see her again, hadn't he? Levi had to shake his head.

Levi opened the front door and held it open for Adriana, who walked out in front of him.

They both eyed the car suspiciously, but what were they going to do? They had to drive it. Levi climbed underneath and gave the undercarriage a cursory once-over. Same with under the hood.

"You don't think…?" Adriana trailed off.

"We would have seen someone mess with it, the short amount of time we were in there."

At least he hoped so.

"It's fine." He paused. "You wait until I turn it on before you climb in, though, okay?"

She stepped back onto the front deck.

He started the car. Nothing happened.

She hurried and climbed in beside him. "I never

should have let you do that. I didn't like that at all, thank you." Her voice was tight and tense.

"I didn't want to put you in danger."

She didn't comment, just stared at him, like maybe she didn't love the idea of him being in peril, either. Something was thick in the air between them and Levi waited, but Adriana didn't say anything. The look in her eyes, though...

Could he read women anymore? More importantly, could he read *this* woman? Because everything in her eyes said she cared about him. That maybe it would be more than professional courtesy to be upset if he'd blown up. And he had to admit that he cared about her, too.

He mattered to her. The thought was a weight on his chest. He had let someone down the last time they'd mattered to him. He must have, surely, or his wife wouldn't have been unfaithful, wouldn't have left him.

He could vaguely hear Ryan's voice in his head, disputing that. His family had told him it wasn't his fault. His pastor, too, had reassured him.

Still, some part of him repeated the lie like the echo of a beat on a bass drum.

Your fault. Your fault.

Adriana couldn't look at him that way. He didn't deserve it.

But unless he was wrong...she was. He looked away, tried to break whatever pull there was between them.

"What did you think?" she finally asked after a few minutes of neither of them speaking.

"About Nathan Hall?"

"Yes."

He shook his head. "I can't believe he'd do that to

his wife or Raina. I couldn't stand to listen to him try to explain."

"Do you think he knows anything, though? About her disappearance?"

Levi shook his head.

"I agree." She hesitated. "On both counts. Did…? I mean… You know what, it's not my business, never mind."

"What?" he asked as he drove toward the police department. Since the trip to talk to Nathan had mostly been a bust, he wanted to pick up information about the other victims to take back to Adriana's house to work on. Of course, she didn't know that yet, but he was hoping she'd be okay with the plan.

He'd toyed with the idea of moving her to a safe house but knew she'd be resistant to that. Sure, they could work on the case at the police department, but she'd still have to go back to her house to sleep. They might as well work from there now. She wasn't less safe there than she was anywhere else. The attacks could have happened anywhere.

"Nothing."

Clearly it hadn't had anything to do with the case, so Levi let it go. It was surprising, though, that she'd think to ask what seemed like it must have been a personal question… Wasn't it?

He needed to finish this case and get some distance from Adriana. Because it was getting more and more difficult to keep her at arm's length.

TWELVE

"Anything yet?" Adriana asked from where she sat across from Levi at her dining-room table. Levi had asked if they could work on going over case files at her house and she hadn't argued. Especially because he'd promised her Chinese food for dinner.

"Nothing is jumping out at me." He rubbed his head with his hand.

Adriana had been reading an update from her SAR team about what they'd been working on that week, but the look of near defeat on Levi's face made her want to help him. Even if she was eager to get back to the life she was familiar with.

At this point, even if he asked her to step down, she'd fight him on it. He needed her, whether he wanted to or not.

And she needed to know, strangely, that someone was looking out for him. So far, in all her interactions with him, it had been clear that he was used to being alone. Fending for himself.

Was it wrong to want to be the one who helped him out? Who cared about him?

She had tried over and over again to tamp down those

feelings, but so far it hadn't worked. Adriana was close to giving up. To just letting herself care about him, even if he never let her get close. Even if the feelings were never reciprocated.

But what if she got hurt again…?

"I can try looking, if you think it might be worth it," she offered with a shrug.

"I'd appreciate it more than I can say." He exhaled and reached out to hand the papers to her. "Here."

Her fingers brushed his as she took them. Completely accidental, but she was aware of his touch in a curious kind of way.

"Thanks." She cleared her throat, then looked down at the documents. At first she focused on the things she already knew about the victims. Age. General build. It was all what Levi had told her it was.

Goose bumps sprang up on her arms the third time she read over them. Victim number three had been married.

"This woman was cheating on her husband, according to the notes of people who were interviewed. Some friends, but also the man she was cheating with, confirmed it. It's all personal testimony, but it seems pretty for sure."

"Really?" Levi was frowning. "Is nobody faithful these days?"

Adriana shook her head. "That's not it. Some people are. Would be."

That's when he met her eyes, his own eyes widening.

"So… We're looking at a biased cross section of society."

She stopped what she was doing.

"What are you saying?" Adriana asked.

"What if that is one of the things our victims have in common?" he said aloud, and Adriana felt her own eyes widen as she started shuffling through the pile at double the speed. Levi scooted his chair toward hers and starting looking also.

"Victim number four was also dating a married man."

The same as Raina Marston, though it had only been one date.

How had the killer known? Had they discussed his marriage in the coffee shop? They needed to go back and ask Nathan that.

"Can we link all of them to infidelity of some kind?" Adriana was breathless at the thought that she might have found the link.

"It's looking like it."

Victim one—reports indicated she'd been unfaithful.

Victim two—unknown, but they were curious if more digging would turn up something.

"We need to go back and look at the older murders also."

"If those aren't in the case files, like that kind of information, probably no one knows anymore. Or people would rather not admit to it however many years later."

"Almost thirty years. You have a point."

"Is that what the killer meant, then? As far as rationale?"

Levi stood up and walked across her living room. Then walked back. It was an effortless pace, not frustrated or overly anxious, but it seemed like somehow just the motion of moving helped him to think. And it made Adriana smile because it was just one more part of his personality she thought was fascinating.

"It could be."

His words were hesitant. But his eyes were shining.

They might have finally found a lead. Her heart skipped. She smiled.

Then she yawned as adrenaline finally started to crash and reached up to cover her mouth with a hand. "I'm sorry, this has been fun but tiring."

"Let me order dinner."

She didn't argue with him. He ordered and half an hour later they were eating in relative silence.

"Thanks," Levi said around bites. "For helping with this case, and just being a partner sort of these last few days."

"You don't miss working alone?" she teased him, a smile on her face so he wouldn't misread her tone.

He didn't smile back, though. Instead, he seemed to be thinking. She almost made a joke, anything to lighten the atmosphere that had gotten entirely too serious, but instead she waited, half holding her breath.

"I'm alone too much."

His words were simple, said with a vulnerability that tugged at Adriana's heartstrings. That he could be so honest about something like that attracted her even more, and she found the courage to ask something she hadn't managed to ask before.

"Why haven't you gotten married? I don't believe there hasn't been an opportunity." She didn't need to list his good qualities. Surely he was aware of them.

"I have, actually."

And this was why she had to remember to keep her mouth shut and stay out of other people's business. The quiet hum of the fridge was the only noise, besides the drumming of her fingertips on the tabletop.

She hadn't realized she was drumming. She stilled her hand, shoved it into her lap.

"I am so sorry," she said, shaking her head. She felt her facial muscles tense as she wrestled with regret. Not just for causing awkwardness; she could handle that. What she hated was that she'd hurt Levi. He was one of the people she'd grown to trust and she'd never wanted to cause him pain.

"No, it's okay." He shrugged. "It's just that no one knows, except Judah, of course. I kind of came here to start over."

Something else they had in common, though he didn't know it. Maybe it would be her turn next to share her story.

Rather than being awkward, though, the silence felt full. Adriana took another bite of food. Levi said nothing. They finished eating.

Adriana stood up, took her plate to the sink and was about to ask Levi if he wanted to call it a night and work more in the morning when she heard a noise outside. Sort of a half shuffle, half thump.

Something that sounded very much like someone in her backyard.

"What was that?" she asked, her voice quiet.

Levi's face was unreadable. Completely blank.

"Get in a closet. Somewhere away from the windows. Now."

Fear choked her almost immediately, her throat closing so much that it made swallowing difficult. The events of the last few days, the bodies they'd found, all combined to become an overwhelming force suffocating her body's desire to breathe.

She had to do what Levi said, to push through the panic enough to take shelter.

The pantry was the first place that caught her eye, and she didn't wait for him to tell her twice. She jumped from the table, then flung open the door and fell to the floor. Blue and Babe followed after her. Even with the addition of the dogs, there was room for at least two more people. Not that there were that many of them there who needed to take shelter.

"Levi, aren't you coming in?"

"I need to get whoever this is."

It was like earlier, when he'd insisted she not get in the car and then had started it up on his own. She'd stood there on the deck, farther away from danger, and it had made her feel sick. It felt wrong to let him shoulder all the risk, alone. Even if she was only working with him temporarily, that wasn't what partners did. Not at all.

"No, come in here," she insisted.

"I need to—"

"Levi!" The tone that she used wasn't one she'd heard in ages, probably years. It was every ounce of bossy and "don't take no for an answer" that she possessed, and it worked, because he came to the door and looked at her.

"If you leave, I'm unprotected here. At least, for my sake, stay here." She tried that tactic and saw by the look on his face that he accepted it.

He sat down, pulled the door closed. "Thank you."

She buried her hands in Blue's fur, loving the feel of it between her fingers, fluffy and full.

Levi had pulled out his phone, the light illuminating the mostly dark pantry. The bulb had gone out months ago and she'd never gotten around to replacing it. "Judah, listen, it's Levi. Someone is here, at Adriana's house.

Outside. I saw a shadow and Adriana heard a noise. I've got her in an interior closet, the pantry, away from the windows, but I don't like that someone has escalated to stalking."

Was the serial killer escalating, if he'd added stalking to his list of crimes? It was a lesser charge than murder, but it was a different one than those he or she had been committing. Adriana found herself wondering, mostly to keep her mind occupied.

"Thanks," Levi said and disconnected, rubbing the back of his neck. "Someone will be right over." He looked at the door again, like he was considering leaving.

"Please," she said again. He nodded. She reached for his hand, truly more for reassurance than anything. She only meant to squeeze it once. But he tightened his grip.

And didn't let go.

His phone screen went black. They were back in the dark.

Then there was silence again. Levi broke it, in a voice barely above a whisper.

"I was married once."

He felt closer in the darkness. The conversation felt more natural.

"What...?" Her voice trailed off, curiosity making her ask the question and then self-consciousness making her immediately wonder if she should have. She wanted to know. But she didn't want him to feel like he had to tell her.

She could still barely breathe, though the pressure on her chest had eased slightly. Listening to his voice seemed to do that, make her calm down.

"She divorced me, five years ago. After she cheated on me. Then died a couple of years later. Car accident."

To have had a loss doubled like that... Adriana couldn't even imagine that, so didn't say anything.

"I guess you probably... I mean, I guess it answers your question. I did try the marriage thing. I wasn't very good at it. So. Now you know."

Adriana could barely breathe. Her chest was tight with his pain, with knowing that he blamed himself. Adriana wasn't stupid. She knew that every relationship took two people and when a relationship broke up both usually had roles to play.

But she'd also seen friends' marriages end without their permission, despite everything they'd desperately tried to patch up that someone else had willingly broken.

"It wasn't your fault." He'd said the woman had cheated on him. Couldn't he see that took the blame away from him for their broken relationship? Did he see that he could have a second chance, start over?

Her heart pounded in her chest, suddenly aware of his proximity in a way that related to more than just safety.

"I wasn't good at marriage. I guess some people just aren't meant for relationships." All she knew was that rather than say all that she was thinking, Adriana leaned toward him. Then she caught herself. Was she really doing this?

She could see the silhouette of his face in the dark, close to her, but not close enough. He moved another inch or two toward her.

She reached up, brushed his cheek with her hand, feeling the stubble along it. Definitely not just a friendly gesture.

There was no going back now. Adriana lifted her face to his and met his lips with hers. It was a kiss unlike any she'd had before. A whisper of reassurance in the dark, something not slow and lingering, but not fast and passionate, either. It was firm. Steady. Soft.

The man might say he wasn't good at relationships, but man, could he kiss. Adriana kissed him back, leaning closer to him as she did so.

For the first time since she could remember, she felt like she wasn't alone.

She felt safe.

Levi didn't know how they'd gone from talking about what a failure he was to kissing, but then her lips were on his and he couldn't have argued with that if he'd tried.

He did know when to pull away, though, and did so, although he felt breathless. When she'd kissed him, he'd forgotten his questions about whether there was something wrong with him that made him too broken for relationships. No, when she kissed him, nothing in him felt broken. She was like healing and wholeness, or at least the reminder of the fact that those could be possible, wrapped up in one beautiful package... One who was kissing him. Alone. In a dark closet. That was why he'd needed to pull away.

Because he wanted to do this right. He wanted to be good at relationships, starting with making sure he didn't promise something more than he was willing to give right now.

Besides all that, she might still be in danger. He needed every sense on alert right now for what might be happening outside.

When she was kissing him? She was all any of his senses noticed.

She was certainly a distraction.

He swallowed hard.

"I'm not sorry," she said, head still close to his. Their foreheads were almost touching and he could feel her breath on his cheek. "Please, please don't say you're sorry. Are you?"

He wouldn't, because he wasn't. But, oh, what had he been thinking? They'd been working together so well, and everything could be jeopardized because of that kiss.

But everything was possible because of that kiss, too. The second chance he'd never really thought he could have was sitting in front of him in a darkened pantry.

His phone beeped.

"My brother's here." Levi stood, and Adriana did, too. They were still close together. And somehow it didn't make Levi want to back away. Instead, he fought the desire to pull her toward him and kiss her again.

"Are you okay?" she asked, softly, like the walls between them were gone. Like she cared and wasn't afraid to show it and wasn't afraid who knew.

"Adriana?" He turned to her, intending to speak, but her full lips caught his eye, and he closed his eyes to kiss her one more time. Softly, with purpose.

"Yes?" she answered after breaking off the contact, sounding as stunned by the entire situation as he felt.

"That question you asked earlier? I'm not sorry, either," he said and stepped out into the light of the kitchen, heading toward the front door.

His heart was still pounding when he got to the front door, and not from the danger, either. This time it was something else entirely.

Some*one* else.

How many years had he known Adriana and just been driven crazy by things about her that now made him feel captivated? Timing was a funny thing.

Maybe he hadn't been ready before.

Was he now? He shook off the question before it could fully land, the feeling of her lips on his still fresh in his mind. The way it felt to have someone look at him like he mattered, like they trusted him.

He wanted to be the type of man she clearly thought he was.

Someone knocked on the door. He took his hand off his sidearm, where he'd placed it just in case, moved the blinds up from the door to confirm that it was Judah, then unlocked the door and let him in. "Thanks for coming," he said. "Nothing out there?"

Judah shook his head as he stepped inside. Levi locked the door behind him. "No *one* out there, anyway. I wouldn't say there was nothing."

"What does that mean?"

Judah handed a note to him. Levi frowned. Whoever was after them had already shot at them and blown up his car. A note made no sense if the killer had appeared to be escalating.

Stop working the case. They deserved their judgment. It was necessary punishment. You and your girlfriend have done nothing wrong, but you have made yourself a target if you won't leave this case alone.

Levi blinked. The words were typed. So writing it must have been premeditated. It was essentially the same message of the phone call, but with more urgency.

The serial killer felt justified for what he or she had been doing. It didn't surprise Levi too much. It was a special kind of insanity, but this was consistent with it.

It made the person that much more dangerous, though, because they had a level of determination that someone committing a general crime of passion might not have.

"So whoever is behind this sent me a warning. And Adriana, too."

Judah nodded.

He could handle the threat against himself. It certainly wasn't the first time. But the idea that Adriana's life was in danger grated at him, and would have even if they hadn't kissed earlier.

What had made the killer assume she was his girlfriend? Was it a sarcastic comment? Or had someone seen them together so much they'd truly assumed that?

Either way, she was in danger, which Levi hated.

She had done nothing to deserve that kind of threat. She wasn't even officially after the killer. *He* was.

Maybe Judah had been right. He should never have let her get involved.

All the places he'd taken her, the danger he put her in over and over, went through his mind. From the darkened woods where they searched for bodies, to the fact that he'd taken her with him to the coffee shop and to talk to Nathan Hall, frustration boiled over. He couldn't believe himself.

What had he been thinking?

He needed to talk to Nathan Hall again. If they were being warned off the case *now*, there had to be a reason. Something about their investigation today had triggered the serial killer's rage.

Which meant that they were getting close. But he wasn't taking her with him this time, not when it could put her in more danger.

"I've got to go somewhere." Levi glanced over his

shoulder, in the direction of Adriana. "Can you stay here with her for me?"

Judah nodded. "No problem. You'll be careful?"

"Yes."

Levi gathered his things and headed for the front door. Outside, there was a replacement patrol car that one of the officers had brought by earlier.

He stopped one more time before walking out.

"Watch out for her." Levi met his brother's eyes, which were overflowing with questions. Yeah, well, he'd answer them later. Or maybe not. Right now he needed to know she'd be okay long enough for him to have the conversation with her that he needed to have.

"I will." Judah nodded.

And God, if You're listening, please take care of her, too. He added the prayer as he reached for the door, trying in one tiny step to trust the God he had walked away from.

"What's going on?" Adriana walked into her entry-way just in time to see Levi reaching for the door. He was leaving? Without saying goodbye?

"I've got to go talk to Nathan Hall again." He hesitated, then walked toward her. "My brother is staying here with you. Be safe and don't go outside, okay?" He pulled her toward him, like it was something he'd done a hundred times, and kissed the top of her forehead. It felt familiar. Like he'd done it a hundred times before. Safe. Warm. Loving? "I'll be back soon."

Judah locked the door behind Levi and looked back at Adriana.

Her cheeks heated under his gaze and she heard his unasked questions.

"Please be careful. I don't want to see him get hurt," Judah finally said, bypassing anything resembling a question and going straight for his point.

She fought the urge to be offended, which was balanced by her appreciation of how much Judah cared about his brother.

She nodded. "Okay."

Judah considered her again. "He's been hurt before."

"He told me," she said, wanting him to know that she wasn't being casual about this. And from the way he'd pulled her close, it didn't feel like it was casual to Levi, either.

"He's never going to stop being a police officer," Judah said.

Why would he? Adriana had had the privilege to watch him this week, and he was good at his job. She'd never ask him to do that.

She frowned. "Right, I know."

"Good." Judah nodded once, like that was all he needed to hear. "I've got some work to do on my computer. If you don't mind, I'd rather stay inside where I'm closer to you."

She would prefer that also. Adriana nodded. "Thank you."

True to his word, Judah walked away to the living room. Adriana went toward the kitchen. Strange that he'd brought up Levi being a police officer. Was that related to what had gone wrong in his marriage? She didn't feel like it was her place to ask necessarily…

But she meant what she'd said to Judah. She would never ask Levi to give that up, even if they started some kind of relationship.

She reached for a dish in the sink and started to scrub

Levi was at this minute at the house of a man who could be a murderer. Maybe he wasn't. But he could be.

Okay, if she thought really hard about it she could understand why a woman who cared about a man wouldn't love him being in constant danger. She and Levi, though…they weren't anything yet.

Adriana just needed to know if she could live with that.

She reached for another dish, scrubbed harder and tried not to think.

THIRTEEN

"You didn't tell me everything earlier," Levi said once a surprised Nathan Hall had opened the door and invited him inside.

The other man looked like a weasel, his eyes wide, his nose practically twitching with nerves. Levi supposed that was what happened when you were trying to live a double life and half of it kept trying to catch you out.

"I didn't," he admitted.

Good. Levi liked it when people didn't bother to argue with him or lie to him. It made his job much easier that way.

"We talked about why you were out dating, and then we left to investigate another lead. I didn't ask you how you and Raina parted, and as it turns out, that is very important also."

"Like, was she mad? Or…?"

"No." Levi shook his head. "Did you walk her to her car at the coffee shop? Did you drive her to your place? Her place? Where did you go after coffee? And where did she go?"

Now he wanted to lead the man, as it was all too easy

to guess that he'd gone back to one of their houses and they'd done things he didn't want to admit to.

"Nothing happened" was all Nathan said.

Levi stared. Kept staring.

The guy finally broke after a few tense seconds. "We were supposed to go back to her place, okay? But you can go there and search it, however you guys do, and you'll know I was never there. I waited in the driveway for a solid half hour, and she never showed. Do you know how embarrassing that is? It's not like it was even my home, where I could go about my business—I'm just sitting in some woman's driveway and she's who knows where."

"Getting murdered, probably, in this case." Levi didn't sugarcoat it.

Nathan paled.

"I need you to tell me every detail you remember about your conversation."

He nodded, then swallowed hard. "Okay, I can do that."

Forty minutes later, Levi left again. According to Nathan, he and Raina had hit it off at the coffee shop. They'd started talking and he'd thought things were going well. That's when they'd made the plan to meet back at her house. They'd left at the same time. She never showed up.

If he was telling the truth, something Levi generally had a fairly good sense about, then she had been abducted somewhere between the coffee shop and her house.

There had been no cell phone on her person when they'd recovered her body. If there was, they could have used the GPS to track her movements. As it was, that wasn't an option. So he had to think through others.

The presence of more traffic cameras in town would have made everything easier as another option. But Raven Pass didn't have many. Without the cell phone tracker or cameras to work with, they would need to talk to anyone who was in the area at the time.

How had someone known to come after Raina, though? It was another hole in the case he needed to figure out. Had someone recognized one of them and then decided to enact what they saw as justice? Or had someone heard them talking in the coffee shop and then decided to kill her?

He thought about the barista's binder. Was there a chance they could find someone that way, through the receipts? Only if they'd paid by credit card. It was a possibility, but not a good one.

It might be a better decision to work the case from another angle.

Levi drove back to Adriana's house, the thought of facing her again making butterflies dance in his stomach. Since they'd kissed, he'd been focused on this discussion with Nathan.

Now he had a chance to think about what they'd done.

And he still wasn't sorry.

He parked the patrol car in the driveway, beside his brother's, and knocked on the door. Judah answered it, and Levi walked inside.

"Everything okay?"

"It's been quiet. Nothing going on."

Levi looked at his brother and tried to gauge what else he wasn't saying. He wouldn't have talked to Adriana about that kiss Levi had given her as he left, would he?

Thinking back on it, though, yes, he might have. Because Levi hadn't just hugged her like a casual friend. He'd pulled her to him and kissed her head like she was his to embrace and say goodbye to and expect she'd be waiting for him. It had been the gesture of someone who was part of a couple. Not friends. Not coworkers.

"Did you say something to her?" he asked, his suspicions high.

"I just don't want you hurt."

Well, that answered that question.

Levi shook his head. "Don't mess with my personal life, okay? I don't need your interfering." Would he always feel like the little brother? He had no problem being younger, not in theory. He'd be in good shape longer and would be able to work longer, both of which were perks. But he was tired of being the one looked down on as less experienced.

It was partially his fault for not making wise choices earlier in life. But he was doing better now.

"Never meant to interfere." Serious as usual, Judah shook his head and started toward the door. "I figured it was you at the door, so I got my things together. Officer Koser is watching her house tonight, so let me know when you're planning to leave and I'll send him over."

Or maybe Levi should call Koser himself, so his brother didn't know exactly what time he left and question him about that. Wisely, he kept those thoughts to himself and just nodded.

He didn't want to antagonize Judah. He just needed him to treat him like the adult he was.

"Have a good night." Levi offered a small olive branch.

"You, too," Judah said, and then he left. Levi locked the door behind him.

Levi walked into the living room, expecting to see Adriana, but she wasn't there. He frowned and walked toward the kitchen.

She was scrubbing at the top of the oven, which looked perfectly clean to him.

"Everything okay?" he asked quietly so he didn't scare her.

She still jumped and he didn't blame her. It had been a tense few days. "Levi, you startled me."

"You're all right?" Was she upset about the kiss? The danger they were in?

About nothing at all?

It had been so long since he wondered what a woman was thinking, he'd forgotten exactly how relationships worked. Did he push her to tell him or let it go?

See, he really wasn't very good at this. A good reason if there ever was one to apologize to Adriana for the kiss and gracefully bow out of whatever it was he had started.

But if he did that, he'd lose her. And that wasn't a good option, either.

Levi took a deep breath and waited. Better let her answer before he stressed too much.

"I'm okay," she sighed, then shrugged. "I was just worried."

He stepped toward her. "Judah was here. You were totally fine."

She looked up at him and he stepped closer. They were close enough to touch, but they didn't—but he still felt her closeness as much as if they were.

"I wasn't worried about me, I was worried about... You know what, it doesn't matter." She smiled. "Never mind."

"You're okay now?" he asked.

She smiled and nodded. "I'm okay."

He reached out, rubbed her shoulder, and she moved closer toward him.

"Levi?"

Her eyes asked him questions that her lips never asked. What were they doing? Was this the start of something or just a weird reaction to the pressure they were under and all the time they'd been spending together?

He didn't have answers to any of it, not tonight, so instead of trying, he just hugged her close to him, loving how much smaller than him she was. She melted into his embrace and he felt his shoulders relax, even as his mind grew firmer in its resolve.

He had to protect this woman he was slowly coming to love.

Had to.

"It's all going to be okay," he told her, hoping that he was telling her the truth.

Usually at night, Adriana was asleep moments after her head hit the pillow, but tonight she heard every creak of the house, every car door slamming from down her street, every strange dream-inspired noise that Blue made.

Levi had *kissed* her.

And then walked into the house of someone they weren't sure was innocent of murder. He'd faced down a possible killer, giving little to no thought for his own safety.

She had meant what she said to Judah, that she could never imagine asking Levi to give up his job. But she hadn't expected to spend the next hour after that unable to concentrate on anything as worries for Levi clamored for her attention in her head.

Could she let herself fall for a cop? She'd already lost one man she'd loved. And Robert had had a desk job, working for the Alaska Department of Fish and Game. But his hobbies had been full of risks, and ultimately one had been responsible for the loss of his life. Should she let herself fall for someone who put himself at more risk than that on a regular basis? Knowing the danger he would be in every day he went to work and even on his days off?

The darkness held no answers and she turned over again. Blue cuddled closer against her. She'd once had a no-dogs-on-the-bed policy, but Blue had broken her of that. Babe preferred to sleep on the floor, have his own space.

What do I do, God? Do I keep moving forward with whatever this is? He hadn't kissed her good-night, but the way he'd held her still made her feel the closeness between them. Everything was different now. Funny how one small kiss could break down so many walls.

They'd decided to spend the next day with Blue, checking out the four sites where they knew the killer had buried bodies, in case there had been additional victims. It could be a pattern.

The more evidence they found, the better their chances of catching the killer got. If Adriana and Blue could find what Levi thought they would tomorrow, they'd have enough for him to finish building his case without her and her dog's help. It might be the last day they would need to work together.

Was it because he was developing feelings for her that he was pulling away with the case? Was he trying to keep her safe and out of it?

It had to be that, because nothing about the way he'd

behaved tonight implied that he wanted to see her less. If anything, it was the opposite.

She turned over again. Men were confusing. She needed to fall asleep so she could wake up for work. At least her job made sense.

FOURTEEN

The drive to the site of the first body was much like it had been days before.

"You ready for today?" Levi asked her, and Adriana nodded and petted her dog.

"I hope so." She patted Blue, trying not to let her nerves show in her voice. They were going to see whether they could find three, or even all four, bodies in one day.

It would be a lot for Blue, and for her, but she had dog treats and toys for the dog; she'd ordered herself a new ebook to read in the bubble bath she was planning to take tonight.

They parked the car and climbed out, then headed to the trailhead. Waiting for them there were Wren and Judah.

"I asked Wren to meet us up here today, in case we were successful," Levi explained after hugging his cousin and nodding good-morning to his brother.

Adriana said hello, too, and found herself wishing she could have been alone with Levi on what would likely be the last day before he went back to work on his own.

They were both busy, driven people. Wasn't that a recipe for drifting apart?

They'd stalled out before they began.

Maybe.

She and Levi had discussed the way she worked and decided that today it was better for Blue to be on a leash. Her dog could otherwise catch a scent of another body, if any others were buried out here; they wanted to focus on the specific area they were suspicious about, not just shoot blindly.

The pressure of the dog pulling on the leash was comforting and familiar to her this morning. With so many other aspects of her life feeling like question marks, the relationship with her dog was a constant.

"It's about half a mile up ahead," Levi said.

"That's it?"

He nodded. They walked in silence. Judah and Wren were behind them, but they weren't talking much, either. Adriana caught them looking at Blue once or twice, which was a good thing. Judah had always been one of those officers who didn't put a lot of stock in what her dog said. It would be good for him to watch them work.

Adriana had given Blue the scent at the parking lot, and she knew what she was looking for. Levi had asked how that worked, for a cadaver dog, and Adriana had explained that they sometimes used artificial scents when training the animals. Blue was trained to alert to both deceased bodies and live missing persons whose scents she'd been tracking, so when they were searching for cadavers, Adriana liked to give her that synthetic scent to remind her which they were looking for. Adriana watched her take in the area, with her nose, her eyes, her ears. All senses were engaged.

Blue's demeanor changed. She perked her ears and held herself more upright, even as her face somehow got sadder. The facial expression was not a standard search-dog alert technique, but Adriana felt she knew her dog.

"She's got it," Adriana said and checked her GPS watch. They'd gone just about half a mile.

Right where they'd wandered about last time. She stole a glance at Levi. His expression was intent, determination in his eyes.

They were so close.

"Good girl, keep going," Adriana said as Blue nosed the ground, still moving forward. They followed her, cutting through the low vegetation. Adriana tried to step as carefully as possible. There was no sign of anyone walking this way recently, but then again the bodies they were looking for were from several decades ago. The ground would have healed.

The families who didn't have closure would not have.

Blue whined, low and long, and dropped to her stomach.

Bingo.

Adriana nodded. Levi stopped and they waited for Wren and Judah to catch up.

"That's it?" Wren asked.

"Yes," Adriana confirmed.

Wren walked toward the site, paced around where Blue was lying down, looking like she was studying the ground itself.

Wren cleared the ground as best she could and studied it again. Then she started to dig.

Adriana stood and watched as long as she could, though heaviness pressed against her as she thought of what they were doing, of what had been done and how evil people could be. She just wasn't cut out for this kind of work, and it had never been more apparent to her.

Many of her acquaintances who were in law enforcement all seemed to handle it better than she did. But Ellie had confided in her once that she'd been in law enforcement before coming to Alaska. She hadn't offered any more details than that, and Adriana hadn't asked for them.

It was part of the bond of the far north, in a way. People who came here had reasons, some of which people didn't want to talk about. But you understood, even if none of you spoke of them.

"You okay?" Levi asked. Had he really learned to read her that well over just a few days?

Adriana shook her head. "I'm going to walk a bit."

Levi nodded. "Let me come with you."

"No, I'm okay."

Judah approached. "I'll go, then."

Levi looked at his brother.

"I know you want to see what Wren finds," Judah reasoned. "And I also know Adriana doesn't need to be alone. Especially not here."

Adriana didn't argue, just started walking across the open alpine landscape. Whichever brother followed her was fine with her because she didn't necessarily want to be alone right now, anyway. Not so close to where a killer had already buried one victim.

What if he was watching? He already seemed to know so much about where they were, what they were doing.

Were they being followed?

She shook her head and took a deep breath of fresh air, trying to clear her mind of all the clutter from the case.

"I'm behind you, just so you don't get startled," Judah called.

"Thanks." She didn't mind that Levi hadn't come. She didn't want to talk right now, anyway.

No, right now she wanted to think about the world they lived in, where some person would end someone else's life. Where hikers got lost and were found dead, with hands zip-tied.

Where her fiancé could be out for a fun snowmobile ride and never return.

Why did God let it all happen? It wasn't like this was the first time she'd asked—she'd asked many times over the years—but the need for answers pressed heavy on her now, with this case added to her questions.

It was time for her to decide what she believed still, about God. For years she'd wrestled with the discomfort of knowing God had allowed tragedy into her life. With a deep personal knowledge that God allowed bad things to happen.

She felt more than ever like this case was drawing her toward a decision point. Did she still trust Him, or not?

And still, that resounding question she had. Unanswered. *Why?*

Why? Why? Why?

God didn't answer, through either a small voice or any kind of booming thunder. Instead, there was just wind across the mountainside tundra. A marmot calling somewhere.

A beautiful, gorgeous world God had created.

Adriana stopped trying to wrestle with these big questions. Right now she bent down and scratched her dog behind the ears.

"You doing okay, sweetie?" she asked her.

Blue looked up, big brown eyes kind. Concerned.

"Yeah, I'm okay if you are," Adriana whispered. "It's

just not my favorite way to spend a day. But three more and we are done."

She walked back toward the site of the body and found that they'd unearthed a large object wrapped in trash bags. Exactly the right size to be a body. Adriana looked away.

"Judah, if you'll stay here while Wren finishes up, Adriana and I will move on."

"You're going to look at the three other places?"

Levi nodded.

This was the body closest to Raven Pass. There was one more a bit farther away, then one closer to Girdwood, which was only about a fifteen-minute drive, maybe twenty. The farthest away was near the town of Hope.

That meant they'd have to spend the entire day together, in order to make all those drives.

And surely they wouldn't excavate each body? It was fall and so the sunshine was no longer endless. Days had their nights now, natural stopping points for work. "We won't be able to unbury all of them today, right?" she asked, hoping the answer was no. This had felt enough like an eerie backward burial to her, and she couldn't handle the weight of any more of them today.

"No. We'll mark them with GPS coordinates so I can come back when you aren't with us."

Apparently he'd read all her struggles on her face. And while Adriana didn't like feeling like the weak link, it was okay. She nodded. "Thanks."

They hiked back in silence and wasted no time getting to the second location.

Blue found the next body within an hour of starting their hike, though this time it had taken her a little longer to pinpoint the exact location. It was about fifteen feet, Levi had said aloud earlier, from where they'd found a body during this most recent investigation. The last one had been twenty feet away, so it appeared the exact distance between the two bodies wasn't part of an MO, but the fact that there were two indicated a pattern.

She'd learned more fascinating facts about serial killers, their inconsistencies and idiosyncrasies, during the last week than she'd ever wanted to know.

"Want to go to Hope or Girdwood first?"

North or south. May as well get the easy one out of the way so they could devote the rest of the day to the one that would be more of a challenge.

"Girdwood, then Hope," she suggested.

He nodded his agreement, and they climbed back in the car with Blue and started the drive.

They had quick success with the body just off the popular Winner Creek Trail in Girdwood. He remembered being there when this crime scene had been worked a few years ago, for the body they'd found then. They'd been on high alert as it had been berry season at the time and grizzly bears were thick in these woods. Now it was late enough in the year that bears should be thinking about bedding down, but he still didn't let his guard down, not until they'd entered the GPS coordinates and made it back to the car.

Only the body in Hope was left. As far as Levi could tell, Blue was doing better today. Her general body language still seemed good and she was wagging her tail, chewing the caribou antler Adriana had given her for a treat after they'd loaded back up in the car.

She'd told him in one of their earlier conversations that while working animals were usually given a treat after making their find, many cadaver dogs wouldn't take the treat in the presence of a body. They could tell just by the smell that something was wrong, and it made them feel disconcerted. Off.

Adriana seemed to feel the same as the dog. She was the main reason he was in a hurry to get this done. While he'd enjoyed the time spent with her, he'd watched her over the last few days and this case was adding shadows underneath her eyes that he didn't like to see there. Not because they hurt her beauty at all—they didn't. She was gorgeous no matter what. But because they were a reflection of how she felt inside and he didn't want that tiredness or hopelessness for her.

"Are you going to be okay for one more?" he asked as he turned left onto the Seward Highway from Girdwood. This road would take them back past the turnoff for Raven Pass and then onward to the Kenai Peninsula and Hope. He'd only been to the town of Hope once, years ago one July, when Jim had talked him into going fishing there. He'd had some fun, but the fishing was better down near Soldotna, at least in Levi's opinion. The longer drive was worth it to him.

"I can handle one more." She said the words like she was hoping she believed them.

"Thank you for doing this."

"Well, we need to finish." She allowed a small smile.

"I meant all of it. You didn't have to help at all, but frankly I'd have been lost without you. And not just because if I'd had to find that first burial site near the lake without you, I'd probably still be looking. Nothing

I know of substitutes for a search dog in cases like that. I owe you, really."

She shook her head. "You don't. I wanted to help."

The air between them was thick and Levi wasn't sure what had happened between last night and now, at least between them.

Eighteen or so hours ago they'd been kissing in her pantry, hardly any space between them. Now she was quiet, her answers short.

And he was no expert at relationships, but it still felt to him like something was wrong.

"While we're driving," he began, keeping his eyes on the road, "we should talk."

"About?"

"We kissed last night." Remarkably, he got the words out without tripping over them, though when he thought back to that kiss, his mind felt like a muddle of all good things and it was hard to focus. It was a wonder he'd been able to talk even semi-articulately about it.

"We did." She matched his tone with her own unflinching one, which he appreciated. That was one of the things he loved about Adriana, her confidence.

He...what?

Levi swallowed hard. "We, uh…" And now any focus he'd had was gone. Love? *Love?* Sure, he'd been planning this conversation, hoping to ask her to date, but now…

The calm he'd felt was gone, evaporated like morning dew. In its place was a feeling of being tossed about, akin to the waves he was watching in Turnagain Arm right now as they drove down the highway. The water was a churning steely gray.

That was what his mind felt like when it thought for

too long about the word *love*. Love hadn't been good to him, not so far. Friends, he could do. Kissing he could do, at least with Adriana. They'd proved that.

But he'd wanted to date her. To what purpose?

Did he not remember he'd tried this relationship road before and failed?

"Was there something you wanted to talk to me about, Levi?"

Suddenly, something slammed into the back of him, sending his car jerking toward the center line.

Adriana screamed and grabbed her dog, who had slammed into Levi's shoulder in the initial impact.

"Hang on!" Levi corrected himself toward the right, got them back in their lane quickly enough to avoid the large moving van that had been coming toward them in the other lane.

"What was that?" Her voice trembled, betraying her fear in its unsteadiness, and Levi had nothing with which to reassure her.

This serial killer usually killed his victims up close, forensic evidence said. But Levi had felt relatively calm when he'd been shot at because from the beginning, it had somehow felt like a warning to him. Then the bomb had happened and it had confirmed his suspicions.

Their lives had only been in a semblance of danger.

Now, the real thing began. Because the killer was almost within arm's reach. And for the many victims who had come before, that point was exactly when they'd died.

Levi wasn't going to let that happen, not to Adriana. At least not without a fight.

He glanced over at her.

He wouldn't let anything happen to her dog, either.

She'd never forgive him if he did. And she didn't deserve to lose anyone else she cared about.

The car slammed into him again.

Levi jerked the wheel left, into a parking lot near Portage, trying to lose the car, but it followed. He floored it back onto the highway.

"What are you doing?" Adriana's voice, coming from between clenched teeth, demanded an answer.

"Trying to keep us alive."

"And you think getting involved in some kind of high-speed chase is the best way to accomplish that?" she asked, her eyes on the side-view mirror. He knew that because he'd looked over at her before.

The car was getting closer.

There was little other traffic today, but he was still worried there would be some kind of casualties if he didn't get off the road soon.

Clearly their would-be killer wasn't giving up easily.

"Get your phone out and call 911," he told her, trying to keep his voice as calm as he could.

Adriana did what he asked, and he was proud of her for the way she relayed the information like the trained professional she was.

That was the thing about her he didn't think she realized. She might not like the darkness. But she sure could withstand it better than almost anyone he'd ever met. She buckled down, found some kind of strength inside, maybe from God, and made it through.

Yeah, no matter how scared it made him, he loved her.

And he might have missed the chance to tell her. You didn't get a second chance to say some things.

He hoped he got a second chance for that conversation that he'd handled badly.

Because if he lived, he was going to ask Adriana if she'd be willing to date a guy who wasn't very good at relationships, since there was a very good possibility that guy was head over heels for her.

FIFTEEN

Adriana watched the speedometer creep over eighty, so she gripped the door handle of the car tighter. Eighty might not be fast on some roads, but on the notoriously dangerous Seward Highway, with sheer cliffs on one side and ocean on the other, it was terrifying.

"We've got to figure something out," Adriana said as they advanced on a Winnebago camper and Levi passed it, cutting it close. The SUV chasing them followed and advanced on them again.

They were going to be hit again, while going… She glanced at the dashboard again.

Ninety miles per hour wouldn't go well. This wasn't working. It was too much of a risk, and besides, staying on the road would endanger the other drivers.

Did they have other options? she asked herself as she dug her fingers into Blue's fur, trying not to grip too tightly, and fought to maintain some semblance of composure.

They could pull over, but with as few cars as were on the road today, there wouldn't be many witnesses. They could be killed in plain sight and still it was possible that no one might see.

They could keep going, but it might cause a wreck, hurting innocent people, one that she and Levi couldn't survive.

"We could go back to Raven Pass?" she offered, but it was still another few miles up the road.

"That's my plan."

Adriana kept looking in the side-view mirror. Then she looked up at the road. One or two more miles to Raven Pass.

Levi eased off the gas. Put his right turn signal on.

And made the turn off the main highway.

The SUV kept going straight.

His hands free, Levi called the police department and reported the incident.

Adriana's heart raced in her chest, maybe worse now. She was usually okay during an immediate crisis that required her focus, she'd learned.

Now, though, now that there was a break in the danger, she felt like she was going to be sick.

"I never should have let you do this."

Levi's voice was emotionless. Numb.

Yet somehow, the words still cut her to the quick. "You just told me you couldn't have done it without me." Something warned her not to talk, to be patient, to be kind. But she ignored that. How could he have said that less than half an hour earlier and now be claiming he never should have let her help?

It made no sense and it was insulting. Not to mention pointless. Clearly they couldn't change the past. So why waste time saying things that would only hurt people's feelings?

"I... Maybe I couldn't have. I know it would have

taken ages longer, but I had no right to ask you to risk your safety."

"You didn't ask, I offered," she reminded him, feeling her patience wearing thin. She heard it in her voice, the harsh edges of frustration. It wasn't anger with him, she reminded herself. It had been a traumatic experience just now. A traumatic week, really.

"But I—"

"You know, Levi, you can't make other people's decisions for them. You can't decide that I shouldn't have helped you. You can't decide anything except what has to do with you. You can't decide that because you were married once and it ended badly that you're never going to let anyone else love you." The last part came out in one big whoosh of breath.

Adriana gasped as she realized what she'd said. Had she consciously known she loved him until she said that? No, but she did. It was true.

But it didn't need to be said now, not in a long tirade like that when she'd thrown his past in his face, even if it was meant to be an encouragement that he could one day have a better future. And it wasn't like she'd even had the courage to say she loved him, to tell him he could have a future *now*.

She'd just tossed out his past failure and berated him with it.

"I'm sorry. I'm so sorry," she said quickly, but not quickly enough.

Pain had etched itself across Levi's face.

Subtlety had never been her strong point, but she didn't generally go for the jugular in conversations. She'd hurt him just now, mentioning how his marriage had ended badly. She'd unintentionally used that as a weapon. She hadn't meant to, but that didn't mean it was less painful. And there was nothing she could do to undo that.

"Levi…" She trailed off. All her apologies would go unacknowledged.

He nodded. "Yeah, you're right."

She stilled. "Oh, yeah?"

He turned down one street, then another. Then onto hers.

He parked in her driveway and met her eyes. "I can't decide not to let anyone love me, but I can sure decide not to love anyone else."

She felt the words stab her heart like a knife. Like hers must have felt to him earlier. She nodded. Swallowed hard. "Thanks for driving me home."

She had so many questions that weren't going to be answered. Why had the SUV tried to run them off the road and then backed off? When Levi ran the plates, who would the car come up as registered to?

He was the officer. He would learn the answers to those questions and have no reason to tell her. Because even though it hadn't been said, Adriana knew she was done with this investigation. Levi would leave the last burial site alone, or go without her.

They were finished, too.

Whatever of "them" there had been. It was just a kiss or two. Nothing that should have rocked her world the way it did, but maybe it was for the best. She didn't know why right now, but the empty platitude was all she had to offer herself.

A verse about God working for good to those who were "called according to his purpose" came to her mind. She didn't remember where it was from, but welcomed the reminder that God works things out for His people.

Maybe things would work out. Or maybe this *was* them working out.

"Goodbye, Levi."

He nodded to her. "I'll stay until someone else gets here."

Adriana nodded. She'd long since stopped fighting the extra security. She wanted to *live*.

And she wanted to fall in love again. Even if that meant risks.

She'd wanted to let herself fall in love with Levi. Actually, she already had. It just looked like she was the only one who'd let her mind go there.

"Thanks." She opened the car door and exited with Blue. "For everything," she said with finality, and then walked inside.

Once the door was all the way shut, she finally let herself cry. For Levi, for Robert, for all of it.

Idiot. Idiot. Idiot. Levi didn't know what he was upset with himself for most. Starting that conversation in the car? Abandoning it when he'd panicked? Or planning to tell Adriana that he loved her and then blowing up any chance they'd had at a relationship after she'd made a careless comment that had hurt him?

Calling it careless wasn't exactly true. He was pretty sure she'd meant it to hurt him, at least in some way, but they'd just had a near-death experience. She'd been tense, angry, boiling over with frustration.

Instead of answering in a kind voice and calming down, he'd reacted, too. And now it was too late to fix anything. He'd seen the shuttered look come over her eyes.

He wasn't the only one who had been hurt in the past. And now they'd both hurt each other again.

See, this was why he should focus on his work and not people. Because people did let you down, even when they loved you.

He had no idea how some people made it work. Like his parents, who had been married for thirty-five years. Or Jim, who'd been married for somewhere around forty at this point. His thirty-fifth anniversary had been when he'd still worked at the police department. They'd had a cake for him.

He should call her and apologize, and see if there was any way they could...

What? There was nothing to do. Nothing to patch up.

Did he call and try to mend their friendship at least?

Judah was at her house now. He'd tried to get another officer to do it, but had finally had to accept that he was the only one with the time.

"Just leave her alone about me, okay? There's nothing going on anymore," he'd said to his brother.

Judah had just raised his eyebrows. "I'm not your dating coach."

Sure, *now* he wanted to be uninvolved.

Levi had gone to the police department to meet with Wren, who had information on the bodies they'd recovered today. She'd called in some colleagues to help with the sheer volume of work, but all three victims were from over two decades ago. Female.

More details would emerge with time, but so far they fit the profile.

One victim from the first set of murders. One victim

from the most recent set. None in between. When Adriana had the idea to help, Levi had been so sure he'd find a link between both cases, and that the link would be in the form of murder committed between then and now.

Instead there were no bodies from that time frame.

The killer had truly stopped killing for over twenty years.

Levi paced his office, then sat down in his chair. He'd promised himself he wouldn't bother Jim and would let the man enjoy his retirement, but there was one question he wanted someone else's perspective on.

And now he couldn't get Adriana's.

He picked up the phone, dialed and listened to it ring.

"Levi, how are you doing? How's the case?" Jim's voice was warm, as usual, with a smile.

"I'm good. A little stuck, actually, on the case, so I wanted to get your thoughts on something."

"Please do. I'm stuck at home watching romance movies." He lowered his voice. "And if I have to watch another one I'm going to lose my mind."

Levi suppressed a laugh. He supposed that was one small bright side of how badly things had ended between him and Adriana before they even began.

Then an image of her, tucked into a fleece blanket, on his couch watching a predictable Christmas movie crossed his mind.

It almost made it hard to breathe; that was how much he wanted the future he envisioned. How much he wanted her in his life.

He'd go back over tonight and talk to her. Maybe she wouldn't forgive him right away, but surely he could have one more chance, right?

Adriana was special, different. The only second chance he wanted in his life. He didn't want to lose her.

Jim cleared his throat. "You okay?"

Levi hadn't been paying attention, and as usual his old partner had noticed. The man seemed to notice everything.

"Yeah, uh, I'm fine. Listen, Jim. I meant to leave you out of this case and let you just enjoy being retired."

"Like I said. Watching made for TV movies. Please, ask me."

"So what would make a serial killer stop killing for more than twenty years?"

Silence.

"Jim?"

"He, uh, the killer, uh…stopped for over twenty years?"

Had he told his old partner about the cold case he'd found? Levi wasn't sure now. He filled him in with vague details. No need to get bogged down.

"Huh… So the first case was—"

"Nearly thirty years ago," Levi told him.

"That's strange." Jim's voice was softer now, like he was holding the phone farther away from his ear. "Listen, Levi, this case, maybe you should…"

The call dropped.

Levi frowned. Then called back. It went straight to voice mail.

Was Jim having a heart attack? He was in good shape but it wasn't completely impossible. Levi didn't know what else besides sudden illness would have made him respond that way.

Surely if the killer himself had walked into the room Jim would have exclaimed, not tried to be subtle.

Levi mentally replayed their conversation. No, he had no idea what the problem was. But he didn't like it. The more he thought about it, the more he wondered about the medical-problem option.

He called 911 and asked for a welfare check with EMTs. If Jim was sick, they were the best ones to see about him. Did Levi dare go over there, knowing it was dangerous to be where Levi was right now, with a serial killer after him? Levi could be putting Jim in danger. Nah, he wouldn't do that to Jim. He'd wait and let the EMTs do their job and then talk to him later.

He'd already dragged one person down into this danger with him. And he wished with everything inside him that he could get her out. But it was too late.

"I just want to take her on a walk." Adriana tried again, having been told by Judah five seconds before that under no circumstances was she going anywhere. She'd been sitting in the house for hours. She'd left Judah outside in his car for a long time, then finally had gone outside a few minutes before to see if he wanted some coffee. He'd said yes and come inside.

It was then that she'd very calmly suggested that she might like to go for a walk.

He hadn't responded very calmly.

"And am I correct in saying that it was only earlier today you had someone following you and trying to kill you?"

He wasn't wrong. She exhaled.

"Fine. I can let her out to go to the bathroom in my own backyard, correct?"

"Of course." Judah stood from where he'd been sitting on the couch. "I'll go out with you."

Arguing with him wasn't going to get her anywhere, she knew, so she just nodded. "Okay, thank you." She wasn't foolish or shortsighted enough that she couldn't see that he was doing something nice, helping keep her safe.

She exhaled in the cool night air, walking around the yard as Blue did. Babe had done his business for the night already and refused to come outside with them. Adriana was glad Blue had needed the trip out; she was beyond claustrophobic at this point and the fresh air was already helping her relax. As much as she could in this situation. Her house was on one of the edges of Raven Pass, and she could walk straight from her unfenced backyard—her dogs were trained to stay close to her—into the woods and hike endless miles of trails.

That thought had always comforted her, since she'd always loved the outdoors, but with the time she'd spent in the backcountry this week, unburying bodies and secrets, it felt like an eerie thought.

She wasn't so far removed from them as she wished she was.

"Almost done, sweetie?" she asked Blue, then looked around to find Judah. He was still in the yard, but farther away.

Blue trotted toward her.

"I'm heading in, okay?" she asked Judah.

He nodded. She headed for the door. She was almost there when Blue stopped, turned her head to the right and let out a long, guttural howl. Blue moved toward the side of the house and out of view.

Adriana frowned. Looked at where Blue had gone, then back at Judah. She wanted to be responsible, but she wasn't going to let her dog run away, either. She needed Blue.

"I've got to get her." She motioned with her hands. He was shaking his head, she could see that even though he was far away, and hurrying toward her now, but she needed to get to her dog.

She rounded the corner of the house. Blue was lying on the ground like she'd just alerted to a body. Adriana was wracked with guilt. Had she pushed her too hard? What else could have…?

"Hello."

She heard the voice at the same time as she felt a knife enter her side.

It was a woman.

And Adriana was fairly certain, as her vision started to swim in darker and darker shadows, that she was the one responsible for all the murders.

The serial killer had found her.

And Levi was nowhere nearby to save her.

SIXTEEN

"Did you guys get there yet?" Levi had called a friend, Isaac, who was an EMT with Raven Pass.

"We did. No one is home."

"I told you he hung up. Can you break down the door or something?" He felt a little absurd asking—no doubt Jim would laugh at him for his excessive worry, but he couldn't shake the concern.

"We got inside. No one is here."

Hard, cold dread fell like ice in his stomach.

If Jim hadn't had any kind of medical incident... He hadn't been taken by the killer, had he?

Levi's mind raced. That last conversation. Jim's strange reaction to what Levi had found. And then the line had gone dead.

All he could think of was Jim's wife... What was her name? Rosie?

Jim's wife must be around sixty years old. Yes, they were both in shape because they liked to hike together.

Surely Jim's wife wasn't...

Levi didn't care how absurd the idea was because it didn't really matter *who*, not at this point. All that mattered was that Jim was in trouble.

"I'll be right there," he told Isaac and hung up the phone.

He hurried to his car and called Judah on the way. On the off chance his crazy suspicion about Jim's wife was correct, he wanted his brother to be on the lookout and not let Adriana be alone with the sweet-looking woman if she came over. Even if he'd ruined his chances with her forever, he wanted her safe. It still felt like his job to protect her. While the phone rang, he navigated the dark roads, hating the fact that fall had stolen the daylight. It wasn't quite all the way dark yet, but it was coming.

"Levi. Something has happened."

Judah's voice was gravel rough. And not hopeful.

"You heard about Jim already?" Levi asked.

"No." Silence.

"Judah. What?" Levi couldn't keep the tension from his voice.

"It's Adriana. She's gone."

"She's—" Levi couldn't breathe. It felt like he'd been gut punched. Except this time he'd never be able to catch a full breath again.

"They took her."

Alive. She is still alive. Not dead, like he'd assumed from his brother's phrasing.

"You were supposed to watch her!" His voice raised in volume and he didn't hold back any of his frustration.

"I was. She went to get her dog and I ran after her. When I rounded the house, something hit me over the head and knocked me over."

"How long were you passed out?" Levi was still biting back anger.

"Not long. A minute? Maybe not at all but I was disoriented. I'm sorry, Levi."

It could have been one minute or thirty. Judah had no way of knowing, and Levi knew it wasn't his brother's fault.

"I'm on my way," Levi said and hung up.

Levi swallowed hard and hit the gas, changing his course for Adriana's house. His old mentor could handle himself—at least Levi hoped so. But Adriana wasn't used to people like this and had no training for dealing with a killer.

Why had he left her at all? Oh, that's right, he'd been afraid of the feelings growing between them and scared he'd be right back where he'd been years ago, torn between his job and a woman. Except this time, he should have realized, there was a difference. Adriana hadn't asked him to give up anything. She hadn't complained. She hadn't questioned.

All she'd done was care.

And he'd let her down.

He bit back anger. Barely. "I'm on my way."

Her side hurt. It was strange, how one part of her body could throb in exhausting pain while the rest of her felt fine. Adriana would have thought all of her would hurt, but no, only the stab wound.

Was that how death was, too? she wondered.

"Walk faster." She was shoved forward, farther down the dark trail behind her house. She'd never walked very far this way before. They'd hiked in for a little while, ten minutes maybe, and then turned left. Adriana had always turned right, toward the developed trails. Left led to private land, so she'd never explored that way.

Because of that she had no concept of how hard or easy she would be to find.

Was there a body there from nearly thirty years ago? she wondered in passing. Was she going to be the new body?

Now her head throbbed, too, joining the stab wound in vying for her attention.

"Where are we going?" Was that her voice, groggy and wounded?

Please, God, let Blue lead them to where I am. She prayed as she waited for an answer. She'd issued a sharp command for Blue to get inside right after she'd been stabbed, and her dog had listened. Hopefully, Blue might lead a search party to her.

Levi? Would he be the one looking? Her SAR team?

She knew how this part went. The search grids. The agonizing minutes turning to hours, the knowledge that if a person wasn't found soon, exposure could kill.

All of that, plus this week's knowledge about humanity's depravity, was too much to handle. Adriana had seen death up close this week, what this woman's rage had done, all the lives it had ended.

She didn't want to be another casualty. She didn't want to be part of this killer's twisted plan.

"Why are you doing this?" Adriana asked. Her captor hadn't talked much, and Adriana didn't recognize her. The woman was older than she'd have pictured a killer, somewhere in her sixties, but fit. Smaller than Adriana, and built like a woman who spent her days hiking mountain trails.

And burying people on them.

All those victims—*this* woman had been responsible?

Still, she didn't answer. Instead, she shoved Adriana again, harder. She tripped on a root and fell to the ground. Pain knifed in her side, where her wound was, and she grabbed it with her hand and tried not to cry out. When she moved her hand away, there was fresh, sticky blood.

God, help me not die here, she prayed.

"If you're trying to be the biggest pain and slow me down so I let you go, it won't happen. I could kill you now, you know. I've killed many, many times."

How did you explain the feeling of hearing those words? Adriana wondered. There was no way to articulate the amount of evil in what should be a normal, pleasant voice. Or the way she could almost feel the... void behind her. Like the woman had traded in her humanity for something else altogether.

It was eerie. Terrifying.

Please don't let her kill me. She prayed, willing to beg God however much she needed to. Adriana wasn't ready to die. Too much of the last few years had been suffocated under thoughts of death. Robert's. The people she helped find. She needed a few years in full sunlight. In hope.

With Levi. Please, with Levi.

Please, not yet.

"I'll walk faster," Adriana promised, doing her best to get her legs to cooperate. They were heavy.

"Do that."

They hiked in silence. Another ten minutes, Adriana guessed. How far had they gone? It was hard to judge her pace when she knew she was walking more slowly than usual. More importantly, how fast could Levi hike it? And could Blue find them?

Was there still hope? Or was it really lost now?

She couldn't let herself think that, she reminded herself as she took more hurried steps into the darkness.

She had to believe there was still a chance. Levi knew she was missing by now; he had to. And she'd asked God to save her. Sometimes He allowed tragedy to strike, she knew that.

Yet sometimes God stepped in with miracles. And Adriana needed one of those right now.

Levi banged on the front door of Adriana's house with a closed fist, anger loaded and ready. It took Judah more than a minute to answer.

"Where is she?" Part of him needed to see that she was really gone, or he'd keep hoping maybe she'd just stepped into another room, maybe Judah hadn't seen her, maybe she was really fine.

Maybe he hadn't messed this all up. *Again*.

"I don't know. We were in the backyard, taking her dog for a walk."

It wasn't unreasonable, Levi knew that in his head. Still, he felt his fists clench. "You let her outside?"

"It was her backyard, Levi. I was with her. You couldn't lock her up forever."

No, he couldn't have. And with any other person in danger he'd have agreed with Judah. Quality of life was important and Adriana's had been smashed all to bits this week. He loved the idea of her outside in her own yard. Safe in the outside air. Finally relaxing a little.

Except he knew how this ended.

"When did she get away from you? How? Did someone come? Did she leave?"

Blue came trotting in from the living room, whining. She jumped up and put her paws on Levi's shoulders.

He didn't remember Blue ever jumping up on him before. She was far too well trained for that. Stress from her owner being missing?

"She went around the corner of the house." Judah nodded toward Blue. "The dog acted weird. Sort of howled and ran and then she followed and was gone." He shook his head. "I ran that way, and someone hit me. The dog came back, barreled right into me, actually, before I hit the ground, and then I passed out. When I got up, Adriana wasn't there."

Levi bent down, scratched Blue behind the ears and looked into her eyes, willing her to communicate with him somehow. Adriana did this all the time, right? She made it look so easy, but the truth was she was a talented woman. Talented and gorgeous and funny and brave.

He needed her to be okay.

"Please tell me something," he muttered at the dog.

"You're not talking to the dog, right? We'll find her, Levi. Let's go. I've already put a BOLO out for her and I've got everyone in the department looking for cars they don't recognize."

Levi shook his head. "Except that may not be our biggest danger."

Judah stilled. "We know the killer?"

"I'm not sure." Levi couldn't quite shrug, as it wasn't a casual shrugging situation, but he felt every bit as puzzled as his shoulders wanted to convey. "Jim's missing. I was on the phone with him, and he reacted really oddly to what I told him and then disappeared."

Blue whined and jumped up on Levi again, then ran toward the back of the house. Ran back. Again.

Levi frowned. "You want us to follow you."

"You're talking to the dog again," Judah said. "And the isn't *Lassie*."

Blue barked.

Levi nodded. "All right. Come with me, Judah. I'll fill you in on the way, but we're following the dog."

"Following…" Judah's voice trailed off, but Levi was already hot on Blue's heels as the husky ran ahead, then pawed at the back door.

This had to work. Levi swallowed hard against fear, desperate to do something to help Adriana. If she trusted her dogs, then…

Maybe he needed to do that, too.

Levi opened the door, said a quick prayer.

Without hesitation, the large white dog ran for the woods behind the house.

Woods. Levi swallowed hard and felt his chest compress. *Please, don't let me find her like every other woman I've found in the woods lately.*

Surely the killer wouldn't murder Adriana. Not if he—well, more likely *she*—was motivated by a sense of justice. If the killer was truly motivated by infidelity, by making that right somehow, then Adriana had done nothing wrong. She shouldn't be a target.

And wouldn't have been, if he hadn't gotten her involved in this case.

Shoving aside guilt that would do him no good, he hurried after the dog. Prayed he wasn't too late. And that this actually worked.

Please, God, let this dog actually know what she's doing.

The glow of a light from a cabin would have been a welcome sight any other time, but right now it only added to Adriana's sense of foreboding.

She wasn't dead yet; that was a plus. However, the

wet, sticky blood staining the side of her shirt served as a reminder that she could be. She had no idea how much blood she'd lost, no idea how much was too much. All she knew was that she was fighting waves of dizziness, but it could easily be panic.

"Now we wait for your boyfriend." The woman stepped ahead of Adriana and looked back at her with a look of bored hate. "Then you can die. Try to stay alive 'til he gets here. This works best if everyone knows how much their actions have made other people suffer."

The words reminded Adriana of what Levi had told her about the phone call, the fact that the person killing seemed to think they were doing something good, righting some kind of wrong. Is that what this person was referring to?

The door to the cabin pushed open easily against the woman's weight. There was no lock on the door, common in Alaskan cabins like this, something that should help Levi and anyone he might bring with him. *If* they got here. She'd lost track of how many turns they'd taken and there hadn't been a way to subtly mark their path with someone right behind her. At first she'd done her best by snapping twigs with her feet, but when the woman had become impatient, Adriana had decided that keeping her calm was her first priority.

She trusted Blue. If anyone could find her, Blue could. The question was whether or not Levi would trust the dog to do so, and if he could read her signals.

"Who is this? What did you do, Rosie?" a raspy male voice called from the corner of the room. A man sat in a chair, hands bound, tied to it. His feet were bound, too.

"Shut up, Jim."

Jim? She'd heard of Jim, hadn't she? Where had she heard that name lately?

"You did this, Jim. I didn't do this, *you* did."

The woman turned to the other corner. Adriana looked over there for the first time and saw another woman, not much younger than Adriana herself, tied up like the man. The only difference was that the man looked tired. Resigned. And the younger woman, who bore a resemblance to Rosie and Jim, looked terrified.

Adriana struggled to put the pieces together. Frowned.

Levi's old partner? Had his name been Jim?

"You did this, too, Jenny." Rosie turned toward the other corner and advanced. "You should have known better. *You* were raised better."

Now she spun around, back to Jim. "Unlike you, apparently."

"Rosie, I said I was sorry. A hundred times, I said it. I showed you every day. And it was over thirty years ago. And I stopped seeing her…"

Rosie shook her head. "Not. Soon. Enough."

Adriana watched as Jim's expression wavered, as understanding dawned.

"You…didn't…"

"She was the first to die. The others committed the same sin she did."

So Rosie had been the killer all those years ago.

But why…

Adriana watched the family drama unfolding before her, hoped for answers, but more than that, hoped for escape.

"You sit there." Rosie grabbed her arm, the one Adriana had kept pressed against her wound, and pulled her toward a chair.

Adriana sat. Put her hand back against her side. Blood stuck to her skin.

"Why did you stop?" Adriana asked, knowing she had little to lose by at least getting answers.

Rosie jerked her head toward the young woman. "I spent years raising her. Pouring all my energy into raising the perfect daughter." Her face contorted into a sneer. "Only to have my daughter follow in her father's footsteps with her bad moral choices. Dating a married man! Just like that other woman who wrecked my marriage. No better than she was. Then I realized I could never stop killing. That there would always be more people who had been unfaithful or helped someone else be unfaithful, people who needed to die."

Wrong as infidelity was, the woman was sick. Adriana felt nauseous as her stomach churned.

"Why me, though? I haven't done anything wrong."

Although, yes, it was madness that the killer was justifying her actions, Adriana had to keep her talking if she wanted to live. At least that was her theory.

"You kept interfering. You and your boyfriend."

He wasn't her boyfriend, Adriana wanted to say, but denying it was hardly going to help her now, was it?

Besides, she loved him. There was no point in denying that now. Either to herself or anyone else.

She. Loved. Him.

The woman grabbed a rope and started to tie Adriana up as she continued, "Seeing you die will hurt him. Which will hurt you." Rosie turned to Jim, her husband, and glared.

Okay, maybe knowing they weren't a couple could help, much as that truth hurt Adriana. "We aren't together. Killing me gets you nothing."

Rosie shrugged. "Maybe, maybe not. But I've been watching. I see the way he looks at you. Anyway, he will want to save you. And when he gets here, he will die while my husband watches and sees what his sin has cost *everyone*."

Adriana kept quiet.

There didn't seem to be anything more to say.

SEVENTEEN

The dark tangles of the woods surrounded them as they hiked on into the night. Blue looked back at Levi now and then and he nodded at her, trying to convey somehow that he was trusting her. Adriana would know how to do this. She'd led countless searches.

Levi looked at Blue. Swallowed hard. She was a regular search dog, too, wasn't she? Because he couldn't handle the possibility that she'd caught a cadaver scent. Adriana had to be alive. He stopped walking abruptly, tried to catch his breath.

"What's wrong?" Judah asked from behind him, having had to stop suddenly to avoid hitting him.

Levi shook his head. The words brought up such a big fear, he didn't even want to say it aloud.

"She'll be okay."

But his brother couldn't promise that and they both knew it.

Blue whined and trotted ahead again, then came back. Levi was fairly sure this was the same dog she used for all her searches. With that thought in mind to give him the little bit of hope he needed, he moved forward.

He tripped on a root at one point, but stayed focused. Only when they got off the trail did he start to worry.

"You sure about this?" Judah asked.

No, Levi wasn't sure at all. But Blue seemed pretty confident. He hadn't seen her sniffing the ground, like he would picture a search dog doing, but from the little bit Adriana had explained to him, it seemed like the dogs were able to find scent in air. So maybe it didn't have to be exactly what he was picturing.

He needed to trust the dog.

As he walked, questions started to nudge his heart.

Was this anything like trusting God? Following a path that didn't make sense to him, going through things like he'd gone through in the past? Why was he willing to trust a dog, but not the God who had created him and the universe?

Because he was mad. He knew the answer right away. He'd grown up following Jesus, tried to do his best in his marriage, and it had still fallen apart. Now he walked around with his own kind of scarlet letter, at least in some parts of the Christian community, because he was divorced. But his church and friends had never made him feel that way.

So did anyone judge him at all? Or did it just feel that way?

And either way, was God to blame?

No, he knew as he hiked through the darkness. God was not. He was without fault, without blame. He'd been there all the time, waiting for Levi to come to Him with the heartache he'd gone through, and instead of drawing closer to Him, Levi had pushed away.

Why had it taken the thought of losing Adriana, just

when he was starting to believe in second chances, for him to realize it?

God, I'm sorry. Help me trust You. Help me find her.

It may not have been the most eloquent prayer. But as he saw glimmers of light in the distance, like light from cabin windows, he could feel something inside him lighten as well.

Hope. Hope that maybe God had been working everything out, even still was.

Please let that mean that she's alive, he prayed again as the shape of a cabin became more distinct in the darkness.

"Blue, come."

The dog did, went to him obediently, even though he could tell she could clearly smell what she'd been chasing, from the way she danced on her hind legs and whined.

"And be quiet."

She stopped making noise. Levi frowned. How well trained was this dog?

"What's your plan?" Judah asked him, and Levi felt himself stand taller. Shoulders back. For once, his older brother had asked *him* that question. Of course, this time Levi wasn't sure he had a plan, and could have maybe used his brother's help. But he wasn't going to admit that now.

"I think I should stay out of sight for now," Judah offered.

Yes. That was a solid plan. Levi nodded like he'd already thought that through. "You stay out of sight. I'll go in and try to get her."

"You won't be able to just storm in and yank her out. Besides, didn't you say your old partner may be in there, too?"

True. So they'd have an officer going in through the door, one outside. Two hostages. One killer. He liked the odds. The hostages were on his side, but it was still not without risk. If Adriana was still alive, it wasn't because this was a killer who showed mercy. It was because she was somehow worth more to them alive than dead.

That made him uncomfortable, to not understand what they were planning. Also, what shape would Adriana be in? She was a fit woman. If she hadn't managed to escape at her house, then she'd potentially been knocked out, drugged, or worse. He had to factor that in as well.

Levi's mouth was dry and the taste of fear was overwhelming. Adrenaline buzzed down his arms, through his veins. He needed her to be all right.

He needed to do the best he could for her.

He crept toward the cabin, quietly. His feet fell on the ground of the Alaskan woods carefully as he made his way closer.

Blue walked alongside him.

The husky. Did he bring her or not? Adriana wouldn't like her dog being in danger and she might make an impulsive decision if it seemed like Blue was. On the other hand, his chances of being able to save her were greater with the animal for help.

The risk was worth it.

"Don't make me regret this," he whispered to the dog.

They moved as one toward the cabin.

He could hear voices from inside. A woman was talking. The killer?

"If you had never been unfaithful…"

"Rosie, please." Jim's voice.

Levi had never wished so badly to have been wrong, but his partner's wife was the killer. It sickened him to imagine the bodies he'd looked at over the years, to know that it had been her evil and hatred that had ended people's lives.

A gunshot suddenly rang out.

Levi had no more time.

He burst through the closed door of the cabin, the dog at his heels, and hoped that Blue would have some inkling as to how to handle herself in this kind of situation.

"Levi!" Adriana yelled, and as Rosie turned her head to watch the dog, Levi tackled her. The gun fell from her hands and clattered to the floor. As he wrestled her arms behind her back and reached for the cuffs at his side, he looked around.

His assessment had been mostly right. Three hostages. Jim, Adriana and a young woman he didn't recognize.

"Their daughter," Adriana said. Levi nodded but couldn't see if anyone had been shot.

Rosie screamed and fought him, but he finished getting the handcuffs on. "Rosie Johnson, you are under arrest." He continued with her Miranda rights, surprised that his voice was steady as he recited them from memory. She would spend the rest of her life in jail, and the area would finally be free from her terrorizing people and taking some perverted form of justice into her own hands.

Levi's heart beat hard in his chest, but he took slow, deep breaths. It was over. They'd arrested her. He could breathe again.

"No!" Adriana's shout behind him jerked his eyes upward in time to see his old partner, Jim, reach for the gun and aim it at Adriana.

"Jim." Levi's voice was low. Full of disbelief.

Rosie had been behind the killings, right?

"She is still my wife," Jim said with a gasp and Levi noticed for the first time that Jim was the one who had been shot. Blood spattered the right side of his chest. Maybe a fatal wound, maybe not. But enough to slow him down. Not enough to necessarily make him less accurate firing a couple shots of his own. Rosie must have shot him right before Levi had come in. That was the gunshot he had heard.

"Don't do it, Jim." Levi kept his own voice calm. From beside Adriana, Blue growled.

"Make your dog stay put or I shoot her, too. And I hate killing dogs."

Adriana looked down at Blue. "Stay," she told her calmly.

Too calmly. Her voice was quiet, like she was losing strength. Levi looked over at her. The corner of her shirt, on her side… Was it darker than the rest? And if so, was it a shadow or a bloodstain?

With wavering hands, Jim lifted the gun back to Adriana. Trained it straight on her.

"You need to forget this happened, Levi. Bury it somewhere in your memory." Jim was panting between words now—the gunshot must have damaged several organs inside him. Or the blood loss was just too much because Levi could see him fading away. Desperate sadness at losing a man who had been a mentor to him fought against some kind of relief. At this point Jim was at least guilty of attempted murder, and it might be getting worse. He hated the idea of his friend in jail.

He doubted he'd have to worry about that.

"Jim. Put the gun down. It's not who you are."

The window behind Jim. Levi frowned. Did he see something? A flicker of light? Movement?

Judah. It was his brother. Levi felt his shoulders relax even as he kept his eyes trained on the man holding a gun within ten feet of the woman he suddenly realized he loved more than anything on earth.

"Put. It. Down," Levi insisted. As he finished speaking, the glass in the window behind Jim crashed. Jim jerked up the gun and swiveled his head around, so Levi rushed him. He'd come within a foot when Jim leaped back and swung the gun at Levi.

"Levi!" Adriana yelled, and he heard the noise of her chair moving, scraping against the wood floor of the cabin, but there was nothing she could do, nowhere she could go.

No, this was all on Levi until Judah could get back around to the side of the house. The cabin window was too high for him to climb into, but Judah had been brilliant to cause a distraction the way he had and trust Levi to do something with it. It was a kind of teamwork that he couldn't remember having experienced in a long time. They were equals who still needed each other.

Having a partner sometimes wasn't so bad. And he wasn't going to let his brother down now by getting shot and messing this up.

Levi lunged toward his former partner, as he tried to fight him off. Levi jerked hard one final time, tightening his grip on the man's arm as he pushed it down. The gun fell to the floor, again, and this time Levi kicked it to the side, out of the way.

Now. *Now* it was over.

Judah ran in the door, ran over to him. "You got him?"

Levi nodded. "Got him."

"I called the PD. They're sending backup, lots of it. They should be here soon."

Then it would truly be over.

Jim breathed hard, losing strength as Levi kept him restrained but cuffed him carefully with the handcuffs Judah handed him. He could hear the man crying.

Jim had made bad choices, most of which Levi probably didn't know about, and it would be a struggle to forgive him, Levi knew. But he could ask God to help him with that.

At least he had his life ahead of him. The woman he loved...

"This is your fault!" Rosie screamed in Jim's direction.

The woman in the corner, tied to the chair, was crying, too.

"And you are?" Judah walked over and asked her.

"Jenny. I'm their—their daughter..." She trailed off, started to cry again.

"She started killing after Jim had an affair," Adriana said. "And then stopped killing while she raised her daughter."

"I thought I could stop! I thought I could make it right by raising my daughter to be a good woman, not the kind of man stealing..." Her voice trailed off.

"She stopped until her daughter made the same mistake as her father, by seeing a married person." Adriana's voice was quiet.

Levi looked at all of them. His former partner, struggling to breathe. The sobbing woman in the corner.

The angry murderer still sitting on the floor.

And then back at Adriana. The shadow at her side was darker now. There was no more denial. "You're bleeding." He felt himself struggle to breathe as panic overwhelmed him. He had to get her out of here now, back to Raven Pass, to a doctor.

Because he hadn't come this far to lose her now.

Adriana remembered falling asleep, as consciousness played at the corners of her mind. Her side hurt, ached. Throbbed.

She had woken up on a stretcher, in the woods, and had the sense that she was being carried through the forest, probably by the backup that Judah had called.

Thoughts crowded her mind.

"Blue?" she remembered asking.

"She's fine. I've got her." Levi's voice. Calm and reassuring.

She'd fallen back asleep, let the darkness take her.

Now she blinked her way toward the light again. The bright fluorescents of the hospital room where she appeared to be were harsh.

There was Levi. Standing beside her.

"You're awake," he said and smiled.

She loved him, she realized again. She'd never loved someone quite this way before. It was different than the love she'd shared with her fiancé. Not because she'd loved Robert any less, but because they'd had a relationship at a time in her life when she hadn't known as much about loss and the cost of love. In some strange way, loss had taught her to care more deeply.

"I love you," he said to her, quietly.

She blinked.

He grinned wider. "You okay? Did you hear me? I love you, Adriana. And if I'm bad at relationships, I'll work on that, and I won't give up, because I love you. And that's not what love does."

She smiled back at him. "I love you, too," she said to him as she met his eyes.

They stayed that way, staring, for what seemed like minutes but could have been seconds. Her perception of time was still off.

She frowned.

"I'm in the hospital?"

"The doctors wanted to check your stab wound. You needed a little bit of blood, but you're going to be okay. I'm so glad. I love you so much."

Adriana nodded, tried to sit up a little against the pillows.

"I learned some things about the case," he started, then paused. "Did you want to know this now?" Adriana nodded, but also suppressed a small laugh. This was what life with Levi would be like. They'd be talking about something serious, talking about their love for each other, and then he'd bring up a case. She knew it as surely as she knew anything else. And it was fine with her. She wouldn't change the way he was for anything.

"What did you learn?" she asked.

"I sent a team down to try to see if there was a body near where the very first one was discovered. Outside the town of Hope."

"Did they find something?"

He nodded. "Yes. Fifteen feet away from the site of the original body was another."

They were the same measurements, same MO of having two bodies buried near each other. That was a strange element of Rosie's MO they'd probably never have an explanation for, but it had been consistent through each body Adriana knew of.

"Anything else?" She could see that there was in the way he looked at her, with his eyes lit up. He nodded again.

"The body we found this time was a woman who was from the town of Hope. She appears to have been killed before the first body we found there." His face turned serious. "She was the woman Jim had an affair with. Rosie admitted to it once she was down at the station. She seems to have no desire to plead innocent, which is driving her lawyer crazy. She was only too happy to confirm what we knew and tell us some information we didn't know yet."

"That's why we were run off the Seward Highway the other day," Adriana commented. "Because if we had started talking to that victim's friends, the investigation would have uncovered Jim's affair. Then we would have started asking questions of Jim. And his wife."

"And we would have figured out it was her," Levi confirmed.

Adriana closed her eyes. What a broken world they lived in, she thought. And yet a world full of good things, too. She never wanted to forget that and let the bad weigh her down. There was always a glimmer of hope to be found.

"She also told me that Jim met the woman he had an affair with at a coffee shop."

"That's why Rosie found her victims there?"

Levi nodded. "Women who were cheating or helping someone else cheat. Always taken from a coffee shop as a kind of sick memorial to what Rosie's husband had done to her with his betrayal."

Another detail of the case explained. Adriana had wondered.

Sick, sick woman.

Adriana shook her head, still overwhelmed with sadness. She looked away from Levi. A few minutes passed in heavy silence.

"Adriana?"

She turned to him, noting the seriousness in his voice.

"I don't want to date you."

She raised her eyebrows, waiting for him to elaborate. He'd told her five minutes ago that he loved her. And now...

"I want to get married."

If she hadn't been lying down already, she'd have needed to sit. The words stunned her, but filled her with more hope and happiness than she could explain.

"You want to marry me?"

"I want to marry you," Levi said again. "Will you please do me the honor of becoming my wife?"

He was down on one knee now, and in her mind Adriana knew the scene looked ridiculous, with her on a hospital bed, under a pile of blankets, and him down on one knee.

"I don't have a ring yet. I've been in the middle of this crazy case, see. I'll get a ring, though, as soon as we can. You can pick it out, or I can. I think I could do a pretty good job. I love you, Adriana. That's what matters to me..."

Adriana pushed herself farther into a sitting position.

"Levi?"

"Yes?"

"The ring doesn't matter." Well, it would be exciting. And she'd love seeing it as a sparkling reminder of promises on her finger, but it didn't matter as much as Levi himself.

He looked at her. Eyebrows raised. Anticipating her answer.

"I would love to marry you, Levi Wicks." She laughed as he reached out his arms and hugged her in the gentlest way possible, careful not to press against her wound.

"I know it's fast, but we've known each other for years." He nodded. "I know we can do this, Adriana. We make a good team. And we'll make a good team together."

It was another vote of confidence Levi being convinced that they would make this work, that their love would only grow stronger. She loved him even more for it.

"Are you sure?" His eyes flickered with a tiny hint of vulnerability. "It would be forever."

"Forever with you is exactly what I want," she assured him, and she put her hands on either side of his face, cradling his jaw, as she leaned forward into his kiss.

EPILOGUE

Never had Levi been prouder than at the sight of both of his brothers dressed in suits, for him. Ryan was performing the wedding ceremony, and Judah was his best man.

Neither he nor Adriana had wanted a long engagement, so as soon as she was fully healed, they'd started to plan the wedding. It was just over three months since that day in the hospital when he'd asked her to marry him.

And he loved her more than ever.

Levi looked at his older brothers and smiled. But as he caught Judah's eye he smiled a little wider.

They had never explicitly talked about Judah's tendency to treat Levi like he was perpetually in need of his help, but somehow after that night at the cabin, when Judah had come through for him without making him feel less than capable, everything had turned out okay.

He stood at the front of the church, eyes fixed on the door at the back of the room. In a few minutes, Adriana would come through those doors. He couldn't believe that only half an hour or less stood between him and forever.

Despite his past hurts, today was only a celebration. Of the fact that they'd survived the hardest case he'd ever worked, of their love and that he'd found a team-mate for life.

The doors opened. She walked in, looking beautiful in a dress that highlighted her curves in a subtle way that he found so beautiful.

That word. *Beautiful.* It was everything about her, but not just her. It was everything about their story.

He'd stopped trusting God after heartache, then had finally tentatively tried again. And God had blessed him beyond his wildest dreams.

"I love you," he whispered to Adriana as she came closer.

Her eyes met his. They flickered, full of hope.

Again, that word. *Beautiful.*

"I love you, too."

They were the best words Levi had ever heard.

* * * * *

Sharee Stover is a Colorado native transplanted to Nebraska, where she lives with her husband, three children and two dogs. Her mother instilled in her a love of books before Sharee could read, along with the promise "If you can read, you can do anything." When she's not writing, she enjoys time with her family, long walks with her obnoxiously lovable German shepherd and crocheting. Find her at shareestover.com or on Twitter, @shareestover.

Books by Sharee Stover

Love Inspired Suspense

Secret Past
Silent Night Suspect
Untraceable Evidence
Grave Christmas Secrets
Cold Case Trail

Visit the Author Profile page at LoveInspired.com.

COLD CASE TRAIL

Sharee Stover

And ye shall know the truth,
and the truth shall make you free.
—*John* 8:32

For my daughter, Andi. Your love for K-9s and their law enforcement handlers inspired Magnum's story.

Many thanks to:

My amazing editor, Emily Rodmell, for her encouragement and support.

Trooper Levi Cockle and K-9 Cole for their expertise and service.

ONE

He's been in my apartment, I'm sure of it. Is he watching me now?

Forensic psychologist Justine Stark glanced over her shoulder and shivered. A slight breeze rustled the oak tree leaves near the pasture, and the wind chime overhead sang softly. She searched for movement in the inky night but spotted nothing out of the ordinary. Her surroundings stilled, and she returned her attention to the diary's worn brown leather cover. Somewhere within its pages, she'd decipher the clues to develop a criminal profile to catch the killer.

First, she had to compartmentalize her emotions, a liability for any investigation. Except her throat tightened at the sight of her best friend's flamboyant handwriting, as whimsical as the woman who'd penned the contents. Worse, Justine almost heard Kayla Nolan's terrified voice in each entry, even a decade after her death.

Justine wrapped herself in a hug, warding off the chill, though the summer air was balmy. Slowing the old porch swing, she noted Kayla's fear escalation and stalker-related entries. The shrill ring of her cell phone sent her pen skidding off the paper.

A nervous chuckle escaped, and she glanced at the screen. Caller Unknown. Was the Nebraska State Patrol investigator in charge of Kayla's case finally returning her call? Or had Harry Dante found time to harass her from prison again?

A second ring. She contemplated letting it go to voice mail, except she wanted to talk to the investigator. "Hello?"

Silence, then heavy breathing.

Her irritation increased. "Give it up, Harry."

A responding dial tone.

She sighed and set the phone atop the notebook. Her extensive profiling and criminal-trial testimonies produced a growing list of haters, but dealing with the harassment never got easier.

Dante had sworn revenge on everyone involved in his sentencing hearing. Over the past year, he'd bombarded Justine with not-so-anonymous hate mail and a steady stream of untraceable calls. Certain Dante used a burner phone, she'd contacted the warden. He'd disregarded the claim, stating prisoners had access only to landlines.

Changing her number had proved futile because the calls continued. The final straw—the vandalism of her car outside her Lincoln apartment—prompted her relocation three hours away to the rural twelve-acre, fixer-upper ranch in the far northeastern part of Nebraska.

Justine resumed swaying, focused on the abundance of fireflies dancing in the night sky to the cadence of crickets and cicadas. The sweet scent of lilacs wafted from the overgrown bushes bordering the two-story farmhouse wraparound porch, calming her.

You're safe here. She rehearsed the comforting mantra, relishing the haven where she fostered dogs for the overflowing animal shelter in town.

Lifting the diary again, Justine angled the page, allowing her to read by the soft glow of the porch light. She donned the persona of a clinician, shoving aside the guilt-ridden heart she had for failing to save her best friend.

Kayla's scribblings testified to a nameless, faceless psychopath, who'd tormented her by leaving bizarre gifts inside her apartment. Though she'd tried to report the incidents, no one except Justine had believed her. The authorities had classified Kayla's death as suspicious, claiming it was an overdose after a drug buy gone bad. And they were wrong because Justine knew her friend never used drugs. Kayla had been murdered. But why?

What she hadn't done ten years ago, she'd accomplish now and ensure Kayla got justice. The diary was a beginning, but Justine wanted the investigator's evidence files, even if it meant storming his office door.

Clover stretched out a reassuring paw before consuming the rest of the porch swing with her furry body.

"Am I in your way?" Justine ruffled the overweight calico's velvety fur.

Sharp, piercing barks emitted from the renovated barn, sending Justine's pulse racing. She placed a hand over her chest. "I'd better go to bed before every noise gives me a heart attack. What is going on with the boys?"

Clover yawned, indifferent to the commotion.

"Thanks for your support," Justine teased, pushing off the swing. She stepped down to the lawn and rounded the house, aiming for the barn—affectionately dubbed the Dog House—with Clover accompanying her.

An ambient glow stretched from the building's ajar

door, slowing Justine. Hadn't she locked up after feeding the boys?

Uneasiness crept between her shoulders. She paused, turned and scanned the surrounding trees, casting shadows with their canopy of leaves.

You're safe here.

The dogs continued barking in an uneven banter.

A rustle sent the calico darting off, startling Justine. "Stop that," she admonished herself.

Too bad Clover wasn't an attack cat.

Should she enter? And what other choice did she have? Mr. Richardson, her closest neighbor, lived a half mile adjacent from her. The unpleasant man was more interested in taking ownership of her property rather than helping her.

Justine still clutched the diary. She shoved it into the large pocket of her khaki cargo shorts. Inhaling a fortifying breath, she pushed wide the door and, in a single stride, stepped inside and flipped on the overhead lights. "Gentlemen, what's with all the hullabaloo?"

At her entrance, the barking ceased and five tails wagged in greeting. A quick scan confirmed an empty room, except for the motley crew of mutts. Justine studied the door, accepting she'd earlier failed to close it properly.

Or a raccoon got in, explaining Clover's sudden departure. The varmints had discovered the building held an abundance of food, making them a recent nuisance.

"It's bedtime." Talking to the dogs calmed her.

Justine double-checked each kennel and resident, providing a few minutes of attention.

She saved the neediest patient for last. "Hey, Barney,

how're you feeling?" Justine knelt beside the senior basset hound recovering from a broken leg.

He gave her a rhythmic thump of his tail while lounging on his doggie cot, his big brown eyes pleading.

"I promise you'll return to the house once you're able to climb the stairs again."

Barney harrumphed and laid his head down, dangling his long ears over the edge.

She chuckled and exited the kennel, giving the space one last perusal. A countertop on the far side, along with a sink and cabinets, held the dogs' food, treats and medications. Her part-time ranch hand's accommodations were cordoned off on the right. The barn was spotless, and since the installation of the air conditioner, the temperature remained comfortable.

Next year she'd install the same amenities in the old farmhouse, but that was a luxury she'd have to save up for. Barney's unexpected arrival and medical treatment, the renovations for the Dog House, along with canine flea and tick medications, had consumed this year's funds.

"That's enough ruckus for one night. Go to sleep and I'll see you tomorrow." She exited the building and pulled the door shut.

From the shadows, Clover reappeared.

"Did you chase off the raccoon?"

The calico's tail stood tall as they traversed back to the house.

Will Percy, her hired hand, would arrive in the morning. He worked hard, but his busy schedule and her lack of money made his assistance sporadic at best. There was never enough time, cash or able-bodied help to keep up with the ranch. Dreams might tarry, but she'd invested everything to breathe life into hers.

Her shoes thudded against the rotting porch wood as she rounded the house. Gathering her notes and phone from the swing, she tugged open the rickety screen door. A wave of humidity and stuffy air spilled out, and the grandfather clock chimed ten o'clock from the corner of the living room. After flipping on every light between the entrance and the kitchen, she determined to read the diary a half hour longer before going to bed.

The lights flickered, then went out, thrusting Justine into pitch-dark. She pivoted on one foot, eyes focused on the door. Probably just needed to reset the fuse box.

In the basement.

A lump formed in her throat. "Clover?" Justine squeaked, hating the quiver in her voice. "Here, kitty-kitty."

Because the cat could reset the fuse box? Were raccoons responsible for the blackout? Doubtful. The hundred-year-old house offered a variety of creepy noises, and functional errors happened occasionally.

You're safe here.

Why hadn't she brought Barney inside? Perhaps calling for help would be wiser. And say what? *My lights went out, and I'm a big baby and don't want to go into the basement by myself*?

Justine threw back her shoulders and stood taller. No, this was just another part of living in the country as an independent woman.

Inching across the kitchen, she felt her way to the junk drawer and groped for a flashlight. At last, her hands gripped the cold metal, bringing a small measure of comfort. She flipped the switch, exhaling relief at the responsive beam.

"You are always with me, Lord."

A resounding meow blazed a voltage through her heart, and she laughed nervously.

"Clover, you about shot me through the roof." Justine wedged the flashlight under her armpit and lifted the cat, stroking her fur.

The knife block beside her had Justine considering her options.

"Stop that."

Clover fidgeted, forcing Justine to set her down.

"Sorry, not you." She snagged a butcher knife and, gripping the flashlight, made her way through the kitchen. "Nothing but a blown fuse. Get a grip."

Her footsteps echoed on the creaky floors—a multifunctional feature, making the home endearing in the daylight and eerie at night. She tugged the basement door open, releasing dank mustiness into the hallway.

Justine reached in and flipped on the light switch, hoping against reality it worked.

Nope.

She swiped her clammy palm on her shirt, readjusted the flashlight in her left hand and clutched the knife in her right. Justine descended the steep cement steps, trying hard not to think about the encroaching darkness. A wisp of something grazed her face. She swatted away the sticky substance, but the spiderweb remnants clung to her skin. Justine shook them off and wiped her hand on her pant leg.

At the bottom of the steps, she inhaled and swung the beam, illuminating the fuse box. Destination in sight, she sprinted for the corner of the cinder block basement and reached for the metal door.

A shadow shifted in her peripheral vision.

Justine spun, her nose connecting with someone's fist. The force thrust her into the wall.

The flashlight toppled to the cement floor with a thud before dying.

Grasping the knife, Justine screamed a battle cry, flailing the blade blindly around her. She kicked in every direction and a resounding "oomph" from the invader confirmed she'd made a connection.

Justine fought, slashing the knife in front of her, unrelenting. Though he never spoke, her attacker's labored breathing echoed around her.

Then everything stilled.

Had he fled? She squatted, groping for the flashlight. Her fingertips touched the cold metal.

A tackle from behind flattened Justine against the cement floor, jolting the knife from her hand.

The intruder restrained her wrists behind her back and secured bindings on her ankles.

"Where is it?" he growled.

Did he know about Kayla's diary? Had he watched Justine reading? She swallowed. The weight of the small book in her pocket anchored her.

"What are you talking about?"

"Fine. We'll do this the hard way." He slapped tape over her mouth, restricting breathing to her nose, and covered her head with a hood.

Lord, what's happening? Help me!

Strong arms gripped, lifted and inverted her, gravity rushing blood to her brain. He ascended the stairs. Heavy footsteps reverberated on the wood floor, indicating they were in the hallway. Justine forced herself to focus on the details. She'd need them to escape. Hysteria wouldn't help. If there was ever a time to lean on her psychology training, it was now. She'd outwit the perpetrator and flee. Somehow.

He crossed the living room and descended the porch steps. How had he gotten to the ranch? She'd have seen him driving up to the property. Had he waited by the Dog House? Was that what had riled the boys?

She bounced against his shoulder, nausea building.

The man paused.

Justine squirmed to break free, helpless against his tightening hold.

"Knock it off."

A familiar beep, like a key fob release. In a swoop, he dropped her, and she landed with a hard thud. Rough material brushed against her arms and legs. Carpet. She was in a trunk.

A slam, and his footsteps faded.

Justine calmed her breathing to combat the panic of the smothering tape and hood. She tugged against the restraints and tried scooting out of the hood, using the carpet.

To no avail.

Several long minutes passed. What was he doing? Would he kill her?

Finally, a second slam and the engine roared to life. Justine sniffed, inhaling the bitter scent of fertilizer. She'd loaded the bags earlier in the day. He was using her car to kidnap her.

The vehicle reversed.

Justine focused on the details. She'd find her way home once she escaped her bindings.

He shifted again and drove forward, leaving her property. The connecting dirt road was rough. If the man was a local or if he'd cased her place, he'd be aware of the large pothole left over from the last major flood.

She braced, waiting. Sure enough, the car dipped into the rut, slamming her face into the floor. A blast of pain coursed through her nose. Not a local. She made the mental note, beginning her depiction tactics. She didn't need to see his face to create a profile. He would not get away with this.

Justine shifted to her back, with the coordination of a wounded caterpillar. The vehicle slowed, rolling her to the side. He'd turned left onto the major county highway, heading east.

If she freed her hands, she'd grasp the trunk release. Every car had one, or so she'd read.

Justine tugged her arms apart, trying to break through the zip ties. She kicked, extending her efforts there, but the plastic tore at the tender skin around her ankles.

The car accelerated.

Lord, please get me out of this!

Nebraska state trooper Trey Jackson was about to walk into an ambush. The perfect ending to the worst day ever. And he'd chosen it willingly. As if postponing his K-9 partner Magnum's recertification exam wasn't bad enough, his nemesis, Eric Irwin, had offered to fill their spot in the meantime. Thankfully, Sergeant Oliver had declined, but not before warning Trey their assigned work area needed a capable K-9 team soon. To top it off, Justine Stark would slam the door in his face when he arrived unannounced at her house in less than ten minutes.

She detested Trey.

Rightfully so, after he'd failed to respond to their mutual friend Kayla Nolan the night of her murder. He should've been the first to arrive at her apartment. No excuses. Still, he wished Justine had allowed him to explain.

Kayla was high-strung and openly communicated her feelings for Trey to anyone who would listen. He hadn't reciprocated, and finally confessed he was interested in Justine. Kayla refused to accept that fact. Trey assumed Kayla had told Justine how he felt, especially when the trio's friendship grew tense shortly thereafter. He interpreted the change as Justine's rejection of him. Still, Kayla never gave up on trying to win him over.

The night Kayla called with wild claims of a stalker, Trey and Magnum were working their first manhunt. Unable to leave, Trey sent his brother and fellow trooper, Slade, in his place. But when Kayla saw Slade, she slammed the door in his face.

Trey's reasons for not showing up that night might've seemed justifiable from the outside, but he willingly bore Justine's disdain along with his own guilt.

He allowed his thoughts to return to Irwin, not wanting to consider the possible outcomes with Justine yet.

Trey was all for healthy competition, but Irwin played on his anxiety. A forced recovery risked reinjuring Magnum. Not an option. Regardless of his insecurities over the possibility of losing their position. Grip tightening on the steering wheel, Trey pictured the last interaction with Irwin.

"Magnum's past his prime. You should retire him," the younger trooper had commented.

A new wave of irritation flowed through him. "Over

my dead body," Trey grunted, feeling the urge to slug Irwin's smug face the next time he saw the man.

The Belgian Malinois whined from his temperature-controlled space and poked his triangular head through the truck's divider.

Trey reached up and scratched his scruff. "Sorry, boy. Thinking about Irwin."

Magnum gave a sympathetic and well-timed bark of understanding.

"See, you totally get it." Trey rewarded him with a good ear scratching. "But Oliver thinks he's Mr. Helpful. More like a vulture circling its prey."

Magnum rested his head on Trey's shoulder.

"Don't worry, buddy. You're healing fine, and we'll be back in the saddle. Right now, though, I need a little courage to handle the blast from my past. You know, this could go really bad. I mean, worst-case scenario, Justine slams the door in my face. Hopefully, we'll get the best-case scenario and she'll hear me out once she sees the files I brought."

Almost ten years had passed since their last inter-action, and that hadn't been pleasant. They'd scarcely spoken at Kayla's funeral, and the death daggers Justine had shot from across the room were enough to kill.

Sergeant Oliver hadn't forbidden Trey to make the long commute to Justine's home, though his disapproval at the personal visit hadn't gone unnoticed.

"What choice do I have, Mags? If I'd called first, Justine would've hung up as soon as I said my name. She hates me."

And he deserved it. If he'd been there for Kayla, she'd be alive.

Trey glanced at the cold-case file box riding shotgun

beside him, contemplating for the hundredth time if this was the wisest action. Were Kayla's files enough incentive for Justine to listen to him?

The shorter and less painful option was a phone call. And cowardly.

The face-to-face meeting was his one chance to right the wrong. However pitiful the step might be. "Let's pray for the best."

Magnum sighed and slipped back into his space.

"Thanks for the reassurance."

Trey's phone rang.

"Call from Sergeant Oliver," the automated voice announced.

Trey answered using his hands-free device. "Boss."

"Where are you?"

"Almost to the Stark residence, if Callista correctly recorded the address." The patrol secretary, Callista Neff, was knowledgeable and a valuable asset. However, her attention to detail and customer service skills ebbed and flowed depending on her mood of the day.

"Jackson, you should've returned her call." His placating tone reemphasized disapproval, but Oliver wasn't privy to Trey and Justine's history, and he didn't need the details.

"No worries, Sarge. Magnum and I wanted to get out of the office anyway."

"Understood. Besides, after the way Callista treated Miss Stark, it's probably not a bad idea to do some damage control."

"Ouch."

Oliver grunted. "Yeah, I only heard half the conversation, but it was less than cordial. Monday, I'll be meeting with Callista about her attitude. Again."

"Those are becoming a regular occurrence."

"Don't remind me. I'm headed to the lake for the weekend, but let me know if Miss Stark provides any leads. Although after—what?—nine, no, ten years, I seriously doubt she'll have anything to offer."

"Except she's a highly qualified forensic psychologist now. The patrol didn't pursue criminal profiling back then. Maybe her skills will help us solve Kayla Nolan's case."

"You don't have to sell me on the idea. That's my hope, Jackson."

Tension lessened in Trey's shoulders. His boss's support bolstered his confidence.

"How's Magnum doing? I assume he's enjoying the ride along with you?"

"He's eating up the attention and relaxing. I considered leaving him behind, but the last time he got depressed. He likes working, even if it's not to his full capacity."

Oliver chuckled. "I appreciate a dog's need to be useful, but watch that he doesn't reinjure his paw. You've only got two weeks until the next K-9 recertification."

As if Trey needed the reminder. "Roger that. Thanks again for letting us work cold cases."

"It's the least we can do for him," Oliver replied. "If he needs more time, Eric—"

"Mags will be healed in time, boss." Trey cringed at the rude interruption, but the last thing he wanted was another rendition of Eric the Vulture's brilliant and magnificent capability. "We'll make our recert."

"I have no doubt."

"Thanks."

They disconnected, and Trey exhaled relief. Magnum was getting into his senior years, but he was far from retirement. They were in their prime, a solid team with the highest takedowns, manhunt recoveries and drug interdictions. At least, they had been. On their last case, Magnum cut his front paw on debris in the sewer tunnel where the subject was hiding.

Be anxious for nothing. The soft reminder floated in Trey's mind. "You're right, Lord. Worrying won't solve anything. You've got this case, and You've got us."

The automated GPS voice advised Trey to take a left in a mile. He crested the hill and was blinded by oncoming headlights. The vehicle sped in Trey's lane, swerving at the last minute to avoid a head-on collision, then whipped past, accelerating.

"I don't think so, dude." Trey flipped on his sirens and lights and made a U-turn, pursuing. He closed the distance to read the license plate and radioed in the information.

The sedan skidded around the corner, merging onto the highway.

"You're seriously trying to outrun me?"

As if the driver heard Trey, the car slowed, right-turn signal blinking as he edged to the shoulder.

"What an idiot. Drive out to the highway, where there's traffic, instead of stopping on the safety of the side road?" Trey mumbled. Whatever. This guy had earned a ticket tonight. "Well, that was uneventful." He pulled behind the sedan, deactivated the siren, but left his overhead lights swirling to warn oncoming traffic.

Trey grabbed his uniform hat, placing it on his head, and collected his flashlight. "Five-five-nine-nine, 10-82," he spoke into the radio, notifying the dispatcher of his badge number and the ten code for pulling over a vehicle.

A couple of cars heading westbound passed, and Trey waited until it was clear to exit the pickup. Flashlight on, he approached the sedan's passenger side. A change in recent years after multitudes of officers were struck by motorists during routine stops. He watched the driver for any sudden movements.

One occupant. Probably a texting-and-driving situation—another development responsible for accidents lately. The front passenger-side window lowered.

Trey leaned closer. "Good eve—" His intro was cut off as the driver lifted a gun and aimed it in his direction.

Trey dropped and flattened against the gravel road, reaching for his weapon.

"Plates are registered to—" Gunfire exploded, drowning out the dispatcher's voice in his earpiece.

"Shots fired! Shots fired!" Trey hollered into his shoulder mic, simultaneously army crawling backward and staying low to the ground.

Once he reached the safety of the vehicle's quarter panel, he glanced up and returned fire, then ducked again.

Headlights beamed from an oncoming SUV, cresting the hill. If he didn't get control of the situation, an innocent passerby might be killed.

A long silence motivated Trey to peer around the car.

The driver ran from the sedan, turned and fired, then bolted for the SUV, waving down the motorist.

Trey sprinted after him.

Too late. The driver stopped, and the shooter flung

open the door, yanking out an elderly man who rolled helplessly onto the highway. The subject sped away in the stolen truck.

"Sir, are you okay?" Trey helped the victim to his feet.

"I don't know what happened," he said, weaving unsteadily.

"What's your name?"

"Edwin Smith."

On the way to his patrol vehicle, Trey collected information from Mr. Smith and called in the carjacking, issuing a BOLO—be on the lookout—for the subject. The criminal couldn't outrun the radio.

As they neared the sedan, heavy thuds sounded from the trunk. Trey ran to his pickup and closed Magnum's divider, then waved over Mr. Smith. "Please wait inside for me."

Trey withdrew his weapon and inched closer to the car.

The thudding increased.

Carefully, Trey released the trunk and stepped back, gun at the ready.

A woman lay faceup, arms tucked under her and ankles bound. She jerked awkwardly, trying to kick him, desperation in each movement. Muffled screams indicated she was gagged under the black hood covering her head.

"Ma'am, my name is Trooper Jackson. I'm here to help you. You're safe."

She stopped flailing, her frame rigid.

"I'm going to remove the hood."

Trey leaned in, gently pulling the fabric free, over her head.

She wrenched back. Dark tendrils streaked her face, and her wide hazel eyes pierced him, terror written on her expression.

Several seconds ticked by as he absorbed the sight.

Finally, he found his voice. "Justine Stark, is that you?"

TWO

Justine blinked, then attempted to answer, only to find her words stuck in the tape covering her mouth.

"I'll rip off the tape, but it'll sting."

She braced, and true to Trey's warning, the tape didn't disappoint. Justine inhaled, filling her lungs with fresh air. "Thank you. I heard gunshots. Is he—?" She didn't finish the sentence, allowing her gaze to search for the kidnapper.

He sliced through her bindings, then helped her out of the trunk.

"I planned to meet at your house, but I guess this works," he quipped, flashing a dimple in his smile.

Justine's expression must've spoken questions and disapproval, because he quickly sobered.

"Why were you coming to my home?" She spun, searching. "Did you arrest the man who kidnapped me?"

A small wince crossed Trey's face. "No. He carjacked Mr. Smith's vehicle and got away."

He gestured to a patrol K-9 pickup behind them, with strobing red-and-blue lights. An elderly man sat in the passenger seat, his mouth set in an O shape.

"But I have a BOLO out for the subject," Trey added. "We'll get his identity from the registration on this—"

"It's my car," Justine inserted.

He did a double take. "He used your car to kidnap you?"

"Yes."

"Are you okay? I'll call for an ambulance." Trey reached for his shoulder mic.

Justine shook her head. "I'm fine. Really." Untrue, but she didn't need medical care or the accompanying expense. Her hand brushed the pocket containing the diary. For a millisecond, she considered telling Trey about the evidence, then decided against it. Not until she'd spoken with the case investigator.

Trey held out a notepad. "Can you identify the subject?"

"Nope. One minute, I'm in my house, trying to reset the fuse box. The next, I'm in the trunk of my car, fighting for my life." Justine wrapped herself in a hug, warding off the chill that had nothing to do with the temperature and everything to do with the terror she'd encountered.

A second patrol vehicle pulled up, contributing to the strobing lights.

"Give me a second while I ask the trooper to take Mr. Smith's statement. Then I'll drive you home. We'll have your car towed back." He rushed off without giving her a chance to respond.

Justine walked to the driver's side, slid behind the wheel and adjusted the seat. The familiar road sign ahead assured her they hadn't driven far from her ranch.

Trey appeared at her window. "Planning on racing off?"

She glanced up. "The perp was much taller than me. Easily over six feet, based on where the seat was when I got in."

"That helps." He withdrew a notepad and marked down the information. "You might be surprised what details you remember when we do the report."

She stifled her groan. He needed a full accounting of the event, and though she'd never admit it to him, the thought of returning to her ranch alone was a little disconcerting. The dogs! Had the kidnapper hurt them? "My boys! I have to go home. Now!"

Trey's eyes widened. "Your boys?"

She started the engine.

"Are you sure you're okay to drive? You're still shook up."

"I'm fine." Why did everything she say come out so harshly? Because being in Trey's presence was unnerving. "I appreciate the offer though," she added, nearly whacking him with the door as she pulled it closed.

"I'll follow you, then."

Justine waited for him to reach his pickup before she merged onto the road. He slipped behind her, sans strobing lights.

What was Trey doing in this part of the state? Not that she kept tabs on him, but the law enforcement circles were small. There was no denying the one advantage of Trey's unexpected return to her life was his access to Kayla's case files. She'd insist on his help and wouldn't take no for an answer.

He owed her.

No. He owed Kayla. Trey and Justine were Kayla's closest friends. When she'd called him that night, claiming someone was stalking her, Trey hadn't bothered showing up. But then, neither had Justine.

The thought was an arrow to her heart. No. That was different. Justine had been out of town. Besides, Kayla had made it clear—she only wanted Trey's help. She'd laid claim to Trey early on, eliminating any opportunity for Justine to share how she felt about him.

Just as well. He'd failed Kayla when she needed him most. Like Justine's ex Simon, who'd betrayed and stolen from her. Proof that letting down her guard was unwise. Justine pushed aside the unwelcome thoughts, returning to Kayla.

The night replayed in her mind, an endless spooling reel of Kayla's frantic phone call. They'd talked into the early morning hours, Justine refusing to hang up until Kayla de-escalated. She'd rambled on about her feelings for Trey. Justine chalked up the hysteria of his nonarrival to her friend's theatrics. Especially after Kayla apologized and said she'd gotten scared over nothing.

That was the last time they'd spoken. Two days later, Justine returned to Lincoln. She'd driven from the airport straight to Kayla's apartment, only to find it cordoned off with police tape. She hadn't spoken to Trey since Kayla's funeral. It had been all too raw that day. But a decade was a long time.

Refocusing her energy, Justine processed the questions barreling full speed at her.

Why would someone kidnap her? In her own car?

She gripped the steering wheel. "Thank You, Lord, for rescuing me. Although, for the record, You could've chosen someone else. Your ways, not mine. I need Your help. Kayla deserves justice."

As she neared Vincent Richardson's ranch—her only

neighbor and a cantankerous man she'd nicknamed Mr. Personality—she slowed, searching for a vehicle. Richardson's cows meandered the perimeter, and the house was hidden beneath a canopy of mature trees. She'd contact him in the morning and ask if he'd seen anyone lurking around her property. Mr. Personality's less-than-cordial attitude made the possibility of a stranger parking his pre-kidnapping vehicle on his land improbable.

Had the perp watched her? Justine replayed Kayla's words about a stalker and shuddered as she pulled into the detached two-car garage, triggering the motion-sensor lights.

Trey parked behind her, blocking her in. Annoyed but focused on the boys, she exited the car and headed for the barn. Most likely, the kidnapper hadn't bothered the dogs, but she'd feel better after confirming that with her own eyes.

Trey started toward the darkened farmhouse as she hurried past him to the barn. "Wait. Where are you going?"

She waved him over. "In there."

He hurried to her side, confusion etched in his blue eyes. "Your children are alone in a barn?"

That brought a laugh to her lips. "Sort of. Foster dogs." She pulled open the door, welcomed by a rendition of barks. Justine led him through the building, releasing each dog from their kennels. "There are five males, so I refer to them as the boys."

In a tail-wagging flurry, the canines rushed to greet the newcomer. He gave each one attention, and she marveled at the ease in Trey's demeanor. Did he have to be great with animals? It was getting harder to maintain her animosity.

Trey moved slowly around the perimeter and seemed to linger at Will's meager accommodations. A large section of plywood separated the mini living quarters furnished with a twin bed, table and light. She started to explain, then reconsidered. Trey didn't need information about her life.

He crossed the room to her. "Are they okay with outsider dogs?"

"Yep. We're working on socialization, and it's gone well."

"In that case, I'll release my partner. He could use a bathroom break."

She did a double take deciphering his request. She followed him out, the boys bounding along.

Trey jogged to his truck and opened the back door. He turned, cradling a Belgian Malinois with a gauze-wrapped right front paw.

Justine's heart melted against her stony exterior. "Aw, what happened to him?" Her feet rushed forward against her brain's reservations.

"Magnum cut his paw on a manhunt. He's healing ahead of schedule though." Trey gently steadied the dog on his three good legs. "Where can he use your, uh, facilities?"

She pointed to the grassy area beside the garage, where two of the boys sniffed the ground.

"May I pet him?" She reached out, then quickly retracted her arm. "Sorry, never mind. Police dogs aren't allowed to socialize."

Trey laughed. "Magnum never received that memo. However, he's got intuition like no other. He can sniff out a criminal in an auditorium filled with people. I must warn you, he's a horrible flirt."

Much like his master. Justine stifled her reply and squatted. Magnum hobbled to her and dropped to a sit. She allowed him to sniff her hands. Then, at his approval, she petted his soft fur. "He's beautiful."

"And he knows it."

So incredibly not fair. She could've resisted handcuffs, demands, even a hostage negotiator, but Trey used the ultimate incentive. An adorable and wounded animal. For that, she had no defense.

"He doesn't mind other dogs?"

"Not unless they're breaking the law."

"My boys are legal, just in need of a little rehab. I'm grateful that creep didn't hurt them."

"Aren't you worried they'll run off?"

"This is Club Med for them, probably the best life any of them have known." The dogs' sorrowful histories gave her pause. Part of the reason she labored and sacrificed for them. "Their electric collars and underground fencing keep them quarantined on the premises, allowing them to run freely without leashes. No escape attempts yet."

"You live here alone?"

"Yep." She stepped away, avoiding the conversation.

Her heart bubbled with love for the canines frolicking on the ranch. Between the bounty of repairs, neverending projects, and her consulting and expert-testimony schedule, Justine was too busy to bemoan her nonexistent love life, not that she'd give another man her heart. Instead, she lavished attention on the only creatures worthy and capable of unconditional love. In turn, they never judged her by the scars on her heart or body.

At the reminder, Justine tugged down her sleeves and whistled for the boys. "Give me a sec."

Magnum moved to Trey's side. "Need help?"

"No, this is our routine." Justine finished securing each dog and locking the building, then walked to Trey.

"That didn't take long."

"Nope, got it down to a fine art." She swatted a persistent mosquito. "Let's go inside. There's no air-conditioning, but we won't become dinner for the local insect population."

He lingered before following her. "What happened before the kidnapping?"

"The boys were riled up, and the Dog House door was ajar."

"Was that strange? Do you leave it open?"

Justine led the way across the property, with Magnum and Trey keeping pace. "The barn's temperature controlled, so I keep the door shut. Especially with the recent raccoon invasions. Clover tore after something, and I assumed she chased a raccoon. The boys were fine, so I locked up and headed into the house."

"Clover?"

"My cat." Justine gazed out toward the pasture. "She's around somewhere."

When they reached the porch, Trey carried Magnum up the steps. "This place is nice. Reminds me of my folks' house."

"Needs work, but I love it."

"Mom and Pops would make homemade ice cream—they came up with wild combinations—and we'd spend summer evenings eating their latest concoctions on their wraparound porch, playing games and singing horribly out-of-tune songs."

Justine remained silent at Trey's wistful comment. What must it be like to have a loving family connection?

She'd never know. Her fingers traced the burn scars on her upper arm—hidden, like her painful and embarrassing past—beneath the long-sleeved thin cotton shirt.

A twinge of jealousy niggled, but the solid reminder of who she was and what she needed to do for Kayla refocused her thoughts. She and Trey weren't friends hanging out and socializing. They existed in different worlds. Once he took her statement, he'd be out of her life.

Justine's front door stood open, exposing the darkened rooms inside, her haven no longer. "Guess locking up before he abducted me was too much to ask," she said sarcastically.

The roar of an engine interrupted them. Headlights beamed from the county road. A lifted diesel dually turned onto her property, almost taking out her fence.

"Are you expecting someone?"

"No." Was the kidnapper returning? Certainly not with a cop there. Except Trey's patrol vehicle wasn't visible from the oncoming truck's view.

Trey withdrew his gun and stepped in front of her. "Go inside and lock the door. Call for help if this goes bad. Magnum stay." He descended the porch, gun in hand.

The truck accelerated, kicking up gravel and dirt. Aimed right for her house.

Blinded by the oversize headlights on the Silverado 3500, Trey shifted, then dived to the side, before he became part of the colossal push bumper. He scooted to his feet and turned as the truck skidded to a stop, inches from colliding with his patrol pickup. This guy was out of control.

He glanced over his shoulder.

Justine stood on the porch, watching.

"Get in the house." Unable to view inside the cab, Trey approached with caution. "Driver, put your hands where I can see them."

"I want out of this death trap!" a man bellowed. The passenger door flung wide, and a cowboy boot emerged.

"Slowly," Trey demanded.

The sixtysomething man disembarked awkwardly, straightened his black Stetson, then tossed out a back-pack. "Arrest him! That boy tried to kill me!"

"Driver, shut off the engine and climb down with your hands visible to me at all times." Trey stood at a distance, maintaining visual on the driver and passenger.

"His name is Nathan Yancy. Just got his license, and his dad assured me he was capable. I saw my life flash before my eyes ten times in five miles!"

A nervous-looking teenager held up shaking hands, his body turned sideways to exit. "Sorry, sir. I'm not used to my dad's pickup." His voice quivered over the engine's rumble.

"Don't go blaming the truck, boy!" The passenger stormed toward Trey. "I'm Will Percy. I work for Jus-tine." He started for the porch, halted by Magnum's growls. "You got another dog? What's wrong with this one?"

"Nathan, turn off the engine and join me." Trey kept one eye on Will. "Mr. Percy, that's K-9 Magnum. Stay where you are and keep your hands visible at all times."

"I ain't no criminal!"

"Will's my employee. Do what Trooper Jackson says," Justine stated.

The willowy teenager killed the diesel and in almost slow motion jumped down, landing steadily on his cowboy boots, arms in the air, looking more of a gymnast than frenzied novice. He shifted from one foot to another.

Trey holstered his gun. "Relax and lower your arms. I need to see your driver's license."

The boy produced the identification with a shaky hand. "I gave Mr. Percy a ride—"

"You tried to kill me!"

Trey took the card and silenced Will with a look. "Hmm, got it today?"

"Yes, sir." Nathan swallowed, bobbing his Adam's apple, and nibbled on a nonexistent fingernail.

"Congratulations." Trey handed back the card and lowered his voice. "The day I got my license, I sank my dad's new truck, trying to impress a bunch of girls at the lake. Thought I could load the boat on the trailer by myself. Accidentally left the truck in Reverse. Went down faster than the *Titanic*."

Nathan gasped. "Wow." The boy's cheeks flushed a bright red and his eyes were wide as dinner plates. "My dad woulda grounded me forever. Same as he's gonna do when Mr. Percy tells him about tonight."

"You'll be fine. Just take it easy. You're free to go."

"Thank you." Nathan nodded so vigorously Trey thought the kid's head might bounce off his neck.

"He's gonna kill someone!" Will used his Stetson to gesture at the pickup.

"Sir, you must calm down." Trey focused on Magnum and spoke the cease command. *"Nein."*

Will clamped his mouth shut, fury in his expression.

"Will's harmless," Justine whispered.

Maybe so, but Trey never second-guessed Magnum's instincts.

"I didn't think you'd be here until morning," Justine said.

"Finished at Yancy's early." Will's eyes stayed on Magnum.

Justine smiled. "Great. I'll get on the road sooner."

The roar of the diesel's engine captured their attention as Nathan performed an excruciating forty-point turn near the garage. After several near misses—including the barn, fence and a tree—the dually rumbled at a snail's pace from the property.

"Yancy better pay up his auto insurance," Will grumbled, appraising Trey with obvious disdain. "Who're you?"

Trey bristled and bit back a smart answer, extending a hand. "Trooper Trey Jackson. Is Will short for William?"

"Wilbur."

"Trey and I know each other from a long time ago," Justine replied. "He's here on a professional visit."

"In the dead of night?" He harrumphed. "I'm heading to bed."

"Okay. List is on the fridge."

Will grunted, hefting his backpack. With a final adjustment to his Stetson, he walked to the barn.

The guy bugged Trey, giving rise to a hundred probing questions. He started with the most significant. "He doesn't stay in the house?" The farther the proximity to Justine, the better.

"No. His accommodations are in the barn."

"What's Will do?"

Justine lowered her voice and waved Trey around the porch to the front door. "He works part-time for me and other ranches in the area wherever the labor takes him. I'd hire him full-time, but that's not possible right now."

Was Will involved in Justine's kidnapping? "How long have you known him?"

"About nine months." She raised a hand and brow. "Don't go there. He cares for the boys when I go out of town."

"Seems like a real animal lover." Trey didn't try to hide the sarcasm in his voice.

"That's a defense mechanism. He's a softy and a hard worker."

"Let's talk in private. After I take your full report, I'll explain why I was coming to see you this evening."

She hesitated by the door. "Can I borrow your flashlight? I think the kidnapper messed with my fuse box to lure me into the basement."

"I'll reset it. Point me in the direction. I'd like to clear the house."

She folded her arms, but her tone held relief. "Basement door is in the hall on the right."

"Magnum, stay."

The dog whined but obeyed. Poor guy loved building clearance, but with the stairs in the multistoried farmhouse, Trey couldn't risk a reinjury.

He started with the upper level, making his way to the basement, avoiding the personal items and an abundance of file boxes spread across the floor.

Finally, he located the antiquated fuse box and the fuse the subject must've removed. He inserted the fuse, illuminating the musty space. Trey collected a butcher knife and broken flashlight from the ground and returned to the kitchen, where Justine stood, Magnum dutifully keeping watch.

The lights made the destruction worse than he'd first

glimpsed, and by her pained expression, it was a shock to Justine. "He was busy while I was in the trunk."

"What was he searching for?" Trey placed the knife and flashlight on the counter.

"Hard to say."

Except her mannerism said otherwise.

She led him to the sofa and perched on the far edge. "It's late. What do you need to file the report?"

He sat and Magnum lay at his feet with a sigh. Trey withdrew his notebook. "What happened right before you walked down to the basement?"

"I was reading, and the lights flickered, then went out." She hesitated, hand on her khaki shorts pocket, drawing attention to the small book-sized bulge he'd noticed before. "Wait. Why were you coming to see me?"

Pops said relationships were like bank accounts. You had to deposit trust before you withdrew. "Kayla Nolan's cold case."

"You're not the investigator." Her accusatory tone bit, and he absorbed the blow. She winced. "I didn't realize you worked cold cases."

Trey glanced at Magnum. "We're on a hiatus until his paw heals. Besides, the original investigator retired a long time ago."

"Isn't there a conflict of interest?"

Why the third degree? A chance to fling guilt knives for his failure to protect Kayla? Trey shoved away his defensiveness. He'd own his failures. "Sergeant Oliver assigned me and sends his apologies for Callista's behavior."

Justine's posture softened. "She wasn't very nice."

"Don't take it personally. She was in a hurry to get

out of the office on a Friday afternoon. Anyway, what made you call in?"

Justine bit her lip.

Trey's impatience won out. "We'll get a lot further if we put down the shields."

She pulled a brown leather journal from her pocket and held it up but out of his reach. "I found Kayla's diary this afternoon, moving stuff from the Dog House. No clue how it's gone unnoticed all these years or why it was in my things. Although, Kayla stayed at my place a lot before…" Her voice trailed off. "Anyway, she must've left it by accident. Based on some of her entries, I'll develop a profile to help identify the killer or narrow down possible suspects. I'm certain they were acquaintances."

"Her case is identified as a suspicious death, not murder."

"Semantics. And no matter what they said, Kayla didn't use drugs."

Was Justine in denial about her friend's addiction? She knew Kayla better than he, though Trey didn't recall witnessing Kayla in an inebriated state during their social gatherings. "Who else knows about the diary?"

"I told Kayla's parents when I contacted them about reopening the file and asked to meet with them."

Wealthy and prominent in the Lincoln community, the Nolans weren't exactly down-to-earth folks, from what he'd heard. "Did they agree to speak to you?"

"After some persuasion." Justine fidgeted with a thread on the couch. "I'm sure my call came as a shock."

"I'll take that as a no."

"I'm not quick to judge. Like some people." She narrowed her eyes. "Trauma affects people in unique ways. Dredging up old memories is painful."

Trey noted the Nolans on his list of possible suspects.

Magnum's ears perked up, and he got to his feet, sniffing the air by the open window. He roved in deliberate precision around the room before pausing by the door.

"Hey, Mags, what's up?"

"Probably needs out," Justine said.

Trey didn't agree. Magnum's actions indicated unease, but he didn't want to scare her. "I'll be right back."

Trey glanced out the side window before opening the door.

Fireflies flickered in the distance, and the porch light illuminated a small area. Had the kidnapper been stupid and returned?

Stranger things had happened. "Lock the door behind me. If I'm not back in ten minutes, call 9-1-1."

THREE

Trey set Magnum on the grassy area beside the porch steps. "Have at it."

Magnum took off at a modified pace in full-search mode. Perhaps he should've leashed the dog, but giving him free rein on the property seemed to energize him.

The Belgian Malinois ducked into the tree line on the north side of the expansive ranch.

"Magnum!"

Traversing the uneven ground in the dark was challenging, but Magnum appeared undeterred and determined. He actively sniffed his way into a thicket of overgrown weeds, bushes and dead branches.

Trey activated his weapon's attached flashlight and swept the beam across the darkened area. He spotted Magnum's tail as he disappeared into the thick brambles where ticks and other things Trey preferred to avoid lived in abundance. "Ah, dude, do you have to go in there?"

He groaned and caught up with Magnum, slowing at the forest opening. Long branches heavy with green summer leaves hovered like arms. Bushes reached up in a wild stretch of thick briars restricting his entrance.

A breeze rustled the foliage and something buzzed past Trey's ear. He swatted it away.

"Magnum." Worry niggled through him. Trey called louder, "Magnum."

Sweeping the light across the thicket, he spotted Magnum sniffing the earth beneath a large oak tree. He circled the wide trunk, disappearing behind the massive circumference of bark. Trey hurried to the space, stomping over the knobby roots and rock-covered ground. He dodged a tangle of low-hanging twigs and gripped a branch before it clotheslined him.

His fingers brushed something thin, and Trey jerked back his hand.

Snake?

Magnum barked, startling Trey and regaining his attention. He shifted the light to the dog. A length of rope dangled from above. Trey traced the braid higher to the leftovers of a makeshift tree house situated between the branches.

Magnum scurried to the opposite side of the trunk, and Trey followed him around the base of the tree to get a better look. Spotting nothing of concern, he leaned down and snapped on Magnum's leash. "No more of that, mister. We don't need any further injuries. Sorry, but you're going to have to stay with me."

A plank of wood tumbled from the tree house. Trey ducked and turned just as an explosion of pain to the back of his head sent him stumbling forward.

A dull thud and fluttering on the opposite side of the tree had Trey swinging the light downward. Magnum rushed to investigate, and Trey caught a glimpse of something nestled in the tall grass. A soft whizzing emitted.

Magnum tilted his head and swayed slightly.

A snap above drew Trey's attention. A second plank toppled, striking Trey's face and exploding pain. He dropped the leash, covering his bleeding nose with his hands.

The plank landed beside him. Trey stepped forward, caught by a tightening around his throat that yanked him back. His fingers groped, desperate to stop the rope from strangling him.

The force dragged Trey against the tree, then pulled him upward.

He kicked, girded his weight and dug his boots into the trunk for leverage. The deathly battle had Trey doing a strange backward climb up the tree to keep from being strangled while groping for his weapon. The criminal pulled higher, cutting off Trey's air flow. Panicking, he wrapped his hand around the rope with one hand and grappled for his gun with the other.

At last, he tugged the weapon free from his holster.

The perp jerked harder, and Trey lost his grip on the gun. It plunged to the ground, out of reach.

The need to breathe outweighed everything else.

Stars danced before his eyes.

Trey fought to stay conscious as the perp hefted him higher.

Forced to stand on his tiptoes, Trey gasped for air.

He was fading. His body flattened against the trunk.

Where was Magnum? Why wasn't he barking?

Trey tried to look up, but the hold was too tight. He could barely move. His head brushed against the rough bark, scraping his scalp.

His eyes bulged from their sockets.

Desperate for air.

Desperate to stay conscious. He continued stretching his arms upward, grasping at the rope. It grew tauter.

Justine. He had to stay awake for Justine.

Lord. Help!

Trey's lungs burned. Gravity tugged his arms and legs down.

The darkness swooped in, consuming him.

Dragging him into the abyss.

Consumed by the shadows, Trey closed his eyes and surrendered.

"Hey! Wake up!" A voice hovered from somewhere far away.

Magnum's familiar bark.

A slap and a sting on his face jolted Trey conscious.

"Trooper! Wake up!"

A second slap caused his eyes to fly open. Trey blinked against the blinding light, shielding his face from the brightness.

With a groan, Trey shifted, pushing himself up from the hard ground, and took in his surroundings. Magnum barked furiously from beneath a nearby tree. His leash was wrapped around a low-hanging branch.

The light altered, and Will moved in front of him, staring down. "'Bout time you come to," he grumbled, offering a hand to help Trey stand.

After steadying himself, still woozy, Trey rushed to free Magnum and stumbled over an exposed tree root. "What happened?"

His head swam and a dull headache pulsed at the base of his neck. He leaned down, checking Magnum for any injuries, grateful to find none. But that didn't explain how his dog had ended up bound so far away from him.

Trey recalled the whizzing sound before Magnum went silent. Had the perp drugged his dog?

He untied the leash, and Magnum shifted protectively in front of him, creating a barrier between him and Will.

Had Will attacked him from the tree house?

Magnum didn't rush at Will, but his hackles were raised.

Trey needed information, and at the moment, Will was the only one capable of providing that benefit. "Why was my dog tied up over there?"

Magnum emitted a low growl.

"You gonna call him off or not?" Will groused.

Keeping a wary eye on Will, Trey reached for his gun, then remembered he'd dropped it.

"Whatcha looking for?"

"My gun," Trey confessed.

Will shifted the flashlight, illuminating the area, and Trey scanned the ground for his weapon.

Magnum's disposition grew edgier. "My dog sure seems to have a problem with you. Any idea why that is?"

Will seemed oblivious to Trey's concerns, his blank expression as hard to read as invisible ink. "I don't speak dumb mutt."

Trey's gaze moved to a pistol resting in Will's waist-band. Was Will a friend or foe?

"You're welcome," Will grumbled. "Look here, Trooper, I just saved your life. Least you can do is call off your dog."

"You know the funny thing about animals? They tend to pick up on cues and nuances humans miss."

"That so? They also chase squirrels and bark at leaves."

Will crossed his arms. "And your dog didn't wake you either."

Trey chuckled despite his hesitation. "Can't argue that. Magnum, *nein*."

Magnum dropped to a sit beside Trey. "Thank you for helping me."

If Trey had to guess based on their short interactions and his cop instincts, Will was the kind of guy who enjoyed riling a person, then when he got punched, claimed he was attacked unprovoked. At least he was consistent in his rudeness. *Kill 'em with kindness*, Pops would say. And right now, Trey needed details. "I'm at a loss, so anything you can tell me would be helpful. Starting with, how'd my dog end up over there?"

"Couldn't tell ya. He was rabid, and I wasn't going anywhere near him."

Magnum was far from *rabid*, but Trey didn't correct Will since he was volunteering information. "How did you know I was out here?"

"I didn't. Your dog barked up a storm and woke me out of a dead sleep. Came out here to give you a piece of my mind and found you sprawled cold under the tree. I figured the mutt wouldn't let me near enough to release the leash, so I left him tied up over there, then helped you."

Trey returned to Will, standing where the assault had occurred. Two planks of wood lay on the ground. His gaze traveled up the trunk to the tree house. "There was someone hiding there. He ambushed me."

"So, that's where you got the bloody nose."

Trey glanced down. The dark uniform hid the crimson stains, but his nose ached with confirmation. "Yeah, whacked me with a plank, then tried strangling me."

Will pointed the flashlight into the tree. A rope swung, tethered by a pulley near the remnants of the tree house. "Why would someone go to all that effort?"

Trey jerked to face the farmhouse. "Is Justine okay?"

"Why wouldn't she be? Ain't seen nobody around here, and other than your dog's rowdy caterwauling, it's been quiet. I sat here trying to wake your sorry self up for the past fifteen minutes."

Had Justine told Will about the kidnapping? Trey scoured his mind, recalling the interaction. No. She'd never mentioned it. If Will was involved, was he playing dumb? Or did he not realize Justine was in danger? Anxious to get to her, Trey headed out of the brambles. "How long was I out?"

"Couldn't tell you." Will joined him.

"I need to check on Justine."

"Seems to me you should be more concerned with whoever attacked you." Will grunted, shifting the light to illuminate a path.

"Unless they did it to get me out of the way." Trey shot Will a quizzical glance.

"Of what?"

Trey kept walking, unwilling to give him any unnecessary information, still unsure of the man. Magnum remained close to his side, and they cut across the pasture.

"Why are you here, Trooper?" Will persisted.

Trey didn't look at him, his focus fixed on the farmhouse. No lights shone from inside. *Please let Justine be safely asleep.* But Trey's instincts warned that wasn't true. "Justine and I are working on a case. I've known her a long time."

"Funny, she's never mentioned you."

Trey winced. Not speaking of him was better than

telling the whole world how much she detested him. He hadn't spotted a Trey-shaped dartboard. That was a positive, and although she hadn't been oozing with kindness, she'd been decent in their communications.

"I haven't seen her for a while."

"This yours?" Will called.

Trey halted and turned, then walked to where Will stood beside his gun.

"Yes." Snagging the weapon, Trey checked the bullets. All removed. Convenient. And how did Will just happen to know where to find it? Trey tucked the Glock into his holster. Why remove his gun and then leave it lying on the ground? He continued the trek across the pasture. "Did you see anyone?"

"Nope. In case you ain't noticed, Trooper, light isn't really plentiful out here."

"Did you hear anything? A vehicle?"

Will snorted. "You got dirt in your ears? Your dog was it."

Trey increased his pace, desperate to get to Justine. They reached the edge of the yard just as an ear-piercing blast exploded.

The force had Trey ducking and protecting Magnum.

Trey turned, shielding his eyes from the consuming flash of light engulfing the house. Ears ringing with agonizing intensity, Trey pressed a hand against his head to still the noise. He blinked to clear his vision. "Justine!"

Jumping to his feet, he bolted for the home, Magnum running beside him in an awkward three-legged gait. Why were his limbs so heavy? Trey pumped his arms, willing his body to get to Justine faster.

Please, God, let her be alive.

His mind raced. Less than an hour since finding Justine, and he'd lost her.

Why had he left her alone? He'd stood not more than twenty feet away, wasting precious time with Will while some maniac hurt Justine.

Trey had failed to protect someone.

Again.

She would die tonight. Justine squeezed her eyes against the blinding explosion of light emitting from her farmhouse and prayed the home didn't go up in flames.

Lord, not fire. Please not ever again.

Even from her position beneath the canopy of trees at the far side of the ranch, her ears rang from the blast.

She recognized the diversion tactic, a sort of flashbang, typically used by law enforcement. Though how her captor had managed to set it off from a remote detonation device eluded her.

"That'll keep 'em busy." Her captor chuckled.

"Don't hurt them!"

He snorted. "Shut up. You better be grateful I didn't kill the cop and his mutt." Under his breath, he mumbled, "Shoulda double dosed the dog though. We coulda been long gone by now if he hadn't barked and woke the old codger."

He'd drugged Magnum? That explained why he hadn't alerted Trey.

The man glared at her. "Woulda saved us both some trouble if you'd just handed over the book. I came prepared this time."

Justine jerked to look at him, his comment confirming he was the same man who'd abducted her earlier in the evening. She watched in horror as Trey, Magnum and

Will bounded from the far pasture. Grateful they were alive, she stared helplessly as they called out her name.

They'd search the house, and by the time they realized she wasn't there, she'd be dead. The overgrown foliage that bordered the north side of her property provided the camouflage her captor needed and prevented the men from seeing her.

Had the whole scene not been terrifying, she'd assess the criminal's distraction as rather ingenious. Though she wasn't gagged, the sharp tip of the gun's muzzle pressed against the back of her head kept her quiet and at his mercy. What recourse did she have but to obey him and pray she found a way of escape? Or if she gave him the diary, maybe he'd let her go.

No superhero to rescue her.

She was on her own.

The man made no effort to disguise himself. An indicator he intended to kill her.

Dead people couldn't testify.

"There's nothing in the diary. Why do you want it?" she blurted, working her negotiator-skills training for all it was worth.

"Too late. You had your chance to hand over the book. Now you can deal with them."

"Them?" Who did he work for? *Keep him talking.*

"Justine!" Trey's cries carried across the land, tearing at her heart.

"Hel—" Her plea was cut off by her captor's boa constrictor arm encircling her neck. The gun pressed harder against her temple.

The man dragged her deeper into the tree line. His hold squeezed the air from her lungs. She kicked, fighting to breathe.

He loosened his grip and shoved a gag in her mouth, then secured it with a piece of tape. He finished the adornment with zip ties around her wrists. Her one advantage was he didn't bind her arms behind her. But timing was crucial.

"Don't get no bright ideas. Try to run and I'll break your legs."

Somehow, she didn't doubt his threat, and since he hadn't bound her ankles again, she'd take the win.

"You can be a good girl and shimmy between the wires. Or I'll just throw you over."

Justine swallowed against the gag that eliminated any chance of speaking. She nodded.

"Smart." He went first, ducking between the fence cables. His beefy hand gripped her arm, yanking Justine forward.

She maneuvered through, catching her shoe on the wire and stumbling. She reached out to stop her fall, but the man's grip tightened, and he tugged harder, sending a volt of agony up her arm. He jerked again, nearly pulling Justine's shoulder out of the socket.

The gag muffled her cry of pain.

He lugged her to a four-seater UTV parked and hidden behind a large bale of hay. Justine recognized Richardson's three hundred acres. A cow mooed nearby, as if confirming her supposition.

Would Richardson hear her if she screamed?

"Don't even think about it," the perp warned, as though hearing her thoughts. "Make one sound, and they're all dead. Including your mutts."

Justine's mind whirled with possibilities and none of them pleasant. She had to escape before they got in the UTV.

"Get in."

An idea bloomed. He was at least a foot taller than her. She'd need to stand on the floorboards to be eye level with him.

Justine clamped her hands together, forming a large fist, while he assisted her onto the UTV. She turned and thrust her bound wrists upward.

The crack of his nose confirmed solid contact.

He swore. Then, in a flash, he retaliated by smacking her with a powerful slap across the face.

Justine flew backward, landing hard on the ground beside the UTV. She scrambled to her feet, and using the vehicle as a barrier, she scurried around it.

"I'm going to kill you!" The man stalked her, arms outstretched like a wide net. He dodged from side to side, cackling as he toyed with her.

Justine surveyed the distance. For all his bulk, she prayed he wasn't fast.

She jumped to the right, faking him out, then lunged in the opposite direction, straining for the freedom beyond the fence line. Her bound wrists made running difficult, but Justine pushed on.

Heavy pounding and breaths behind her propelled Justine to run harder.

Almost there.

The diary beat against her thigh, hidden inside her khaki shorts pocket.

Justine's fingers grazed the fence just as the man tackled her to the ground, knocking the wind from her lungs. His hands were on her ankles in an instant. He yanked her back, flipping her over.

"You'll pay for that." He hefted Justine into the air and hoisted her over his shoulder.

The impact and constant jolting of her stomach sent a wave of nausea through her. She swallowed down the rising bile burning her throat. With her bound arms, she stretched out her fingers, grasping the corner of the tape, and tugged. The tape ripped the gag out too, and she dropped both.

Justine tried to scream, but the lack of breath diluted the sound.

The man's massive torso was like a brick wall, yet she was unrelenting. Justine fought and kicked against his stranglehold on her legs. He squeezed tighter, and shooting pain exploded through her thighs.

She refused to give in.

With her bound hands, she beat on his back, aiming for his kidneys. Twice she made contact, and the man jerked in spasm. On her third attempt, she struck pay dirt.

He lost his hold, dropping Justine. She landed on the hard ground next to the UTV. Air whooshed from her lungs, and she gasped.

Before she could respond, the man's Texas-sized boot settled on her chest, pinning her in place.

He reached up and grabbed something from the front seat. Then he squatted beside her, smothering her face with a cloth.

Her nose filled with a sickening sweet smell.

Ether.

Justine held her breath, willing her body not to inhale the anesthetic. She had only seconds before she'd be forced to breathe.

She wriggled, turning her head from side to side. He was linebacker huge and unyielding.

The battle to stay conscious warred with her body's

desperation for oxygen. Justine's vision blurred, and her eyes bulged from the pressure. Her lungs were ablaze, exploding behind her rib cage.

Not yet.

Her attacker knelt on her chest, pressing the cloth harder over her face.

If she didn't get free, she'd pass out for real.

Air. She needed air.

And fast.

Lord, I can't hold on anymore. Please help me.

Fake him out. The thought sprouted to her mind unbidden, providing the only option left. Convince him she'd gone unconscious. Justine stopped fighting and closed her eyes, allowing her other senses to heighten.

The boot weight lifted from her chest, and he hoisted her up in a fireman's carry.

The cloth fell to the ground, and Justine inhaled slowly so as not to draw attention, though her lungs begged for more. He laid her across what she assumed was the back seat of the UTV. Then the vehicle rocked as he slid behind the steering wheel.

Justine opened her eyes.

The engine roared to life.

This was her one chance.

When the UTV lurched forward, Justine rolled off the seat, onto the floorboard, and pushed up to her knees. She leaped off the side and into the pasture.

With hands still bound, she sprinted for the fence.

"Trey! Will! Help!"

The UTV turned, headlights beaming behind her. He was coming back!

Justine swerved, rounding a hay bale, and lunged for the fence line.

She reached the wires and ducked between them.

"Trey! Will!"

Light bounced from the porch, a beacon calling her home.

Justine ran with everything in her. "Help!"

Barks erupted, and she aimed for the familiar sight of the Belgian Malinois hobbling across the property.

The UTV stopped, changed direction, and the whir of the engine faded behind her.

Justine didn't look back.

"Justine!" Trey closed the distance between them, but Magnum reached her first.

She fell to her knees, chest heaving with exertion, and fought to catch her breath.

Trey braced and helped Justine to stand. "What happened?"

"He. I. Eth." Justine couldn't get out the words.

"It's okay. Just breathe," Trey said, holding on to her.

She crumpled against him. Needing his strength.

Will hurried up beside them. "What happened?" The grumpy exterior was gone, and he reached for her. "Are you okay?"

Dizziness consumed Justine, and she swayed. Finally catching her breath, she said, "The same man from earlier. He got away. On the UTV. Richardson's land."

"And he used the flash-bang to distract us," Trey assessed.

Justine nodded.

"Let's get you inside."

The group made their way across the property and into the house. The smell of smoke filled the living room, increasing Justine's nausea. Childhood memories flooded her mind, creating a vise over her chest.

"I need air." She rushed to the swing and inhaled long and deep, clearing her lungs. Justine gripped the banister, anchoring her shaking body to the porch.

Trey joined her. "We have to leave."

Justine shook her head. "No. Not until I'm sure the boys are safe."

"They're fine, and I'll be here to watch over them," Will assured her.

"See?" Trey pleaded. "Justine, we need to get out of here. We'll work on a sketch of the guy while your memory is fresh. There's a great artist in Lincoln."

Justine dropped onto the porch swing, gazing out on the inky landscape. Anger ignited. "I can draw the sketch myself. This is my home. No bully is scaring me off my land."

Trey sighed. "Will, would you mind giving us a minute alone?"

She glanced up. Her hired hand hesitated, gaze bouncing between Justine and Trey.

"If the guy returns, we need to make sure we're ready. Do you have any other weapons?" Trey asked.

Will nodded. "Yeah. Ain't no one getting close to Justine again." He stepped off the porch. "I'll check the garage and my stash."

After he'd disappeared around the side of the house, Justine said, "Trey, I can't leave the boys. If anything happened to them..."

"Will promised to take care of your dogs. If I have to ask my brother to come and haul the whole crew to my home, I'll do it."

She laughed at the image.

"I'll request Slade patrol the property personally. Whatever it takes. Okay?" Trey's blue eyes bored into her, embracing her. How long since someone had offered to reach out a helping hand?

No. Dependency was a trap that morphed into a weakness.

Justine averted her gaze and changed the topic. "Slade's still a trooper?" Fabulous.

She'd known Trey's older brother, Slade, only as an acquaintance when they'd attended the same social events. But the family was renowned. The kind of people who'd warn Trey away from less than desirables.

Like me.

"He'd love to see you."

A happy reunion invading her ranch solace, where she'd just escaped with her life, wasn't in her plans. "I've unleashed a monster. Who wants the diary so bad? I haven't seen anything so incriminating it'll pinpoint one specific person. At least, not yet."

"Clearly someone fears the contents."

Justine filled Trey in on the encounter.

"He drugged my dog? That explains a lot." Trey leaned against the spindled porch rails. "How did you get over there?"

"I should've listened to you. I heard meowing from the far side of the house. I always leave the windows open. You've experienced firsthand how stuffy the place gets. Anyway, I was looking for Clover. Thought she locked herself in the closet again. She does that sometimes. When I reached the back room, the sound came from near the window. I leaned out to call to her." She swallowed, shivering at the memory. "He dragged me through before I realized what was happening."

Trey ran a hand over his head. "I never should've left

you. I didn't think the guy would have the nerve to show up again tonight."

"Did he hurt you or Magnum?" Her mind reeled at Trey's breakdown of the night's events. "Thankfully, he didn't kill all of you and Will found you when he did."

Trey hesitated a moment too long.

"What are you trying not to say?"

"Have you considered the possibility Will's working with this maniac?"

She opened her mouth to argue, but Trey held up his hand. "Hear me out."

Justine bit her lip.

"I'll be honest—I'm not sure what to think of Will. He could've killed me and didn't. But he might've lured me outside to give the kidnapper time to get to you."

"No, Will helped you," Justine insisted.

"Consider this. The distance from the thicket to the house is expansive. He couldn't be in two places at once. If Will was the one hiding in the tree, he would've been perfectly placed to knock me unconscious."

She couldn't refute the argument beyond a shadow of a doubt. At least, not to Trey's satisfaction. But in her heart, she knew Will wouldn't do that.

Still, she'd been a bad judge of character once before… Thoughts of her ex-fiancé Simon returned. He'd blinded her with false promises for their life together while stealing everything she owned. Thanks to Simon's betrayal, Justine learned the importance of caution and careful behavioral assessments.

Justine shook her head, then stopped when the world started spinning. "No way. Will isn't like you think. You've misjudged him. You saw how upset he was."

Trey shrugged. "You have to admit the events were conveniently timed."

Justine averted her eyes. No. Admitting Will was a criminal meant she'd inaccurately assessed her employee. Behavioral science was her forte. Her superpower. The one thing besides her animals that gave her life meaning.

Misjudging Will meant she'd failed to identify a traitor under her roof. And if she couldn't spot an offender under her own nose, how could she correctly perform her job in other cases? Most important, how could she develop the profile for Kayla's case?

Failure meant she was incapable of her profession.

Failure wasn't an option.

"I understand you not wanting to leave your home, but I think it's evident whoever is after this diary isn't going to stop."

"I agree, but it's late. Surely the guy won't return tonight."

Trey withdrew his notepad. "Let's run through everything you remember. Did the kidnapper say anything?"

Justine sighed. "He demanded to know where 'it' was. Though he never mentioned the diary, I assume that's what he referred to. He also said I'd have to deal with them. Whoever 'them' is."

"That adds credence to a hired thug."

"I did think it was strange he used my car to kidnap me the first time, and we never saw anyone approach the second. Either he parked nearby and walked the rest of the way or someone dropped him off."

"Will doesn't own a vehicle."

Justine glared, disapproval hanging between them. "Will knows the topography of the area."

"You lost me."

"The kidnapper didn't slow for the big pothole on the road."

"Why is that important?"

"His lack of knowledge indicates he isn't a local. After the heavy flooding from the recent rains, many of the dirt roads were washed away or damaged. Will's familiar with the landscape."

"Hmm. Interesting."

"What's it going to take for you to believe Will is innocent? He'd never hurt me. But I'd appreciate extra patrolling by Slade or whoever if you'd arrange it."

Trey sighed. "Justine—"

"This is my life and my home. I'm perfectly capable of making the necessary decisions." And if she was wrong, she would die at the hands of Kayla's killer.

FOUR

A wct swipe across his face and a warm puff of air dragged Trey to consciousness. He stared at the familiar brown eyes pleading with him. "Mags, I'm a light sleeper. A simple whine works to wake me."

Trey sat up on the living room sofa with a grunt, ruffling the Malinois's mane. His gaze traveled past the padded dog bed Justine had provided for Magnum and landed on the hands of the antique grandfather clock. 5:45 a.m.

He stood and stretched, feeling the repercussions of sleeping on the couch after declining Justine's offer of her spare bedroom. Proximity to the main floor overrode his personal comfort.

A text from Slade buzzed from his cell phone. ETA five.

His brother's overnight security detail had allowed Trey a short but needed rest, and the night had passed uneventfully. Otherwise, he'd be functioning on no sleep, which was worse than a backache.

Magnum whined and thumped his tail in a steady get-moving-please-now rhythm.

"I'm coming." Trey schlepped to the window and peered out before tugging open the door.

Magnum wasted no time scurrying outside.

"Wait."

But the dog was halfway across the lawn, after an almost normal descent down the stairs. He didn't favor his good side as much. A definite sign of healing. "Guess you're feeling better."

A cardinal trilled from one of the maple trees, and Trey filled his lungs with the fresh morning air. He strolled the wraparound porch, maintaining visual of Magnum actively exploring the ranch.

Pastel streaks colored the sky as the sun peeked over the horizon. Ominous land the night before, it now splayed out in a lush green landscape.

"I could get used to this," Trey mumbled to no one, stepping off the porch.

Magnum joined him, nose to the ground.

Slade's familiar blue sedan pulled into the driveway and parked near Trey's patrol vehicle.

"Good morning, sunshine. Packed for a trip?" Slade stepped out of his car.

Trey blinked. "Dude, I just woke up and I'm caffeine deficient. What're you talking about?"

"Those bags under your eyes. If they get any bigger, your head will fall in," Slade teased.

Trey ran a hand over the stubble on his face. "Thanks, bro."

"Brought what you asked for." Slade passed Trey a small bag, which he transferred to his patrol truck's tailgate cabinets. He returned to find Slade offering a supersize fountain drink. "Mountain Dew?"

Trey wrinkled his nose. "Um. No."

"Suit yourself." Slade took a long swig. "This place

is nice, but I can see why you needed the perimeter help. Did you get any sleep?"

Trey leaned against Slade's car. "Yeah, a few hours. If you hadn't shown up, I'd be a zombie."

"Good thing you caught me when you did. Although, you might owe Asia some cinnamon rolls for interrupting my off days."

Trey chuckled at the mention of Slade's wife. "I'll make it up to her. However, you're probably donating this time."

Slade shrugged. "It's all good. I've got your six." His brother referred to the cop slang for defending and covering one another. "Family first. Always. You really should relocate her for now."

"I tried. Even explained the need for a sketch artist while the image of the criminal's ugly mug was fresh in Justine's mind. She refused and said she'd do it herself." Trey paced a short space in front of Slade. "I get it though. She's concerned for her foster dogs."

"You two are a perfect match. Both dog motivated and stubborn."

Warmth radiated up Trey's neck at the implication of being matched with Justine. Ridiculous and out of the question. He was the last person she'd consider dating since she blamed him for Kayla's death. Justine believed Trey had failed to show up when Kayla called. If he'd been there, maybe he could've stopped her from overdosing. Yet he hadn't even known Kayla had a drug abuse problem? No. He wasn't relationship material. Last night's double failure in apprehending the kidnapper proved Trey's inability to protect those he cared about. Romance wasn't an option for either of them.

Oblivious to Trey's internal debate, Slade continued,

"If Justine refuses to leave, Oliver might finagle overtime for security detail."

"Doubtful. He made a point last night of reminding me how short-staffed we are."

"Yeah, little brother, you're still taking after me, even with trouble and impossible odds perched on your shoulders."

Trey bristled slightly at the reminder—always shadowed by his older sibling. It was no secret Trey had looked up to Slade when they were younger, but they weren't kids anymore. Was calling him for help a mistake? Yet what choice did he have?

"Don't get your feathers all ruffled. I'm only teasing." Slade took another swig of soda. "What's Oliver got you working?"

And there it was, the piece Trey hadn't shared. Once he mentioned Kayla's name, Slade's older-sibling, unwanted advice would spill out.

Trey inhaled. "Kayla Nolan's case."

"Murder."

"Technically, no. It's labeled a drug buy gone bad resulting in a suspicious overdose death. Kayla was attacked in her apartment. Murder isn't out of the question. Justine's developing a profile of the killer." Before Slade could interrupt, Trey launched into an explanation regarding the diary and their planned visit with the Nolans later in the day.

A beat passed. "Just curious, but what does she hope to gain by meeting with them?"

"Something about a clinical perspective versus conclusions based off memories from things Kayla had shared."

"I guess that makes sense. Memories have a way of tainting everything."

And they dredged up pain you'd forgotten existed. Trey shoved away the thought. "Should've seen the look on her face when I asked what time 'we' were heading out."

"She didn't want you along for the ride, I'm guessing? How'd you convince her?"

"With my brilliant power of persuasion." Trey chuckled.

"No, really." Slade quirked a brow.

"Well, there is the fact that the files belong to the patrol, and I can't just hand those over and leave."

"'Possession is nine-tenths of the law,'" Slade quoted teasingly, then lowered his voice. "Dude, are you sure being involved in this case is a good idea?"

There it was. Big-brother judgment. "What choice do I have? I owe Kayla."

Slade shook his head. "Trey, her death wasn't your fault. You didn't have any other options. Let it go."

Heaviness weighted his chest. "Too late. I'm committed to getting justice for Kayla. Justine's profile and the diary might provide the missing leads, after all these years."

"Do what you need to. Just let me know if you want me out here again tonight."

"Thanks. Hey, one more favor?"

"Sure."

"Run a background for me?"

Slade surveyed the grounds. "On who?"

"Justine's hired hand, Wilbur Percy."

"Stetson Man? He trolled the property until late last night. Is he a problem?"

"I'm not sure. I need evidence to either kill my suspicions or convince Justine he's not the man she thinks he is," Trey said.

A creaking drew the men's attention.

Slade gave a jerk of his chin. "Speaking of."

Four of the five canines lumbered out of the barn, scattering in all directions. The basset hound Justine called Barney followed Will outside. He knelt, stroking the dog's head, and spoke too softly for Trey to hear. For all his complaining about the animals, he appeared gentle and kind with them.

Contemplating Magnum's earlier assessment, Trey wasn't sure what to make of Will. Still, if his partner found fault with the man, Trey would remain wary. Though this morning Magnum strolled toward the other dogs, undaunted by Will's presence.

As if Will heard Trey's thoughts, he turned and visibly stiffened. Will gave a slight tip of his Stetson before shoving his hands into his jean pockets. Trey didn't miss the pistol tucked into Will's waistband. At least he took his role seriously. Trey waved him over, and Will's reluctance registered in his every step, closing the distance.

"Will, this is my brother, Slade," Trey said.

Slade extended a hand.

"Nice to meet you. Saw you driving around last evening." Will's reply sounded more like a complaint than a greeting.

"Thankfully, it was a quiet night. I'll head out. Touch base with me later, Trey." Slade slid behind the wheel of his car and started the engine.

Will moved toward a midsize brown dog sniffing near a large trash receptacle. "Shep, get outta there. You just ate breakfast."

The dog trotted away, tail wagging. Without Justine's presence, maybe he'd get information from the hired hand. "Magnum's always hungry." Trey chuckled.

"Shep's a scrounge. Surprised you're still here."

"After all Justine went through, I wouldn't leave her without a protection detail."

Will harrumphed. "She has me. I ain't afraid of nothin'."

Yeah, except you might be part of the problem. Justine hadn't told Will about the first kidnapping, so he had limited information. Unless he was in on it. "I appreciate your help. Justine does too."

"Well, you won't be here forever, right?"

Unsure how to respond, Trey opted to redirect. "This place is too large for one person to monitor alone."

"Yeah, s'pose that's true enough."

Glad I have your approval.

Will's gaze moved to Shep, who was making a second attempt at the trash can. "Shoo."

"How many of you are there?" Will narrowed his eyes.

Trey grinned. "If you mean siblings, there's five total."

"Eight in mine. Nothing more important than family unless they've done you wrong."

While he had Will's attention, Trey opted to probe for information. "Justine tells me you've been helping her out for a while."

"Yeah. She pays better than most, but with all those critters eating up her money, she can't afford me full-time." Will spit. "Waste of time and cash, taking care of throwaways nobody wants."

And just when he thought he'd misjudged Will, Trey reverted back to wanting to smack him. Maybe the guy had had a bad experience with animals as a child or something. If Will had been in on last evening's danger, motive would be a huge factor. However, if Will resented the foster dogs and viewed them as a threat to his livelihood, was that reason enough?

Testing the waters, Trey said, "Though without them, she'd probably request your assistance less than she does."

Trey almost saw the light bulb illuminate over Will's Stetson-covered head. "S'pose so. But it ain't like this place is lacking for repairs."

A quick survey of the grounds revealed several vacant areas where buildings once occupied the spaces. "Were there many outbuildings?"

"Yep. Tore down three. Course, wasn't much left of 'em anyhow. They were hazards waiting to happen. She wanted the silo gone too. I convinced her it's in good shape and might come in handy if she decides to farm the land." He pointed to a four-story cylindrical brick structure.

"I haven't had a chance to look things over, but it does appear the place needs TLC."

Will grunted. "And money. Nothing's free."

"I know that's right." Before Will interjected another comment, Trey baited him. "She's a nice lady. I can't imagine anyone wanting to hurt her."

"My granny always said your enemies ain't the folks you hate—it's the folks who hate you."

"Yeah, I see her point. Who are Justine's enemies?"

"Why ask me?"

"I'm guessing you have a pulse and historical perspective on the area." Okay, maybe a reach.

Will straightened his shoulders, standing taller, proving a little flattery went a long way. "Age has its benefits. Check out her neighbor, Richardson. He's always bugging her about selling him this land. Been a battle since she bought the place."

"He's the one with the cows next door? Relatively speaking." Since Richardson's property sat a half mile away.

"Yep. His pa sold Justine's acreage in a gambling debt years back. He's worked hard to regain possession. More about pride than the ranch. When Justine started fostering those mutts, she won over some highfalutin folks in town. Made ol' Richardson madder than a nest full of bees."

"Mad enough to kidnap her?" Trey cast the question like a fishing line and waited for Will to bite.

The man glanced away. "Who knows?"

Answering a question with a question. Diversion tactic, or was he innocent of the incident? "Do you also work for the guy?"

"If the money's right. Gotta make a living. Folks want everything for free. I don't work for nothing."

The abrasive man was like invisible ink on a page, impossible to read.

"You never told me why you were here in the first place."

Trey debated. Was it wise telling Will the truth? "I'm working on a cold case with Justine. Found her in the trunk of her car last night after the perp attacked and abducted her from the basement."

Will's incredulous stare lingered on Trey.

Whether the man was sizing him up or digesting the news, Trey couldn't determine.

"You catch him?"

The question, though nonconfrontational, wormed

insecurity under Trey's skin. No, he'd failed to catch the kidnapper. Twice. "Not yet. He escaped."

Will huffed.

"For now. But we'll have an identity on him soon." At least, he hoped so. They had very little to go off of. However, if Will was guilty and conspiring, the not-so-subtle-warning just turned up the heat.

"If he comes back, I'm ready." Will patted his gun. "Never know when unexpected danger will show up."

Precisely why Trey needed to get Justine somewhere safe. "Has that been a problem before?"

Will jerked a chin toward the adjacent property. "Trooper, if you see danger and ain't prepared for it, you're one second too late. I'd say that accurately describes how I found you in the thicket last night."

Trey studied the man. *Or how you ambushed me.*

"You two are up early." Justine cradled Clover and descended the steps. She wore another pair of khaki shorts—gray this time—and a long-sleeved plaid shirt, unbuttoned to reveal the blue tank top underneath. The outfit complemented her features, forcing Trey to avert his eyes.

"Mornin'. I'd better get busy," Will said, excusing himself.

"I didn't want to interrupt. Seems you were deep in conversation."

"Nothing significant." Trey gave his best reassuring smile.

"By the way, Richardson is annoying but harmless." How much had she overheard?

"I called Dr. Curtis, the current medical examiner."

"Just now?" Trey glanced at his watch.

"Yeah. He works strange hours. I couldn't stop thinking about the Nolans declining the autopsy. I requested he exhume and reexamine the body."

"After ten years, though, what're you hoping he'll find?"

"Proof Kayla didn't overdose. She was murdered, regardless of what the paperwork says. The question is, why?" Justine glanced beyond Trey, and he turned to follow her gaze.

The dogs frolicked around Will, who seemed none too thrilled about the company.

"He acts tough, but Will loves them," she said.

"Sure about that?"

She grinned. "Definitely. Anyway, Dr. Curtis agreed, stating how the technology developed since Kayla's death might provide something new to the case. He casually mentioned the prior ME, Dr. Elvin, might've made an oversight. Nice way of saying the guy was incompetent."

Trey mentally added Elvin to the suspect list. Had the prior ME been sloppy or paid to look the other way?

Justine had sat in numerous courtrooms under the shriveling inquisitions of merciless defense attorneys, but Mr. and Mrs. Nolan's penetrating glares were a new level of intimidation. Their exquisite home with its marble floors and vaulted ceilings was an extension of their icy reception and added to the uncomfortable atmosphere.

Justine had mastered the art of feigning confidence as a matter of survival when interviewing criminals who lived to manipulate and terrify. The same tactics applied here.

The Nolans clammed up like two oysters being harvested from the ocean when Trey introduced himself.

Ten long, silent minutes had passed since anyone had last spoken.

Justine straightened her shoulders, pinning Mr. Nolan with her question. "Mr. and Mrs. Nolan, I'd like to review the case file information with you. Were you aware Kayla feared a stalker?"

"She mentioned something about it, but Kayla always had an active imagination," Fredrick Nolan replied in a tone that lingered just a notch above condescending. He sat rigid on the leather chair, in his tailor-fitted black suit and a red power tie. His long legs were set at a perfect ninety-degree angle and both hands rested on the arms, giving him the appearance of Abraham Lincoln's memorial. His auburn hair was styled neatly, and his wiry frame was similar to Kayla's.

By comparison, Susan Nolan bore no resemblance to Kayla—not that she would, as her stepmother. Her dark hair pinned into a tight chignon and pinched lips made her narrow face more severe. "Those were silly attempts to get attention. I cannot tell you the number of ridiculous antics she pulled over the years. There was no proof of a stalker, as I'm sure you've read in Investigator Drazin's notes." She smoothed her pink dress suit and crossed her ankles. "We're busy, Miss Stark. Surely you came here for more than wasting our time with silly repetitive questions. What do you hope to accomplish by reopening Kayla's tragic case, other than drawing unwanted scrutiny to our family?"

Justine blinked, taken aback by the strange comment. Kayla's words traveled from the recesses of her memory, reminding Justine the Nolans' priorities rested on their upstanding reputation in the community. "I'm sorry for

your loss, and I mean no disrespect. I only hope to identify Kayla's killer."

Susan swatted the air. "The police classified Kayla's
death as suspicious, most likely a drug deal gone amiss."

"Were you aware Kayla used drugs?" Trey interjected.

Justine bristled at the accusation.

"Our daughter was an enigma and a grown woman,
Trooper Jackson. We didn't keep tabs on her all the
time." Susan glowered at Trey.

Justine leaned forward. "Finding Kayla's diary was
a gift, and she deserves justice. I'm sure you want that
too."

"You've mentioned this diary. Where has it been all
these years?" Fredrick inquired.

"I found it among old keepsakes I'd had stored," Justine explained.

Susan perched on the end of the chair. "Kayla's personal items are not for public consumption. No stranger
should have access to her private thoughts. The diary
must be returned to us immediately."

Justine was hardly a stranger. Rather, she knew more
about Kayla than either of the parental figures sitting
before her, but arguing with them benefited no one. Regardless, she'd come as a clinician. Though everything
within her longed to defend her friend, she must remain
objective.

"I assure you, Kayla's effects will be treated with the
utmost respect. However, the diary is now documented
evidence," Trey said.

Justine shot him a grateful nod.

"What makes you think you'll find anything worth
dredging up the pain of the past?" Susan asked.

Fredrick adjusted his tie and placed a hand on his wife's arm. "I believe what my wife means is, after ten years without answers, we don't want to get our hopes up."

Exactly the opening Justine needed. "When I compile a profile, I use all the available evidence. Sometimes even the smallest things provide the most significant details. Anything you share with me about Kayla and those last few months is helpful."

"Like what?" Susan asked.

"For instance, Kayla's comments about a stalker and his ways of scaring her appear to reference someone who was familiar with her routines—I believe the stalker and killer are one and the same."

"You're certain the killer is a man?" Susan inquired.

"No. At this point, I can't say that with absolute certainty. However, the person was stronger than Kayla, able to subdue her, which leans toward a male suspect." Justine withdrew her notepad and pen. "Was there anyone Kayla mentioned? A coworker maybe?"

Susan sighed. "I vaguely recall her ramblings about strange gifts she'd received. In light of the drug paraphernalia discovered in her apartment, those are just drivel from an addict."

"Kayla wasn't a drug user." The words escaped Justine's lips before she restrained them. She softened her tone. "In my experience, I never witnessed her under the influence."

"Kayla kept many secrets. We all have secrets, don't we?" Susan's glare made Justine's skin crawl.

"When did you last speak with Kayla?" Trey asked.

"We've already told the police all of this." Susan smoothed her skirt again.

"It would help to get a fresh look at the case," Trey said.

"My daughter and I didn't talk on a daily basis." Fredrick crossed his arms over his chest.

Justine didn't miss the defensiveness in his tone.

"The only person who had regular interactions with Kayla was her boss and our attorney, Alex Duncan. He graciously tolerated her obnoxious personality." Susan rolled her eyes.

Justine smiled. "She was a free spirit."

Susan snorted. "That's just a polite way of saying she was out of control."

Fredrick stood. "I don't see how we can give you anything more. As soon as possible, I'd like Kayla's diary returned. Our daughter made a poor life choice and died as a result. She gave no consideration to how her actions would reflect upon us. I'm not interested in dredging up dirty laundry. I know you'd like to believe a grave injustice or conspiracy is to blame, but Investigator Drazin agreed the evidence suggested a bad drug confrontation, resulting in an overdose." A chime interrupted Fredrick, and he withdrew a cell phone from his suit pocket. He studied the screen and walked away, calling over his shoulder, "Susan, please show them out."

"You'll have to forgive my husband. Kayla's death took a toll on both of us."

"Understandably so. Thank you for your time," Trey said.

Susan led them through the living area into a long hallway. Her beige heels clicked a solemn cadence on the marble floors.

Nothing about the Nolans' home reflected Kayla. In fact, she seemed to have done everything possible to disassociate herself from them.

When they reached the entryway, Susan opened the door. Trey exited first.

Justine followed, halted by Susan's touch on her arm. "May I speak with you? Privately." She lifted her chin toward Trey.

Would she divulge something personal? "Trey, I'll be right there," Justine said.

"No problem. I'll wait in the truck," he said.

Susan closed and blocked the door. Her dark eyes narrowed. "Kayla and I were very close."

She may have viewed the relationship differently, but Kayla had called Susan an overbearing tyrant. Yet she'd striven to be the daughter both parents wanted, always falling short of their demands and expectations.

"No one was more heartbroken than I to have lost Kayla," Susan continued. "I loved her as my own. I adopted her when she was only three."

Justine hadn't known that, though Kayla had never spoken of her birth mother.

"Her death was a tragedy, and I'm sure you understand reopening this case exposes us again to the negative publicity. People can be heartless and cruel. Especially those who would like to use Kayla's misdeeds as a weapon against us."

Though Justine didn't approve of the Nolans' concern for their reputation over bringing their daughter's killer to justice, it was clear their social standing was a huge component of their lives. "I understand the media's ability to negatively affect a family."

Justine forced her arms still at her sides, though the scars itched with memories of the fire. The media had sensationalized the story of her father Ignaseus Grammert's despicable and intentional attempt to murder his daughter and wife. After beating Justine and her mother, Ignaseus set the home on fire. Victoria, her mother, played on the sympathy of the public to gain financial support, and when the attention ran dry, she reverted to pleading for her husband's release from prison, claiming it had all been a horrible accident and misunderstanding. Victoria conveniently forgot about the abuse Ignaseus inflicted on them regularly, as well as his attempt at drowning Justine once before.

Susan continued, yanking Justine to the present, "Kayla's unconscionable acts devastated our hearts. I appreciate your intentions, but the past must remain buried for everyone involved." She touched her nose with a handkerchief produced from her sleeve.

Justine chose her words carefully. "I'm sorry for all you've endured. And it's not my intention to hurt you or your husband. But a killer is still out there."

"I see." Susan's disposition changed, and the grieving mother vanished. "Tell me, dear. If it were your past being dredged up for public review, would you be as adamant? Would you willingly unveil your hidden skeletons for the sake of justice?"

Ice crystals skittered up Justine's back, and her stomach roiled. Had Kayla betrayed her and told Susan about the fire?

Summoning the last of her confidence, Justine replied, "If someone was dedicated to helping and protecting another from the same wretched fate, I would gladly sacrifice my pride to solve the case." She reached for the door, tugging it open.

Susan squinted. "Suffering is certainly a personal experience. Is vindicating a crime, even while you harm others, worth the glory you attain?"

Justine swallowed and blinked. Words eluded her. *Stay strong.* Susan used intimidation to control people. Justine had changed her last name and hadn't spoken to her parents in fifteen years. "Justice is blind for a reason, Mrs. Nolan."

Susan lifted her chin. "Hmm. Perhaps. The skeletons of our pasts tend to rear their ugly heads to destroy our present or threaten our future. It's such a shame when others' choices affect our lives in negative ways. Don't you think, dear?" Susan touched Justine's arm, squeezing a little too hard on the burn scars beneath her sheer blouse sleeve.

"How dare you!" Fredrick stormed in, face red.

"Fredrick?" Susan startled.

Justine jerked free of the woman's hold.

Fredrick lasered Justine with a glare. "You requested to have Kayla's remains exhumed?"

Word spread fast. Justine straightened to her full five-foot-four height. "The examination is a necessary part of the investigation."

Movement in her peripheral vision brought relief. Trey's determined stride said he must've overheard Fredrick's bellowing. She mentally willed him to get there faster.

"Absolutely not!" Fredrick roared.

Trey reached the entryway. "Justine, we're late for our next appointment."

Fredrick's chest heaved. "How dare you disrespect us this way? Get out! Both of you!"

"You won't get away with this," Susan injected. "We'll stop you. Whatever it takes."

Justine backed into Trey as the door slammed shut.

"What was that all about?" he whispered.

"Guess we won't be getting their cooperation with the exhumation."

Justine's gaze lingered on Susan watching from the window, a murderous expression frozen on her face. *The skeletons of our pasts tend to rear their ugly heads to destroy our present or threaten our future.* The veiled threat hovered in Justine's mind, and her arm burned from Susan's rough grip. *We'll stop you. Whatever it takes.*

Would working Kayla's case expose everything Justine had spent her adult life escaping?

FIVE

Trey's instincts blared on high alert at the Nolans' behavior, but his bigger concern was Justine's reaction and unusual silence. She'd also been rubbing her arm since they left. "Did she hurt you?"

Justine twisted to face him, hands dropping to her lap. "What? No. I'm fine. Thank you for interrupting back there."

"I've been told I have impeccable timing," Trey teased, waggling his eyebrows.

Magnum poked his head through the separation glass, panting softly.

Justine stroked Magnum's chest. "He's smiling."

Trey marveled at his partner's ability to calm a person by his furry presence. "I've always thought that about him."

"Great diversion tactic with the second-appointment ruse too."

"Oh, that was real."

Justine leaned forward. "It was? Where are we going?"

"To talk with Laslo Drazin. Fair warning—he's not thrilled about this meeting."

"Why?"

"I interrupted his travel plans." He didn't share Drazin's skittishness on the phone. One of them had to remain objective in the questioning. He'd fill Justine in on his own suppositions afterward.

Trey exited the highway and pulled into the parking lot of the large two-story truck stop. Signs boasted of showers, a restaurant and overnight accommodations. He circled around to the opposite side of the immense facility and parked in front of a wooden sign featuring a cartoon dog.

Trey lifted his phone. "We're here."

"I see you. Five minutes. That's it." Drazin disconnected.

"He's on his way." Trey opened his door, avoiding Justine's quizzical glance.

Magnum sat patiently waiting for assistance.

"Don't get too used to this, buddy. At some point you're going to have to climb down without my help."

The dog tilted his head with what could only be described as a *duh* expression.

They entered the grassy lawn and walked to a picnic bench while Magnum roamed the full thirty-foot span his leash allowed.

A Cadillac SUV pulled in beside his patrol truck, and Drazin exited the vehicle, wearing dark sunglasses. The retired investigator strode toward them. His lively Hawaiian shirt and Bermuda shorts contrasted the scowl on his bearded face.

"He looks cheerful," Justine whispered.

"That's his normal expression." Trey stood to greet Drazin. "Good morning. Thanks for meeting with us."

"As if I had a choice," Drazin groused, dropping onto the seat opposite Trey. "You're the shrink?"

"Forensic psychologist. Justine Stark." She extended a hand, which Drazin ignored.

Magnum returned and sat, allowing Drazin to pet him. "Handsome guy."

"This is Magnum," Trey said.

"Always loved the dogs. Lost my corgi, Chuck, a few months ago. Best friend a guy ever had. Great thing about pups—they aren't disappointed by who you really are." Drazin removed his sunglasses and shifted his gaze, surveying the area. "Look, I gotta make this fast. Trey told me you're working on the Nolan case. So, what do you want to know?"

"I'm developing a profile based on the crime scene and evidence."

"You can get that from my notes."

"I'd like your perspective. The file is marked 'inconclusive suspicious death,' though the Nolans are adamant it was a drug buy gone bad."

Drazin's eyes darkened. "Then you've got all you need."

Justine leaned forward. "Kayla was my best friend. Anything you tell us that might help solve her case is appreciated."

Drazin rubbed the back of his neck. "The Nolans pushed to close the investigation ASAP, but I believed the scene was staged. It was all a little too clean, if you catch my drift. The drugs on the table and Kayla's tox screen pointed to an overdose. Nothing contradicted those findings."

"In my professional opinion, prior behavior speaks volumes, and Kayla wasn't a user," Justine said.

"The case went cold right before your retirement?" Trey prodded.

The man shot him a glare. "I worked every clue until there wasn't anything left. Are you implying I did a shoddy job because I was leaving?"

Defensive. Interesting.

"Actually, considering it was your final investigation, I'd think you'd put all your efforts into solving it," Justine inserted.

That defused Drazin. "Absolutely. Wasn't easy either. The Nolans had their fingers in everything. Watched me like a hawk. Even if I'd wanted to do a less-than-stellar job—which I didn't—they'd never have allowed it."

"Losing their only daughter must've been very hard," Trey said.

Drazin snorted. "The Nolans aren't the type of folks who want scuttlebutt about them airing on the six o'clock news. They were more concerned about their reputations than solving their daughter's case. Talk to Alex Duncan, their attorney. Kayla worked for him, and he spends Saturdays at his office alone." Drazin stood, eyes focused on the truck stop parking lot, and withdrew a piece of paper from his pocket. He slid it across the table to Trey.

"Trey said you're leaving for a trip?"

"Yeah. Canada. Got friends up there."

"My dad always wanted to take my brother and me up to Alaska for a men's vacation. We still haven't made that happen." Trey slipped the note into his shirt pocket.

"Make the time. You never know if you'll get tomorrow. One more thing." A look of contemplation passed over Drazin. "The Nolans have a long arm, and you don't want to be on the wrong side of their favor. Believe me."

"Are you implying they're dangerous?" Justine asked.

"I'm not *implying* anything, because this conversation never happened." Drazin put on his sunglasses and scurried back to his vehicle.

"Well, that was interesting," Justine said. "Since we're here, I'd like to stretch my legs. I'll run in and get a large cup of coffee. What would you like?"

Trey wrinkled his nose. "It's going to be one hundred degrees with ninety percent humidity today, and you want coffee?"

"What's your point?" Justine tilted her head, blinking innocently.

He chuckled. "Would you grab a bottled raspberry tea for me?" Trey reached for his wallet.

Justine's lips curved, and she waved away the offer. "Seriously?"

"What? You thought I'd want a powered-up energy drink?"

"Something like that." The playfulness in her tone sent a strange flutter through Trey's chest.

He cleared his throat, guesstimating the distance to the store was half a football field away, and three semis in the gasoline bays blocked his view. Protectiveness consumed him.

Magnum headed toward an oak tree, tugging on the leash. Trey knew that stride. "Wait up until he's finished doing his business, and we'll escort you into the store." His attempt at sounding casual flopped, based upon Justine's quirked eyebrow.

"I don't need a babysitter. I'm perfectly capable of defending myself. No one will kidnap me from a populated truck stop."

Trey lifted his hands in surrender. "Whoa. Don't kill the messenger. Just being cautious."

Justine frowned and looked down. "Sorry. My limited

sleep is starting to dampen my joyful attitude. Thank you for your concern, but I'll be fine."

Trey wasn't so sure, but she didn't give him a chance to respond. Not that he had anything brilliant to say. He walked toward Magnum, who glanced back with an expression that said "smooth."

"What?"

With one eye on Magnum and the other surveying the truck stop, Trey contemplated following her. The place was busy, so there were plenty of witnesses should anyone try to harm Justine, and as she'd said, it was broad daylight.

Still, uneasiness kept him on edge as Justine disappeared between two large semis.

Too many long minutes passed without her presence.

Disquiet niggled down Trey's spine, with a knowing he couldn't explain. "Mags, I don't like this."

"Officer, excuse me." A woman jogged toward him, waving as if he could miss her. "Officer!"

Trey glanced over his shoulder, anxious to see Justine, but there was no sight of her. He tugged on the leash. "Mags, this isn't a social call. Do what you need to so we can get on the road."

The woman closed the distance between them, invading Trey's personal-space bubble. She pressed a hand against her chest, splaying her extremely long, painted fingernails. "Oh, I'm so glad I caught you." She sidled beside Trey and lifted her blond hair, twisting and securing it up with a clip. Her heavy perfume inflamed his nostrils.

"How can I help you?" Trey shifted to keep one eye on the store.

The woman moved closer, blocking more of his view.

"What a beautiful puppy. Aren't you a lovey-dovey boo-boo? What's your name, handsome?"

Why did people speak to his seventy-pound dog as though he was a toddler? "He's working." He deliberately refrained from using Magnum's name.

She reached out, disregarding everything Trey said. He stepped in her way, preventing her from touching his dog. "Ma'am, we don't recommend socializing." Rarely did Trey discourage Magnum's public interaction, but something about her bugged him.

Magnum shifted away from her in silent agreement.

"He's as handsome as his master."

Where was Justine? "We've got to get going. Have a nice day." Trey turned.

The woman clamped her dagger nails over his forearm. "But, Officer, I need your help." She blinked bloodshot brown eyes wearing heavy makeup. "I accidentally locked my keys in my car."

Trey firmly but gently removed her claw hold. "I'm sorry, but you'll have to call a locksmith."

"Please. You don't understand. A locksmith will take forever, and my little dog, Scriffy, is trapped inside."

A dog locked in the car on a stifling hot day demanded immediate attention. "I'll need to grab my window-punch tool. It'll break the glass though."

"A small price to save my Scriffy," she replied.

"Where is your car?"

The woman pointed to a sedan parked on the east side of the parking lot. It would be faster to run there than to load Magnum.

"I'll meet you there." Trey jogged to his pickup and grabbed his dual-purpose seat belt cutter and window-punch tool from his utility box in the truck bed. He

turned, nearly colliding with the woman standing behind him.

"Thank you so much, Officer."

They reached her car, and Trey confirmed the door
was locked. A small white dog panted inside.

Trey applied the tool, breaking the glass, and unlocked the doors.

The woman raced to the passenger side and scooped
up the dog. "Oh, thank you, thank you!" She lavished
kisses on the animal's head.

"No problem."

With the dog in her arms, she ran to Trey, inching
too close. "I'd like to show my appreciation for you rescuing Scriffy. Maybe I could buy you a cup of coffee?"

Unable to see the convenience store door, Trey
stepped to the side. "Appreciate the offer, but I'm meeting my—" he hesitated, unsure how to refer to Justine
"—partner. Did you see a woman with dark hair walk
out?"

She brushed a stray tendril from her face. "Darlin',
I only had eyes for you. I wouldn't have seen a herd of
elephants if they'd stood right in front of me."

A man came rushing around the corner, waving his
arms wildly. "Hey! Get away from my car!"

Trey jerked to look at the woman. Her mouth hung
open, and her gaze bounced between him and the en-
raged stranger.

"What's going on?" Trey asked. Had she played him?

She lifted a hand in surrender.

The man closed the distance between them, but the
run had clearly worn him out. He bent over, huffing
with both hands flat on his thighs. "You broke. My window," he panted.

"Liar!" the woman argued, hugging her dog closer.

Great. And now he was in the middle of a domestic dispute. "I need to see the registration and both your driver's licenses." Trey didn't have time for this, but that was the quickest way to get to the truth.

The man glared at him. "You should've asked for those things before you broke my window. Don't ya think?"

"He saved my little Scriffy-poo," the woman whined.

"What was your dog doing in my car?"

A gunshot cracked from behind them, somewhere near the long line of parked semis.

Trey spun in the direction of the sound. "Both of you, stay here."

"I'll have your badge. You can't—" the man hollered.

Trey barely heard the rest of the sentence. He took off, sprinting toward the row of trucks.

Justine's mind screamed for her to run, but every cell in her body ignored the command. Her gaze froze on the stranger's pistol, which seemed to grow to the size of a cannon.

"Get into the truck. Now, or the next bullet has your name on it."

Cornered between two ginormous semitrailers, Justine was hidden from the view of any witnesses. The passenger door of one semi stood wide, blocking her escape, and the rumble of the massive diesel engines would drown out her scream. Had anyone heard the warning shot the man had fired seconds before?

You're so stupid, choosing a shortcut between the semis instead of going the longer way around. The condemning voice echoed in her mind, feeding her fears.

No. Justine slid into the mode of a psychologist. "I'll give you my purse. Put down the gun."

"Lady, save it. Just get into the cab."

"No." Justine gripped the bottle of tea in one hand, a large foam cup in the other.

"Get inside the truck. Now." The man's thick, unruly beard covered most of his face, and the stained baseball cap shadowed his crooked nose. His bulging midsection enlarged the cartoon character on his dirty red T-shirt, stretching out the rabbit's head to unnatural proportions. He glanced past her, as if searching for someone. "C'mon, Peggy, we gotta go," he mumbled.

Justine sidestepped, fighting to steady her shaking hands.

"Move!"

Now or never. Justine took a step forward and flung the coffee at the man's face. He yowled and threw up his hands.

Justine bolted past him.

He clamped a brawny hand over her arm, but she jerked free and ran, rounding the trailer without looking back.

In the open, she spotted Trey and Magnum sprinting toward her across the expansive lot.

"Trey! Gun!"

A shot rang out behind her.

Justine ducked in front of another rig, where Trey joined her.

Someone screamed.

"Are you okay?" Trey withdrew his weapon, one hand holding Magnum's leash.

"Yes."

"Stay here." Trey peered around the rig and returned fire.

Movement in her peripheral vision drew Justine's attention. A woman watched from the distance, her gaze nervously darting between Trey and the dog park. She quickened her pace and a husky man stumbled after her, hollering while he cradled a small dog in his arms.

As her eyes connected with Justine, she lunged into a sprint.

"Oh, I don't think so, sister." Justine took off after the woman.

The exchange of gunfire continued, as did Magnum's furious barking.

The warm sunshine beat down on Justine. She pumped her arms, increasing her speed to catch up. She reached the dog park and leaped into the air, tackling the woman to the grass.

They skidded to a stop, and Justine pushed up, pinning the woman's arms beneath her knees.

"Get off me!"

Scanning the area, Justine searched for something to bind her wrists with. Magnum rushed toward her, his leash dragging on the pavement.

"I'll kill you!" The woman wriggled, but Justine restrained her by pushing her head down.

Magnum was with her in seconds, growling, hackles raised.

"Calm down or the K-9 will attack," Justine warned.

"Don't let him bite me," she whimpered, chest heaving with frustration and exertion.

"Don't give him a reason." Justine reached out and Magnum moved closer, allowing her to disconnect his leash. "Good boy."

She wrapped the cord around the woman's wrists.

"Be still," Justine warned.

Magnum shifted protectively in front of her, emitting a low growl.

Trey hauled the gunman into view, approaching Justine.

"Wait. This is all a misunderstanding," the woman interjected.

"Really? You're going that route?"

"Honest. We wouldn't hurt you. All you had to do was go with us."

"Where?"

"Don't you say a word, Peggy," the gunman hollered as they neared.

"Who sent you to attack me?" Justine asked.

"I want a lawyer."

Sirens screamed, announcing help. Within seconds, responding patrol cars screeched into the parking lot. One sped to where Justine and Magnum stood, and a trooper she didn't recognize stepped out. She launched into an abbreviated explanation as the officer helped the woman to her feet, then handcuffed her and returned the leash to Justine. "Resourceful."

She grinned and jogged to where Trey relinquished the gunman to another trooper's custody.

"Are you okay?" Trey asked Justine, surveying her, then Magnum.

"Thanks to him."

Trey took the leash and gave his dog a scratch behind the ears. "What happened?"

"Let me start with admitting you were right."

"I like to think so," Trey teased.

"Whoever is after this diary is determined, and apparently—" she gestured toward the parking lot filled with cop cars and people "—even in broad daylight, I'm not safe." Justine gave him a quick rundown about the shortcut and abduction attempt.

"How'd you get away?"

"Threw my coffee in his face."

"Foiled by caffeine." Trey grinned, revealing identical dimples she'd failed to notice before. "Well done."

Justine shrugged. "Use what you have on hand. Magnum arrived right on time or the woman might've wriggled her way out of my hold. I borrowed his leash to tie her hands."

Trey knelt and checked Magnum's paw. A frown creased his brows. "Buddy, we need to re-dress your wound."

Justine gasped. "Did he reinjure his paw?"

"Probably just overdid it." Trey hefted the dog into his arms, and they headed for his patrol truck.

Guilt sent Justine's stomach roiling. "I'm so sorry."

"You didn't do anything wrong. Mags can't help himself. He saw you running and took off before I could stop him. He's chivalrous that way."

"Yes, he is." Justine smiled, but Magnum babied his paw, driving a nail of shame into her heart. What had she done?

Magnum shot her that irresistible grin as Trey loaded him into the kenneled area before disappearing behind the truck bed. He returned a few seconds later with a bag of medical supplies and expertly bandaged the paw. "Good as new."

Trey filled a stabilized dog bowl with bottled water. Grateful laps followed, and Trey passed her a treat. "Since you two worked the case together, you reward him."

She offered the bone-shaped biscuit and Magnum's soulful eyes pierced her as he gently lifted the treat, whiskers brushing her palm. The acceptance released a stray tear, and Justine swiped it away.

"Whoa. Hey, it's okay. See? He's fine." Trey pulled her into a hug.

She allowed herself to be held for the first time in forever. "I'm so sorry."

Justine refused to let any more tears flow while the weight of the attacks crashed onto her shoulders. She buried her face in Trey's chest, unsure how to respond. The comfort of his strength and his heartbeat calmed her.

"You're a superstar for chasing that woman down."

She lifted her head and forced a smile. "I wouldn't go that far." Her gaze traveled from Trey's blue irises, the color of tropical waters, down to his jaw, strong and firm. He leaned in, his breath warm on her face. She inched up on her toes.

An engine drew closer, and she jerked to see a patrol car approach. Trey's hold loosened, and he quickly shot a glance in Magnum's direction. Justine stepped back, arms at her sides.

The second K-9 vehicle parked beside them, and a trooper exited, then opened the back door, releasing a dog that could've been Magnum's twin.

"Who's that?" Justine asked.

"Vulture," Trey mumbled.

A smirk split the trooper's young face as he rounded the vehicle, his dog moving in stride with him. "Hey, Jackson. Out causing trouble, I see."

"Irwin, are you lost?"

Though the two spoke in jest, a gravy-thick tension hung in the air.

Irwin turned to her. "I don't think I've had the pleasure. Trooper Eric Irwin, and this is K-9 Apollo." He gestured to the Belgian Malinois beside him.

"Justine Stark." She took his proffered hand. "Pleased to meet you."

He responded with a weak single shake, then addressed Trey. "Sergeant Oliver sent us to Supply to pick up materials. Too bad we weren't a few minutes earlier or I could've come to your rescue."

Trey visibly bristled, but his expression remained neutral. Whatever was going on between the two blared animosity. "We're fine."

"Heard the call over the radio. Sounds like you had a serious run-in with some criminals. Was Magnum a help?"

Trey closed the door, creating a boundary between Magnum and Irwin. "He's staying within his light-duty restrictions."

"Good. Thought you were forcing him to work before he was ready. Would sure hate for something to happen and put Magnum out of commission permanently." Irwin patted Apollo's head.

"Trey is diligently watching over Magnum," Justine said.

"Sergeant Oliver wants a K-9 in our assigned work area." Irwin ignored Justine's comment. "Apollo's raring to go."

"Magnum's right on schedule," Trey said.

Irwin faced Justine. "You're the psychologist helping with the Nolan case?"

"Yes." Who was this guy?

"Hmm. Is today's event related?"

"It's a possibility," Trey answered.

"So someone's trying to prevent Miss Stark from testifying?"

"I'm not testifying. I'm developing a profile," Justine corrected.

"Has Jackson mentioned protective custody?" His disingenuous smile irked her.

Trey stepped between them. "So, hey, thanks for stopping by, but we were just leaving. We have an appointment and need to get going. See you around."

Irwin chuckled. "Right. Nice meeting you. Better give Apollo a quick break." He led his dog to the grassy area.

"I'm scared to ask what that was about," Justine said.

Trey moved to the patrol pickup and slid his hand along the undercarriage and wheel wells.

"What are you looking for?"

"A tracking device. How else did the trucker couple know where we were?"

"You don't think Drazin is involved, do you?" Justine joined him, working the opposite side.

"Possible. Got it." Trey held a tiny black square with a blinking green light. He flipped it over and slid a small switch, killing it. "I'll see if I can find the GPS coordinates or anything to show who owns this little tattletale."

They climbed into the truck, and Trey turned up the air-conditioning, cooling the cab's space.

"I got the impression Magnum working is an issue?"

Trey scrubbed a hand over his head. "Technically, he's not allowed to respond to calls right now. The last thing I need is Irwin reporting Mags reinjured himself."

"I see."

"And as much as I detest Irwin, he might be right. You're in danger, and although there's only a select few aware of the diary, it's obviously the catalyst for the attempts on your life. Protective custody would be better."

No way. Did he think her incapable? She'd just taken down a woman in a truck stop parking lot. Justine used her best psychologist voice. "I'm a professional, and I don't run and hide because things get hard. If I did that, I'd never accomplish anything. There's always someone out to intimidate me. All that does is fuel my determination."

Trey chuckled. "I was hoping you'd say that, but I was obligated to give you an out."

Relief coursed through her. "Want to tell me what's going on between you and Eric?"

Trey worked his jaw. "He's a new handler and determined to secure a spot."

"He's circling the injured, vying for your place?"

"You described it perfectly. I call him Eric the Vulture."

Justine chuckled. "Great minds think alike."

Trey glanced at her, then quickly averted his eyes. "I sure hope so."

"Beg your pardon?"

"Nothing. We'd better step up our game. Whoever wants the diary's contents kept a secret is willing to do anything to make that happen. Next stop, the Nolan family attorney, Alex Duncan."

SIX

"I smell smoke," Justine commented as Trey pulled onto the highway.

"What?" He leaned forward, searching through the windshield.

She laughed and swatted at him. "I meant, you're thinking so hard, I can smell the smoke burning in your brain from the effort."

Trey chuckled, settling back in his seat, and passed her a piece of paper.

She scanned the scribbled phone number and address. "Should we call first?"

"Not yet. I don't want to give him a chance to avoid us. It's only about ten minutes from here."

"Interesting the Nolans didn't recommend we meet with him," Justine mused.

"I thought the same thing."

Trey turned into a business district and approached a massive stone-and-glass building. The landscape surrounding the property offered no parking spaces. "Looks like we'll have to go in there."

A large striped bar restricted entrance into the multi-level parking garage.

"Guess we'll need him to give us access."

"I'll call." Justine dialed the number and put it on speaker. A male voice answered on the third ring. "Mr. Duncan, this is Justine Stark. I'm a forensic—"

"I know who you are."

Justine shot Trey a confused glance. He shrugged.

"As the Nolan family attorney, my loyalty lies with them first and foremost."

"Absolutely. I—" Justine began.

"I have nothing to offer regarding Kayla's case."

Justine rushed on. "With all due respect, Mr. Duncan, I believe you do."

A silent second ticked away, and she glanced at the screen, worried Alex had hung up.

"The Nolans are covered by client-attorney privilege."

"We understand that." Justine held her breath.

"I don't see the point."

"The point is justice for Kayla," Trey said.

Alex sighed. "Her death was…a tragedy."

Justine heard the difference in his demeanor. "Yes. And the case has remained dormant. I'd like to change that."

Another long pause.

"I'm sorry."

He wasn't getting off that easily. "Mr. Duncan, I realize you don't know me, but Kayla was my best friend, and she deserves justice. The Nolans deserve closure. Not to mention there is a killer still on the loose. What if someone else is hurt? Please. I'm only asking for a moment of your time." *Lord, help me get through to this guy.*

Alex lowered his voice. "Ah, yes, I do recall her mentioning you. That must be why your name was familiar to me."

Trey gave Justine a thumbs-up.

"Miss Stark, you don't realize what you're asking."

Trey opened his mouth, but Justine held up her hand, silencing him, and shook her head.

"Our conversation will be kept in the strictest of confidences."

"It's not that simple. I won't testify or go on record."

Something in his tone had her redirecting. "Mr. Duncan, are you afraid for your safety? If someone has threatened you, we can help you get protective custody."

Alex snorted. "No amount of protection would suffice. I'll meet with you. Briefly. Park on the second floor of the garage and use the stairwell to walk down. I'll turn off the security cameras there. Come to the north side of the building. There's a door where I will let you in."

The bar over the entrance lifted.

"Thank you," Justine responded, but Alex had already hung up.

Trey parked on the second floor, and the trio exited the truck. Their footsteps echoed in the empty concrete structure; dim light filtered through the drab space. They made their way to the stairwell.

Justine pushed open the heavy steel door and startled as it slammed behind them.

Inside was stuffy and dark, and Justine eagerly stepped outside, welcoming the bright summer sun.

Unlike the dank garage, the grounds of the Nolan Building were professionally landscaped, with colorful plants and flowers bordering the sidewalk. They approached the north-side door marked Personnel Only. Justine raised her hand to knock as it opened.

A bald man of average height, dressed in jeans and a navy polo shirt, stood on the opposite side. His salt-

and-pepper hair was groomed short, and the goatee completed his distinguished appearance.

"Thank you for meeting with us, Mr. Duncan," Justine said.

He ignored her, glancing down at Magnum. "We don't allow dogs in the building."

Ever intuitive, Magnum sniffed Duncan's expensive shoes and sneezed.

"Magnum's got dog immunity," Trey retorted.

Justine stifled a giggle.

Alex shook his head and spun on his heel. "Follow me."

Trey shot her a conspiratorial grin, and Magnum trotted triumphantly beside him.

The hallway was painted a depressing shade of gray and ended at a stairwell door. Justine held it open while Trey lifted Magnum through, then hoisted the dog up each flight of stairs. To his credit, he never complained, but hauling the large animal had to be exhausting.

Finally, Alex stopped on the fourth-floor landing and stepped aside to allow the trio to exit the shaft. They then followed him through the darkened area, still under construction and lit by only small emergency lights.

Alex led them to a closet with three folding chairs. "Have a seat. I apologize for the clandestine atmosphere, but as I said on the phone, I'm uncomfortable doing this. This floor doesn't have security cameras."

Justine sat next to Alex, giving Trey the chair closest to the door.

"Do you fear retribution?" Justine withdrew her notepad.

He frowned. "I've been a faithful employee of the

Nolan family, and they trust me. I'm afraid they'll see this meeting as a betrayal."

"How so?" Trey leaned forward, elbows on his knees.

Alex glanced down and seemed to study the floor.

Justine said, "Mr. Duncan, I realize this isn't easy, but I assure you we will not misuse any of the information you tell us."

Several seconds passed before Alex spoke. "The Nolans are prominent pillars of the Lincoln community."

Justine forced herself not to roll her eyes. She was so incredibly over hearing about the Nolans' fine reputation.

Alex continued, "Kayla fought not to fit into their mold, but I adored her. She was a great kid. Hard worker too. She had a good eye for business and accounting. One month in my office, and she'd done what the previous accountant hadn't accomplished in twenty years."

"Did you work closely with Kayla?" Trey asked.

Alex snorted and lifted his chin. "I'm a corporate attorney with enough responsibility, but Mr. Nolan reassigned the accounting division to report to me with the specification I supervise Kayla. I'm not sure if that was punishment or favor. I certainly didn't have time for babysitting. Not that Kayla needed one."

An attorney overseeing the business financials was unusual but not completely out of the question. "Had something prompted that reorganization?" Justine asked.

"Mr. Nolan is obsessive about money. Under the previous accountant, he became aware of several errors. Nolan tossed the man out before he knew what hit him. Kayla was an accounting major in college, so he got his academic money's worth in having her work for him. His words, not mine," Alex explained.

"Did Kayla locate the source of the errors?" Trey pressed.

"No, but she implemented a system of checks and balances to prevent it from happening again."

"Was the previous accountant charged?" Trey asked.

"How could he be? There was no proof he was responsible or had done anything blatantly illegal. He covered his tracks well."

"I'm confused with what that has to do with this surreptitious meeting," Trey said.

Alex narrowed his eyes. "Tell me, Officer, would you be happy knowing your most trusted confidant talked with the police about the investigation of your daughter? How do you think the Nolans will take that bit of news?"

"If they trust you, and you've got nothing to hide, why worry?" Trey straightened his shoulders, gaze unwavering from Alex.

Justine intervened before the men threw punches. "Mr. Duncan—"

"Alex, please, dear," he said in a voice smooth as ice cream.

"Alex, my goal is to develop the profile of the killer. I'm most interested in the clues available to help me do that. What can you tell me about Kayla's state of mind the week prior to her death?"

"Agitated. You were her friend. Did she mention a stalker to you?" Alex addressed Justine.

"Yes."

"Was there any proof of her claims?"

Justine hesitated, unwilling to share details from the diary. "Only gifts the stalker left."

Alex frowned. "Did she show those to the police?"

"No, sir, she threw them away."

Alex shook his head. "That was unwise. Might've helped her since her parents didn't believe the stalker allegations. They viewed them as another of her attention-seeking antics."

"Why would she need to seek their attention?" Trey asked.

"Why does any child?" Alex sighed, annoyance written in his expression. "She put them through the wringer in her teenage years. Always so rebellious and wild."

"Did she get into trouble with the law?" Trey asked.

"No, never like that. But she worked hard to embarrass and annoy them. Once at a country club event, Kayla showed up accompanied by a motorcycle gang! Can you imagine? They drove over the golf course, tearing up the greens. She strutted into the dinner, wearing black leather, on the arm of a hooligan twice her age, as though it were the most natural thing in the world. That girl was a force to be reckoned with. Susan tried to corral the wild child and make her a respectable young lady."

Justine shoved down a grin, picturing Kayla pulling such a stunt.

Trey interjected, "Did you witness Kayla using drugs?"

"She died of an overdose. I'd say that answers your question," Alex bit out.

Justine bristled. "However, that's counter to her normal MO. Did she have visitors at the office?"

Alex seemed to ponder that. "No, but she took long lunches several days in a row. Caused quite the uproar with the other staff. They interpreted it as her taking advantage of her position as a Nolan."

"Did she meet with anyone?"

Alex shrugged. "I'm not accustomed to following my personnel on their lunch breaks."

"Did Kayla report to work under the influence of drugs or alcohol?" Trey probed.

Justine glared at him. *Let it go already.*

"Who could tell the difference between Kayla's boisterous ways or intoxication?"

"So, no," Justine concluded.

Trey quirked a brow. "Were any of the employees who viewed Kayla's role as nepotism vying for the same position?"

Alex nodded. "As a matter of fact, yes. Grant Barron was so angry about being passed over, he threatened to quit, until Susan offered him a considerable pay raise."

Had Barron sought revenge by stalking Kayla?

"Look, the Nolans are very good to me, and I will not speak ill of them. However, I liked Kayla. She was refreshing in a monotonous environment and brought life to the office. Kayla was one person Mr. Nolan couldn't tame, and they fought often. They were quite accustomed to getting whatever they wanted. Mr. Nolan still is." Alex hesitated. "You didn't hear this from me, but Mr. Nolan's temper is an issue. Susan's confided her own fears about her husband to me. She said he was desperate to deal with Kayla."

"We've seen a glimpse of Mr. Nolan's temper," Justine said.

"Oh, yes, the exhumation. He already contacted me about that. Expect a motion to dismiss, by the way," Alex said with the ease of a weatherman reporting the forecast.

"Why did the Nolans decline an autopsy? Wouldn't

that be a normal course of action in a suspicious death?" Justine continued.

Alex snorted. "Why bother when the intoxication-panel screening showed she'd overdosed? I understand your hope for due diligence, but let me share a tidbit that may change your mind. Kayla demanded her inheritance early, expressing a desire to travel the world. Naturally, Nolan viewed it as Kayla throwing away her career. They had a big fight the night before her death. Susan tried to intervene, but he threatened her."

Kayla had never mentioned a trip, her inheritance or fearing her father. "Are you implying Mr. Nolan killed his own daughter?"

"Absolutely not," Alex said. "Simply that Kayla had the gift of manipulation. Something she learned from Nolan, no doubt. Isn't it ironic we detest most in others those traits we see in ourselves?" Alex locked eyes with her. "However, I don't believe traveling was her intention. Rather, Kayla got involved with the wrong people, not realizing the cost."

"You think she owed a drug dealer who retaliated when she couldn't pay?" Trey clarified.

"Yes."

"That sounds out of character for Kayla," Justine insisted.

"Except I also never shared that Kayla came to me, desperate for money. I gave her a few hundred dollars, as it was all that I had on hand. Such a sad situation."

Justine wasn't convinced, but arguing with Alex was futile. Any noncash deficits in Kayla's financial records would confirm or refute the man's claims.

"Additionally, the Nolans want Kayla's diary. I'm sure you appreciate the significance of such a personal item."

"And when the investigation is finished, they'll be able to take it," Justine explained.

Alex frowned, glanced at his expensive imported watch and stood. "There's nothing more I can offer, and I have another appointment today, so I'll see you out."

Justine rose. "Thank you for meeting with us."

The departure was solemn as they went back down the stairs and out of the building. Alex paused, his hand bracing open the door. "Oh, I forgot my briefcase. Please go on ahead."

Trey shot a look at Justine. "Okay…"

Once they were belted in the pickup and Trey had started the engine, Justine said, "I'm not sure I believe him about Kayla asking for her inheritance."

"Me either."

Trey backed out of the space and drove down the ramp, exiting the garage.

A blast from behind them rocked the ground. Concrete rained around the truck.

Trey sped from the property, and Justine twisted in her seat as a massive chunk of cement landed where the pickup had been only a second before.

Dust and debris clouded the space.

Trey parked at a distance.

Justine gaped in disbelief at the decimated structure. "We could've been killed! Was Alex inside there?"

Trey threw open his door. "I don't know. I'll check. Stay here."

"No way. I'm going with you."

"If there's a secondary device, I don't want you hurt. And I won't risk Magnum getting reinjured."

On cue, Magnum poked his head out of the divider between them. She wanted to argue but couldn't disagree. The dog might hurt himself on the rubble. Justine acquiesced for his sake. "Fine."

Trey stepped out of the vehicle, cautiously working his way toward the garage, disappearing into the fog.

"Lord, keep him safe."

Her phone rang, and she glanced down. Alex's number. "Alex? Where are you?"

"If I hadn't forgotten my briefcase, I'd be dead! I told you it was dangerous to meet. Now do you believe me?"

Trey's emotions seesawed between anger at himself and Alex Duncan. Thankfully, Sergeant Oliver offered to handle the garage-bomb investigation after reaming out Trey for endangering Justine. The fire investigators located the ignition source in Alex's luxury sedan, and Trey shared the information with Justine. Oliver concluded by commanding they return to the ranch ASAP. The berating added to Trey's self-loathing for his failure to protect Justine.

They sat eating a quick meal at Trey's kitchen table before he packed a few essentials, and they got on the road again.

"That bomb was intended for Alex," Justine reminded him, invading his internal tirade.

"Except it was convenient he forgot his briefcase, disconnected the security cameras so we wouldn't have any footage to refer to and stayed in the building where he wouldn't be affected by the blast."

"What will your boss do about Alex's plea for confidentiality? If he pushes the man, we might lose any leads if the bizarre story he told us has any credibility."

Trey worked his jaw. "For now, he's agreed to keep Alex's involvement under wraps." That hadn't been an easy request. Oliver, like Trey, found the events a little too coincidental. After some discussion, Oliver conceded Duncan had a bead on the Nolans and they couldn't lose that connection.

His phone rang. Oliver. Great. Round two. "Boss."

"As if today hasn't been enough fun, the captain just advised you have seventy-two hours to provide sufficient evidence to continue working this case or you'll be reassigned," Oliver said.

Trey pulled the phone away from his ear and stared at the screen, praying he'd misunderstood. "Hold on."

Justine paused, hamburger in hand, midbite.

He covered the receiver. "Be right back." Trey stepped outside and closed the sliding glass door before continuing, "Sarge, that's impossible. This is a decade-old cold case. How am I supposed to solve it in seventy-two hours?"

"You just need to come up with evidence to justify working on it."

"I assumed an unsolved murder of an innocent woman sufficed. Not to mention dodging kidnappers and a bomb in between conducting interviews."

"Save your snappy comments for someone else. Who besides the Nolans and Duncan have you spoken to?"

Trey hesitated. "Off the record, Drazin."

"If you got Drazin to poke his head out from the retirement hole, I'm impressed. Can't say I blame him. When I retire, I plan to revert to smoke signals and will toss my cell phone into the lake before casting my fishing line."

Trey opted to cast a line of his own. "He wasn't very forthcoming and was nervous talking to us. He also left just prior to the attack at the truck stop."

"The man's devoid of personality, but that doesn't mean he set you up."

"Any word on the GPS device I found?"

"Nope. Techs are still working on it."

"Okay, but Drazin retired right after Kayla's case went cold, and rumors were he came into money thereafter."

"Kayla's investigation was the needle that broke the camel's back for him. He was already a foot out the door before it happened."

Trey grinned at Oliver's way of confusing clichés.

"What're you getting at?" Oliver asked.

No point in dancing around the question. "Did Drazin accept a payout from the Nolans to close the file?"

"Your accusation is based on the indisputable evidence you've found to support it, right?"

Trey grimaced. "Negative."

"Then until it is, don't go there."

"Roger that. I've got a long list of suspects but not enough on any of them to haul them in for questioning. Although Duncan tops that list, Justine is adamant the guy is terrified and might be imperative to the investigation, since he offered new information."

"Thought you didn't buy his story?"

"I don't. At least, not in its entirety, but he did offer details no one else has thus far." Trey sighed. "Okay, when does the clock start?"

"Already did. Captain advised he doesn't appreciate the waste of resources on this case."

Heat boiled up Trey's neck. "Since when is a murder investigation a waste of resources?"

"Suspicious death. Based on our short conversation,

I'm thinking those would be the regurgitated words from the governor."

Trey paced the small concrete patio. "Why is he involved?"

"If I had to take a guess, the Nolans started making calls."

"So what? I just pack up and leave the case unsolved? Sarge, someone is trying to stop us, and Justine's in real danger."

"I don't disagree with you, but the governor's unwavering."

"Does he know about the attacks on Justine's life?"

"Does Miss Stark have enemies outside of the Nolan case?"

He'd tried talking to Justine last night, but she'd been shaken up and asked to hold off until morning. "Yes. I'm looking into every possibility."

Hopefully, Slade had information on Will Percy.

Oliver sighed. "Jackson, you and I debating this isn't going to change a thing."

Trey turned and spotted Justine reading through Kayla's journal. "The only evidence we have is Kayla's diary, but it's inconclusive."

"Oh, yes, the captain mentioned the Nolans want the diary returned to them."

"It's evidence."

"I'm aware of that. Has Miss Stark completed the criminal profile?"

"No. We're headed back to her ranch and will focus on reviewing the details this evening."

"And Slade is still helping with security?"

Trey hesitated. Would Oliver be upset with them?

"Give me a break. I know how Team Jackson works.

I'm trying to get overtime authorized. Might finagle comp time, if nothing else. Miss Stark needs the protection detail, but with the upper echelon hovering like vultures, I don't see that happening."

Interesting Oliver would choose the same metaphor Trey referenced with Irwin. "We'll take care of her security."

"Keep me informed."

"Will do." Trey disconnected and pocketed his phone. Three days to solve a ten-year-old cold case. Next they'd want him to explain the Bermuda Triangle.

He turned and spotted Justine, hand perched on her hip and an expression that mirrored his mother's look of disapproval. He followed her inside. "What has to happen in seventy-two hours?"

Trey exhaled the ridiculous order in one breath, expecting Justine to explode. Instead, she gathered the remnants of their fast food. "If the Nolans intervene with the exhumation, that'll stall progress, and we can't afford the delay. We have to get on top of this and do a little preemptive work. Let's meet with Dr. Curtis and explain the urgency. Then we can use the drive to the ranch to sort through the evidence."

He blinked. She was relentless and amazing. "Right. Okay, let me finish gathering our stuff." Trey broke off a chunk of burger and handed it to Magnum, then stuffed the last bite into his mouth.

Justine paused. "Trey, I appreciate everything you've done and don't want to appear ungrateful, but you have a job to do. You can't be my personal bodyguard forever."

Trey pushed in his chair. "Sure I can. I just need my toothbrush."

A corner of Justine's lip lifted. Kneeling to pet Magnum, Trey overheard her say, "Does he ever wait for someone to respond before leaving the room?"

He chuckled. No, because he wasn't willing to leave her unprotected.

That was the reason, wasn't it?

Before the phone call, Trey's thoughts hovered around the almost kiss that Vulture Irwin had interrupted. No time for that kind of thinking now, but even as his mind raced with the impossible seventy-two-hour order and the Nolans' interference, he returned to that single consideration. Justine had softened toward him.

Hadn't she?

That made no difference. She was off-limits, and he wasn't worthy of a woman like her. As much as he detested Irwin, his arrival probably had kept Trey from doing something stupid and unacceptable.

Head in the game, Jackson.

Ten minutes later, Trey returned to the living room, duffel bag in hand. "Well, the diary is our go-to for now. Care to share what you've discovered?"

"So far, not much. However—" She pulled out the book and flattened it on her lap. "Kayla really seemed to enjoy working with Alex. At least, I'm assuming that's who she is referencing by *A*."

"She mentions this *A* a lot?"

"No, but always in a good light. Seems *A*, or Alex, was encouraging." Justine met Trey's gaze. "She tried hard to gain her family's approval, but she had bigger dreams. I remember her saying employment under her dad would be a last resort."

"What changed her mind?"

"Honestly, I don't know. She never talked about work." Justine closed the diary and gathered the case files. "I don't mean to speak ill of Drazin, but he didn't have a long list of witnesses or suspects. Gives the impression he wasn't looking particularly hard."

"I'd like to dispute that, but I can't."

"If the Nolans are trying to interfere, let's warn Dr. Curtis."

"Sounds good." Trey locked up, and they loaded into the truck.

They'd driven only a mile before Justine said, "I've debated bringing this up, but since it appears we're going to be together for the next few days, we should probably talk about what happened at the truck stop."

Trey focused on the road a little too hard, not daring to breathe. "Okay."

"I'm not trying to make excuses. Or maybe I am. But I don't normally break down like that. In my defense, I've never had guns pulled on me so many times in a twenty-four-hour period."

"No judgment here." Good—she wasn't going to tell him how out of line the almost kiss was. No harm. No foul. He exhaled relief.

"Kayla was in love with you."

Not what he'd expected. Denying Kayla's multiple romantic overtures would be childish. "She was open about her feelings."

"You didn't reciprocate?"

Trey considered his words carefully. "No. She was a good friend, and I enjoyed spending time with her in group settings. I was interested in someone else." *Chicken.* Why not tell Justine the truth?

"Kayla never mentioned that."

She'd never told Justine? Trey recalled Kayla's disregard for his rejections, subtle at first. When she hadn't taken the hint, he'd had to spell it out and confess he liked Justine. Kayla had exploded. "I did." Weak, but it was the best he could offer.

"Oh, gotcha. She didn't take no for an answer. Kayla was used to getting her way." Justine closed the file and settled back in the seat.

Her cell phone rang, and Trey had never been more grateful for an interruption.

"Hey, Will, what's wrong?" Justine paused and gasped.

His relief was short-lived.

SEVEN

Justine's heart thudded with worry. "What's happened? The dogs? Are you hurt? Wait. You're not quitting, are you?"

"Most people start with 'hello,'" Will huffed.

"You never call unless there's something wrong."

"Quit jumpin' to conclusions. I haven't said anything yet."

Justine sat back. "Sorry, you're right. I'm catastrophizing."

"Your cat ain't got nothing to do with this."

That brought a grin to Justine's lips.

"Barney—"

"What's wrong with Barney?"

"Justine—"

"Sorry, go ahead."

"He's being ornery. Acting strange and refuses to come out of his kennel. Can't even get him off his bed to eat."

"Did you try—?"

"Yes, I tried those special bacon treats."

Barney never turned down a meal. He was the most food-motivated animal Justine had ever seen. "I'll call Dr. Abernathy."

"Now, hold on there. That money monger will charge you an arm and a leg for showing up. You've got good instincts. See what you think before you spend the bucks."

"But if he's sick—?"

"Don't get yourself all worked up. Barney ain't dead. Just seems a little down in the dumps, which ain't far for an overweight basset hound to get down to."

Justine grinned, despite the sobering topic. Will knew her too well.

"Wondered if there's medicine or something I'm supposed to give the mutt."

"No, but I'm glad you called. I'd feel better checking on him."

"It's probably best if you return home rather than staying overnight somewhere anyway."

Was that Will's reasoning for calling her? He'd never been overly protective before, but the last twenty-four hours had thrown them all into uncharted territory. "Will, what aren't you telling me?"

A long sigh. "Richardson came by looking for you."

"And?"

"I told him you were working a case."

"The man never gives up." Justine rolled her eyes and stared at the cab's ceiling.

"Yeah."

"Thanks, Will. We should be there by nightfall."

"That trooper's staying here again?" Will's irritation was palpable through the line.

Trey's presence wasn't Will's business, but Justine shoved down the snarky reply threatening to escape. "Yes. We have evidence to review."

"In that case, you don't need me around this evening. 'Sides, I've got personal dealings to tend to. Text when you're an hour out, and I'll kennel the boys. They'll be fine until you return."

Justine hesitated. "Everything all right?" Not that Will shared private matters with her. In the time she'd known him, their conversations had revolved around work-related topics.

"Yep."

"I may need to leave again tomorrow though."

"No problem. I'll be back in time."

"Okay. I'll text with tomorrow's schedule."

"Fine."

She disconnected and faced Trey.

"Not that I was trying to eavesdrop, but I take it from the conversation, something's wrong with Barney?"

"Will says he hasn't eaten, and he needs to handle a personal matter."

Trey's lip twitched, but his eyes remained on the road. "Does he normally abscond when he's supposed to be taking care of the dogs and ranch?"

She gave a dismissive sigh, not wanting to encourage Trey's skepticism. "I'd say *normal* flew out the window after I was stuffed into the trunk of my own car. Besides, I have you." Heat flushed her cheeks at the words, and she averted her eyes. "I mean, he's aware you're providing protection detail."

"I'm sure that was a huge relief for old Will," Trey said, sarcasm thick in his tone. "Is he always so concerned for your welfare?"

"Will's rough around the edges, but he has good intentions. However, it's clear nothing I say will convince you, so change topics."

Trey turned north and accelerated. "I'm sorry about Barney."

Was Will using Barney as a means of checking up on her? Regardless, if the dog wasn't doing well, she wanted to be there. "Poor guy. Maybe he's depressed."

"Has he been that way before?"

"Not since he first had the surgery, but that time, he had an infection."

Justine busied herself organizing the file. "It's like Drazin hit the brakes and gave up."

"Did he contact you in his investigation?" Trey asked.

"Nope. Strange, right? I considered mentioning it in our meeting with him, but he was already defensive." Justine watched the countryside passing by her window. "I should've pushed harder when Kayla died."

"Hey, don't do that to yourself."

Logically, Justine understood the words were meant as encouragement, but at that moment, Trey's comment struck her as one more person throwing up their hands in helplessness while her best friend was ignored by the people who should care the most.

The irrational wave overflowed before she could stop it. "Is it better to pretend no one is responsible for Kayla's death? That it's a too-bad situation? Nobody is taking it seriously or dirtying their hands. Not then. And not now. We all went on with our lives, didn't we?"

Tears welled in her eyes, and she blinked them back.

"You're right," Trey said softly.

She balled her hands. Hating the way her emotions interfered with her professionalism. Maybe this was a mistake. She wasn't strong enough to fight for her friend.

"Justine, I need to tell you something."

She exhaled, talking her brain off the ledge. "Okay."

"I deserve your blame and anger over Kayla's death.

I'll never try to minimize that, but please know I tried to help her. And I've always regretted not doing more."

An excuse. "Let's not talk about this any longer."

"It's the unwelcome elephant sitting between us."

As if on cue, Magnum poked his head through the divider and lapped Justine's cheek. His intrusion immediately de-escalated her mood. "You always know what to do." She stroked the dog's soft ears.

"He's great about that."

"Since you brought it up, why didn't you respond to Kayla that night? I realize she was a lot to handle at times, but she was adamant about wanting your help."

"I know."

"There were very few people she trusted. And in all fairness, she'd gone to the local police. They ignored her concerns about a stalker, especially after she told them she'd thrown away the few 'gifts' he'd left. Kayla told the officer she had a bad feeling, and he shut her down. Said he couldn't investigate feelings. Your disregard by not showing up was the final devastation."

Justine withheld her own regrets, because doing so meant admitting her jealousy. Kayla's intentions toward Trey superseded her friendship with Justine. Kayla only wanted Trey's comfort.

Not that Justine could've been with her. She'd been a state away at a conference. Would a better friend have jumped a plane and raced to Kayla's side? How could Justine know that Kayla's call would be the last?

If Justine's selfishness hadn't overridden her intelligence, Kayla wouldn't have been alone and murdered. But saying those words made all the ugliness true, and Justine couldn't bear to speak the self-condemning accusation.

Trey invaded her mental diatribe. "Let me start with a disclaimer. The night Kayla called, Magnum and I were assigned our first case together, a manhunt. We were out in the middle of a cornfield in the center of nowhere Nebraska. I couldn't leave."

She wanted to dispute his words. To attack him and blame him, but how could she? His reason was valid. Yet she returned to the safety behind the stony exterior of her heart. "So you ignored her?"

Trey frowned. "No, I sent Slade in my place."

Kayla had never mentioned Slade showing up. Justine swallowed. "And did he find anything?"

"Never got the chance. Kayla refused his help, literally slammed the door in his face."

A typical Kayla tantrum when she didn't get what she wanted. "I wasn't aware of that." *Apologize.* Tell him she didn't blame him, but the words stuck in her throat. Instead, she said, "No one took Kayla seriously."

"Did you?"

Two words that drove a spear of shame through Justine. Had she taken Kayla's stalker claims seriously? Her friend, for all her whimsical ways, did have the tendency to overdramatize. A quality Justine admired, but one that prevented her from responding to Kayla's "emergency" calls. And she couldn't ignore the omission of Slade's arrival from Kayla's story. Or was her own memory faulty?

Did Justine blame Trey? Or herself?

"You did what you had to do," Justine said, silencing her own condemning thoughts more than replying to Trey. "Let's focus on finding her killer."

The remainder of the drive was unbearably quiet, and

Justine exhaled relief as Trey pulled into the medical examiner's parking lot.

Entering the building, her day was progressively getting worse.

Justine halted at the sight of Dr. Curtis and Susan Nolan conversing at the far end of the hallway. Susan's hand rested on Dr. Curtis's arm, and she tilted her head, exuding playful laughter. He nodded in agreement with whatever Susan said, their voices too soft to be overheard from the distance.

"She's gotten to him," Justine whispered, dragging Trey around the corner and out of sight.

"We could interrupt them."

"No. I don't want to gang up on him. Or have Susan lose it and make a scene. He said he'd do the exam and has always been a man of his word. I'll call later."

But Justine's instincts warned her Susan Nolan would win.

Dusk had fallen by the time Trey turned onto Justine's long gravel driveway. His headlights beamed off the darkened barn and house as he pulled in front of the garage doors, activating the motion-sensor lights.

He'd barely shifted into Park before Justine was out of the truck. "I need to check on Barney."

"Wait up." Trey hurried to climb out and release Magnum.

Justine had already reached the Dog House by the time they caught up to her. Clover did figure eights around her legs. "I think she missed me."

"For a short person, you walk extremely fast."

Justine chuckled. "Sorry. I'm a woman on a mission."

She unlocked the door, unleashing a rendition of barked greetings. "Couldn't sneak up on them if I wanted to."

They stepped through the doorway, and she flipped on the overhead light.

"Well, hello. I've missed you all too. Would you mind releasing the boys for me, Trey?" she called over her shoulder, beelining for Barney's kennel.

"Sure." Trey scanned the spotless barn, making his way to Justine while Magnum reacquainted himself with each new friend.

"Hey, buddy, what's going on with you?" Justine knelt beside the basset hound.

Barney responded with a couple of slow tail thumps but remained lying on his side. He glanced up at Trey, blinking a brown soulful eye.

Justine smoothed his long ears in steady strokes, speaking softly. "I hear you don't have an appetite." She gently touched his bandaged leg. "Doesn't appear to be in pain. I know what'll do the trick."

Trey leaned against the kennel as Justine grabbed dog biscuits from the cabinet, passing treats to each animal, saving Barney for last.

Magnum inched beside Barney.

"Moral support?" Justine held out biscuits, and each dog eagerly snarfed down the treats. "That's the Barney I know."

He blinked innocently as if to say "who me?" Barney scooted off his bed and gave a good shake, jowls swaying.

"You big faker. Were you playing Will?" She laughed.

Trey opened the door, and canines burst through. Clover, Magnum and Barney took up the rear with humans trailing.

"I thought Will made it sound as if the dog was on his deathbed," Trey said.

Justine shrugged. "I think Barney may be at fault. Played Will like a fiddle."

Did Will use Barney to encourage Justine's return to the ranch? Or had Will's personal business forced him to leave? Slade hadn't found anything on the man, but Trey remained unconvinced Will was the stellar individual Justine perceived.

Which was why Trey needed evidence. "I'm going to grab our things."

Justine nodded, eyes on the meandering dogs.

After gathering his duffel bag, the bag Slade provided earlier containing the minicams and the box of case files, he locked the vehicle. Will's absence gave him the perfect opportunity to install the cameras. He set down the items on the porch.

Fireflies danced in the night air, and crickets chirped happily from the pasture.

Justine strolled along the gravel driveway, her gait relaxed, hands in her pockets. Peace oozed from her, and her smile beamed serenity. She was beautiful. Smart and compassionate. Everything Trey remembered her to be.

"I'll be right there." Justine gave a shrill whistle. Canines appeared from all directions, rushing back to her.

Trey waved, disappointed the moment had ended. He schlepped to the barn and hovered in the doorway while Justine tucked each canine into their kennel.

If he placed a camera above the door, he would have a great visual of the dogs' quarters and entry.

Not yet. She'd never agree to him invading Will's privacy without a good reason.

"Night, boys." Justine turned off the light and locked the barn. "I smell smoke again."

He chuckled at her reference to his thinking expression from earlier. "Sorry. Considering possibilities."

"Like?"

"Better, now that you've seen Barney's okay?"

"Much. Here, let me carry something."

Trey passed the duffel to her and adjusted the file box. The charm of country living and hard work encompassed the old farmhouse. "I see why you love this place."

"It has a peaceful ambience, doesn't it? I picture a large family here. Kids running around, laughing and playing. Barbecue on the grill." Her tone was wistful. "Someday."

Everything she'd said spoke to Trey's wish list too, but he dared not interrupt the precious glimpse into her thoughts. Their footsteps crunched on the gravel driveway, transitioning to swishing in the grass. Justine and Magnum beat him to the porch steps, taking them two at a time. "He must feel better too," Trey said.

Justine stumbled forward, and Trey caught and steadied her. "Careful."

"Clumsy me." She bent and inspected a board. "Another thing to add to Will's list."

Instinct had the hairs on Trey's neck rising, and he set down the stuff. "Let me clear the house before you enter."

"Don't be silly. It's an old house and boards are always lifting." Justine stood and gripped the screen door handle. She tugged it open, and Trey held it with his foot while she inserted her key.

A soft click sounded.

Trey snagged Justine, falling backward onto the porch floor, shoving Magnum with them.

The screen door slammed shut.

An explosion of wood and debris rained down.

Heart thundering against his rib cage, Trey turned, Justine still wrapped in his arms.

A large hole gaped in the center of the front door, and the screen hung by one hinge.

Magnum rushed to Trey, licking his face. "We're okay, Mags." He released Justine.

"What happened?" She scooted to a sitting position, arms around her knees.

"Wait. Keep low." Trey got to his feet. "Mags, stay."

The dog moved protectively beside Justine.

Trey withdrew his gun and flattened his back against the wall. He kicked open the remnants of the door.

A shotgun swung, suspended from the ceiling, its barrel aimed at Trey.

"Stay here while I clear the house."

Justine nodded.

Trey swept through each room on the main floor, then the basement, moving swiftly. His pulse thundered in his ears. Finally, he climbed the stairs to the upper level and paused outside Justine's closed bedroom door.

Once more, he flattened against the wall.

Gripped the knob.

And, with a fortifying breath, shoved open the door.

Silence.

Trey reached around the corner and flipped on the light switch. A soft glow emanated from the overhead fixture, filling the room.

Something blazed by Trey's face.

He ducked and swatted at it.

The object fluttered to the floor.

Trey inspected the small black bat. A laugh escaped

his nervous lips. He rushed to the bathroom and grabbed a trash can to trap the creature. "I'll be back for you in a minute."

He returned to the bedroom, where the queen bed, white side table and a large oval colorful braided rug took up most of the tidy area. The door to the closet was open, and Trey quickly cleared it. Nothing beyond the bat was out of order.

Exhaling relief, Trey finished the upper level and walked to the living room.

Justine stood inspecting the gaping hole in her front door. "I can't believe this."

"I need a piece of cardboard."

Justine quirked an eyebrow. "I think wood might be a better repair."

He laughed. "No, for the bat in your bedroom."

"Thought you were going to say *belfry*. Wait. Did you say a bat?" She shivered. "Gross."

Trey followed her into the kitchen, and they cut a portion of cardboard from a box in her pantry. "Be right back."

He jogged to the second floor, slid the cardboard under the trash can, creating a seal, and hauled the unwanted visitor outside, freeing him.

Trey returned to the empty living room and walked to where a light streamed from the back room. Justine removed files from the box.

"Our batty friend is gone."

"Thank you. I don't like them, but the poor thing must've gotten trapped in my room. I'd like to say that's a new development, but I'm afraid the attic needs repairs, and in the meantime, those creatures seem to find their way inside. Another addition for Will's list."

Trey leaned against the desk. "Convenient Will was called away for personal business tonight."

Justine spun and pinned him with a glare. "Why would Will set up a snare gun?"

That was the hardest question to answer. "Okay, who did?"

"I don't know, but it had to have happened after Will left."

"Any other visitors?"

"Mr. Richardson came by looking for me, but I told you, he's harmless."

"He wants this land. That's motive."

"But why now?"

Exactly. Will was the best suspect. "How did the person know Will wouldn't be here?"

Justine shrugged. "Maybe they assumed he'd gone to bed."

She had an answer for everything, but Trey remained suspicious. "I'm just saying look at the evidence objectively."

"I need to call Will." She withdrew her phone. "He's not answering. Must be asleep."

"Or wondering why you're not dead," Trey inserted.

"Stop. I told you. Will wouldn't do that." A shrill ring interrupted them. "It's Will."

"Ask him about anything unusual and put it on speakerphone," Trey insisted.

Justine frowned but did as he asked.

"Sorry, I was busy. Is something wrong?" Will's voice sounded genuinely concerned, but Trey had heard better actors.

"Yes!" Justine launched into a speedy explanation of the snare gun.

Will grumbled a few choice words, most of which were unclear. "I left when I got your text. How'd someone get into your house to set it up?"

"Was there anything out of the ordinary today?" Justine pressed.

"Nothing except Richardson's visit."

Justine's shoulders slumped.

Trey focused on her expression. Was this a regular occurrence? Had she filed harassment charges on the neighbor? He fought the urge to speak, not wanting to stifle Will. Better if he thought Trey wasn't listening in.

"I'll head back tonight," Will assured her.

"No. It'll be fine. Trey's here."

"Oh, good to hear *Trey's* on the watch," Will snapped.

"See you in the morning?" Justine asked.

"Yep."

They disconnected, and she faced Trey. "Is this ever going to end?"

"Let's talk about Richardson. Does he threaten you?"

Justine sighed. "Never."

They walked out to the living room.

"Would he go to this extreme?" Trey slipped on a pair of latex gloves from his uniform pocket, took several pictures with his phone, then carefully removed the gun

"No. He prefers incentives. Killing me is a little excessive, don't you think?" Exhaustion showed on her face.

"Go rest. I'll work on repairing the door."

"It'll go faster if we do it together."

Rather than argue, Trey followed Justine to the garage to gather supplies. They worked in tandem to cover the hole.

"It's not pretty, but it'll do for now. I'll order a new door tomorrow," Justine said.

Trey placed his hand on her shoulder. "I'm sorry you're going through this."

Justine nodded. "It's overwhelming."

"Would you allow me to take a few preventative measures?"

She tilted her head. "Like?"

Trey removed the cameras from the bag. "We'll place them strategically, with views of the house and barn giving you 24/7 surveillance." He held his breath, ready for her to argue.

"That's a great idea."

He blinked. Had he misunderstood?

Justine smiled. "What?"

"I'll set them up." Working quickly, Trey assembled the small cameras and placed them over the barn and both house doors.

He booted up his laptop and sat on the porch swing, checking the links to ensure they all worked.

Justine dropped beside him, the sweet smell of lavender wafting from her. "Wow, those work great."

"Yep, and they're adjustable to focus on other areas too." Trey demonstrated the features. "The software will also record, so you can reference it later."

She leaned closer to the screen, and Trey fought the urge to inhale deeply. "I love this. Wish I'd thought to do this a long time ago. Although, I'm sure Will won't fully appreciate us watching him."

Trey moved the mouse, shifting the barn camera to face the door and kennels. "There. Now we're not invading Will's privacy."

"You're brilliant."

"Don't tell my boss. He'll expect me to work harder."

Justine chuckled. "We should tell Will though."

"Do me a favor and wait on that."

"Trey—"

"Please. See what the footage captures first. If I'm wrong, I'll buy the man a brand-new Stetson."

She grinned at him. "Fair enough. Thank you for doing this. I only wish we'd had them installed when whoever did that was here." She gestured toward the door. Her phone rang, and Justine rushed inside to grab it. "Hey, Will." She frowned. "No problem. Tomorrow afternoon is fine. Good night." Justine addressed Trey. "Will can't get a ride here until later."

Convenient. Trey called Slade, keeping near to Justine.

"Hey, everything all right?" Slade asked.

Trey explained the snare-gun incident. "Did you see anything out of the ordinary?"

"Negative. I've watched the perimeter and saw nothing more exciting than a cow in the pasture. Who could've rigged that up in the time between Will's departure and your arrival?"

He chose his words carefully, opting for the ten code on criminal history. "Exactly. Did you run the 10-29?"

"Yep. Nothing. Percy's a drifter, seems to bounce between locations in the area, but that's not a crime. I can't see him doing that, can you? It's too close, makes him suspect number one."

Trey frowned. If Will wasn't behind the attacks, who was?

EIGHT

The dead keep their secrets, and in a while, we shall be as wise as they—and as taciturn. Justine recognized Alexander Smith's quote inscribed inside the diary cover. The apropos message propelled her quest. Kayla had something to tell her, and she'd find a way to decipher it. The familiar shroud of guilt hovered over her for invading the sacred pages.

"Have you been up all night?"

She startled at Trey's entrance and glanced toward her office window, where the sun crested the horizon. "I couldn't sleep, so I was going over the evidence. Listen to this." Justine read the quote to Trey. "I can't help but wonder if she anticipated her death."

Justine wrapped and unwrapped the book's leather strap around her finger. "Here again, she says 'He's following me. Today I found a black rose—'"

"That would prove someone had been in her home. The police should've followed up."

"They probably would've if she hadn't tossed it in the trash. Regardless, a rose isn't a death threat. It's an intimidation technique. Everything points to Kayla knowing her killer. No forced entry, nothing stolen from her apartment and Kayla hated roses." Justine made a note in her notebook and took a sip of coffee. "It was a warning."

"About what? An enemy or a friend?" Trey slid onto the desk.

"Most murders are committed by people the victim knows," Justine advised.

"True." Trey walked to the evidence board hanging on the wall and seemed to study the haphazardly tacked-up Post-it Notes, her sketch of the kidnapper and a few quotes from Kayla's diary. He gave a low whistle. "Impressive. And since I'm apparently several hours behind you in working, care to walk me through what you've found so far?"

Justine moved closer, the diary in hand. "There's not much to go off, but I've managed with less."

"That's good news. We could break this down into—"

"No offense, but I use a methodology."

"I'm all ears."

Justine grinned while respectfully disagreeing. Trey Jackson was far more than just ears.

His flawless appearance showed no traces of sleeping squished on her couch, as if he'd folded himself into a drawer and unfolded again this morning. Ironically, the same could be said of Trey's return to her life. Between him and the diary, she was getting a double dose of facing the past.

A very handsome part of her past.

Trey's dark hair and blue eyes shadowed by thick lashes gave him a boyish appearance, but his stature and physique emphasized a commanding presence—the ultimate blend. Worse, he was kind, brave and thoughtful. The combination reminded Justine of the long-ago feelings she'd tucked away when Kayla first confessed her crush on Trey. Best friends didn't overstep those boundaries.

Even after one of them was gone.

His presence might put her on the precipice of confronting her own long-term issues, but it certainly wasn't unpleasant. In fact, though she'd never admit it to anyone, she was starting to enjoy being with him. She'd forgotten how charming Trey could be and how adorable those dimples were when he smiled.

"What?" Trey blinked. "Why are you looking at me like that?" He swiped a hand over his head, drawing attention to his well-defined bicep.

She glanced away and gave herself a mental slap. Not the time. Place. Or person. "Sorry, lack of sleep and I zoned out. Right. Methodology. Simply put, we assess how the murder occurred, why someone wanted Kayla dead, and that will tell us who."

"If you'd told me that prior to your kidnapping attempts, I'd have conceded Kayla's murder was a random drug buy gone bad. Wrong-place-at-the-wrong-time type of situation. But I think we've surpassed that."

"What if Kayla was overdosed against her will? I never saw her ingest anything wilder than Tabasco sauce. If my theory is correct, surely Dr. Curtis's new exam will confirm a struggle." Except Dr. Curtis still hadn't returned her call.

Trey nodded. "This is a lot of discussion prior to caffeine consumption though."

Justine laughed. "I have a single-serve coffee maker. Help yourself. Pods are beside it."

He scurried out of the room, and Justine focused on the evidence board. Within a few minutes, Trey returned, mug in hand. "Now I can function. However, you're not going to like what I'm about to say."

"I love when people start out conversations that way."

He chuckled. "I don't disagree with your exhumation idea, but the Kayla I knew was a little unconventional."

Justine grinned. "That's putting it mildly. Kayla's personality filled a room before she entered. She was uninhibited. Daring. Fearless."

Unlike me.

Kayla's openness was a strength Justine didn't possess and everything she wanted to be. "I admired her." The confession surprised Justine. Why share that?

"How can you be certain she never used?"

Justine shrugged. "Experience and faith. If Kayla's death is the result of an overdose, I don't believe it was voluntary."

Her cell phone rang, and Justine reached for the device. Unknown number.

"Justine Stark."

"This is Susan Nolan."

Confusion mingled with excitement, and Justine waved her arms and put the call on speaker. "Mrs. Nolan, good morning."

A sniffle. "I need to talk to you and Trooper Jackson."

"What's wrong?"

"Not now. In person. I have information regarding Kayla's death. Information that will get me killed if he finds out."

"Who?"

Susan continued, ignoring the question. "Meet me in Valentine, at the bridge on the Cowboy Trail. Five o'clock."

"If you're in danger, the police—"

"Just be there."

The line disconnected.

"At least she gave us time to make the drive," Trey grumbled. "That's halfway across Nebraska."

"It's only four hours away."

Trey sighed. "What's she up to?"

"She sounded genuinely fearful."

"But why come to us now? Why not go straight to the cops? And who is 'he'?"

"Maybe the bombing at Alex's office scared her into speaking up? Plus, this works in our favor. We'll explain the need for the exhumation and get her to back off. She could stop the stupid seventy-two-hour time limit too."

"I hope you're right. I hate to be a downer, but unless Susan gives us something substantial, we're stuck at square one. There really aren't any other earth-shattering clues."

"Kayla deserves justice. You can't just say 'If we don't find something, oh well.'"

"Then this meeting has to count. If we can link your profile to someone Kayla knew, we'd have evidence to demand more time."

Justine shook her head. "It doesn't work like that. I can't go in with the intentions of pinning it to a specific person. That's a bias all by itself. We have to work every clue fresh."

Magnum strolled into the room, favoring his good side.

"Good morning, sleepy boy," she said, ruffling his fur.

"Glad you could join us," Trey teased. "He was zonked out when I woke."

"Poor guy. We did have a stressful day, and sitting in that truck must get old."

"He gets breaks, but I could let him stay inside."

"On a hot day, are you kidding?"

Trey stepped forward. "Patrol canine vehicles are equipped with a thermostat-control safety feature. If the interior exceeds the temperature, the windows automatically roll down."

Justine rose again. "Every vehicle should offer that."

"I agree. And see this?" He pointed to the small black box on the front of his tactical vest. "If I push the button, Magnum's door opens and he's trained to run to me."

"That's too cool." She leaned against the desk, considering her next words. "He did wonders for Barney's attitude last night. Why not leave him at the ranch? He enjoys exploring the property with the boys. It'd be good for them."

Trey visibly bristled. "No way. Magnum is my partner. He goes where I go."

Justine held up a hand. "Magnum shouldn't move around a lot with his injury. And you installed cameras, so you'll be able to keep an eye on him. I'm only thinking of his best interest."

"As if I don't?"

"I never said that."

"I'm not leaving my partner with *Will*." Trey spewed the man's name as if it tasted bad in his mouth.

Justine stiffened, fixing her eyes on Trey. "Will takes great care of the boys. I'd never leave my dogs in the custody of someone I thought would hurt them. I trust him implicitly."

"Even after last night? The snare gun?" Trey gave a

dismissive snort, crossing his arms. "Will is one factor we'll have to agree to disagree about."

Justine dropped onto her chair, hesitant to share her painful history with Trey. But he needed to understand. "I'm careful about those I allow into my inner circle. I learned at the wise age of nineteen how damaging misplaced trust can be."

He uncrossed his arms, the defensiveness deflating in his posture. "I'm listening."

"Simon and I were engaged for two months. I'd fallen hard for him and never considered he'd abuse my trust. Imagine my surprise when he cleaned out my bank account and disappeared with the few things of value from my home."

"I'm sorry."

"It took me a long time to listen to my instincts, and it's partly why I chose psychology. It became a shield for me. I may not do a lot of things well, but human behavior is something I understand. You don't have to like Will, but at least respect my competency in choosing him to watch over my animals."

Trey sighed. "Your expertise is never in question. I wish I saw him the way you do, but too many details point to him being involved with the attempts on your life."

"Or your perception is painting that picture. Magnum would be fine here with Barney and the boys."

Trey shook his head. "Magnum is fine. I'd never compromise his recovery. He needs the interaction and enjoys working. Being left behind depresses him, and he's already contributed immensely in this investigation, even while recouping. Of all people, I'd think you'd appreciate the mental and emotional components of his total healing."

The words were like daggers. If he thought her opinion was valuable, why did he refute and shoot down everything she said? The tension hung thick between them, sucking the air from the room. Justine turned her back to Trey and busied herself with the evidence board.

"Justine, I don't mean to sound ungrateful."

"No problem."

He placed a hand on her shoulder. "Truth is, I'm probably more in need of Magnum than he is of me."

She nodded, still feeling the sting of his words.

"I'm truly sorry for what Simon did to you."

She forced a smile. "Experience gives us the wisdom to make better future choices. I resolved to never compromise myself by being codependent. If I ever entrusted my heart—and, believe me, that's a big-fat-hairy-green *if*—it'll be after I've accomplished my goals and done the things I want. I know that sounds selfish, but Simon tried to steal my dreams. I won't give someone that power again."

Trey's gaze moved downward. "But a healthy relationship encourages a couple to work together, ensuring their hopes are realized."

Rebellion and fear swam, conjuring images of her tyrannical father and cowering mother. "Not in my experience. Relationships are detrimental. I've got no interest."

Trey's smile never reached his eyes. "Sure. I get that. Me either. Got too much to do before I consider settling down."

Magnum whined.

"I'd better take him outside." His footsteps faded down the hallway.

In one conversation, they'd gone from teasing light-heartedness to high-towered distance. Just as well. They were working a case. Nothing more.

She glanced at the diary, her eye catching Kayla's script. *Justine keeps me grounded.*

Great. Killjoy Justine and Whimsical Kayla had fit together like two halves of the same book, almost as if they'd completed the missing pieces for one another. Justine had seen a side of Kayla most people hadn't—subtle and gentle. Something she'd hidden from her affluent parents. They'd bonded over the complexities of family dramas and agreed vulnerability was an intolerable weakness.

"I miss you, Kayla." Justine perched on the end of the old wooden desk.

This was the one chance she had to prove how much she cared for Kayla.

Trey strolled with Magnum outside the window, conversing with the dog. Tenderness for him flowed through her. If she did think herself capable of romance with someone, Trey would be at the top of her list. But he was off-limits. Wouldn't falling for him be the ultimate betrayal to Kayla? Friends didn't do that to each other.

Objectivity without emotion was the recipe for a successful profile. If only her feelings understood what her brain knew.

The door shut, and the clicking of Magnum's feet on the hardwood floor announced their return.

She'd not allow another man to prop her up, because that gave him the power to tear her down. She'd come too far, sacrificed too much to heal.

Never again.

Not even to Trey Jackson—the one man who held her heart in his hands, regardless if he knew it.

"Where are you taking me?" Justine leaned forward, hands braced on the dashboard. Golden tassels waved from the peaks of the sea of cornstalks. "Isn't there a parking lot closer to the bridge?"

Trey never took his eyes off the road. "I agreed to this meeting, especially if she's got something to offer in the investigation, but we're not advertising our arrival."

"So we're hiking through acres of corn to get there?"

"I'm still not convinced this is the best idea. We could be walking into an ambush. My only consolation is the trail is wide, giving me a good visual, and we're taking an alternative path to the bridge."

"You know this area?"

"Somewhat. I have one condition to this expedition."

"What's that?" Justine busied herself collecting her purse and the diary.

"If I see anything that concerns me, we're out of here."

Justine slid Kayla's journal into her khaki pants pocket. "Okay."

"Why not leave that locked in the truck?"

"As ridiculous as this might sound, having the diary with me is like keeping Kayla close. Gives me courage."

"You're the last person I'd think needed a dose of courage."

Justine grinned. "See? It works."

He chuckled, but something in his eyes said "choose your battles." And she'd agree. After the morning's dissension, this was small potatoes. "I have to say again, for the record, I'm not sure this is a good idea."

"What choice do we have? Susan sounded desperate, and you heard Alex. If Fredrick is a tyrant, he could've killed Kayla. Susan might provide the missing piece to give us the break we need."

Trey worked his jaw but said nothing more. He turned off the road and parked in a small area tucked between rows of corn. The stalks enveloped the truck, camouflaging it.

"If you didn't know this place was here, you'd drive right past it."

"Exactly. We're hidden."

"Do you think that's necessary?" Justine second-guessed herself. Was meeting Susan naive?

Trey gripped the steering wheel. "I don't know."

"Well, now I feel all warm and fuzzy," Justine teased, attempting to lighten the mood. "Come on. We'll make this quick and get out of here." She stepped into the towering plants and around to where Trey stood at the tailgate.

Magnum wagged his tail, rocking a cornstalk.

"After you."

Trey led the way. Grasshoppers bounced between them, and the excessive temperature plastered her shirt to her back. They traipsed through the field until it opened to a dirt lot, eventually leading to the Cowboy Trail. Trees surrounded them on both sides of the red gravel path bordered by yellow and purple flowering plants.

"This is pretty."

Trey didn't respond, focused on surveying their surroundings.

"I appreciate your dedication to our safety, but it's a little perplexing."

He stopped and lifted the binoculars, scanning the distance. "I promise to be better company once I'm certain there's no one out to ambush us."

"It even smells nice." Justine leaned down, sniffing a flower, birds chirping cheerfully above her. "I remember seeing pictures on the news about the river flooding here this past spring. It was devastating, but to see it now, you'd never know it happened."

"Nature has a way of recovering from tragedy." Trey started walking again, and she hurried to catch up with him.

"It's like we're the only two people out here."

Trey paused. "Let's hope so."

"You're making me nervous."

"Just being cautious." Trey stooped and removed Magnum's leash, giving the dog free rein. "He'd spot someone before I did."

"Good idea. How far is the bridge?"

"Probably a half mile or so, which is why we're here extra early."

They made their way along the path tucked between lush green foliage. Focused on the scenery, Justine spotted a mulberry tree and moved toward it, nearly tripping over Magnum as he paused beneath it. "Sorry, sweetie."

Trey rushed to her side and reached for Magnum's collar. "Mags, no. He loves mulberries."

Justine snickered. "Ah, let the poor guy have a treat. Besides, who passes on fresh mulberries?"

Magnum snatched more abandoned berries, proving her words.

"Want one?" Justine picked a couple, popped them into her mouth and relished the sweet fruit.

Trey smiled. "We loved gathering them as kids. My

grandmother had rows of mulberry trees. She made it sound fun, but I'm sure we were cheap labor. Will work for mulberry pie." He waggled his eyebrows, and Justine couldn't help laughing.

She gathered a handful of the plump purple berries and held one between her fingertips, lifting it to Trey's mouth. He hesitated, then accepted the offering, grazing her skin with his surprisingly soft lips.

The touch felt like a battery-jumper-cable jolt, and she fought not to jerk away her hand, instead giving him a shaky smile.

Had the contact rattled him in the same way?

Trey collected more of the berries, snacking on them. "I'd forgotten how good they are."

Apparently not.

Justine joined him, filling her hands. "We could just eat mulberries all day."

Trey chuckled. "Maybe after we meet with Susan."

"Right. Almost forgot why we're here." Justine walked past him. Magnum trotted ahead. The fine red rocks crunched beneath their feet. "It's hard to believe we were fighting for our lives less than twenty-four hours ago." She inhaled. "I'd be content staying here and forgetting my cares for a few days."

"The outdoors does that for me too."

The irony that she and Trey enjoyed so many of the same things wasn't lost on Justine, but the weight of the diary in her pocket reminded her that her feelings for Trey weren't allowed. She wouldn't do that to Kayla.

Or to herself.

The path curved around a bend.

"Before we go farther, let me do a little recon." Trey

pointed to a long line of trees ten feet to the right. The branches were wide and varied, perfect for climbing.

She followed him off the path through knee-high grass, the tip of Magnum's tail leading the way. Trey's easy climb up the tree made him look more like a young boy than a seasoned trooper. She glanced up and caught sight of him watching through binoculars and leaning out too far on a branch.

"Well?"

"There's a sports car parking. Susan's arrived," Trey called.

"Is she alone?"

"Appears so."

Trey moved down the tree. "She's early, so let's head to the bridge."

The trio returned to the path, quickening their pace. "I wonder what she has to tell us."

Justine slowed at the sound of rushing water. The rock path became wood and connected with a large steel bridge ahead. Trey and Magnum continued walking, not noticing her hesitation.

She swallowed against the dryness in her throat, willing her body to move until she reached the railing. Her hand clutched the warm metal, and she clung for dear life, fear rising like the waters flowing swiftly below. She peered over the edge, keeping as far back as possible, unable to take another step.

Lord, I can't do this.

"Are you coming?" Trey called, but his voice sounded distant.

One step at a time. Justine lifted her one-ton-heavy foot. Forward.

Her pulse raced.

She advanced two more steps onto the steel-beamed floor and halted. Every muscle in her body locked up. She'd bit Trey's head off at the house, declaring her competency. How could she tell him water terrified her? Rather, death by drowning.

Trey rushed to her, alarm written in his eyes. He lifted the binoculars, surveying the area. "What's wrong? Did you see something?"

"I didn't realize the river was so high," she squeaked.

Trey leaned his hip against the railing and whistled for Magnum. The dog bounded to his side. Trey secured his leash. "At one time, the bridge was under water. Normally, the river is shallow enough to walk in, only up to your knees, but this part is abnormally deep."

As if that was a comfort.

He pointed to the edges where a wall of jagged sand cascaded, leaving only a few inches between the riverbank and the waters. "It's a great place for kayaking, although that wouldn't be wise today. River's moving a little swift."

Justine held tight to the bridge, immobile, words eluding her. *Say something. Anything.*

"Not into water sports?"

She'd waited too long. *And now you've done it. There's nothing to be ashamed of.* But she refused to voice her fears, instead opting to change the subject. "This is really pretty. Except for the graffiti someone so lovingly added." She pointed to the beams marred with spray-painted words and images.

"People have to find a way to ruin things." Trey sighed, turning to face the water again.

Magnum barked and tugged on his leash, sniffing the underside of the bridge.

Justine followed closely, grateful when her feet hit solid ground. "What's he got?"

"I'm not sure. He's on to something."

Magnum sniffed vigorously, inching along the bank and moving toward the tree line. She and Trey trailed, their feet sliding on the bank's shifting sands.

A rustle in the leaves made Justine pause.

She jerked and turned.

Only the sound of the water reached her ears.

"What's wrong?"

"I don't know. Thought I heard something. Probably just my overactive imagination," she said, brushing aside a stray hair.

Magnum spun and lunged, barking at the tree-lined path.

"You're not overactively imagining anything," a man said, emerging from between the trees, gun aimed at them.

NINE

Trey gripped Magnum's leash with one hand, reaching for his gun with the other. Magnum barked furiously, straining to attack the stranger.

"Touch your gun or make a move, and I'll shoot your dog before I shoot her."

Any other day, Trey would've unleashed Magnum, but his injury might delay his reaction time. He couldn't risk losing his partner.

"Shut that stupid mutt up!" the man ordered.

"Nein." Trey tugged Magnum back and shifted to cover Justine.

Justine gasped. "What do you want?"

Shadows hid the man's face. "You're smarter than that. Toss the diary to me."

"The diary is police evidence. Why would we bring it along?" Trey inserted.

Magnum inched closer, a low growl rumbling.

"Nein," Trey whispered again.

A click behind him had Trey twisting to investigate. A second assailant stood on the opposite side of the bridge, partially hidden by the trees. The sunlight glimmered off his gun. Had he been watching them the entire time?

"My friend would love to kill you where you stand. Then your body can float downriver. Along with your dog's," the first man warned.

"We can't take you to the diary without moving, genius," Trey said.

"No, but there's no need to go far, is there? Your lady friend has it in her pocket." The man fired. The bullet zinged off the metal bridge.

Justine hopped back, bumping into Trey. He steadied her, and his gaze moved to her khaki pocket above the knee. The diary bulged inside.

They were cornered. Unless...

Trey's eyes traveled to the rushing waters, following the river into the low-hanging trees as it curved and disappeared from sight. If they jumped in and let the current carry them around the bend, they'd be hidden in the tall grass and could escape to where he'd parked the truck.

The diary would be ruined, but what choice did they have? Would Justine agree?

And how to get Magnum into the river too?

They'd need a running start to clear the sandy bank before diving. The guy had already threatened to shoot them, so turning their backs was unwise. But Justine's body language on the bridge had told him she feared the water.

Justine faced Trey. "What do we do?"

"Walk up here, lady," the man ordered again.

If Justine went first, Trey could grab his gun and cover her. At least, he prayed he would.

Right now, he needed a way to communicate the plan. "Justine, you know we can't get away from them," he said loudly. "It's hopeless. What're we going to do? Jump into the river? The current would drag us away."

Her eyes widened with what he hoped was under-standing. "You're right," she said, maintaining the ruse. Then she mumbled, "I can't swim."

So that was why she'd locked up on the bridge.

Magnum continued growling.

"He can," Trey whispered.

Justine glanced down. "Okay." She gave a slow nod and turned her back to him, facing the gunman. "Don't shoot. I'm coming."

"Yeah, yeah, hurry up," the man said, annoyed.

"The ground is steep. Let me help," Trey offered.

"I don't need you. Just her."

"True, but if she slips and falls, and you have to help her, you can't do that and keep your gun on me."

"That's why I have a partner, *genius*."

"Fine. Have it your way." Trey leaned closer to Justine and whispered, "Take a step toward him, then turn, run and aim for the river. I'll be right behind you."

She shook her head. "I can't."

"Yes, you can. Don't panic when you hit the water. Magnum will help you," Trey whispered. "On three."

"Knock off the whispering and get up here!"

"Okay, I'm coming," she called.

Trey pressed Magnum's leash into her hand. "One, two—"

Justine executed the plan perfectly. "Magnum!"

The dog jumped in beside her.

"Stop!" Curses accompanied bullets from both at-tackers.

Trey returned fire, his gaze ricocheting between the assailants and Justine.

He shot several consecutive rounds, then launched

into the river, gun still clutched in his hand. Justine and Magnum had rounded the bend, taking them from sight.

Trey swam with fury, allowing the current to provide an extra boost.

The men continued shooting, forcing Trey underwater. The murky water was impossible to see through and he sprang to the surface. Algae stung his nose, and sticks brushed his fingers.

Ahead, the river forked. Justine and Magnum clung to a beaver dam made of twigs and branches on the right, but they had to keep moving downriver or the men would catch up.

Justine inched toward the edge, using a fallen tree.

Trey increased his strokes. "Wait."

She turned, eyes wide with fear.

He reached for her. "I've got you. Kick your legs."

"There!"

A barrage of hissing *pffts* surrounded them as bullets hit the water and sandy bank.

Trey pulled her toward the fork, aiming for the opposite waterway. "Keep kicking."

Magnum swam with ease beside him, and they continued downriver and slid behind a marshy area with tall cattails.

After several seconds, the gunfire stopped. Trey lost visuals of the men and prayed they weren't able to see him and Justine.

They climbed out and slipped into the brush. Magnum gave a thorough shake, flinging water from his fur.

Trey checked his magazine. Not enough ammunition for a second shoot-out. He holstered the weapon. "Stay silent and low."

Hidden in the tall grass, they hunkered down while Trey used the binoculars still hanging around his neck.

The men searched for them on both sides of the river.

He motioned for Justine, and they crept along the tree line until the men's voices faded completely.

Once more, they paused, and Trey exhaled relief at the shooters running in the opposite direction. No doubt from where they'd parked before ambushing the trio earlier.

"Think they've gone?" Justine whispered.

"Doubtful, but we're not far from the pickup."

Concealed by the thick mass of trees, they walked toward the north. Familiar rows of corn promised they were almost free. Entering the fields, they startled grasshoppers, which pinged in all directions. To her credit, Justine didn't make a sound. Even Magnum seemed to understand the magnitude of the moment and remained quiet. Nearing the edge of the cornfield, they stopped. Trey's truck sat parked five feet away.

But was it safe? Were the men watching?

"Wait here."

Trey stepped out, binoculars raised, and surveyed the area. A soft wind rustled the crop.

Nothing.

He lifted his key fob, hoping it still worked, and pressed the button. The door locks clicked. *Thank You, Lord.*

One more check.

Trey rushed to the vehicle and searched the undercarriage, wheel wells and every place it was conceivable to hide a GPS or bomb. Convinced all had remained safe, he waved over Justine and Magnum.

They made record time getting into the cab and exiting the area. Trey used his patrol radio and called in the gunmen, giving the best descriptions possible with the little information he had. "They won't catch the losers."

"What about Susan? Do you think they hurt her?"

Instead of commenting, Trey withdrew his cell phone. The black screen of death, and dripping water confirmed the diagnosis. He dropped it into the closest cup holder.

"Rice," Justine said.

"What?"

"Put the phone in a bowl of rice. That might fix it."

"I appreciate your optimism, but there's not enough rice in the world to help this. It's insured and everything's backed up to the cloud, so I'm not panicking yet. However, I need to borrow yours to call Slade."

"Well…" Justine held up her cell, water oozing from the device.

"Probably should've left that in the truck too," he teased.

"Right?" Justine leaned back and pulled out the diary from her pocket. She placed it on the console, open and soaked. "I should've listened to you."

"I saw a show where books were recovered from sunken ships. Once the pages dry, they may be legible."

"I love your optimism."

"You're a good influence. First stop, phone store."

"Susan was in on the attack," Justine said.

"I'm glad you're seeing things my way. As soon as I reach Sergeant Oliver, I'm bringing her in for questioning."

"I hate to agree, but I agree."

"She set us up. The assailant on the opposite side of the bridge got there ahead of us or crossed the river farther upstream and walked down."

"And the Nolans are the ones insisting on getting the diary. Have they been responsible for the attacks?"

"That's my theory." Trey accelerated, grateful as the highway came into view. "I want as much distance between us and those criminals as possible before stopping. And I'll ask Slade to do recon at your place after we check the cameras."

"No argument here." Justine finger-combed her wet hair.

Within thirty minutes, Trey pulled into a phone store.

"We're a mess." Justine gestured at their rumpled clothes.

"Act natural," Trey teased.

They purchased replacement phones and ignored the curious look from the clerk. Returning to the truck, they plugged the devices in to charge, and as soon as they came to life, message notifications chimed for both.

"Trey, Dr. Curtis returned my call." Dread hung in Justine's tone.

"Maybe he has good news." He waited as she activated the voice mail on speaker.

"Miss Stark, I've reevaluated the evidence in Kayla Nolan's case, and I do not believe an exhumation and reexamination are warranted. I apologize for the miscommunication." Dr. Curtis's tone was robotic.

Justine's cheeks burned crimson. "Oh, that woman!"

"Susan's very busy, and we're about to fix that problem." Trey dialed Slade, and before his brother said "hello," Trey blurted out the day's events.

"Unbelievable. What's your next move?"

"Questioning Susan and charging her with multiple counts of everything I can find. In the meantime, would you run recon at the ranch?"

Slade exhaled loudly. "Oliver called me in to help serve a warrant."

Trey's stomach tanked. "Oh."

"You've got the cameras set up, though, right? Maybe stay in Lincoln tonight instead? Or at the house with Asia."

After all they'd endured, Trey wasn't endangering his sister-in-law. "We'll see."

"If we finish early, I'll head to the ranch."

"I appreciate it." Trey disconnected and called Sergeant Oliver.

"I love that we talk every day, Jackson. Don't whine about Slade. I had no choice. We're low on manpower."

"Actually, boss, you'll want to hear this." Trey explained Susan's luring them to the bridge and subsequent ambush.

"Whoa. Are you sure she was there?"

Trey reconsidered what he'd seen. "Susan drives a sports car, and a woman got out of the vehicle."

"But did you see *Susan Nolan*?" Oliver pressed.

"Whose side are you on?" Trey bit out.

"Jackson, you'd better have evidence before you accuse her of ambushing you. I'll call and request she come in to meet with you. Irwin's handling supply duty, so he'll be around and can run interference until you arrive."

Great. Irwin the Vulture to the rescue. "Roger that. If she doesn't have an alibi, that helps me."

"Don't hold your breath."

"One other thing. Justine and I witnessed Susan talking with Dr. Curtis. Now he's refusing to do the exhumation. At the very least, that's impeding an investigation."

"This is unreal. I hate bullies, and the Nolans are

the quintessential example of bullies. I want that diary secured and this case solved! Whatever it contains has someone losing their mind." Oliver grunted. "District Attorney Madeline Hansen owes me a favor. Never thought I'd be using it on this though." He rattled off a phone number. "Tell her I sent you."

"Thank you."

"Transfer Justine to a safe house."

Trey smiled, eyes focused on Justine. Gold highlights shimmered in her raven hair. "Negative, sir. Her options are limited because of her dogs and the unpredictability of her hired hand. However, I installed surveillance cameras at the ranch. We're headed back ASAP."

"You've got a good handle on things. I'd prefer her in a secure location, but I understand her hesitancy. I hate to add to the stress, but Captain's unrelenting on the seventy-two hours."

"Yes, sir. Which is why we need that exhumation order."

"Agreed. Keep me updated."

"Roger that."

They disconnected and Trey pocketed his phone.

"Your boss isn't gung ho about questioning Susan?" Justine asked.

"He's bringing her in. Just cautious."

The diary lay on the console, pages slowly drying in the warmth of the summer sun. "Dr. Curtis was in total agreement about the examination. Without his cooperation and expertise, it's hopeless."

Trey's heart hurt at the dismay weighing down her shoulders. He squeezed her hand. "Did the infamous Dr. Justine Stark say *hopeless*?"

She smiled, but it never reached her eyes. "I'm not a doctor."

"Ah, close enough." He chuckled. "Are you kidding? We're just getting started."

"The Nolans have money and influence. They're beating us to every punch. It's impossible."

"Nothing is impossible," Trey said. "You pray and I'll make some calls. It's time to pull out the big guns." He dialed Madeline's number.

After four rings, she answered.

"Mrs. Hansen, I'm sorry to bother you. This is Trooper Trey Jackson. My sergeant, Mitch Oliver, authorized me to contact you. I have a predicament."

A long pause hung in the air before she spoke. "If Mitch sent you, I know it's important."

"Yes, ma'am." Trey rambled off the situation and requested the exhumation.

"I'm familiar with the prior ME and his misgivings. As well as the Nolans' influence. I'll expedite the order to you."

"Thank you."

Trey faced Justine and started the engine. "Done. The DA is issuing a court-ordered exhumation."

Hope danced in her hazel irises. "Thank you!" She squealed, diving over the console to wrap her arms around his neck.

Trey hugged her slight frame and chuckled.

Her cheeks blushed a soft pink. "I'm sorry. I just—"

"Don't apologize. I'm thrilled too."

"I'd given up."

"No way. We're our only cheerleaders."

She grinned.

Trey shifted into gear, his arms still warm from holding Justine. She'd fit so perfectly in his embrace, and he hadn't wanted to let her go. But the reaction was simply excitement for the win.

He had to keep telling himself that or he might do something stupid like blurt out his feelings.

They fell into a comfortable silence, allowing Trey to replay their earlier conversation. His heart stuttered at the glimpse into her past and his regret for being a huge jerk and shooting down her idea of leaving Magnum with Will.

But the discussion had established a firm boundary, and he'd respect it. Justine had made her feelings very clear. She wasn't interested in him or anyone. They were partners. Nothing more. Regardless of his traitorous emotions.

Get your head in the game, Jackson.

His phone rang with Oliver's icon. This couldn't be good news. "Boss."

"Word travels fast," Oliver said. "Just spoke with Madeline. The Nolans are fighting the order."

Trey gripped the wheel. "They can't do that."

"They'll stall, but they won't win."

"What do we do?"

"Keep moving forward. Use that Jackson charm at Susan's interview and get her to agree to the exhumation."

"Ugh." Trey hung up. "You'll never believe this." He shared Oliver's news.

"If they refuse, and Dr. Curtis is ordered by the judge, he might drag his feet on the examination." She lifted her phone. "My turn. I have a contact at the FBI, a forensic anthropologist, Dr. Taya McGill-Stryker."

"An independent exam. Great idea!"

"Exactly. And the Nolans won't intimidate her."

"How dare you!" Susan hugged herself, arms shaking. Her seething glare could've burned a hole through Justine.

The defensive posture conveyed an attempt to hide deception.

Trey leaned closer, invading Susan's space. "The call will trace to your phone. There's no point in denying you lured us out there."

"I did not!"

Justine spoke calmly. "Mrs. Nolan, I can see you're upset."

"Don't placate me with your psychological babble!"

Alex sat beside Susan and Fredrick at the far end of the table. He wore a stoic expression and hadn't defended or denied Trey's accusations, disengaged from the event.

"My client is distraught over the reopening of Kayla's death investigation," Alex intervened. "As to your accusation regarding Mrs. Nolan's involvement in an ambush, be assured there is no way she could've contacted you and traveled to— Where was it you were at?"

"Valentine," Trey offered.

"Oh, yes. *Valentine*—" Alex made a note on the yellow legal pad beside him before resuming "—*and* made the trip to Lincoln in time to attend the Friends of Friends Charity lunch."

"And even if you trace a call to my phone, which you won't, there's no proof I made the call, which I didn't," Susan reiterated for the third time in ten minutes.

Alex shrugged. "In this day and age, anything electronic can be tapped and manipulated." He whispered something to Mr. Nolan, who responded with a single nod. "Let's end this ridiculous treasure hunt and prove my clients' compliance."

Alex withdrew an iPad from his briefcase and swiped at the screen, revealing a social media site for the Friends of Friends group. He played a video of the Nolans cutting the ribbon at the ceremony and pointed to the time stamp. "Proof Mr. and Mrs. Nolan were in Omaha during your alleged attack."

"There. You see?" Smugness covered Susan's face.

Justine stuffed the frustration threatening to explode. "Why would someone dressed as you entice us to meet up?"

Susan's lip twitched, and her gaze flicked to Fredrick. "I'm certain I don't know."

Trey jumped in. "Mrs. Nolan, we also saw you with Dr. Curtis, the medical examiner."

Fredrick glanced up. Was this news to him?

Susan gave a one-shoulder shrug, defiance in her eyes. "You're following me?" She turned to Alex. "That's a violation of my rights!"

He responded with a slight head shake and whispered something to her. She clamped her mouth shut, pinching her lips tightly together.

"I'm curious why you'd meet with the ME." Justine egged on Susan.

She leaned forward, her tone icy. "None of your business."

"If you're interfering with an investigation, it is all my business," Trey countered.

Susan jerked to look at him. "What else would you like to blame on me? World hunger? The financial deficit?"

"Susan—" Alex said.

"The audacity to drag us down here with claims of ambushing, attempted murder and impeding an investigation, meant only to smear our good daughter's name, is unconscionable! They want to desecrate Kayla's final resting place for selfish reasons!" Susan screeched.

"The exhumation is necessary and will be handled with the utmost care and respect for you and Kayla." Justine worked to steady her voice.

"Don't try that with me. Your sword is two-edged and too late. Dr. Curtis assured me he wouldn't exhume Kayla's remains," Susan argued.

"How much did that cost you?" Trey asked.

Susan transferred her glare to him.

"Now you're insinuating she paid off the ME?" Alex snorted.

"Yes." Trey never broke eye contact.

Like a serpent focusing on its prey, Susan slithered her gaze to Justine. "May I remind you, Justine Stark, disputing the prior ME's conclusions has disgraceful repercussions? You provided expert testimony on several cases with him, didn't you? It'd be a shame to have those files reopened and reexamined too."

The venomous words sucked the air from Justine's lungs, and her chest tightened over her racing heart. "I only want what's best for Kayla."

The satisfaction in Susan's expression preempted her next attack. "Let's not pretend you're concerned about anyone besides yourself. Isn't that how it's always been for you? Take care of number one? After all, what do you know about family?" Susan's lips formed into a knowing smirk.

The adrenaline rush caused Justine's ears to ring.

She lowered her shaking hands beneath the table, hiding them from view, unwilling for the Nolans to witness her anxiety. The jab struck so deeply she could scarcely speak. She interlaced her fingers in her lap to prevent grasping her burned arms.

They knew about her father. It wouldn't be hard to find the details, the court records, the newspaper stories. How far would they go to keep her from investigating Kayla's case? Justine averted her eyes but caught a glimpse of Trey's bewilderment.

Her mind raced. Hadn't she spent her life helping others? Hadn't she devoted her work to gaining justice for victims?

Trey spoke again, but Susan's words blared in Justine's brain. What would happen if the district attorney reviewed every case she'd worked with the prior ME? Justine had addressed any mistakes she'd made with the authorities, hadn't she? Nothing egregious that would overturn a conviction, but it might create reasonable doubt. Not only in his work but in her testimony.

Run, her instincts screamed.

"That's enough! I have far better things to do than to sit and listen to this nonsense!" Fredrick shoved his steel chair across the linoleum floor, piercing the space with a loud screech.

Trey stood. "We're not finished."

"Trooper, you've wasted too much of my time. I've already missed an important meeting, and if you're determined to continue this ridiculous round of questioning, I need to notify my next appointment," Fredrick challenged.

"Maybe a small break would be good," Justine offered, hoping to de-escalate the conversation and desperately needing to escape Susan.

"Ten minutes," Trey conceded.

Fredrick stormed from the room.

"I hope you're happy with yourselves." Susan threw up her hands.

"Let's take a short walk and get a cup of coffee," Alex encouraged.

Justine had a new appreciation for the lawyer's way of calming Susan. She busied herself making notes, avoiding Susan's eyes, and remained seated until she and Trey were alone.

The quiet click of the door infused her lungs with breath.

"Are you okay?"

"I have to get out of here." Justine stood and beelined for the exit, then through the parking lot, sucking in the humid evening air.

Trey kept in step. "Better?"

"Nothing like drinking your oxygen." She forced levity into her response, but it fell flat. Justine roamed to a tree and faced the patrol office. "What if she's right?"

"You mean about recalling your cases?"

"Yes. No. It's just an intimidation game." Justine crossed her arms.

"By the look on your face, it was effective."

"Ugh. That bad?" Justine pressed a finger against her temple where a dull headache thrummed. "I worked several investigations with the prior ME. If his findings were off on Kayla's, they could be wrong on the others, as well. If they're all reopened, what will happen to those victims?"

Trey blew out a breath. "Tough call. Don't give Susan

the satisfaction of getting inside your head with what-ifs that may never happen."

Justine's stomach twisted in knots. "I can live with the stain to my reputation. I mean, I don't want that, but it's the lesser of my worries. Trey, I've testified in some horrible cases. Court puts the victims through the wringer." A reel of the heinous stories, those especially involving innocent children and their families, played before her. "They trusted me. How would they endure it again?"

Trey placed his hands on her shoulders, grounding her. "First, the future of others is out of your control. Second, if the Nolans are this emphatic about exhuming Kayla's body, I want to know why. We're getting close to a breakthrough." He stepped back. "I'll stand beside whatever you decide. Maybe we don't need the exhumation."

She studied him, allowing his promise of support to feed her broken soul. She'd always fought alone. What would it be like to have someone in her corner? Strength infused her, and she shook her head. "We're not giving in. Outside of the—" she lowered her voice, glancing around "—diary, the exhumation is the only physical evidence we have. I'm not letting her intimidate me out of this investigation."

"I'm so glad you said that." Trey grinned.

Fredrick walked out of the building, engrossed in a phone conversation.

"We'd better get in there."

"After you." Trey gestured with one arm.

Once inside the air-conditioned building, Justine spotted Susan and Alex at the far end of the hallway, holding cups of coffee. Susan lifted her chin at their entrance and pivoted on her heel, turning her back to them.

"Ever wonder if she'd drown in a rainstorm?" Justine whispered.

Trey chuckled. "That's the Justine Stark super-warrior psychologist I know."

She grinned. "Sorry. That was rude."

"Nah, I'd say it's pretty accurate. And it's given me an idea. Let's do a little divide and conquer."

"How?" Justine worried her lip.

"Follow me."

Trey headed for Susan and Alex, Justine trailing.

Susan stiffened at their approach. "What?"

"We apologize for upsetting you, Mrs. Nolan."

"You should." She sniffed, dabbing at her eyes for effect.

So incredibly fake. Barney could take lessons from Susan. Justine forced a neutral expression.

Trey continued, "Your husband's still on the phone outside. He's a busy man."

"He's very important," Susan said with a dismissive wave.

"It's obvious you bring strength to the relationship. He was pretty quiet in there. Letting you handle the questioning."

Susan shrugged. "Fredrick expects that."

Trey put his hands into his pockets and rocked back on his heels. "You're a nice woman to support him. I'm sure it means sacrificing so much of yourself. Even when he's undeserving of such kindness."

Justine studied Susan's body language. Her shoulders lowered. Oh, Trey was good.

"It's my duty as his wife."

"And you're clearly the rock in the relationship. Pure class." Trey laid it on thick.

Susan's expression softened slightly. "It's not always easy, you know? Fredrick has quite the temper."

"Yes, ma'am. I've done a lot of interviews, and I must say, I can see that brewing beneath the surface. That got me to thinking—" Trey glanced toward the door. "Would you mind if we spoke privately for a moment?"

"Not without Alex," Susan countered.

"Oh, absolutely. You should always have your counsel present. That's why you make the big bucks, right, Mr. Duncan?" Trey shot him a grin.

Alex frowned and fidgeted with his watch. "Okay."

The group returned to the interrogation room, and once seated, Trey said, "Susan, something in your eyes earlier spoke fear to me."

"I'm not afraid of you," she bit back.

"Oh, not me. But I sense there is someone you fear."

Susan glanced down, then at Alex.

He nodded and patted her hand. "It's time. Tell them about Fredrick."

Susan's steel exterior melted, and her lips quivered. "Fine. The truth is, I did make that call to meet you, but Fredrick overheard and threatened to kill me." Her eyes darted nervously to the door.

"Let us help you," Justine said.

"You can't. Leave this case alone. Please. I don't want to end up like Kayla."

Justine shot Trey a look. Was she implying Fredrick had killed Kayla? "We can protect you."

Susan tilted her head. "Alex told me what happened at the garage. You don't understand the kind of man I'm married to. He'll do whatever it takes to stop this investigation."

Trey nodded. "We don't want to endanger you."

Justine forced her mouth shut. What was he saying? Surely, Trey didn't buy these lies. Everything about Susan spoke deception.

Trey continued, "I'm certain you're aware of the seventy-two-hour clock ticking on this case?"

Susan had the decency to nod. "Fredrick contacted the governor."

Trey shrugged. "Perhaps time will just run out. Justine, if Mrs. Nolan fears her husband, what else can we do?"

Justine tried to comprehend Trey's ploy. "May I speak with you outside?"

"Yes, of course. Please excuse us."

They exited the room. "What are you doing?" Justine hissed.

"Follow my lead."

Mr. Nolan reentered the building, and Trey scurried to meet up with him. "Sir, could we speak with you privately?"

He hesitated, then nodded. Trey pulled him into a different interrogation room and closed the door.

"Sir, I'll speak candidly. The evidence implicates you in Kayla's death and the garage bombing," Trey said calmly.

Fredrick jumped to his feet. "What? Are you insane? What evidence?"

"A witness has come forward," Justine inserted. Susan's accusation most likely was a lie, but Justine didn't add that part.

"That's absurd! I've never hurt anyone, especially my own daughter. I must speak with Alex immediately!"

Trey remained seated. "I'm not saying I believe it, but we need proof you're not involved. Signing the exhumation order would be a step in gathering additional evidence to exonerate you."

"With the most recent events, Susan admitted to fearing for her own life," Justine added.

Fredrick blinked. "She's worried someone will try and hurt her?"

Trey nodded. "We have to find the real killer and protect Susan. I know you want what's best for her."

Fredrick slid onto the chair, shaking his head.

Several long seconds passed.

Finally, he said, "Yes, of course. The truth is the sole means to exonerate me from this ridiculous accusation and protect my wife. What do you need from me?"

"Your cooperation," Trey said.

"What about the governor?" Justine asked.

Fredrick nodded. "Consider it done. Bring me the forms needed to authorize the exhumation."

"Thank you, sir." Trey bolted from the room and returned with the documents in seconds.

Once Fredrick had signed the forms, they returned to where Susan and Alex sat waiting. "You're free to go."

Susan quirked an eyebrow, her gaze bouncing between Fredrick and Trey. "What's going on?"

"I've authorized the exhumation," Fredrick said.

Susan jumped to her feet. "No! You can't do that. Fredrick, no!"

"It's for the best, darling," Fredrick pleaded. No longer the strong businessman, now a concerned husband.

"Alex, stop him!"

"I can't, Susan."

Susan pointed a finger at Justine. "You won't get away with this! Dr. Curtis won't perform the examination."

"Dr. Curtis's services aren't needed," Justine said triumphantly.

FBI forensic anthropologist Taya McGill-Stryker was already on her way. For once, Justine had an ally in high places.

TEN

Justine tucked the pillow under her head, exhausted. The bright blue LED letters of her clock read 1:00 a.m. Clover padded across the bed and curled into a ball beside her, purring.

Winds ushered in the promise of a rainstorm, whipping tree branches against the house and waving her bedroom drapes. Justine shoved off the covers and walked to the open window, pausing to glance over the pasture. Fresh air laced with humidity filled her senses, and she tied back the curtains, inviting the breeze in.

"Thank You, Lord." Gratitude overflowed her heart. They were close to solving the case. With Mr. Nolan's capitulation on Kayla's exhumation order and his promise to contact the governor and remove the ridiculous seventy-two-hour restriction, they'd made huge strides. Even Will had happily—or as happily as Will did anything—reported Barney had returned to his food-motivated self.

Things were definitely looking up.

Trey settled on the couch downstairs gave her a sense of comfort, though he probably longed to sleep in his own bed. Everything was coming together, and life would get back to normal. A bittersweet reminder that once they'd completed the investigation, Trey would be gone.

She sighed. That was best for everyone.

Sliding under the cool cotton sheets, Justine exhaled contentment and closed her eyes.

Sleep beckoned, and she willingly drifted off.

A thunderous roar jolted Justine awake, and she glanced at the clock. Nearly 3:00 a.m. Clover's spot was vacant. Probably off hunting for mice somewhere. Lightning splintered the night, illuminating a shadow near the window.

Justine jerked upright, hand groping for the table lamp. The sensation someone watched her sent a shiver tingling down her spine. She flipped on the light and scanned the empty room.

A second roll of thunder and the sky opened, pouring down rain.

Maybe closing the window would be best. Justine scooted off her bed, planting her feet on the cool wooden floor.

Someone grasped her ankles, and she flew forward, landing with a hard thud, and knocked over her side table. The antique lamp crashed and shattered. Hands ripped her backward, dragging her across the old rug.

She clawed at the floor covering, failing to get traction and stop the assault. Her hand caught on a piece of glass, tearing into her skin.

Justine screamed, but the sound was muffled as the attacker smashed her nose into the worn hook braids. She fought, trying to throw him off, but he held her down, smothering her.

Magnum's barks erupted outside the door.

Footsteps and a knock. "Justine, are you okay?"

Trey, help me!

Stars danced in front of her eyes, and she flailed, desperate for air.

The assailant's hand threaded through Justine's hair. He yanked back her head, restricting her cry.

"You should've walked away." He breathed against her ear, then slapped tape over her mouth. A sting in her arm sent a cold tingle oozing through her veins.

Justine jerked, and something toppled to the ground.

He cursed. "No matter. I got enough injected to shut you up."

Dizziness consumed Justine, and her mouth numbed.

The room spun, blurring her surroundings. Her arms were heavy, impossible to move.

"Figuring it out now?" The intruder cackled, something oddly familiar in his tone. He stayed behind Justine. "Don't worry. You'll be wide-awake to enjoy your demise."

"Justine?" Trey knocked again.

In one swift motion, the man hefted Justine, then tossed her onto the bed. He rolled her over and pulled the sheet to her chin, tucking her in. Darkness and a black balaclava disguised his face. "Sweet dreams."

Movement around the room ratcheted up her terror.

And then she smelled it.

Gasoline.

Justine turned her head, heard the splash of liquid hitting the floor.

Oh, Lord, no! Help me!

"Justine!" A thud against the door.

The intruder sat on the windowsill. "He won't get in

to save you." A flash of lightning silhouetted his terrifying presence.

Thunder crashed, just as the man dropped the match, igniting the trail of gasoline. Like a speeding race car, the blaze zipped from the window to the door.

Frantic, Justine tried to roll, willing her body to move, but the quicksand of her bed held her down.

"Justine!"

Three repetitive thuds.

Smoke filled the space, burning her lungs.

A macabre dance of orange flames engulfed the room, a juxtaposition to the torrential downpour outside.

And the memories came crashing in, surrounding her with their terrifying claws. Dragging her back to the night of her father's attempt to kill her and her mother.

But then, rescue had come in time.

Tonight, she would die.

"Justine! Hang on!" Trey called through the fog in her mind.

"Hang on," a voice repeated, sounding so much like sweet Mrs. Scranton, the brave neighbor who'd pulled her from the inferno.

The woman who'd rescued Justine not just from the flames but from her nightmare childhood.

But Mrs. Scranton wasn't here now.

Smoke stung her eyes, and she squeezed them shut. *Lord, fight for me.*

The heat intensified around her.

"Magnum, stay back!"

Strong arms lifted her. She was flying.

Then moving swiftly. Justine couldn't open her eyes.

"I'm here. I'm here." Trey's voice carried to her.

Water splashed onto her face, and she sucked in a breath.

Painful coughs racked her body. Trey rolled her to the side, and she wheezed, gasping. Her lungs fought against the smoke's intrusion.

"Are you okay?" Trey leaned closer. "Can you sit up?"

Justine blinked, rain cascading down her face. Unable to move, she watched the long wisps of fire reach out from her bedroom window.

"Send rescue. Structure fire, one party injured," Trey said. "Help's on the way. There's—"

Barking in the distance. Justine turned her head and spotted flames from the Dog House.

Trey was already running across the property.

This wasn't happening.

Her boys! Justine forced her energy into moving her hand, finally gaining a weak response from her fingers. The progress infused her with hope.

Frantic barks from the Dog House tore at her heart.

Were they okay? *Lord, help Trey!*

She couldn't see him, and he'd been gone too long. Where was Will?

Tingling returned to her hands, and Justine groped at the wet ground, nails grazing the grass and digging into the dirt beneath. The fire danced into the night air, stretching too close to the tree beside the house. She forced herself up and crawled across the lawn.

Six canines and Clover bounded toward her, then smothered Justine in a flurry of licks, wagging tails and the comfort of wet dog smell.

Trey rushed back to her side. "They're all okay. Can you stand?"

"Will," she gasped in reply.

Trey helped her up on wobbly legs. He braced her with an arm around her waist. "Will." She coughed.

"He wasn't in the building. In fact, he's nowhere to be found." The accusation in Trey's tone struck a fresh wound to her heart.

Will wouldn't do this.

Would he?

Sirens screamed in the distance, and the strobing lights of the fire truck and ambulance added to the fire's radiance. The rescue vehicles pulled onto the property. Trey hoisted her into his arms, running for the two medics who'd burst from the rig.

"I think she's been injected with something. She's struggling to move and speak." Trey placed her onto the stretcher as a female paramedic leaned in.

The woman ran her hands over Justine's arm. "I see a puncture wound. Ma'am, do you know what you were injected with?"

Justine shook her head.

"We need to get her to the hospital."

No. She couldn't leave the ranch. Her boys. "No!" Justine said, startling herself. "It's. Wearing. Off," she stammered.

Trey corralled the dogs, securing their leashes. He moved them away from the burning buildings.

Justine gaped at the fire raging all around her.

Would the nightmare ever end?

Trey stood beside the garage. A mixture of fury, self-disdain and sorrow weighed down his shoulders.

A firefighter approached. Trey tried to remember his name but came up blank.

"It's clear. We restricted the flames to the bedroom

where they started, but there will be smoke and water damage throughout the house. Once daylight hits, the fire marshal will come and check it out."

"It's arson," Trey said.

"Yep, accelerant marks around the bedroom prove that. Miss Stark is refusing to go to the hospital." He gestured to where Justine sat on the lawn, gaping at the house.

"Somehow, that doesn't surprise me." Trey shook the man's hand. "Thanks for everything."

Trey surveyed the damage as the firefighters and paramedics exited the property. Thankfully, the rains had helped stave off the flames, but the structures appeared badly damaged, and his heart hurt for Justine. Wet ash and soot lingered in the air, mingling with the fresh smell after the storm.

The constant condemning thoughts battled for attention. How had he let this happen? Who would do this?

He'd fallen asleep, but not before doing a full walk-through of the home and surrounding buildings. How had he not heard the intruder? Even Magnum hadn't warned him. Had the interloper been inside the entire time, waiting? Or had Magnum not reacted because he was familiar with the man?

And if that was the case, Will topped his suspect list. Trey had issued a BOLO for Will, who'd mysteriously disappeared after they'd spoken last night.

Fury boiled his blood.

The sun would rise soon, and they'd determine the full extent of the loss. And their next steps.

Justine walked toward him, caressing Clover and accompanied by all five rescue dogs, keeping watch over their rescuer.

"Hey. Feeling better?"

Justine shrugged. "Whatever the jerk injected me with wore off quickly. The paramedic said he must've missed or failed to get it all inside the vein. Still no sign of Will?"

"No, but are you really surprised?" Trey bit his tongue. Now wasn't the time. Once he pulled up the cameras, he'd have the proof against Will to convince Justine.

The rescue rigs disappeared from sight.

"Why would someone do this? Don't answer that. I'm sure it's pretty obvious." Justine turned to Trey's pickup. "If you hadn't suggested locking the diary in your tool-box last night, it would've been destroyed."

Perfect segue. Trey rushed to the truck, dropping the tailgate and entering the code on the lockbox. Justine joined him, and Trey tugged open the drawer, withdrawing the damp book. "Good thing you remembered. It still needs to air out."

She took the diary, holding it gingerly. "I need to keep the pages separated so they don't dry together. Let's go inside and see if there's anything salvageable from the case files."

"Let me grab my laptop."

Justine waited beside the porch steps, apprehension in her expression.

"Ready?"

They moved through the house, Justine's footsteps slowing as they entered the hallway, then walked into the back room, directly below her bedroom. Soot and water dripped from the ceiling. The files were saturated, along with Justine's evidence board.

Trey collected the box, and they went outside. "We'd better head to a hotel."

Justine's laugh held bitterness. "And what hotel is going to take my five dogs and overfed cat?" She gestured to the menagerie. "I'm not leaving."

"You can't stay in there." Trey pointed to the house.

"It's almost daylight. Not as if I'll get a ton of sleep. We can sit out here." Justine slid onto the porch swing.

The sun peeked over the horizon, filling the sky with streaks of orange and blue.

Dropping beside her, Trey placed his laptop on his legs and logged in. "Maybe the cameras caught the perp."

He focused first on the house cameras.

"Got him." Justine leaned closer to the laptop and pointed to a shadow slinking near the side of the house. "He avoids the cameras, as if he knows they're there."

Trey shifted to the barn's vantage point. If he caught Will sneaking out of the structure, Justine would have to believe him. The video showed Will entering the outbuilding around midnight, after they'd parted for the evening. Then the screen went black and remained off.

"Did someone disconnect the camera?" Justine asked.

"Someone who knew it was there," Trey clarified, selecting the footage to before they'd returned to the ranch. He watched with the intensity of a starving hawk.

The screen came to life, revealing Will sitting on the countertop in the barn. His cell rang. "What? I'm working. I'll get the money. Just need a little more time."

He sighed and stuffed the phone into his pocket.

Justine met Trey's eyes.

Motive.

They continued watching as Will walked to each ken-

nel, grumbling as he opened the doors, leaving Barney
for last.

Trey gripped the laptop's edge. If he hurt that dog...

"Boys, I'm in a mess. Y'all are the only friends I
have." Will dropped to the floor beside Barney, and the
other canines surrounded him. "Nobody wants to em-
ploy an old codger full-time, but I can't make it on these
side jobs. I need to move and find real work, but how am
I s'posed to up and leave Justine? She needs my help."

Barney whined and thumped his tail.

"You understand what it's like, being unwanted, don't
ya, boy?" Will leaned against the wall and closed his
eyes. "Lord, You're our Provider. Please make a way for
me and Justine. Even that annoying cop friend of hers.
Justine's trying hard to be a light in a dark world. Bless
her, Lord, and somehow allow me to be here for her. I'm
grateful You're using an old homeless man."

Trey paused the video, loath to speak the words Justine deserved to hear. "I might've been wrong about
Will."

Justine's eyes shone with satisfaction. "Humility is
a wonderful trait." She sobered. "Will's not the monster you labeled him, but it doesn't explain where he is."

Why would Will disappear? Or had the intruder gotten to him? He thought about the tree house incident.
Was Will in danger?

"Let's check out the Dog House." Trey set down his
laptop and led the way to the barn.

The door had been removed by the firefighters, and
it, like the house, dripped wet from the fire hoses. The
dogs wandered in, sniffing around the room.

"Trey, look!" Justine pointed to Will's accommodations. His bed was unmade, and his boots were beside

the bed. "Will's in trouble. He'd never leave without his boots, or that."

They rushed to the black Stetson lying on the floor.

"Magnum." The dog moved obediently to Trey's side. He held out the hat and boots. "Track."

Magnum sniffed both and shot out the door, forcing Trey and Justine to jog to catch up. The Malinois scurried through the property to the old brick silo, circling the building several times, then poked his head through one of the square open spaces. He dropped to a sit and barked.

"He's alerting!" Justine cried.

Using his phone's flashlight app, Trey illuminated the inside of the silo. A familiar form lay still on the ground. "Will!"

Trey squeezed through the space and moved to Will's side. A big gash on his head bled profusely, but his pulse was strong. "We'll have to work together to get him out of here."

Trey gently lifted him and walked to the windows. He and Justine shimmied Will through and lowered him to the ground.

Will groaned.

"He's coming to." Justine ran to the garage and returned with a first-aid kit to cleanse the wound.

"What happened?" Will asked groggily.

"I was going to ask the same question," Trey said.

Will blinked, squinting at him. "A man. Saw him for a second. Then everything went black."

The same intruder? "Do you remember anything about him?"

"No. Something woke me up. I walked outside and got whacked upside the head."

"What time was that?" Trey mentally established a timeline.

"Not long after I'd gone to bed."

Trey helped Will to his feet, and they walked to the porch swing. Justine grabbed bottles of water from the fridge.

"We should get you to a hospital. You need stitches," Justine said.

"I ain't going to no hospital. Slap a Band-Aid on it, and it'll be fine," Will groused.

"Sorry, man. She's right," Trey said.

Will shook his head. "Can't afford no more bills."

"Why didn't you tell me you were having money issues?" Justine asked.

Will's neck jerked up. "Who told you?"

Justine bit her lip and looked at Trey. He sucked in a breath. She'd said humility was a great trait, though he doubted Will would agree.

"After the last break-in, I installed cameras on Justine's house and the barn," Trey confessed.

"Did they catch the creep that did this to me?" Will asked. Then, as if a light bulb appeared over his head, Will's eyes narrowed.

Trey braced for the explosion.

"Wait a minute. You spied on me?"

"It's not like that," Justine interjected.

"I wasn't sure you were trustworthy, Will. I misjudged you, and I'm sorry," Trey said. "By the way, I owe you a new Stetson."

Will opened his mouth, then closed it again. After a few seconds, he said, "No idea what that means, but I can't fault you for wanting what's best for Justine and the boys. So, uh, you saw me, uh, talking to the boys?"

Trey grinned.

Will sighed. "They're good listeners, and they don't charge me to whine."

"Canine therapy is the best," Trey agreed, ruffling Magnum's fur.

"Yeah, I s'pose you get that. Fact is, I'm embarrassed."

Justine touched his shoulder. "Don't be."

Will shrugged. "May as well come clean. Truth is, I've taken every job possible, but there ain't enough hours in the day to get them all done. And I didn't want to leave you in a lurch."

"I'm truly sorry, Will. I should've told you about the cameras." Justine shook her head.

"It's on me," Trey said.

"Nah, this is your property. You got the right to have surveillance equipment, although if they didn't catch the guy, seems they weren't installed properly." Will flicked a glance at Trey.

He absorbed the hit. It was true. The three cameras should've caught something to help them identify the intruder. "He knew to avoid them."

"You think he scoped out the place first?" Will asked.

"Must've." Trey rubbed the back of his neck.

Will frowned. "Could've come around when I wasn't paying attention. That's on me."

"You've been a godsend to me, Will. I'm grateful for all that you've done. Whoever is out to stop this investigation has made it their personal mission to destroy me. I wouldn't blame you for running for the hills right now." Justine glanced down.

"I don't run from nothin' and no one," Will asserted.

"Your insurance should cover the repairs," Trey said. The reply was weak and offered no real solution.

"Let's hope," Justine agreed. "But Will can't wait on a settlement's slow progress. I've got a little savings. We can use whatever's there to get started."

"Nathan Yancy owes me. I'll drag his young self out here to help," Will said.

Trey nodded. "With us in your corner, we'll figure something out. One day at a time."

"Can't take 'em no other way." Will snorted.

Trey chuckled and offered Will a handshake. "So, you're in?"

"You ain't seen nothin' yet. This old dog's still got some fight in him."

ELEVEN

Justine's breath hitched in her throat at the long rows of headstones and the spattering of color where loved ones' flowers spoke of their losses.

"You okay?" Trey asked, parking the truck.

"Yes."

"Will and Slade have things under control at the ranch. We have bigger fish to bake."

"Fry," Justine corrected.

Trey laughed. "Oliver's colloquialisms are wearing off on me."

Susan and Fredrick stood beside the large tractor prepared to tear into the ground.

"Nice to see their out-of-state trip allowed them to return in time for this," Trey said.

After asking for Susan to be brought in for questioning, Trey and Justine learned the Nolans had called Sergeant Oliver to notify him they'd be coming straight from the airport, having been out of town for a fundraising event. Their social media pictures provided proof of their airtight alibis for the night of the fire.

The walk to the grave was somber, and they stood at a distance, watching as the tractor's jaws removed layers of dirt, revealing the casket beneath. The worker hoisted the box from the ground and placed it on the trailer.

Trey and Justine returned to his pickup and drove to the Omaha hospital where Taya McGill-Stryker prepped for the exam.

Entering the area just outside the pathology lab, Justine rushed to hug her friend. "Taya, thank you so much for coming."

They exchanged pleasantries and Taya said, "The remains should be ready. There was a little delay in getting them here. Something about car trouble. However, you won't be allowed in the lab. You can watch through the glass though." She disappeared through the swinging doors.

Justine and Trey moved to the lab viewing-room window. A steel table and a rectangular tool tray sat beside the casket. Taya entered, and the assistant lifted the lid.

A long pause.

"What's going on?" Trey whispered.

"I don't know."

Taya shook her head. She removed her gloves and exited the lab. Within a few seconds, she walked over to Trey and Justine. "We have a problem. There's no body."

"What?" Trey and Justine chimed in unison.

"The casket's empty."

"How's that possible? We were there when it was dug up," Trey insisted.

Taya lifted her hands. "All I can tell you is it's empty now."

"Was it left alone at any time?" Trey pressed.

"Only with the driver." Taya paused, then scurried out of the room.

Trey and Justine followed her to the loading area. The driver and truck were gone.

"Guess that explains the delay in the delivery." Taya shook her head.

Trey slammed his hands on the wall. "Unbelievable!"

Justine slumped onto a hard plastic chair. Her cell rang, interrupting the conversation, and she glanced at the screen before hitting Ignore.

"The Nolans got to the casket and stole the body," Trey said.

Justine's phone rang again with the same number. "Excuse me." She hurried from the loading dock, answering the call. "Justine Stark."

"Miss Stark, this is Mr. Krendal. I'm sorry to bother you during your time of mourning, but I'm the funeral director at Dearly Departed in Omaha, and your name is listed as the guarantor for the Grammert funeral."

"I beg your pardon?"

"Mrs. Victoria Grammert advised you'd be responsible for the bill. I'm sorry, but I must insist on payment before the services today, or we will not be able to fulfill our commitment."

Justine sucked in a breath. "What are you talking about? Ignaseus Grammert is dead?"

"Yes, ma'am, and the services are this afternoon at four o'clock. Without payment—"

"Do you have a number for Mrs. Grammert?"

"Yes." Mr. Krendal rattled off the ten digits.

"Please give me a moment. I'll call you right back." Justine disconnected and dialed the number.

"Hello." Victoria's quivering voice carried through the line.

"Mother, this is Justine. I just spoke with Mr. Krendal."

"Don't worry—I didn't tell him the great Justine Stark, criminal psychologist, was related to the lowly convict Ignaseus Grammert. I simply listed you as the guarantor of the services. A good daughter who would pay for her daddy's funeral."

How did her mother have the power to use Justine's achievements as swords to attack her with? Trey exited the loading dock and paused.

Justine shook her head and held up a hand, signaling him to stay back. "When did he die?"

"Why do you care? You wrote us off for that hag, Mrs. Scranton. But the least you can do is pay for your father's burial. You won't even have to leave the comfort of your home to do that."

The words were tiny daggers to Justine's heart. "When did he pass?" she asked again.

Trey moved closer, but Justine couldn't look at him. Yet she didn't walk away.

A part of her needed his comforting presence.

"Last week." Victoria sniffled.

Always the actress.

"So? Are you going to do the respectful thing? It's a daughter's duty."

Guilt swarmed Justine. She strove to behave honorably in everything. Did she owe it to her parents to absorb the costs? For once, maybe her mother had a point. Justine swallowed hard. "Yes. I'll handle the payment."

"Good." Victoria disconnected.

Justine pocketed her phone, her gaze fixed on the small octagon floor tiles. Her father was gone.

"Justine?" Trey slid beside her. "Are you okay?"

She turned as the ground gave out beneath her. Trey caught her in an embrace. Justine clung to him, allowing the tears to fall freely.

They stood that way until Justine could speak again.

"What happened? Who died?" Trey spoke softly, caressing her hair.

"My father." The words were so foreign. She backed away and dug out a tissue.

"Oh, I'm so sorry. Do you want to talk about it?"

She withdrew her phone. "Give me a few minutes alone, please. I need to call Mr. Krendal."

The need to be in control had Justine shifting into professionalism.

Trey nodded, then shoved his hands into his pockets and exited the room.

Justine secured the total amount for the funeral and agreed to meet Mr. Krendal at the home an hour before the services. She'd pay her respects without the other attendees seeing her and slip out before her mother arrived.

But the cost would drain a huge part of her savings account. What would she do about the ranch? How would she cover Will's labor and the supplies? Her head ached with the overwhelming questions stacking in a towering pile.

Trey returned with a cup of coffee for her. "I talked with Taya and she agreed to stick around. We're not letting the Nolans get away with this. I spoke to the hospital security manager and got footage of the driver, Pete Lucas, from their cameras. Sergeant Oliver is sending Eric the Vulture to bring Pete in for questioning."

"Good." Justine swallowed the lump in her throat. "Mind if we take a walk?"

"Sure. Let's get Magnum too."

With Magnum leashed, they strolled to a nearby park.

"I hate to ask this, but I need a ride to the funeral home later today."

"Of course. Whatever you require."

Justine smiled. "Somehow, I don't doubt you mean that, but you have no idea how much I could ask right now."

Trey stopped and faced her. "I'd do anything for you. I know that's corny, but it's true."

She shook her head. "Not if you really knew me."

Trey took her hand, enveloping it with his own. "Try me."

The need to unburden herself with why her father's death hurt but not like it would for a normal daughter propelled Justine forward.

They walked to a stone bench and sat.

"Sure you want to hear this?"

"Absolutely." Trey petted Magnum. "You have our undivided attention."

She chuckled. "Well, until he spots a squirrel or something."

Trey laughed. "Fair enough."

"My father's name is Ignaseus Grammert. My mother is Victoria. I changed my last name when I was eighteen and took my maternal grandmother's surname. I divorced myself from my parents."

Trey didn't speak and she continued, "You're probably thinking what an ungrateful brat I am."

"Actually, I'm wondering what pain caused you to make that drastic change."

She bit her quivering lip. His compassion squeezed her heart. "My father was physically abusive. Always angry. My mother sided with him. No matter what. Our home put the *fun* in *dysfunction*."

He chuckled. "Sorry."

She smiled. "No, I have to joke or I'll cry again."

He nodded. "I understand. Family relationships are the toughest. The old adage 'hurting people hurt people' applies here, because your parents both lived out of their pain. That's not an excuse."

"Yes. And I agree with the statement. I don't think anyone wakes up one morning determined to destroy another person's life. Even in murder cases I've worked, the act itself was rarely premeditated. More like an emotional volcano that burst."

"Attending your father's funeral would be closure for you."

He didn't understand. She removed her button-up shirt, revealing the matching tank top beneath it, and showed him the burn scars covering her arms. "That night, my father beat me senseless. For the first time, my mother tried to protect me, and he went after her too. We were unconscious when he covered the room in gasoline and lit the house on fire. Our next-door neighbor, a widow named Mrs. Scranton, heard the fire alarms going off and saw the flames." Justine's throat tightened. "She pulled us both from the blaze. One of those things where a person gets crazy strong and overcomes natural odds by sheer adrenaline. Anyway, she saved our lives. But my mother defended my father's actions and stood by him, even after he was convicted."

Trey's mouth hung open. "I don't know what to say."

Justine donned her shirt again, covering the scars. "I forgave them both years ago. At least, I started the process of forgiveness. Days like today, I feel as though

I haven't made much progress. My mother signed my name guaranteeing the payment for my father's funeral."

"If you want to go, I'll be right beside you. If you decide it's too much to deal with, I'll support you. Whatever you need, I'm here for you." The sincerity in Trey's eyes consumed Justine.

She looked down, and Trey took her hands in his, grounding her. "Why are you so good to me?"

"Because you're the most beautiful woman I've ever known. Inside and out."

Captured by his words, Justine was flooded with unfamiliar emotions.

Their gazes held while the rest of the world faded away.

Justine surrendered to her heart's cry, feathering her lips against Trey's. Their kiss was tender, tentative and full of promise.

Trey paced outside the interrogation-room door, his patience waning.

"You're making me nervous," Justine whispered.

"We know Pete's involved in the theft of Kayla's remains. Why is he lawyering up?"

Footsteps at the end of the hallway halted Trey's words. Alex Duncan approached. "I'll be Mr. Lucas's legal representative."

Trey glanced at Justine. "I should be astonished you're representing Lucas, but my surprise-meter is flat pegged out."

Alex held his briefcase with both hands, a smirk playing at the corners of his lips. "I will need a moment to confer with my client."

"Have at it." Trey gestured toward the room.

Justine blocked the entry and shifted out of the way, allowing Alex to enter. He closed the door softly behind him.

"This is ridiculous. Why can't we just haul in the Nolans?" Justine's question was more comment than inquiry.

Trey resumed pacing the hallway until Alex peered out.

"We're ready," he announced.

Justine entered first, and they moved to the chairs across the table from Pete and Alex.

Pete's knee bounced, and he bit a fingernail with nervous vigor.

Guilty. "I'm curious why you're his lawyer," Trey said.

"Pete's worked for the Nolans in the past, and they wanted to help him," Alex said dryly.

Trey snorted. "Now that your *attorney* is here, tell me where Kayla Nolan's remains are."

Alex's blank facial expression matched his monotone response. "My client is only responsible for exhuming the casket, which you both witnessed. He provided that service appropriately and efficiently."

"Right up to the point where he detoured and the contents mysteriously disappeared," Trey snapped.

Pete opened his mouth, but Alex shook his head. "The contents aren't his responsibility."

"They are when he either organized or performed the theft," Trey said.

Pete leaned forward, a bead of sweat easing down his brow. "I only did what I was—"

"Don't say another word or I cannot help you," Alex instructed.

Pete slunk down in the seat and resumed fingernail biting and knee bouncing.

"We have security-camera footage showing Pete pulling up at the hospital twenty minutes after the expected arrival time. That gives him plenty of opportunity to drop off the remains somewhere else. I will recommend charging your client with obstruction of justice, among other things." Trey stood.

Pete jumped up. "No!" He addressed Alex. "You said—"

Alex placed a hand on the young man's shoulder, pulling him down. "I said we would handle this." Then to Trey, "My client may have information on the body's location, but before we say anything, I want the assurance that he will not be implicated in any way."

Justine jerked to look at Trey, desperation in her expression. "We need the remains."

As if that were news, but Trey agreed. Charging Lucas would only delay the exhumation. Still, allowing him to go unpunished somehow rewarded the Nolans. Trey leaned back and crossed his arms. "If I get information—solid, verifiable details—and the remains are recovered in their entirety, I will not recommend charges against him."

Alex slapped both hands on the table and Pete startled in his chair. "Very good. We'll be in touch." Alex stood. "Let's get you out of here."

Trepidation hung in Pete's eyes, but he willingly followed Alex from the room.

Justine rose and peered out the door, then closed it. "What if he doesn't provide anything?"

"He will."

Ten minutes later, a text message rang through with

GPS coordinates from an unknown number. "Chicken," Trey mumbled.

"He sent the information?" Justine looked over his shoulder.

"Possibly. It came from a blocked number. I'll ask Sergeant Oliver to handle it from here. You and I need to leave for the funeral."

Justine glanced down. "Yeah, I guess so."

Oliver answered on the first ring. "Well?"

"Alex Duncan's representing Lucas," Trey began.

Oliver mumbled something unpleasant. "Did he give you anything?"

"Yeah, as long as we don't charge Lucas. I had to agree to it, boss. We need the remains."

"That should've been my decision, but I'd have done the same. And?"

"I'll text you the message with the location that Alex sent over." Trey concluded the call with the request to have Oliver accompany Taya.

"Consider it handled. I'll stay with her through the examination, as well. Please give Justine our condolences."

"Will do. Thanks, boss."

"Everything okay?" Justine asked.

"Yep." Trey offered his most encouraging smile, and they walked out to the truck.

The funeral home wasn't far from the patrol office, and a few cars filled the parking lot. They'd arrived early enough to avoid the mourners.

Trey and Magnum accompanied Justine to the business office, where she paid the bill. He stood outside the door, but his cop instincts took over and he listened in. When Krendal announced the amount due, Trey sucked in a breath. Her mother had apparently spared no expense since Justine was responsible. A slow simmer of anger welled inside him.

Justine made no qualms about it but silently handed over her credit card. Trey wondered how the drain on her finances would affect the repairs to the ranch. As much as he wanted to rush in and settle the bill for her, Trey knew it wasn't his place.

"Mr. Krendal, would it be possible for me to pay my respects before the visitation?" Justine asked.

"Absolutely."

She exited the office with a blank expression. Her gait was stiff, almost robotic, as Krendal led them to the viewing. Soft music played, and an open casket stood at the front of the room.

"Take your time." Krendal closed the doors behind them.

"Would you like me to go with you?" Trey asked.

Justine shook her head.

He waited with Magnum at the last row.

She didn't move for several beats. Then, in painfully slow steps, she approached the casket. Trey's heart squeezed, desperate to help her and completely clueless how to do that.

She'd nearly reached the casket when a slender woman with strikingly similar features to Justine's entered from a side door. "You've got a lot of nerve. Don't touch him."

"Hello, Mother." Justine's voice was steely, but Trey recognized the vulnerability beneath the tough exterior.

He stepped forward. This was Victoria Grammert? "Excuse me."

Victoria's lip curled. "This is *my* husband's funeral. I have the right to say who can and cannot be here, Officer." She practically spit the last word. "Did you handle the bill?"

"Yes," Justine answered.

Satisfaction covered Victoria's face. "Good. Then you're free to go." She waved them off. "Don't waste your time pretending you care about me or your father."

Justine held her chin high. "I'd like to pay my respects."

"Why? I haven't had a daughter for twenty years. You're a stranger, and strangers aren't welcome here."

People began filing into the room.

Justine stood frozen just a few feet from the coffin.

Trey moved to her side. "Let's go."

Victoria stepped forward, blocking Justine. "Get out! You're too good for us. Always have been. You turned your back on us. You kept him behind those prison walls! You stopped him from having a real life, just to hang on to your bitterness." Victoria's voice rose with each word.

Trey put an arm around Justine's waist. "Come on. Let's go."

She nodded, shuffling beside him. A woman ran to the front to comfort the now-wailing Victoria, and the other mourners looked on with curiosity.

The trip to the truck was excruciating.

"I'm so sorry, Justine."

She released a bitter laugh. "I walked into that."

"You did the right thing, and you did not deserve that attack."

"Maybe I did." Justine glanced down, one hand rubbing her arm.

"Don't let Victoria do that to you. She's angry and hurting. I'm sure she didn't mean those awful things."

Trey hoped that was true, but something told him Victoria intended the cruelty and the show.

"Oh, she did." Justine looked up, tears welling in her eyes.

Trey reached for her, and she crumbled into his arms, her body racked with sobs.

He shouldn't have encouraged Justine to attend the funeral. Seeing her hurt was agonizing, and he longed to take away her pain. *Lord, I need wisdom here.*

He turned so Justine's back faced the people filing into the building. Several glanced at them. Did they know Justine was Ignaseus's daughter? A few pointed and shook their heads.

He held Justine tighter, anxious to guard her from their judgmental faces. And in that moment, Trey realized he needed Justine in a way he'd never needed anyone before.

She was much more than a colleague. He cared what happened to her. He wanted her to be happy. He wanted to protect her.

He wanted to be a part of her life.

But what if she didn't feel the same way? She'd established defined boundaries of their relationship.

Yet they'd shared a kiss. One that had rocked him to his core, igniting a place in his heart reserved for only Justine.

Trey's cell phone rang, dragging him to the present, but he didn't move.

Justine leaned back. "Answer it. I'm okay."

"It's Oliver," Trey said, glancing at the screen. "Sir."

"The body has been secured. Dr. McGill-Stryker will begin her examination immediately."

Trey exhaled relief. Finally, some good news. "Outstanding."

"Jackson, you should know the Nolans have gone to the colonel."

"With what?"

Oliver sighed. "They're accusing you and Miss Stark of an inappropriate relationship, claiming it's interfering with the case and the profile."

"That's ridiculous!" Trey paced an area beside his truck, feeling Justine's eyes on him.

Were the Nolans following them?

"I'm a realist, Jackson, and it wouldn't be the first time romance invaded a case," Oliver said, referring to Trey's brother, Slade, who'd fallen for a murder suspect.

"That's not what's happening here. Miss Stark and I are purely professional and platonic. Neither of us has any romantic interest in the other."

Justine faced him, hurt in her eyes.

"See that you keep it professional. Otherwise, I'll have to take you off the case."

"Understood." Trey disconnected.

Justine folded her arms, donning her clinical exterior. "Now what?"

He reluctantly gave her an abbreviated version of the discussion.

"Of course there's nothing going on between us. We shared a kiss—that never should've happened—but surely they didn't see that? Even if they did, it meant nothing." Justine's tone hardened.

"Are you upset with me?"

"No. We're partnered on a case. I appreciate the kindness you offered for my father's funeral. It won't be needed again." Justine gripped the truck door handle. "Let's get moving."

Trey loaded Magnum and slid behind the wheel.

Justine sat erect in the seat, face set like flint.

"There's good news. Kayla's remains have been recovered, and Dr. McGill-Stryker will start the exam immediately."

Justine nodded. "Great."

"You've had an awful day. Let's head back to the ranch so you can rest."

"No, we have to keep working. I need the distraction, and if the Nolans are as unreliable about the seventy-two hours as they have been about everything else, we can't risk running out of time. We have the case files— or what's left of them after the water damage—with us. Let's find a place to go through them."

"We can return to the patrol office so that we're close to where Dr. McGill-Stryker is working."

"Perfect."

The drive was too quiet, but Trey was at a loss for words.

Once seated in the room, they spread out the files.

An insurance document caught Trey's eye. "The Nolans had a life insurance policy on Kayla."

"How much?"

"Seven hundred thousand." He scanned the document. "It was paid out to them—" he pointed to the case file "—just prior to Drazin's retirement date."

"The amount is odd. Not a million or half a million?" Justine asked.

"An off amount would deflect from suspicion?"

"But why? They're not in dire straits. Who's the beneficiary?"

"They are."

"They could've hired someone to kill Kayla or…" Justine hesitated, a pen pressed against her lips. "You said it was paid out before Drazin retired. What if he was the recipient?"

"It should be easy enough to trace." But Sergeant Oliver's warning rang in Trey's mind. He couldn't accuse Drazin of taking a bribe, and as much as he didn't like the guy, he didn't believe he'd murdered Kayla. "We need the Nolans' financial records."

Trey typed an email to Sergeant Oliver, making the formal request.

"May I look at the insurance policy?"

Trey passed her the document.

Justine's eyes widened. "Hmm, interesting. There's a Slayer Rule to the policy."

"You lost me."

"If the Nolans are found to be involved in Kayla's death, they'd have to repay the money. Let's park this for now until we can get a hold of their financial records." Justine's phone rang. "It's Alex Duncan."

"Put it on speaker."

"Hello, Alex," Justine said.

"Miss Stark. I need to talk to you."

"We're here at the patrol office."

"No. You and Trey must meet with me in person. Enough is enough. I have what you need, but if the Nolans discover I'm the one who gave it to you, I'm a dead man."

"Alex, why should we believe you?" Trey asked.

"You shouldn't, but I can tell you that without the evidence I have, you'll never solve the case. With it, you'll have everything you need for a conviction. So I guess you'll have to decide if it's worth it to you."

Justine met Trey's eyes. He gave a slight nod.

"Okay. Where?"

"I'll send you the address. Meet me there at ten o'clock tonight. I have one chance to right the wrong done to Kayla."

TWELVE

"Remind me why we're doing this." Justine walked the perimeter of the abandoned warehouse, her footsteps echoing. The dank smell of dust and mold filled the atmosphere.

"I'm asking myself the same question, but Alex has evidence. Maybe he grew a conscience or got tired of Susan's antics. Who knows? At least this time we're prepared with backup." Trey withdrew his gun and checked his magazine.

"I'm amazed you requested Eric Irwin's help." Justine peered through a corner of a spiderweb-covered window. She searched the parking lot, but Irwin was nowhere to be seen. Not that he would be, since he was hidden, watching the exterior.

A comfort and a concern.

"Okay, let's not confuse technicalities. I didn't request Irwin. I requested backup and Oliver offered Irwin. Big difference," Trey clarified.

She chuckled. "Duly noted. It's progress for your relationship."

"Doubtful." His cell phone buzzed, and he placed the call on speaker. "We're in position."

"Same here," Eric replied. "No one has gone in or out. Sure you don't want Apollo to do recon?"

Trey rolled his eyes and Justine stifled a giggle. "No, we've got it, but if you see anything—"

"We'll come to your rescue," Eric concluded.

Trey visibly bristled. "Or just cover us."

"Roger that."

Pocketing his phone, Trey said, "He's nothing if not enthusiastic. There's still time, if you'd rather stay with Irwin. Magnum and I can handle Alex and you'd be at a safer distance."

"No way." They'd had this conversation ten ways from Sunday already.

"Stay here. I want to do one more run-through."

Justine hopped up onto a cement dock space and watched as Trey and Magnum moved through the small warehouse, clearing it with expertise and precision. An office near the back was void, except for a file cabinet, and the rest of the building was a large open area. A few pallets littered the floor. Otherwise, it too was empty.

Trey returned to her side. "He's running late."

"What's the evidence Alex is holding?"

"I don't know, but it better be good."

Magnum sat panting at Trey's feet, clad in his camouflage-patterned, patrol–K-9 vest.

"Poor guy. It's hot in here. I can't imagine wearing fur and a vest," Justine said, petting the sweet dog.

"The vest gives me a way to carry him in an emergency, and it's bulletproof."

Justine straightened. "In that case, keep it on him. He seems to be moving better, not favoring one side as much."

"I noticed that too." Trey glanced at his watch. "Alex's got five minutes, and we're out of here."

Justine reached into her pocket and withdrew the diary. "Can I borrow your flashlight?"

"How about teamwork? I'll hold. You read."

"Works for me." Justine inspected the book, careful to separate the pages. "It's dry and most of the pages are legible." She flipped to the end and pressed the journal flat on her thighs. "Oh, there's a little damage to the back cover." A corner of the last page was lifted. "Hey, move that light here."

Trey did as she asked, and Justine gently wedged her fingers beneath the crinkled paper. "It looks like these extra pages were glued down on purpose."

"Why do that?"

Justine further separated them, revealing a small silver key. "What do we have here?" She pried the key from the tiny pocket and passed it to Trey.

"It's too small to open a door. A lockbox? Or a padlock?" He handed it back, and she turned it over in her hand.

"I don't know. But it's obviously important." Justine peeled the paper back even more. "And she wrote *Underwood Machler* beside it."

"A name? Location?"

Justine shrugged.

"Did she write anything about the key in the diary?" Trey asked.

"I don't think so. I didn't memorize the book, but I don't remember anything that said 'by the way, I hid a key that has whatever in it,'" she teased.

"Funny."

Justine slipped the key into the diary and dropped it

into her pants pocket. They hadn't talked about the Nolans' accusation or Trey's emphatic denial of a romantic relationship. Logic told her there was nothing wrong
with what he'd said, but her pride stung. The shared kiss
was an impulsive, emotional action. Nevertheless, she'd
enjoyed it and imagined he had too. Still, she wouldn't
jeopardize his career over a kiss, especially because the
Nolans fought dirty.

"I never said thank-you for what you did at the funeral. I'm sorry the Nolans have the impression we're
engaged in inappropriate behavior."

Trey winced. "I hope I didn't offend you by what I
said to Sergeant Oliver."

"No. I totally get it. We're coworkers."

Hurt flashed in Trey's eyes, but he nodded. "Exactly.
Nothing more."

"That kiss never should've happened. It was a fluke.
I didn't read anything more into it. In case you were
wondering." She was rambling and justifying. He'd see
right through her.

"Just a flurry of emotion." Trey glanced at his watch.
"And we're done. Alex isn't coming. This is a joke." His
cell phone buzzed. "Yeah, I said the same thing. Sorry
for wasting your time. We were played. Nah, go ahead
and leave. We're doing the same." Trey pocketed his
phone. "Let's get out of here."

Disappointment weighed down Justine's shoulders.
"I thought we'd get a break in the case."

"There's got to be a clue in the diary about the key,
and now we know to look for it."

They slid off the cement dock step and walked to the
door. Trey gripped the handle. "It's locked." He thrust
his shoulder against it, but the door didn't budge.

"Must've locked behind us." Justine turned. An exit sign glowed from the other side of the warehouse. "There's another door. We can go out that way."

They crossed the space and pushed it open without issue. She paused and peered outside. They were on the opposite side of the building, near a retaining wall with overgrown weeds.

"All clear." Justine stepped out first, her foot brushing something.

Magnum barked and took off running up the sloped ground. He disappeared into the vegetation.

In what felt like slow motion, she turned to Trey.

He lifted her and lunged away from the building.

A blast propelled them into the air, exploding the space with a vicious orange light.

They landed hard on the pavement, and Trey covered her, pressing down on Justine as metal and wood showered them.

She tried not to breathe in the dirt, and her body didn't move for what felt like hours. Her ears rang with a deafening sound so intense her brain throbbed.

Trey shifted, helping Justine to her feet. His lips moved, but she couldn't hear him. He put his hands around his mouth, calling in the direction the dog had run off to. Then he hopped onto the retaining wall and sprinted into the weeds. Justine's legs were heavy and her body ached, but she followed, stepping up to the higher ground. Where had Trey gone?

"Magnum!" Trey's voice broke through the ringing in her ears. The sound distant but strong. A flashlight swept across an area to her right.

Justine jogged to him. His cries for Magnum were growing more desperate and frequent. Worry etched

Trey's face, along with several scrapes and cuts from the blast.

The warehouse continued to smolder below.

Together, they searched the grasslands, taking turns calling his name. The property merged into a large field leading to the highway.

Headlights illuminated the roadway below.

Lord, help us!

Where had Magnum gone? Was he hurt?

In the distance, movement in her peripheral vision caught Justine's attention. She spun and spotted Magnum running. No, he was limping.

Oh, please be okay. Justine took off, and Trey joined her, closing the gap to where Magnum approached, half running, half limping.

Trey lifted him, holding the animal against his heaving chest and burying his face in Magnum's neck.

Justine looked up, scanning the area. "I don't see anyone out there."

Trey shifted Magnum to her arms. "Stay here." He hurried off in the direction from where Magnum had run to them, then returned within a few minutes. "Whatever or whoever he was chasing is long gone."

Justine inspected his paws, and Magnum jerked when she touched his previously injured paw. "He's hurt."

"Let's get back to the truck." Trey took Magnum and cradled him as they traipsed to the warehouse.

Eric's patrol truck sat in the parking lot. He and Apollo approached. "I saw the explosion when I reached the main road and turned around. Already got fire rescue on the way."

Emphasizing his words, sirens screamed in the distance.

"Convenient you were gone when the blast happened," Trey shot.

Justine gaped at him. "Trey—"

"What're you saying?" Eric stood taller.

Trey brushed past him. "Read it how you want. You were supposed to be our backup."

"And you told me to go," Eric argued.

"Yeah, and how was it someone just happened to get an IED trip wire set up in the only exit available and you never saw it happening?" Trey's voice grew louder, and he still cradled Magnum.

"Gentlemen!" Justine stepped between them. "This isn't the time or the place." She faced Trey. "Take care of Magnum."

"He's hurt?" Eric moved beside them, genuine concern written in his eyes.

"Right before the blast, Magnum went after someone, but we never saw who. He must've lost him," Justine explained.

Eric nodded. "I'll take Apollo through there and see if he can get a scent."

Trey and Justine walked to his patrol truck, and Trey worked to inspect Magnum's wound. "Thank you for interrupting back there. We probably would've thrown fists."

"You're upset. Understandably, but at the wrong person."

"Irwin should've seen someone if they set that IED wire."

"Unless it'd been rigged before we got here."

"I have a friend at the ATF. I'll ask him to investigate." Worry creased Trey's forehead. "Mags, are you okay? I'm not sure what happened." The sadness in his eyes tore at Justine.

"He could've stepped on something. A sticker?"

Trey shook his head. "No. It's worse than that. If he reinjured the wound, Magnum may not be able to work anymore." He stroked the animal's neck. "You were right. I should've left him behind at the ranch. What if he's permanently injured?"

"Let's not throw the dog out with the bathwater."

"Now you sound like Oliver." Trey's smile didn't reach his eyes.

"Have his veterinarian check him over before you make any rash decisions."

Trey spun to face her. "Justine, you've seen him. He wants to work, but unless he's out of commission for a lengthy time, I'm not sure he'll ever get back to his normal self." He looked past her where Eric and Apollo were working the hillside. "Maybe it's time for him to retire."

Justine remained silent, unsure what to say.

Trey reached for his radio. "Possible bombing. BOLO for suspect Alex Duncan, believed to be involved," he continued, responding to the dispatcher's request for specifics.

Justine stroked Magnum's ears. *Lord, is all of this hopeless? Please help Magnum.*

Would the key provide any clue?

Trey returned to her. "When I get my hands on Alex—" He slammed his hand on the truck, pacing in front of her. "He lured us here, had that trip wire placed where we wouldn't see it. Even had the door locked behind us."

"You'll get him," Justine assured him.

He sighed, scrubbing his head. "Okay. I'm better."

Trey gently removed Magnum's vest. "You did good, buddy." He stepped back, closing the door, and paused. "Hey, what's this?"

Justine leaned in, and he withdrew a flashlight, aiming it at the smear.

"I think it's blood, but I need an ALS to confirm."

"Alternative light source?" she clarified.

"Yes. If I'm right, the ALS will cause the blood to glow blue. Then we'll ask the lab to take a sample. Magnum must've gotten a hold of the perp!" Hope danced in his eyes.

"I don't mean to be a downer, but wouldn't we need a known sample to run the blood against?"

"One step at a time. Stay optimistic. We'll catch whoever did this."

"Magnum didn't just injure his paw. It's possible the perp hit or kicked him."

Trey's jaw tightened. "Definitely. Let's go to the troop office. They'll have an ALS."

"But will the lab run the sample now?"

"No, but with a little begging, maybe they'll do it first thing in the morning."

THIRTEEN

Dr. Taya McGill-Stryker's announcement worked to drain the color from Fredrick Nolan's face. Like a week-old helium balloon, the man shriveled before Justine. She stifled a yawn, the aftermath of a busy evening and talking late into the night with Taya. There'd been no time to return to the ranch, so Justine had bunked in Taya's hotel room while Trey had lodged with a friend. They'd met with the lab after confirming the smear on Magnum's vest was indeed blood. And the day was flying by.

"Are you absolutely certain?" Fredrick's voice cracked with age and shock, dragging Justine to the present.

Susan Nolan's eyes widened, and her cheeks reddened. "You're making that up. Trying to justify the intrusion and desecration of Kayla's grave site."

"I assure you that is not the goal. I am an independent forensic anthropologist brought in to perform the evaluation without bias. My findings are documented and absolute. You may view the report for yourself," Taya said.

"Oh, believe me, we will," Susan bit out.

"Where? How?" Fredrick flattened his hands on the table, as if holding on for dear life.

"I discovered a fragmented tip of a needle embedded in Kayla's spine," Taya explained for the second time.

"But that doesn't prove anything," Susan argued.

"Actually, the location confirms Kayla did not voluntarily overdose. I found traces of the narcotics in her spine, as well. The trajectory makes it physically impossible for Kayla to have injected herself. I'm marking her file as a murder," Taya said.

Fredrick's shoulders slumped, and he covered his face. "My beautiful Kayla. What have we done?"

The strange comment grabbed Justine's attention, and based on the expressions of the others present at the interrogation table, she wasn't the only one.

The shift in Fredrick's pain touched Justine. "Mr. Nolan, with this information, I believe it's a reasonable assumption someone staged your daughter's murder to look like an overdose. But who wanted her dead? Is there anything you remember that might help us?"

"This is ridiculous," Susan argued. "Nothing has changed, from our point of view. Kayla's death was a tragedy, but after all this time, what difference will changing the cause of it make?"

Justine gaped at the woman. "For one, we need to get a murderer off the streets."

"Unless you've found evidence, how will that happen?" Susan shot back.

Fredrick rejoined the conversation, tears pooling in his eyes. "Kayla wasn't using drugs?"

Taya shook her head. "I wish I could answer that to your satisfaction, but there's not enough evidence one way or the other."

"She wasn't," Justine defended her friend.

"I wanted to protect her." Fredrick folded his hands

on the table. "It was my doing. I asked Pete Lucas to steal Kayla's body."

"Fredrick!" Susan said. "Don't say another word."

"It's time we told them." He addressed Justine. "After talking with you, Susan and I had a long discussion and she convinced me Kayla's reputation would be dragged through the mud along with ours. The media outlets were relentless the first time. I wanted to protect my family."

Susan's hand flew to her neck, where a large solitaire diamond hung from a thick rope chain. "You're blaming me?"

"No, I'm stating the facts." He sat back.

"Mr. Nolan, do you realize what you're saying?" Trey intervened.

Fredrick nodded.

"You'll be charged with tampering with the body," Trey added.

"I understand and accept full responsibility. Whatever you need from me, I promise my cooperation."

"I'll try to keep your charges to a minimum," Trey promised.

"Thank you."

"Mr. Nolan, I found something in Kayla's diary and wondered if you'd be willing to help me," Justine inquired.

"Yes, of course."

"Does the name Underwood Machler mean anything to you?" Justine asked.

He started to shake his head. "No, I—"

Susan jumped to her feet. "This is preposterous! My husband is obviously not feeling well and speaking from grief. Which you are taking advantage of. We're leaving. If you need something, contact Alex Duncan."

Trey stood. "We'd love to. The BOLO issued for him is still active. Any idea where he is?"

Susan's lips narrowed into a thin line. She gripped Fredrick's arm and hauled him up, then dragged him from the room, slamming the door behind her.

"Wow," Taya said, facing Justine.

"Thank you again for everything."

"I'm grateful I could help. Kayla deserves justice. I'll be praying for you both. I'll finish my investigation notes and get my finding to Sergeant Oliver today before I leave." Taya gathered her files, and after a hug with Justine and a handshake with Trey, she exited the room.

"Is it me or did Susan seem to go off the deep end at the mention of Underwood Machler?" Justine asked.

"Um, yeah. Not sure if it was the name or the fact her husband confessed to stealing the body," Trey said.

Justine's phone rang. A glance at the screen sent her stomach into knots. Everything within her wanted to ignore the call, but experience had long ago taught her Victoria wouldn't give up. "Hello."

"Justine. Oh, honey, I'm so sorry for how I behaved yesterday." Victoria's words dripped with sweetness.

Typical. Attack. Apologize. Repeat. Justine sucked in a breath. "You're grieving."

"I am, darling, but that's no excuse. Forgive me. After you'd gone, it hit me I'm all alone. And I can't bear that." Based on the sniffles and hiccups, Victoria was crying.

How many times had Justine heard her mother speak those words as justification after Ignaseus's angry beatings? Yet a trickle of hope from her traitorous heart clung to one word. *Family.* Hadn't Trey told her it was time to forgive her parents? Was this the step in doing that? "I forgive you."

Victoria sniffled. "Thank you. Honey, I'll be returning to North Platte—that's where I live."

Justine refrained from saying "I know." Though they hadn't spoken, she'd kept tabs on her parents. "I'm glad you called before you left."

"Thing is, I had to talk with you today."

Justine braced herself. Of course Victoria would call with ulterior motives.

"I did my best to be a good wife and mother. Even after that nasty Mrs. Scranton stole you away from me."

Justine gripped the table with her free hand. Her mother always put down Mrs. Scranton, but the woman had saved Justine's life. Figuratively and literally.

Victoria continued, "We all made sacrifices, and as much as your desertion devastated your father and I, I forgive you too."

Warning signs blared. Victoria was warming up for the kill.

"You're successful and can afford the funeral-service bill. I have nothing. Not even enough to bury the love of my life. The ceremony was beautiful. It's too bad you weren't able to stay."

Justine bit her lip to stop the retort dying to escape, and redirected the conversation. "I wish I'd known sooner."

Victoria sighed. "I'm sorry. But I need a little help to get me by. You see, I lost my job when your father fell ill, but I had to be by his side."

Always Ignaseus's defender, no matter the cost. "How much do you need?" Justine cut to the chase.

"I hate to ask, but ten thousand would be great."

Justine gasped. "I don't have that kind of money. I've recently endured some—" she considered what to tell her mother and opted for limited information "—damage to my house. I could probably swing a few hundred."

"That's just like you. So selfish. Take care of number one! Forget it, Justine. Stay out of my life." Victoria hung up.

Justine stared at the phone, disbelieving.

"I'm scared to ask," Trey said.

The comfort of her clinician persona provided a shield, and Justine slotted Victoria into the role of patient. "Apparently the amount I offered wasn't good enough. I won't hear from her again." She glanced down at her hands. What must Trey Jackson, with the perfect family, think of her pathetic one's brokenness?

"I'm proud of you."

Her head jerked up. "What? You are?" Justine sighed. "I could take out a loan or something."

"Absolutely not."

She looked at him.

"Sorry, that's not my place, but, Justine, going into debt isn't the way to help her. Setting boundaries is healthy for both of you."

Logically, he was correct. Her training agreed. But guilt weighed on her heart. "What kind of daughter refuses her mother?"

"Had you heard from Victoria before today?"

"Not since I moved in with Mrs. Scranton my sophomore year of high school."

"Not once?"

"No."

Trey put an arm around her shoulder. "You did the right thing."

"Is it stupid that a part of me wants to give her the

money, just to be accepted again?" She hated herself for admitting the embarrassing truth.

Trey took her hand. "Every child longs for their parent's approval."

"I want to be worth something to someone." The confession slipped out before she could stop it, and she longed to retrieve it.

Trey dropped to a squat beside her. "Your value isn't based on your mother's inaccurate view of love."

She rose, creating distance between them. "You don't understand. Your family is perfect, and you'll have one of your own someday. I'll always be broken, trying to be normal and never measuring up."

Trey laughed and stood.

Justine startled. "Nice. Laugh at me when I'm vulnerable."

"I'm sorry. I didn't mean to offend you. My family is far from perfect. There's just more of us to carry the chaos evenly."

She grinned. "Whatever."

"Seriously. We've got our own sets of problems and battles. If not for God's grace and a lot of prayer between us, we would've fallen apart many times." He sobered. "You make your own future. No matter what's happened, your parents' dysfunction is not a direct reflection on you. Anyone who knows you has seen you're brilliant, beautiful, compassionate, beautiful—"

"You already said *beautiful*."

"It's worth repeating." That delicious dimple of his reappeared. "We're all responsible for ourselves, accountable for our own actions. You've proved you're an amazing woman."

Justine averted her eyes, cheeks warm. But if Trey

meant all those things, why had he adamantly denied they were involved when Sergeant Oliver called?

"Say it."

"What?"

"I smell smoke," he teased.

Justine grinned. "I don't mean to dispute your kind words, but if you think that, why did you tell Sergeant Oliver we weren't involved? Not that we are, but your emphatic rejection seemed over-the-top."

Trey's brows met in a triangle. "I apologize if I came off that way. I was so angry at the Nolans and thought about Susan's warning to you. I wanted to make sure they didn't have any ammunition to destroy our reputations and careers. If I were responsible for that kind of devastation, it'd kill me. I care for you. Too much."

He cared. For her. What did that mean? It didn't matter. They'd agreed romance wasn't a possibility. He was a nice guy. "Thank you. That makes me feel better." Changing topics, Justine pushed in the chairs. "We should get out of here. Poor Magnum needs an outdoor break." She gestured to where the dog lay dozing in the corner.

"Yeah, he looks pretty eager to move." Trey chuckled. "While we're clearing the air, I have to tell you something."

Justine's heart thudded against her ribs. "Okay."

"I'm sorry for not calling out Victoria at the funeral. Maybe that would've prevented her money attempt."

"Ever the optimist? Rest assured you handled the situation well. Victoria's a drama queen. She would've raised the roof worse than she did if you'd have stepped in."

Trey shrugged and perched on the end of the table.

Clearly, he wasn't leaving the room anytime soon. Justine leaned against the wall.

"Failing to protect people I care about is the one thing I excel at. Always has been."

"What do you mean?"

Trey sighed. "Forget about it. I'm whining."

"I blurted my ugly history and confessions. Your turn. Whine away." Justine smiled.

He grinned. "I guess that's a fair trade." He slid onto a chair, and she did the same, keeping the table between them. "I love my job. Serving the public and working with Magnum is a dream come true for me. But I'm always chasing this ghost from my past."

"Does this ghost have a name?"

"There was a kid, Josh, a senior when I was a sophomore. He was fun, the class clown, football star, but he had major drinking issues. He was nice, and I was thrilled an upperclassman paid attention to me."

"Wasn't Slade already including you in his group?"

Trey shrugged. "It's different. I hated being in Slade's shadow. Josh treated me as an equal, not like Slade's little brother. Ya know?"

She nodded, and he continued, "We were at a graduation party. Josh was there, being his usual corny self, but he disappeared for a while, so I searched for him. Found Josh by the pool, downing a large amount of alcohol. He was drunk, staggering around, and he headed for his pickup. I offered to drive him home. Josh was three times my size. I know it's hard to believe, looking at my athletic physique now, but I was really scrawny." Trey puffed out his chest like a rooster.

Justine laughed.

"Hey, it's not that funny."

"Sorry. Go on."

"Anyway, I tried to stop him. Took his keys and ran away. Not smart. Mr. Football Star tackled me. He lifted me by the shirt, threw a solid uppercut and tossed me into the pool."

The smile fell from Justine's face. "No."

"Yep, it was humiliating. Everyone laughed, and I slunk away to lick my wounds. Josh died that night in a drunk-driving accident."

Justine's hands flew to her mouth. "I'm so sorry."

"Shook me up for a while. Kept thinking I should've done something more to stop him. The same way I felt after Victoria unleashed on you at the funeral."

"Trey, you were a kid."

"That's no excuse. I should've called the cops or flattened his tires."

"Is that why you joined the patrol?"

"Yep. I wanted to protect people. But we see how well that's turning out."

Justine rounded the table and perched on the edge beside Trey. "No one controls another's destiny. You did what you could with what you had."

Trey didn't look up.

"Do you remember Nathan Yancy?"

That got his attention. "The kid who drove Will to your place."

"Yes. Can you imagine tagging him with the guilt of a classmate's death?"

"No."

"Exactly."

"But it's not just Josh. Kayla too. I should've done more. I spend so much of my life with *should've, could've, would've*. So what? I'm not helping anyone."

"You make a difference daily. I've never been in more danger than I have in the past few days, and you're always there. I'm grateful for your presence. But I understand reliving the pain of the past. I'll give you the advice I remind myself of. 'Absolve yourself for that night and receive God's forgiveness for any shortcomings you're clinging to. Because He's not holding them against you.'"

Trey smiled. "You're smart."

"I know, right? I have student loans to prove I paid to learn all that smartness." She grinned.

"Now, if only we'd get the results from the blood from Magnum's vest."

At the mention of his name, Magnum stretched and opened one eye.

A single knock preceded a trooper peering around the door. "This just came in." He handed the paper to Trey and disappeared.

Justine moved beside him. "Well?"

"It's the results of the blood test."

"And?"

"No known match."

Trey leaned back and closed his eyes, frustration oozing through his veins. They'd spent hours reviewing the case evidence with no leads. He glanced again at the lab test. "How's it possible to have blood—DNA proof—from the perp who set that IED and still have nothing?"

"All we need is a comparison sample."

"You make it sound so simple."

"Trying to stay optimistic," Justine said. "And we have the key." She smoothed the diary on the table and flipped to the back cover. "That wasn't visible before."

Trey leaned over, spotting a sticker depicting a stylized blue jay.

Justine's eyes widened.

"I smell smoke."

She jumped to her feet and glanced at her watch. "We have to hurry before they close."

"Where?"

"I'll tell you on the way." Justine shoved the case files into the box and hurried out of the room.

Trey leashed Magnum. "Sorry, buddy, the boss lady says we've got a lead."

His partner lazily opened an eye, peering from beneath his eyebrows, then slowly pushed to a sitting position. Guilt coursed through him. Magnum should stay behind at the patrol office. "Hey, Mags, sit this one out."

Magnum stood and gave a thorough shake from head to tail in an emphatic disapproval of the offer.

Trey grinned. Or not.

Justine was already down the hall by the time he and Magnum caught up with her.

"I love a good mystery, but since I'm driving, think you could clue me in to the details on this one?" he teased, loading Magnum into his kenneled area.

"Hurry!" Justine slid onto the passenger seat and closed the door.

Trey rushed to get behind the wheel.

A huge smile played on Justine's face and her hazel eyes sparkled. "Pierce."

Trey blinked and started the engine. "I'm going to need a little more information."

"The town of Pierce."

"Because—"

"If my suppositions are correct, we need to open a safe-deposit box from the First Bank of Pierce."

"And…" Trey headed toward the highway.

"Kayla left the diary for me to find. I'm positive now."

"Why?"

"Why else put the Pierce Bluejays emblem inside the diary? She knew I grew up there, and I'd pick up on the clue."

"But why not tell you what was happening?"

"Kayla might've been gathering information, and I was her fail-safe. Or, fearing someone was after her, she might've protected me."

That made sense. On the drive, they pondered the possibilities of what the safe-deposit box might hold. Trey pulled into the First Bank of Pierce parking lot at ten minutes before six o'clock. "Go on ahead of me. I'll get Magnum and meet you."

"Okay." Justine bolted from the truck and through the bank's glass doors.

By the time Trey and Magnum entered the building, Justine was talking with a customer service representative. A nameplate on the round marble desk read Rachel. She appeared apprehensive and Trey overheard her say, "I'm sorry, ma'am. I cannot give you access to someone else's account."

"But it's a murder investigation," Justine insisted.

Rachel looked at Trey, sizing him up. "You're the trooper working with Miss Stark?"

His uniform pretty much answered that question, but he nodded. "Yes, ma'am. I apologize for our late intrusion, but we really need to get into the safe-deposit box. We believe there's information directly applicable to this case."

Rachel frowned. "I'm not supposed to open it for anyone but the party, unless she listed someone else."

Justine leaned over the counter, nearly touching noses with Rachel. "Could you check the file?" Impatience in her tone evident.

The bank employee sighed and typed something into the computer. "What did you say your name was?"

"Justine Stark."

"May I see identification?"

Justine rummaged in her purse, then produced her wallet and driver's license. Rachel inspected the IDs, taking longer than necessary before handing them back to Justine. "You're listed on the account. I remember this one. So strange. Kayla Nolan paid for the box with a note to release it to you when you came."

Justine turned to Trey, the confusion on her face no doubt mirroring his own surprise.

"Let me get the keys." Rachel stepped away from the desk, returning a few seconds later with a ring of them in hand. "Please follow me."

They fell into step behind the woman, walking to a back room. Black safe-deposit boxes lined the walls on all sides and a large table in the center provided a place to view the contents. Trey and Magnum moved aside as Rachel inserted a key. Justine then inserted the key from the diary.

He held his breath. Would this solve Kayla's murder?

Rachel pulled the box free from the vault and placed it on the table. "I apologize for rushing you, but we will be closing in ten minutes. I'll give you some privacy." She exited, shut the door softly behind her.

Trey stepped closer.

Justine opened the box, revealing a stack of folded

papers, which she flattened on the table. "They're statements from an offshore account in the Bahamas." She pointed a finger at the name. "Underwood Machler is listed as the owner."

Trey leaned forward, reading beside Justine. "Wow, that's a lot of money."

"Why would Kayla have copies of bank records for this Machler?" She passed a set to Trey.

He scanned the documents, homing in on a line repeating several times each month. "Look, there are transactions from Nolan and Associates to this account."

Justine flipped through the rest of the papers. "These are invoices for business meetings and services, but there are no details listed and the contact for the company is Underwood Machler."

Trey glanced up. "What's the last date on the invoices?"

"July 26." Justine withdrew the diary and laid it on the table. "One week before Kayla's final entry."

"Who signed them?"

"Alex Duncan." Justine folded the papers. "This is fishy. There's an address on this account here in Nebraska."

"Let's go pay Mr. Machler a visit," Trey said.

"Should I assume you will not be needing the safe-deposit box anymore?" Rachel asked as they exited the room.

"No, ma'am. We'll take the contents."

"Very well."

Justine handed her the key and thanked Rachel for her help.

Once in the truck, Trey entered the address listed on

the bank statements into his patrol GPS app and started the engine.

"I've never heard of this town," Justine said.

"It's in the middle of nowhere. GPS shows a two-hour drive from here."

"Let's get going."

"First, I need to make a call." Trey chose Slade's number.

"Hey, Will and I finished cleaning out the barn. The damage wasn't as bad as we thought," Slade said by way of greeting.

"That's great news. But I have a favor to ask."

"Aren't you out of those yet?"

"If this lead pans out, it'll be my last one." Trey gripped the steering wheel, anxious to get on the road.

"I'm listening, baby brother."

Trey sped through an explanation, hitting the high points and ending with the newfound information. "I'd like backup just in case. I have no idea what I'm walking into."

"Talk with Oliver first?"

"Not yet, but I will. Can you meet me out there?"

Slade sighed. "Yeah. I'll be on my way ASAP, but I'm more than two and a half hours away. Hang tight when you get close. We'll connect a mile out from the address and go in together."

"All right."

"Ask Oliver for backup," Slade repeated.

"But I don't know what I'm walking into. Could be absolutely nothing. And most likely he'd recommend Irwin again. I'm still not sure I trust him after the warehouse explosion," Trey confessed.

"I think the guy's good. A little obnoxious but not

dirty. Promise you'll wait for me before you go charging into the place. And you'll give Oliver a heads-up."

Trey shook off the irritation at Slade's bossiness, conceding he was probably right. "I'll send you my location, and you can track me on the patrol app too."

"Roger that."

Trey typed a text to Oliver notifying him they'd be following up on a lead and he'd report in with an update ASAP, then shifted gears. "Now we're in business."

FOURTEEN

Trey parked in front of the decrepit structure and glanced at the dashboard clock. His phone had no service, and according to the patrol GPS app locator, Slade was running late. Dusk had settled in the valley, and they'd be hard-pressed to check out the old farmhouse before dark. Waiting on Slade wasn't an option.

Abandoned long ago, the neglected structure sagged on its crumbling frame. Dying trees with naked branches stretched out their limbs in a sad protectiveness around the home. Forest land bordered the property on every side, rising with the gentle rolling hills.

"Pretty," Justine quipped, one hand on the truck's door handle.

"Yeah. Think old Underwood Machler actually lives here?" Trey withdrew his weapon, checking the magazine.

"Um. No. But there might be clues to his actual location in there. Or the house will fall in on us while we're looking." Justine gave him a shaky smile.

Trey surveyed the property. "Maybe Machler used this address for the money laundering or whatever is going on. Wouldn't be the first time that's happened."

"True."

Trey put a hand on her arm. "Wait. Slade will be here soon. Stay inside the truck and lock the doors. I'll clear the house, and if it's empty, I'll come and get you. If I'm not back within three minutes, drive up to the hill, and as soon as you have reception, call Slade."

Justine shoved the diary into her pocket. "No way am I staying out here alone. Two eyes are better than one."

"In that case, I'll take Magnum with me. He's got two great eyeballs and a power sniffer."

On cue, Magnum popped his head through the divider, but Trey didn't miss the exhaustion in the animal's demeanor.

"Nice try. Not gonna happen. We're a team."

As much as he loved the sound of that, Trey made one last plea. "You do realize if something happens, we're too far from civilization to get help. The whole area is forest for miles."

"You're a terrible salesman."

He chuckled. "Sorry. Just giving you the facts."

"I appreciate the effort, but we're so close I can taste it."

Trey scratched Magnum's ear, concerned about the way he babied his injured paw. "Maybe I'll leave Magnum here."

"In a hot truck?"

"You forget the safety temperature controls." He gestured to the thermostat device between them.

"Right. Are you sure the windows will roll down? And you've got that gadget to open his door if things go bad in there and we need Magnum?" Justine asked.

Trey pointed to a small black button on his vest, trying not to think of scenarios that might prohibit him from using the device. Like an ambush. "Yep, the engine stays running. Mags gets to chill in the AC, and we've got a quick getaway if needed."

"See? What do we have to lose?"

He turned up the air conditioner. "Mags, hang tight, buddy."

Magnum whined and slipped into his area. Trey slid the divider closed. Then they exited the truck, and he locked the doors.

"Follow me." Trey's pulse beat in his ears as they crept toward the house.

Thick air without a hint of a breeze had his shirt plastered to his back. Dead silence hedged about them, as if the elements held their breath.

Trey activated his weapon's flashlight, and they climbed the fragments of porch steps. Hypervigilance had him constantly surveying the area. "Stay close."

The comment was unnecessary since Justine was near enough he heard her breathing.

He gripped the rusty knob on the rickety door. Locked. Trey moved to the window and peered inside. It appeared abandoned. He returned to the front door and slammed his shoulder into the rotting wood, forcing it open. He scanned the threshold in search of any IED trip wires, then carefully crossed over, entering the living room. Only a moth-eaten sofa filled the space, and the floors creaked beneath his boots.

He quickly cleared the area and whispered, "Wait here."

Justine shook her head, and he shot her a pleading look. She conceded, moving farther into the room as he eased into the hallway and across to the kitchen.

"Trey!"

He spun, sweeping the flashlight beam off Susan's pistol, pressed to Justine's temple. Where had she come from?

"Drop your gun, or I'll shoot your girlfriend."

"Then I'd have to return fire," he countered. His mind raced. They'd diligently watched for anyone following them on the way and had seen no one for miles. How did Susan know they'd be here?

"You're wondering how we knew you'd show up." Susan's lip curved in a sneer.

We. Who was with her? "Something like that," Trey said, focused on the open front door and his pickup parked in the distance.

"You'd be amazed what information money will buy, Trooper." Susan laughed.

Gun unwavering, he slowly raised his left hand up to his tactical vest, to Magnum's emergency-door-release button.

"Put down your weapon!" Susan screeched.

"I wouldn't test her, Trooper." Alex's familiar voice was accompanied by the jabbing of a gun barrel in Trey's back.

He dropped his hand. "Glad to see you manned up and came out of hiding, Alex. But you'll never get away with anything. There's a BOLO out for your arrest," Trey warned.

The sun had almost set, darkening the room.

"We? Is Underwood Machler here with you?" Justine's voice took on that professional sound.

Susan chuckled. "Some secrets are too precious."

"Secrets Kayla discovered," Justine said.

"If she'd minded her own business, she would've lived," Alex inserted.

"You killed her," Justine replied.

"He did what had to be done," Susan defended.

"Drop your gun and kick it to me." Alex pressed the gun harder.

"Don't do it, Trey," Justine cried.

"Say another word and I'll finish you off," Susan bit out, slamming the butt of her weapon against Justine's temple. She yelped and met his eyes, pleading.

Trey lunged forward, halted by a warning shot near Justine's foot.

"Drop your gun or the next bullet is for Justine," Alex warned, stepping closer.

"Okay, calm down." Trey glanced toward the door.

Justine's eyes widened with what he prayed was understanding. He sank to a squat, placed the gun on the floor beside him and used the diversion to depress Magnum's release button.

Barks resounded.

Alex cursed and shoved Trey down, stomping on Trey's hand as he lunged, and slammed the door shut before Magnum reached the porch.

Trey jumped to his feet and tackled Alex to the ground. Alex's gun slid toward Trey.

Out of the corner of his eye, he saw Justine spin, elbowing Susan in the nose.

Relentless, Magnum snarled, clawing and butting the door.

"It's over. Get up!" Trey ordered.

A warning shot rained bits of wood and plaster on Trey, and he turned.

Justine knelt on one knee, a sliver of crimson sliding down her face.

"It's far from over, Trooper." Susan shoved her weapon

against Justine's head. "Put your gun down now, or I'll shoot her."

Magnum slammed against the door again, barking furiously. Without an injured paw, he'd easily jump through the window, but Trey prayed he wouldn't try as he set down his pistol.

"Move to the couch," Alex ordered.

Trey complied. "So, you're Underwood Machler?"

"Oh, please. We're not going to have one of those last-minute-revelation discussions."

"But even if you kill us, we have the evidence to put you away," Trey stalled.

Alex sneered. "I doubt that. And by the time your cohorts figure out you two are missing, we'll be long gone, lounging in the Bahamas."

Magnum continued hitting the door and barking.

"Shut that dog up before I shoot him!" Susan raged.

Fury showed in Justine's eyes, locking with Trey's. A silent acknowledgment to fight.

"Too bad dogs can't open doors. I'll take care of the cop. Get what you need from Justine. And do whatever it takes," Alex ordered.

Susan dragged Justine down the hallway.

Alex stepped closer, kicking Trey's Glock under the couch.

Trey dived for the man's legs, tackling him with such vigor they went through the rotting floor and landed on the dirt below.

Alex lost his hold on the gun, but the attorney was more agile than Trey anticipated.

He kicked Trey back and scurried up from the ground.

Trey punched Alex, landing several uppercuts, but Alex hooked a foot around Trey's leg, tripping him.

Alex jumped on Trey, punches flying.

Trey dodged a jab and gained the top position. He drove a fist into Alex's stomach and ribs.

Alex clocked Trey, igniting fury.

With three quick hits, Trey pummeled Alex, knocking him unconscious, and then got to his feet, stepping out of the hole.

Trey yanked open the door, and Magnum bolted inside, rushing to Alex and growling at the unresponsive man. "Good boy!"

Darkness had settled, and shadows covered the landscape. How would he find Justine?

Alex groaned, and Trey pulled him through the broken floor and slapped handcuffs over his wrists. He collected his gun from under the couch and grabbed Alex's weapon, then slid it into his waistband.

Magnum sniffed the room. He'd have to rely on the dog's ability to track Justine and Susan. They moved through the house and paused in the kitchen at the open back door. "Magnum, seek!"

The dog bolted outside, and Trey hurried after him. But Magnum sped over the ground and disappeared into the forest.

Please, Lord, let Magnum find Justine. They couldn't have gone far.

Trey ran, debating whether to call Magnum. He didn't want to alert Susan, but he'd lost sight of the dog.

As if on cue, familiar barks echoed.

Magnum had found them!

Hope surged through Trey, fueling his search.

The forest was thick, reaching high, with a canopy of branches and leaves blocking the moonlight.

Trey sprinted, arms outstretched to thwart the low-hanging limbs slapping at him from all directions. There was no path to follow, and the ground was covered with brambles and exposed roots, forcing Trey to move slower.

Ears straining, he aimed toward Magnum's barks. The sound seemed to come from everywhere and inky night smothered him, confusing his sense of direction.

Trey paused, activated his weapon's flashlight and whistled a response.

A gunshot exploded.

Justine glanced down at the creek separating her from Magnum's scent trail. She'd heard him rushing through the leaves, but he hadn't reached her before Susan had forced her across the water. She prayed he'd lead Trey to where she'd dropped the diary and know they'd crossed over.

Susan grew more agitated, escalating her irrational behavior. Pain seared from the bullet-grazing wound of Susan's last warning shot.

"Why not kill me here?" Justine pressed.

"Walk!" Susan seethed, but something in her attitude hinted that things weren't going as planned.

Trey's whistle echoed, a comforting reminder he searched for her in the enveloping darkness, Magnum's barks promising to find her.

But would that happen before Susan killed her?

"I can't see where I'm going." Justine clumsily traversed the sloping ground.

"Shut up and walk."

Stumbling through the brambles, Justine determined to keep Susan talking. "Where are you taking me?" The leaves and pine needles crunched beneath their shoes.

"Where they won't find your body." The iciness in Susan's voice sent a shiver down Justine's back.

Magnum's barks faded. Was he going the wrong way?

Though her eyes had adjusted, she couldn't see two feet in front of her.

Lord, help them find me.

Her head throbbed from where Susan had struck her with the gun.

"Where is he?" Susan murmured, confirming Justine's suspicions Alex was the brains behind everything.

But why?

"Alex will give you up. He's already in custody," Justine surmised, praying she was right.

"You don't know anything." Susan's voice quavered.

"Don't let him get away with killing Kayla. I'll go in with you, explain how he manipulated you."

"Shut up! I need to think!"

Justine paused and turned.

Susan stood close behind her.

She was breaking down. Whatever plot she and Alex had was unraveling. Justine used her most soothing tone. "Susan, there's time to stop this. I'll give you the diary. We can talk to the police together. You don't want another murder on your hands."

A streak of moonlight pierced through the trees overhead. A silent second ticked by and Susan faced her, a murderous glare lasered on Justine. "You think you're so smart, don't you?"

"If you surrender before Alex does, you'll have leverage."

"I'll be gone before that happens. Alex served his purpose."

The woman bounced between calculating to unsure. Had she been the one behind the psychological games against Kayla? Justine stepped closer, hands outstretched. "Susan, I want to help."

From the depths of the night, Magnum's barks grew stronger.

Susan turned, and Justine barreled into her.

They slammed into a tree.

Justine grasped the woman's gun-wielding arm.

"No!" Susan screeched, the weapon swaying dangerously above them in Susan's attempt to maintain control.

Justine thrust Susan's hand into the trunk, and Susan accidentally fired the gun a second time.

Like a beacon to their location, Magnum's barking drew closer.

"Magnum!" Justine held on tight, unwilling to release Susan's arm.

The woman kicked, striking Justine's injured leg.

Pain exploded, and she buckled but refused to let Susan go.

Fury infused Justine with adrenaline, and she straightened and headbutted Susan. The gun toppled to the ground, and the impact sent them both stumbling.

Magnum's barks ceased. Had he left?

Justine's vision clouded, but she couldn't stop. She swung hard, landing a blow to Susan's face.

Susan wasn't giving up easily. She lunged, tackling Justine, and pinned her down.

Susan swung wildly. Two strikes to her ribs stunned Justine as she fought to dodge the attacks.

She tucked her knees up, prepared to shove Susan off.

A blur of black appeared from the brush, and Susan flew to the side.

Justine bolted to her feet.

Magnum stood on guard, teeth bared, hackles raised.

"He will attack," Justine warned through painful breaths, though she wasn't sure he'd act on her command. Where was Trey?

Susan froze, braced on all fours, chest heaving with exertion.

"Justine!" A light bounced in the distance.

"Here!"

Trey sprinted through the dark, rushing to her side. He jerked Susan to her feet.

"Good boy, Magnum." Justine hugged him.

Susan huffed, hands cuffed behind her. "Wait. I'll give you a cut of the money."

"Forget it. Trey, can you hand me that flashlight?"

He swept his weapon light across the area. Justine pressed an arm against her ribs. "I can't find her gun."

"Magnum, evidence."

The dog scurried, nose to the ground, moving beside a thicket, then dropped to a sit. Trey shone the beam on Susan's weapon.

Justine eased out of her outer shirt and used it to pick up the gun.

Sirens blared in the distance.

"Oh, sure. Now big brother shows up," Trey teased, leading the group through the woods.

As they neared the creek, Justine asked, "Did you find the diary?"

Trey nodded. "Yep, got it in my pocket. Great idea, by the way."

Susan gaped but said nothing.

They hiked back to the house, using the strobing lights to guide the way. Entering the clearing, Justine exhaled relief at the two patrol cars parked beside Trey's pickup.

Eric Irwin hauled a swaying and stumbling Alex from the house.

Trey shot her a look.

"Be nice," she whispered.

He grunted.

"What happened to Alex?" Justine asked.

"He made the mistake of trying to keep me from you," Trey said.

She grinned, grateful he couldn't see the warmth radiating up her neck.

Slade rushed to their side and took custody of Susan. "Thank God. We didn't know where you'd disappeared to."

"You've got nothing on me. Alex forced me to do this. He's the mastermind," Susan ranted across the property.

"Lady, save it for your next attorney." Slade assisted her into his patrol car and closed the back door. He turned and faced Justine and Trey. "I'd ask why you didn't wait for me, but that seems to be a moot point."

"Sorry, but it all worked out." Trey grinned.

Slade snorted.

"Why'd you call him?" Trey jutted a chin at Eric, approaching from the side.

"You're welcome," Slade replied. "Instinct. I tracked your location and saw you'd ignored my suggestion and gone into the valley. I requested backup, and Irwin was the first to respond."

"I'm sure he was," Trey grumbled.

"Bro, he's cool."

Justine watched the interaction as Trey sized up the other trooper.

"Did you tell him?" Eric smiled wide.

"Tell me what?" Trey asked.

"Eric did a little background search on this property. Turns out it belonged to the Underwood family," Slade explained.

Justine and Trey exchanged glances.

"And?" Justine invaded the pregnant pause.

"And Underwood was Susan's maternal grandmother's name. She left the property to Susan, who 'sold' " Eric made air quotes with his fingers "—it to Underwood Malcher. They made up the name, used a fake Social Security number and created a false identity."

"You discovered that tonight?" Justine queried.

Eric shrugged. "The internet is full of mystery. Besides, it's all a team effort, right?"

Trey ducked his head and held out a hand. "Outstanding work. I owe you."

Eric guffawed, shaking his hand. "I want that in writing."

"Alex and Susan embezzled money from the Nolans' business into the offshore account. When Kayla found out, she made the copies of the documents," Justine clarified.

"And they killed her before she ratted them out," Trey finished. "But how do we prove who actually injected Kayla with the drugs?"

Slade laughed. "Alex is rambling like a babbling two-year-old. He flat out admitted he didn't mean to kill Kayla. He'll turn on Susan in a heartbeat."

"The dream team stole the show." Eric beamed, slapping Trey on the back a little harder than necessary, based on the accompanying wince.

Justine stifled a giggle.

"Unless you want the honors of booking Alex, I'll take him in," Eric offered.

"He's all yours," Trey said.

"Fantastic." Eric jogged to his patrol car.

"Hey, Eric?" Trey called.

He turned.

"Hold off a few minutes."

"Roger that." Eric saluted and resumed walking to his vehicle.

"See?" Slade put a hand on Trey's shoulder.

"I really had him pegged as a vulture," Trey admitted.

"Nah, bro, he's just young and eager. Can't blame a guy for wanting to jump in and swim." Slade fist-bumped his brother, then turned to Justine. "Will's doing an amazing job at the ranch. You'll be able to sleep in your house tonight."

Justine covered her arms with her hands, suddenly self-conscious of the exposed burn scars and grateful for the dark atmosphere. "Thank you, Slade, for everything."

"That's what family does." He grinned.

"I want to talk to Alex while he's still chatty," Trey said.

"I'll meet you at Booking so you can wrap up here." Slade rounded his patrol car and slid behind the wheel.

Trey and Justine walked to Eric. He opened the back door to where Alex sat.

"She made me. I tried to talk Susan out of it all, but she insisted. What else could I do?" The hope in Alex's eyes was almost comical.

"Let's skip the part where you deny any knowledge of this whole situation," Trey said.

Alex slumped in the seat. "All Kayla had to do was

leave it alone. Susan said we'd just scare her. Use the stalker thing to get Kayla off the trail and make her look unstable."

"You used terror to control her, but it didn't work. Kayla was too strong for you," Justine said.

Alex blinked. "I really did like Kayla, but she locked us out of the Underwood account. That sent Susan over the edge."

"So all this time, you haven't been able to get to the money?" Justine asked.

Alex nodded. "Then, when you called about the diary, we figured she'd hidden the information in it. If you'd just given it back, none of this would've happened."

"You're not seriously blaming me?" Justine gaped at the man.

He shrugged. "No one had to die."

"Who injected Kayla?" Justine pressed.

"If I tell you, will you cut me a deal?"

"You watch too many crime-TV shows." Trey shook his head and reached for the door.

"Wait! There's more! Susan set that IED at the warehouse. I wasn't even there."

Justine leaned against the quarter panel. "Except you were."

"No. I wasn't. Honest."

"Prove it," Trey said.

"Sure! How?"

"Let me see your leg."

Alex's eyes widened. "Why? What's that got to do with anything?"

Magnum sat beside Justine with that knowing smile of his.

"I can get a warrant, but we both know what I'm going to find," Trey said.

Alex shifted, placing his leg on the outer edge of the door. "Stupid dog."

Eric leaned in. "Now, Apollo won't like that kind of attitude," he said, pointing to the dog's kenneled area beside Alex.

The man paled.

Trey lifted Alex's pant leg. A bite mark on his calf screamed the truth. "Magnum, is that your handiwork?"

The dog wagged his tail.

Alex tucked his leg in the truck.

"Thanks, Alex. I'll see you in Booking." Trey grinned.

"Got what you wanted?" Eric asked.

"Yep. Meet you at the office." Trey slammed the door and Alex startled.

Eric exited the property, Slade behind him.

Justine giggled. "Thank you."

"For what?"

"For showing up at the perfect time. Susan might've killed me."

"Nah, you had her."

She grinned and leaned over, inspecting her leg.

"You're hurt!" Trey squatted beside her.

"It hurts worse than it looks," she teased.

Trey lifted her and carried Justine to his pickup. Setting her down, he pulled out a first-aid kit and cleaned the wound.

"Nice." Justine inspected the bandage.

"Still need to see the doctor."

She smiled. "Magnum's rescue more than proves he's K-9 material. The bite is solid evidence against Alex."

"He did a great job, didn't ya, buddy?" Trey ruffled

Magnum's mane. "Too bad that doesn't count for the recertification."

"He's earned a little R & R. Let's see how he does after that."

Trey shrugged. "The funny thing is, I'm okay with whatever happens. I can train a new dog, and Eric deserves to work Apollo. Regardless, Mags is my partner, and even if he's forced to retire, he's staying with me."

"I love the way you think."

Trey chuckled. "See, that optimism of yours totally wore off on me. It's one of the many things I love about you."

Justine blinked. Her mouth went dry, and she rubbed her arms, longing for her long-sleeved shirt to cover the scars.

Trey covered her hands with his. "I love you, Justine. If you feel the same, I'll wait a year, ten years, whatever it takes, but I want to be with you. Forever. You've always been the one."

His words burst through the floodgates of her heart, and Justine melted into his embrace. Had she hidden behind Kayla because she feared falling for Trey? Would Kayla approve? Justine tipped back, her gaze meeting Trey's.

Yes, her friend had known how Trey felt. It was time to release the past.

Justine leaned in.

Trey's mouth parted, and she paused, their lips a breath apart. She whispered, "I love you too," and initiated a kiss.

This time, the connection was no longer tentative.

But deepened with acceptance and promise for their future.

EPILOGUE

The stifling summer heat was unbearable, but Justine wouldn't be anywhere else. She stood at a distance, watching as Trey and Magnum worked through the re-certification exercises.

Anxiety oozed through her and she transitioned from biting her fingernails to worrying her lip, whispering, "Come on."

They'd babied Magnum for the past two weeks, just for this day.

Eric, Sergeant Oliver and Slade stood to one side of Justine, Will on the other. As Magnum and Trey completed each section, the group shouted, "Yes!" and exchanged fist bumps.

But their enthusiasm didn't compare to the boisterous Jackson clan, cheering behind them.

"One short break, then the final test," Slade explained.

"They're an amazing team." She glanced up to see Fredrick Nolan approaching. "Hi there. What're you doing here?"

"I heard this is where you and Trooper Jackson were today."

"We'll give you some privacy." Eric ushered Slade toward the Jackson group and said, "Introduce me to your younger sister."

"No way." Slade laughed, shaking his head.

Fredrick gazed out at the course. "I wanted to say thank-you."

"I'm glad everything worked out."

"Took a little bit for me to accept Susan and Alex betrayed me. Worse, I didn't want to believe they were responsible for Kayla's death."

Justine faced him, compassion warming her heart. "I'm so sorry."

"My new attorney says Susan will be forced to repay the life insurance money."

"The Slayer Rule," Justine interpreted.

"Such an appropriate name for it, don't you think?" Sadness filled Fredrick's eyes. "The money was withdrawn in cash portions, making it untraceable. We're guessing she used it to pay off those she'd recruited to support her quest to stop Kayla and the investigation."

Though Justine and Trey suspected Laslo Drazin was one of those people, there was no paper trail to prove it.

"But that's not why I came. Kayla loved life. She wanted everyone to be happy and joyful. She brought sparkle to everything she did. I miss that most about her."

Justine nodded, emotion thickening her throat.

"She would be happy for you and Trooper Jackson."

Justine startled. "Beg your pardon?"

"Miss Stark, I'm an old man but not a blind one. Trooper Jackson is in love with you. Don't waste a second denying your heart."

Tears filled Justine's eyes at the familiar saying. "Kayla said that all the time."

"Yes, she did. And it was good advice." He winked. "I also came to deliver this." He passed an envelope to Justine.

She startled at the whistle. "They're beginning again." They focused on Trey and Magnum's final part of the course.

The pair eased through the last portion, finishing before the allotted time.

"They did it!" Justine jumped to her feet.

Raucous yelling from the Jackson crew drowned out her cheers, and Fredrick laughed.

Trey stopped to praise Magnum and rushed to Justine. "We're back in the game!"

"Outstanding!" Justine lunged into his arms. Then, remembering Fredrick beside her, she released her hold. "Look who came to support you."

"Mr. Nolan, it's good to see you."

"Fredrick, please." He knelt and petted Magnum. "You all were amazing out there."

"It's all Magnum. I just hold the leash." Trey beamed.

"He is a beautiful creature."

Magnum did the adorable smile that tugged at Justine's heart. She looked down at the envelope. "Fredrick brought this."

"Yes, please open it."

Justine unsealed the envelope and gasped at the amount written on the first check made out to the victims' advocacy center. "Sir, this is very generous."

Fredrick bowed his head, hands in his pants pockets. "I can't bring back my daughter, but I can help others in her memory so women facing stalkers or trouble might have the resources they need. The resources I should've encouraged Kayla to take part in."

"I'm sure they'll be very grateful," Trey said.

Tears filled Justine's eyes.

She froze at the sight of the second check made out to her. "Sir. I can't. It's too much. I can't—"

Fredrick lifted a hand. "Miss Stark, after Trooper Jackson told me about Susan and Alex's horrendous efforts to silence you and the extensive damage they caused your ranch, I could not turn a blind eye. Please accept the money. In Kayla's memory. I'd be hurt if you refused."

Justine nodded and bit her quivering lip. "Thank you."

He grinned brightly. "You all have a good day." He turned and walked away, happiness in his step.

"The suspense is killing me," Trey said.

Justine showed him the check, and his eyes widened. "I've never seen that many zeros before a decimal point."

"It's more than enough to fix my house, the barn and pay Will two years' full-time salary!"

Trey pulled her into his arms. "That's fantastic. Now that Mags and I are finished with the recert, I have one important thing to take care of."

"Oh, yeah? What's that?"

Trey released his hold and withdrew a box from his tactical vest.

Justine gasped as he opened it to reveal an antique diamond ring.

"It was my great-grandmother's. She and my great-grandfather were married seventy years." He dropped to a knee and everything went silent around Justine. "Would you do me the honor of becoming my wife?"

Justine couldn't speak over the lump in her throat, so she nodded her head vigorously instead.

"Is that a yes?" one of his sisters called from behind them.

"Yes!" Justine finally found her voice.

Trey embraced her and she melted into him.

Whoops and hollers cut the kiss short as the Jackson clan, Will, Sergeant Oliver and Eric surrounded them, enfolding Trey and Justine into the family she'd always longed for.

* * * * *

HARLEQUIN
PLUS

Announcing a **BRAND-NEW** multimedia subscription service for romance fans like you!

Read, Watch and Play.

Experience the easiest way to get the romance content you crave.

Start your **FREE 7 DAY TRIAL** at <u>www.harlequinplus.com/freetrial</u>.

LOVE INSPIRED

Stories to uplift and inspire

Fall in love with Love Inspired—
inspirational and uplifting stories of faith
and hope. Find strength and comfort in
the bonds of friendship and community.
Revel in the warmth of possibility and the
promise of new beginnings.

Sign up for the Love Inspired newsletter
at **LoveInspired.com** to be the first
to find out about upcoming titles,
special promotions and exclusive content.

CONNECT WITH US AT:

f Facebook.com/LoveInspiredBooks

🐦 Twitter.com/LoveInspiredBks

LISOCIAL202

SPECIAL EXCERPT FROM

LOVE INSPIRED SUSPENSE
INSPIRATIONAL ROMANCE

*An FBI agent who is undercover as a bank robber
must risk his cover to keep a teller alive.*

Read on for a sneak preview of
Christmas Hostage *by Sharon Dunn,*
available October 2022 from Love Inspired Suspense!

Even before the shouting and the woman's scream, Laura
Devin sensed that something was wrong in the lobby of
First Federal Bank. The bright morning conversation
between bank employees stopped abruptly, but it was
what she saw on her computer screen that told her they
were in the middle of a bank robbery. All the alarms and
cameras had been disabled, just like with the other small-
town banks that had been robbed in the last two years.

Her back was to the open door in the room next to the
lobby, where she was working at a computer. When she
whirled her chair around, she could only see the back of
one of the tellers. Then she saw a flash of movement on
the other side of the counter.

"This is a bank robbery! Do as I say, and no one will
die here today!"

Even if one of the tellers had time to push the silent
alarm, it had been disabled. The police would not show up.

Laura's gaze jolted to her purse across the room, where her phone was. The door was open. If she went for it, they might see her. Closing the door would alert the robbers to her presence that much faster. But she had no choice.

She sprinted across the carpet and grabbed her phone, pressing 911.

"Hey, there's somebody in that room! Get her!"

The operator came on the line. "What is your emergency?"

"Bank robbery—"

A hand went over her mouth. She dropped the phone before the thief could grab it from her. He must have seen that she was making a call, or at least heard the phone when it landed on the carpet. And yet, he didn't tell her to pick it up. Maybe it was still on and the operator could hear what was happening.

He whispered in her ear, the fabric of the ski mask he wore brushing over her cheek. "It's going to be okay. Just do what they say."

Don't miss
Christmas Hostage *by Sharon Dunn.*
Available wherever Love Inspired Suspense books and ebooks are sold.

LoveInspired.com